WEAVE A CIRCLE ROUND

kari maaren

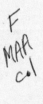

TOR

a tom doherty associates book

new york

WEAVE A CIRCLE ROUND

Copyright © 2017 by Kari Maaren

All rights reserved.

Designed by Greg Collins

A Tor Book
Published by Tom Doherty Associates
175 Fifth Avenue
New York, NY 10010

www.tor-forge.com

Tor® is a registered trademark of Macmillan Publishing Group, LLC.

The Library of Congress Cataloging-in-Publication Data is available upon request.

ISBN 978-0-7653-8628-1 (trade paperback)
ISBN 978-0-7653-8629-8 (ebook)

Our books may be purchased in bulk for promotional, educational, or business use. Please contact your local bookseller or the Macmillan Corporate and Premium Sales Department at 1-800-221-7945, extension 5442, or by email at MacmillanSpecialMarkets@macmillan.com.

First Edition: November 2017

Printed in the United States of America

0 9 8 7 6 5 4 3 2 1

For my sister Jan,

who gave Mel her supremely
unruffled demeanour
and quite a bit of her logic

acknowledgements

This book has been a long time coming. I wrote it in 2010 and finished the first round of revisions in 2011. It was accepted by Tor in the spring of 2015 and published in the fall of 2017. Therefore, my acknowledgements—as is proper for a book with a debt to fairy tales—go back seven years. Okay, let's do this. *Cracks knuckles*

I owe a lot to Andrew House, Helen Marshall, Ben Fortescue, and Peter Buchanan, the other members of the writers' group to which I belonged while I was writing *Weave a Circle Round*. Extra thanks go to Andrew, who went over the whole manuscript and made detailed notes on it when the first draft was done, and Helen, who was responsible for connecting me with David Hartwell of Tor.

Thanks also go to David for taking a chance on a completely unknown writer whose claim to fame was that she had written a silly song about everybody hating elves. David passed away unexpectedly in January 2016, and his loss has reverberated through the SF community. I would also like to thank his brilliant assistant editor, Jennifer Gunnels; the wonderful Diana Pho, who took over from David and Jennifer in early 2016; Jamie Stafford-Hill, the designer of the book's beautiful cover; the people at Tor in general; and my patient, attentive agent, Monica Pacheco.

A special note goes out to my parents, George and Jean Maaren, for their support through an extremely difficult time in their lives. Mum died in December 2016 after a long struggle with Alzheimer's disease. As well, I would like to thank my sister Jan, always one of the first people to read all my manuscripts, and Paul, Lindsay, and Aaron, Jan's awesome family.

Thanks to the many friends who have supported me in all my grumpiness for the past seven years. I'm not going to list you because there are a lot of you, and I'll inevitably leave someone important out, and then there will be tears and recriminations, and it will end badly. However, you know who you are.

And finally, thanks to the city of Burnaby, British Columbia, in which I grew up, and which I have, in this novel, callously replaced with the fictional municipality of Roncesvalles. I haven't lived in Burnaby for ages, but I miss it a lot.

prologue

Freddy never knew exactly how well she remembered that encounter in the park. She hadn't done much with the memory—taking it out whenever she touched the key, but not for more than a few seconds at a time—and she sometimes thought she preferred it vague. But she found it varied much more than her other memories did. Some things that had happened to her she remembered sharply, as if she had stepped away from the time of the memory only just now, while some had faded to a fuzzy grey. Mel told her once that this was supposedly normal and had something to do with synapses, but Freddy didn't pay much attention to Mel when she used words that were bigger than she was. The encounter in the park was sharp and fuzzy at the same time. She could feel the wood of the bench digging into her legs; she could see the key flashing between the woman's fingers. She thought she remembered every word they had spoken. Maybe she was just pretending she did. A lot of the images were blurred, incomplete.

She thought it had gone like this:

The voices from the house faded behind her as Freddy

tore across the front yard and the street, heading into the park. She had run into the park a lot lately. Her parents didn't ever really talk any more. It was all screaming, broken by intervals of icy silence. But until today, she had never heard either of them mention what Mel and her friend Jonathan called "the D-word." Jonathan's parents had been D-worded since he was five. Three years later, he had a world-weary air about it all. Mel tried to copy him. Freddy couldn't.

It was one of the hottest days of the summer so far. The sun beat down on Freddy's skin as she stumbled across the brown grass towards the trees. There was a whisper of breeze, but not enough to cool her. Her vision was breaking up into prisms and quivering flashes of sunlight. She swiped impatiently at her eyes. She didn't like crying, but she never seemed to be able to stop herself. She had once overheard her teachers telling her parents she was "sensitive." Freddy didn't want to be "sensitive." Sensitive people ended up cringing behind doors as their parents shouted at each other, then running blindly into the park to bawl like six-year-olds. Sensitive people got stomped on by life. Not for the first time, Freddy wished she were about a foot taller and could bring herself to try the cigarettes her cousins were always sneaking in her backyard when they came into town for Christmas. She had never asked them. She had told herself they would just say she was too young. She knew she was doomed to be sensitive forever.

She had a favourite place in the park, a big clump of evergreens with a path through them and a bench near the path. Whoever had designed the park hadn't thought very hard about that path. It didn't go anywhere; it twisted into the trees for a bit and stopped. People only took it when they were looking for privacy, and they weren't heading for the bench. The path went on past it for a hundred me-

tres or so, finally ending in a small clearing that teenagers used for
parties and . . . other stuff. Freddy's cousins told her she wasn't old
enough to know about the other stuff. Freddy's cousins told her she
wasn't old enough for a lot of things. She did know, though, and
she avoided the clearing, though it was technically more private
than the bench. People didn't pay much attention to her when she
sat on the bench. It was set a bit back from the path, under three
cedar trees whose needles she was always having to brush off onto
the ground. If she squinted straight ahead, she barely noticed the
grey strip of the path in front of her, seeing only the trees, sheathed
in underbrush, poking into the sky. She could spend hours there,
completely alone, even the sounds of cars and the neighbourhood
kids muted by the trees. A thirty-second walk would take her back
out onto the street. She could pretend it wouldn't, though.

Freddy wasn't supposed to go into the woods alone. It was a rule
she'd been ignoring since kindergarten. No one had ever tried to
hurt her here.

It was cooler under the trees, but not by much. No one was in
the woods. Freddy reached the bench and slid down onto it and
curled up and squinched her face into her knees, and then she just
cried for a long time. A crow gave a short, harsh caw from somewhere close, and she thought, *Go away,* and then, *It's not fair. Why
can't they just . . . ?* She didn't think they would ever be able to *just.* It
hadn't always been like this. They had fought before, but everyone's
parents fought. It was this last year that had been all screaming and
freezing and throwing things. Maybe the D-word wouldn't be such
a bad thing. *No, that's not true. They're supposed to love each other.*
People could stop loving each other. Jonathan's parents had, and
Rochelle's. *But it's not fair. This isn't how it's supposed to work.*

She wrapped her arms around the backs of her knees and drew in a shuddering breath. She really hated crying like this, fighting not to make a sound while the tears streamed down her cheeks to pool on her thighs, but she hated crying the way Mel did more. All that noise was just embarrassing.

The crow cawed again. Freddy became aware she was not alone on the bench.

She wasn't sure what she noticed first. She couldn't have sworn the person hadn't been there when she arrived; in fact, thinking about it afterwards, she was almost certain the bench had been occupied all along. But the cawing was a sound from outside her net of misery, and it made her notice other sounds, too, and one was the slight scrape of a foot against gravel, not far away. Freddy turned her head slightly without raising it from her knees and peered out through swollen eyelids and her mane of curly hair.

A woman was sitting on the other end of the bench. She was one of the things that would seem both fuzzy and sharp to Freddy when she thought about this day later on, perhaps because she had cried her eyes into a semi-functional state by then. There was nothing particularly unusual about the woman herself, but something was wrong with her clothing, which looked as if it had been through a shredder. It was, thought Freddy, pretty good clothing: the kind of blouse and slacks her mum wore to work, plus flats and a little green purse. Or that was what it had been until recently. Afterwards, Freddy would remember staring at the rags that the blouse had become and thinking about how the fabric looked almost new. The slacks were in ribbons. One of the blouse's arms had been yanked almost entirely off, and the front of the blouse was gaping open, hanging together only by its two remaining buttons. Freddy twisted her neck a bit farther to the right, shifting her eyes up towards the woman's face. The woman was gazing straight ahead of her, off into the trees, apparently oblivious to Freddy's presence. She had dark brown hair, neither long nor short, that had also been through the shredder, then tangled into knots and shoved down over her face.

Freddy sat up, still blinking away tears. She couldn't go to pieces with some stranger here.

At her movement, the woman spoke. Still staring into the woods, she said, "Have you ever had one of those days where everything goes so stupidly wrong that you find yourself saying every five minutes, 'Now, this can't possibly get any worse'? And then it *does*?"

Freddy edged very slightly away from her. She knew she wasn't supposed to talk to strangers. She didn't *like* talking to strangers. Strangers always wanted to make conversation, and Freddy could never see the point.

"What am I saying?" The woman was still gazing raptly at nothing in particular. "The desperate crying indicates you're having one of those days now. I sympathise, though if we had a pity party, I think I would win."

"Your pants have a tear in them," said Freddy. Even as the words came out, she knew it was a dumb thing to say. The woman's pants were one giant tear.

"I expect they do," said the woman. "There was a thing that happened just now."

Freddy edged a bit farther along the bench.

Now the woman turned towards her. Freddy saw two bright eyes peering through the hair. "Your parents have told you never to talk to strangers."

Freddy nodded.

"I don't count," said the woman. "I was sitting here already when you came howling through the trees. If I'd had a predatory intent, I would have joined you afterwards and promised to show you a puppy."

"A pred . . . ?"

". . . atory intent. It means I drive around child-friendly neighbourhoods in a van with blacked-out windows and snatch innocents off the streets. Or it would if I did. You're too young to be getting any of this, aren't you?"

"I'm ten," Freddy said indignantly. She hated it when people assumed she was Mel's age. She knew she was too small.

The woman nodded. "I can see that. So why all the wailing and carrying on?"

"It doesn't have anything to do with you."

"That's why I'm interested." The woman leaned forward. More hair fell into her face. It was beginning to bother Freddy that she didn't just push it back. "I need a distraction from my own woes at the moment. You're handy. Why were you crying?"

It was just an ordinary summer day, hot and still, with a lone bird calling in the trees. The moment Freddy would remember most acutely afterwards, however, was this one: the roughness of the bench, the woman facing towards her in a polite sort of way. The only other part of the memory with nearly the same power would be the bit with the key. But the one thing Freddy could never recall was why she answered the woman's question. She knew she should just leave. Instead, she found herself saying, "My parents are getting a divorce," and the tears started again. The crow cawed once more.

"Ah," said the woman. "That would explain it. Do you think they shouldn't?"

Freddy gulped back half a sob. "*Yes*. I mean, *no*, they shouldn't. They're my parents!"

"Your answer is somewhat lacking in logic," said the woman. "I approve of it. Is there ever a better reason for not wanting two people who spend most of the time longing to drive steak knives into each other's hearts not to get as far away from each other as possible? 'They're my parents' is about as good as you're going to get in this situation. Does crying help?"

"What?"

"Does it help?" The woman waved a hand in a lazy circle. "Does it make you want to sing show tunes in the street?" When Freddy just stared at her, she added, "Does it make you feel better?"

"Yes," said Freddy.

"Does it really?" The woman leaned back on the bench and looked off into the trees again. "I know everyone says it does, but isn't it really just that you scream tears all over yourself until you're on the point of throwing up, then stop out of pure frustration because nothing has really changed? What *good* does it do? It's not going to stop the divorce. You're off doing it in private, so no one who matters is even going to notice it's happened. No magical tear fairies are likely to turn up, feel sorry for you, and make everything go *poof*. As far as I can tell, crying about something you can't change is a slightly more sophisticated version of throwing a tantrum because the sun has melted your ice cream."

Freddy felt her eyebrows being drawn down into a glare. Crying did help. It . . . helped, okay? Well, all right, she did feel sick already. She felt as if she needed to cry more, on and on, until . . . what?

Maybe it was true. It wasn't as if she *wanted* to be crying, was it? "I can't help it. Could you?"

"Yes," said the woman. "I have a method."

"No one can *help it*," snarled Freddy. "If you don't know that, nothing bad's ever happened to you."

"Bad things happen to me every day before breakfast," said the woman. Freddy recognised the tone; it was the one Mel used when she was pretending she wanted everyone to feel sorry for her, even though she knew no one would. "You can see I had several just now. You need to get over the crying thing. You've succumbed to a victim mentality."

Freddy narrowed her eyes. There were a lot of big words floating around, and she thought most of them were probably veiled insults.

"I'm going to do you a favour, small crying girl I have never seen before," announced the woman, and Freddy saw knowing eyes appear again beneath the hair. "I'm going to teach you not to cry."

"What good will that do?" Freddy was finding it hard to stop her hands from balling into fists. "It won't stop them from . . . from . . ."

Her eyes filled up. "Oh, stop," said the woman. "It's useless and takes us around in circles. Watch this."

She picked up the little green purse, which seemed less battered than her clothing, and opened it. After a few seconds of fishing, she pulled out a key ring so jammed with keys that it didn't even jingle.

The woman ran her fingers through the keys. "So you see, when one of the usual terrible things happens to me and I experience an overpowering urge to throw myself down on the floor and blub, I take out this key. No, not this one. It's in here somewhere. At any rate, there's a key I take out. I don't know what lock it fits; I found it in a gutter somewhere. So I have this key. Whenever I'm in danger of tears, I go looking for a lock."

Freddy's own tears had receded again, though she could feel them lurking. "Why?"

"To see if the key *fits* it, of course." The woman briefly waved the keys about before returning to her search. "It has to fit some lock somewhere. Of course, there are trillions of locks it *could* fit, and odds are I'm never going to find the right one, but you never know, do you? It gives me something to think about besides my own righteous self-pity. It's always, 'Maybe this will be the time, and maybe the lock will belong to a door that lets out into a magical land of sunshine and kitty cats,' and I stop wanting to cry because I'm interested. It's never the right lock, but maybe it will be someday. And anticipating *that* is better than sitting around moaning for some reason I won't even remember tomorrow."

Her fingers slid onto a little silvery key and stopped.

"I can spare this one," she said. "It's another gutter acquisition. I don't have the least idea what it's for."

Freddy watched as the woman tried to force the key off a ring nearly too full to hold it. She wasn't really sure she believed anyone could stop herself crying just by sticking a key in a lock, but . . . *I've stopped crying now. Is that really all there is to it?* It was worth a try. Anything that would stop her from crying herself sick was worth a try.

The key slid off the ring. So did five other keys. The woman regarded them ruefully, then dropped all the keys but one back into her purse. She let the odd one out rest in the palm of her hand. "Take it."

It was a small key; it gleamed in a beam of sunlight that had escaped the green canopy above. It had a straight blade with a little catch at the end rather than the jagged teeth Freddy was used to from house keys, and the part you were supposed to grasp to turn it— she didn't know what it was called—was a hollow circle of metal. Freddy hesitated. She wasn't supposed to talk to strangers, and she wasn't supposed to take anything from them, either.

"It's not poisoned," said the woman. "I have apples and candy bars for that."

Freddy reached for the key. She glanced up at the woman's face as she did.

The slight breeze had, perhaps, been at work; the hair had blown partly back, revealing a pale curve of cheek. "You're bleeding," said Freddy, her hand still hovering in the air.

"What? Oh." The woman touched her cheek gently. "Never put handcuffs on an angry teenager. They weren't *bad* handcuffs," she added in what Freddy thought was meant to be a reassuring way. "There was stuff that happened, and then it went boom. I don't have the handcuffs any more. Take the key."

Freddy took the key. It was just a key. It was warm against her fingers. She closed her fist around it.

"Good," said the woman, rising and picking up the purse. "That's you sorted. Just try the thing with the crying. It works."

Freddy shrugged. She doubted it would. But the solidity of the key against her damp skin was oddly reassuring.

The woman turned away, then back. Her hair had fallen over her cheek again, hiding the long bleeding scrape. "One thing. Whatever you do, don't tell me I've given you that."

Freddy gave her the stare Mel said made people want to apologise for being born.

"I'm serious," said the woman. "It would be *very, very bad*. You see?"

"But you already know you've given it to me," said Freddy. "And you said you didn't know what it was for."

"Still, don't tell me. I might do something drastic if you did. *People could die.* Or you might accidentally kill a puppy."

There were occasionally crazy people in the park. Freddy hadn't thought this woman was one of them, but she'd been wrong before. It was kind of too bad. The thing with the key and the crying almost made sense, in a zigzagging sort of way.

"I won't tell you," said Freddy, "since I don't know who you are."

The woman gave a slight, twitchy little shrug. "No one does, occasionally including me. You have a nice morning, now."

Freddy said, "It's afternoon."

"Have a nice morning *tomorrow*," said the woman. She turned and marched off down the path. One of her shoes made flapping noises at every step. It looked as if the sole had come loose. Freddy listened to the flapping, which was strangely dignified, receding into the trees.

She was pretty sure the woman had been a passing nutcase. But Freddy did keep the key, threading it onto her own ring next to the keys to her house. And the day her mum and dad sat Freddy and Mel down to tell them they were going to live separately, just for a little while, she made herself think about the key the whole time. Once her parents left their daughters alone, Freddy went to the grandfather clock in the living room—the one they had never been able to use because no one could unlock the casing—and tried the key in the lock. It didn't fit. But Freddy didn't cry. She could feel the tears just behind her eyes, threatening to push their way out. The key kept them at bay somehow.

She used the key many times over the next four years. Sometimes it stopped her crying, and sometimes she remembered it too late. As time went on, she forgot less often, and it finally became automatic, then unnecessary. Just touching it was enough to calm her down. She thought of the encounter in the park whenever she grasped the key, but it gradually grew to be just a slightly weird thing that had happened to her when she was ten. She wouldn't have known the woman again if they had met in the street, especially if the woman had brushed her hair and found some new clothes, but Freddy didn't think they ever had.

1

"The house on Grosvenor Street is sold again," said Mel, and gooped yogurt onto her Cheerios, disgustingly.

There was only one house on Grosvenor Street. Freddy vaguely remembered their stepfather, Jordan, calling it a "bizarre accident of city planning" back when Jordan and Mum had still been eating meals with them. Grosvenor was a fairly short street that went through the middle of Roncesvalles Park; then the park ended on one side of it as it made a T intersection with Elm Drive. Freddy's house was on Elm, though the side yard let out onto Grosvenor. Behind it, fronting on Grosvenor, was the one house. It had a couple of vacant lots on its other side, and then Grosvenor—and the park—ended in another T intersection. Freddy had always been fascinated by that house. In and of itself, it was . . . kind of odd . . . but the most noticeable thing about it was that no one ever lived in it for more than a year at a time. It would have been nice if there had been rumours of ghosts or evil disappearing basement rooms, but the reasons the owners had for moving were always more boring than that: the lawn was too big, or the roof leaked, or there was that one useless room that made the house truly unusual but took up way too much space, or it felt too creepy to be living in the only house on a street across from a park. The last owners, the Johannsens, had moved out eight months before and had been trying to offload the house on somebody else ever since. Every once in a while, Freddy would notice a real estate agent showing people around the place, but it hadn't happened for some time now.

"Oh yeah? Who?" Freddy was mashing her spoon into her own bowl of cereal in an angry sort of way. The anger was just something she seemed to be feeling all the time these days. It simmered gently beneath everything she did.

"Dunno," said Mel. "I forgot my magnifying glass, so I couldn't read the fine print on the 'Sold' sign."

Mel had discovered sarcasm at the age of six, though she'd never used it very well. She always sounded cheerful when she was saying something biting.

Freddy said, "There'd better not be little kids."

"The Wongs weren't *that* bad," said Mel. "I liked Horace."

Horace had been the oldest of five boys and the only one, as far as Freddy was concerned, with any self-restraint. "I've still got the scars from where the twins bit me," she pointed out. Mel shrugged.

Someone went thud on the stairs. "Here come the elephants," said Freddy, "again." The anger surged, predictably.

When Roland entered a room, the room seemed to get smaller. It wasn't that he was fat, exactly; Mel was wider than he was, for all she was a foot and a half shorter. He just seemed built on a different scale from other fourteen-year-old boys. Admittedly, fourteen was a funny age for boys. Freddy's classmates ranged from kids barely taller than she was with unbroken voices to hulking giants who had already started shaving. Roland had taken the "hulking giant" option to extremes. He was more than six feet tall. As he shambled through the doorway, Freddy could see him going through his usual failed attempt to make himself smaller by slouching and drawing his arms close in to his sides. As usual, she found herself fighting the urge to push back the table and make space for him.

"Milk," said Roland, who did not do mornings. His black hair was sticking almost straight up, and his eyes were closed to puffy slits.

Mel flapped a hand at the milk. It was useless for anybody to say anything. When Roland was in this state, he would have been able to manage advanced gymnastics more easily than lip-reading.

Freddy and Mel sat at the table and watched as Roland made a lunge for where he may have thought the milk was. His hand caught the edge of the Corn Flakes box and sent it spinning into the air. Freddy winced as it landed upside down on the linoleum. She didn't think Roland noticed. He groped blindly over the table, his bare feet crunching in cereal.

"I hope he puts orange juice on his Cheerios," said Mel, a hint of wistfulness in her voice. Roland had made this mistake once months ago, and ever since, Mel had been longing for a repeat.

Roland's questing hand found the milk carton. He dragged it towards him, popped it open, and raised it to his mouth.

"Oh, hey," said Mel, and Freddy added, "No!" She knew it was no good, but she could never seem to stop herself from speaking aloud to him, even when he wasn't looking at her. She heard Mel's chair scrape, and she turned to see Mel on her feet, signing as hugely as she could, *Stop it.* Mel had started learning to sign about two days after their mum had begun dating Jordan. As far as Freddy was concerned, it was pointless. Roland could read lips. Mel didn't need to humour him with the stupid signing all the time.

Freddy turned quickly away from the signing. *I didn't understand that*, she told herself, as she always did.

Roland lowered the carton and peered over it at Freddy and Mel. His eyes were open most of the way now, though they were still puffy. He glanced from accusing glare to accusing glare. "What?"

"Now we can't drink our own milk," said Freddy. "Thanks so much."

"I was going to put it on my second helping," said Mel, signing simultaneously.

"I didn't gob in it. Jesus," said Roland. The twist in his voice turned the words topsy-turvy.

"It has boy spit in it," Mel informed him, "whether you gobbed in it or not. There are probably harmful microbes."

"There's this cupboard over the sink, right," said Freddy, "and there are all these *glasses* in it and stuff."

"You need to find something else to hate me for," said Roland. He put down the milk, picked up the box of Cheerios, and slouched from the room, trailing smashed Corn Flakes.

"I keep telling you," said Freddy.

Mel sat down heavily. Mel did most things heavily. "It's just that it's morning. He's usually all right."

Freddy shook her head. "He isn't to me. You're too nice to him. I wish you'd stop."

Jordan and Roland had been living with them for almost a year, though Mum and Jordan had got married only four months ago. Freddy knew everyone expected her to have got over her resentment by now. She didn't want to get over her resentment. Jordan was bad

enough, but Jordan, like Mum, was out most of the time and easy
to ignore. Roland was forever thundering all over the house, leaving a trail of destruction behind him. She did know he didn't deliberately mess things up. It was more as if rooms just fell into disorder
whenever he appeared. It didn't make much sense, since to all in-
tents and purposes, Roland was naturally neat. He would wander
into the living room, fold all the newspapers, put several books back
on their shelves, and wander out again, leaving the place in chaos.
Freddy had never been able to figure out how he did it.

The point was that he was *big*. Everything he did was big. If he'd
been small and humble and easy to ignore, she could have lived with
his presence, but wherever he went, Roland was the centre of attention. Okay, he didn't set out to be, but it was all just so intrusive. Their
house had once been quiet, full of private corners. Now, everywhere,
there was always Roland.

"He's nice to me." Mel was gazing sadly at the plundered carton
of milk. "I like playing RPGs with him and Todd and Marcus. Our
latest campaign is this hybrid fantasy-mystery thing set in an alternate dimension, and I just got *piles* of XP for deducing the purpose
of the crystal water sphere."

"They only let you play because they want a fourth player and
don't have any other friends," said Freddy.

Mel regarded Freddy for a moment. "You're *not* nice to me. My
own sister isn't nice to me. It's sad."

"RPGs. You've reminded me," said Roland from the doorway, and
both girls jumped. Another thing about Roland was that though it
was often possible to tell where he was from all the thumping, he
was also capable of standing so quietly in place that no one would
know he was there until he spoke. Freddy caught his eye; he looked

away immediately, his lips tightening. It was lucky she'd been facing away from the door. He must have doubled back almost immediately and heard—well, seen—most of Mel's side of that conversation. He had pretty clearly got the gist.

Roland continued, "We're playing later today, and I need a setting. You're good at that kind of thing, Mel. Where should we go?"

"I thought you had everything worked out," said Mel, sounding mildly scandalised.

Roland smiled. Freddy had to glance away. When he smiled, the sullenness vanished, and he looked like someone who might be nice to get to know. She couldn't hate him properly when he smiled like that. "I know where the campaign is going, but I've procrastinated on the details," Roland admitted. "Please? I just need a place for you guys to explore for a bit. I know what's going to happen to you there—"

"Tentacles," said Mel to Freddy out of the side of her mouth. "It's always tentacles."

"—but I'm not sure what it looks like."

"Well, I dunno. I'm not the GM," said Mel.

"I'm no good at imagining stuff in the morning," said Roland.

Mel hitched her shoulders up towards her ears. "Who is? I guess it's random book time again."

"Random book time never works," said Roland.

"There's a first time for everything," said Mel.

She leaned over and plucked a volume off the chair in the corner that always held a tottering pile of books. People left books there on the way through the kitchen or forgot them there after reading them at the table. Every once in a while, the pile would grow so tall that it would become unstable and fall over. Mel would put most of the books away, and the cycle would begin again. Some books were on the chair permanently; *Bullfinch's Mythology* was the biggest of those. Freddy had read that one a lot in an absentminded sort of way. She wouldn't have described herself as being interested in myths and legends, but she liked reading about them anyway.

Bullfinch's Mythology would have worked well for Mel's purposes, but it was halfway down. The book on top of the pile at the moment was a slender paperback entitled *Selected Poems of Samuel Taylor Coleridge*. Freddy suspected that Mum, an English professor, had been the one to leave that particular book on the chair. No one else in the family went in for poetry much.

Mel eyed the book with apparent suspicion. "Oh well. It may work." She dramatically opened the volume to a place about half-way through. "Behold," she proclaimed, "your setting:

> *"In Xanadu did Kubla Khan*
> *A stately pleasure-dome decree:*
> *Where Alph, the sacred river, ran*
> *Through caverns measureless to man*
> *Down to a sunless sea."*

Mel blinked down at the book. "Hey."

"Give that here," said Roland. "Is there more? It's perfect. How'd you do that?"

"Raw talent?" Mel handed him the book. "There's lots more. You're going to use it to kill us all, aren't you?"

Freddy had had enough. It was excruciating to see Mel and Roland getting along, and worse that they were bonding over role-playing games. Freddy thought there might somewhere on Earth be something more stupid than role-playing games, but she honestly didn't know what it was. She could tell the conversation was shortly going to be all about hit points and XP and other boring, incomprehensible things. She shoved back her chair. As Roland started waxing poetic about caves of ice and damsels with dulcimers and how spot checks would work in a pleasure-dome, Freddy exited quietly through the kitchen door.

It was a cool Labour Day but not—unusually for Vancouver—a rainy one. Freddy crossed the patio to the smoke bush, which she had always thought was the prettiest plant in the yard. The leaves were naturally deep purple instead of green; in a few weeks, they would turn red. It towered over the patio. If Freddy moved around to its other side, she would no longer be visible from the house. For now, she just stood beneath it, breathing in its clean scent. The best thing about the smoke bush was that it wasn't a treacherous genius little sister or a shambling mess of a stepbrother. It just sat there. It didn't drink milk straight from the carton, and it didn't talk back.

Mel was good at dealing with change. She'd accepted Roland as a matter of course almost as soon as she'd met him. Mel accepted most things as a matter of course. Freddy never could. It had been hard enough trying to fly under the radar at school when it had just been Mel cheerfully spreading her weirdness around. Now Freddy had Roland to deal with as well. She'd been relieved—and guilty about the relief—last year when she'd started grade eight and left Mel behind at the elementary school, but Jordan and Roland had moved in in late September, meaning that Freddy had once again found herself living in the same house as someone who went to her school and was no good at flying under the radar at all. Sure, Roland took most of his classes at the School for the Deaf, which was, unfortunately, housed in buildings connected to Roncesvalles High, yet he was always in at least one hearing course per semester, and last year, he'd turned up in Freddy's math class. It was hard to avoid being noticed when you had an almost-stepbrother blundering all over your geometry lessons.

Freddy glowered at the smoke bush. *And it gets to start all over again tomorrow.* She had worked so hard at seeming normal. She knew she *was* normal compared to Mel, who could have been in university by now if she'd wanted, and Roland, who was proud of the fact that he had been voted the School for the Deaf's student most likely to drive accidentally off a cliff within the next ten years. Everyone knew she was nothing like either of them, but it didn't seem to matter. Bits of them clung to her like secondhand smoke.

And there's Mum, she thought. She immediately shoved the thought away. Mum wasn't the problem. She was never around, anyway.

Someone yelped nearby, jarring Freddy out of her reverie. She raised her head. A voice said something indistinct; another voice went, "Sssh!" Someone was in the yard behind her backyard, the side yard belonging to the house on Grosvenor Street.

The yards were separated by a chain-link fence and two rows of cedar bushes, one on either side of the fence. The bushes on Freddy's side were neatly trimmed and rose only to Freddy's shoulders, a fact of which she was a little bit proud, as a year before she'd barely been able to see over them. The bushes on the other side had grown out of control. They towered above the fence, their upper branches spilling over into Freddy's yard. Jordan had tried to get the Johannsens to cut them back, but the Johannsens seemed to be trying to pretend the house didn't exist. Now Freddy ducked around the smoke bush and approached the cedar hedge. If the house had been sold, it was possible the new owners were in the yard right now. She wouldn't be able to see them over the bushes, but she could at least hear what they sounded like.

The people in the other yard were whispering frantically. Freddy paused beside the bushes to listen. She couldn't make out much, though she thought there were two voices. ". . . being obtuse," she heard, and then, ". . . can't chance it. Even this was a hundred to one against. If we . . ." The whispers sank into incomprehensibility. Cautiously, Freddy pressed herself against the cedar branches. ". . . listening! Right now!" hissed one of the whisperers. Freddy jerked back a little. Did the speaker mean her? She—or he—couldn't have. Freddy had moved silently over the grass; these people couldn't have known she was here. "Well, we should go over . . ." said the second whisperer. Something rustled, and there was silence.

It had all been just strange enough that Freddy went out through the side gate onto Grosvenor Street to take a look. But the street was empty of cars, and the house looked as unlived-in as usual, and when Freddy dodged around the big pine and peered right into the yard, she could see there was nobody there.

By noon, shortly after Freddy discovered that the book her friend Rochelle had recommended to her a few months ago was about tragic nuzzling immortal teenagers and deserved to be shredded, Mel and Roland had gone a bit overboard with the whole RPG thing. Their campaign wasn't starting until three, but it didn't seem to matter. Freddy was drearily certain they were going to spend the next three hours talking about nothing else. Then Todd and Marcus would show up, and the game-speak would continue until midnight. Mum and Jordan wouldn't care. They were out already. Typically, they hadn't said where they were going, but had just slid out of the house while everybody else was focussed on breakfast. Freddy had the vague sense it had been days since she had seen them properly. She sometimes wondered whether they got around by tunnelling through the walls.

The problem was that Roland and Mel were having their conversation in the living room, which had been deserted and deathly quiet when Freddy had sat down to read in it ten minutes before. Freddy scowled at her book and tried to ignore the half-spoken, half-signed, entirely earnest discussion about thrice-woven circles and the particular skills of Mel's cleric character. Mel had the Coleridge book with her and apparently felt it was a good idea to read the entire pleasure-dome poem aloud in dramatic tones, complete with signed translation. The game itself was going to be worse. It would inevitably involve screaming and a fistfight. *I wanted to read,* thought Freddy. And she had been here *first.* Deliberately, she brought the book up in front of her face, blocking out the other two and trying to force herself to concentrate on a book that she kind of wanted to throw against the wall or possibly burn.

"I think you should maybe use monsters that *aren't* eldritch tentacled horrors from beyond the depths of space and time," Mel was explaining. Freddy gritted her teeth and read a description of somebody's sweater for what felt like the thirty-fifth time. She couldn't seem to take it in.

"I like tentacled horrors. I'm comfortable with them," said Roland.

Freddy sighed loudly. She knew Mel would notice and Roland

wouldn't. If he had, he would have ignored her. It was their whole relationship: she was helplessly angry with him without knowing exactly why, and he pretended she wasn't there. *Maybe I should just lose it and yell at him for an hour,* she thought. She knew she never would. She didn't confront people. Confronting people was just another way of drawing attention to yourself, which wasn't the best thing to do when you weren't even sure you were right about anything. At school, she had turned not confronting people into an art form. It wasn't always fun to be invisible at school, but it was safer that way.

She peered over the top of her book at Roland and Mel, happily engaged in a discussion involving the logistics of pleasure-dome ice caves. Neither of them was invisible at school. Both of them had friends. Roland had Todd and Marcus, and Mel had Jonathan and Clara, and sometimes they even all hung out together, and there was always a lot of laughter, plus some squabbling and the occasional full-out screaming match. It was all just . . . messy. Freddy was glad she wasn't part of it.

I have friends, too, she thought. She hadn't seen Rochelle and Cathy in weeks. She would talk to them tomorrow, anyway, and they would start doing stuff together again, and she could stop feeling as if she was—

No, thought Freddy, *I am not the odd one out.* She plunged back into the book, which she was genuinely beginning to despise.

"Stop squirming," said Mel. "If we're stopping you from enjoying your pink sparkly book, go read it somewhere else."

Freddy said, "I was here first." She cringed at the whine that had crept into her tone.

"It's our house, too," said Roland, "in case you hadn't noticed."

She opened her mouth, then shut it again. The anger surged, choking off her voice. She saw Roland's mouth quirk in what could easily have been contempt. He thought she was a coward. Maybe he would have liked her more if she *had* yelled at him. Maybe not. She couldn't imagine a world in which she and Roland were friends.

Her right hand hurt. It was in her pocket, and it seemed to be clenched tightly around . . . that key. She had no idea why. Impatiently, she straightened her fingers. "Whatever you say."

"Don't you go and cry," said Roland.

Her hand clenched again. "I don't cry."

Roland laughed derisively. Mel pulled herself to her feet. Outside, there was a crash so violent that even Roland jumped as the impact vibrated through the floor of the living room.

Freddy said, "What the—?" and ran to the window.

"No," said Mel, "not that way. It was on Grosvenor."

She took off into the kitchen. Roland and Freddy shared one glance, then followed, out the door and across the yard to the gate in the hedge that led to Grosvenor Street.

2

There was only one house on Grosvenor Street, but the park tended to have people in it, especially on weekends and holidays. It didn't today. Grosvenor was quiet and deserted as Mel led the others out onto it, or as quiet and deserted as it could be after an accident that had left a small moving van wrapped around a tree.

The van had run headfirst into the pine that separated Freddy's family's property from the front yard of the house on Grosvenor Street. The front of the van had folded in on itself like an accordion. There were creaking noises coming from it, and quite a lot of smoke. "Freddy," said Roland, "Mel should go back in the yard." For once, Freddy agreed with him. It didn't seem likely they were going to find anything good in the driver's compartment. She felt her stomach contract.

"I'm not a baby," said Mel, though when Freddy glanced at her, she saw that her sister had gone white.

Freddy said, "Go—"

The driver's side door swung open. All three of them jumped back. "Jesus," said Roland.

"No no no," said a woman from inside the van, "no Jesus here. Where'd that tree come from?"

"It was standing by the side of the road," a muffled voice replied, "dumbass."

"It was *not* standing by the side of the road," said the first person, still unseen amidst the wreckage. The front of the van belched more smoke, and metal scraped against metal. "I was looking specifically. There's got to be something illegal about trees that appear out of nowhere and jump on top of your van."

"Do we hit trees for fun now?" asked the second person, his voice cracking on the fourth word. Freddy recognised that crack. Most of the boys in her class had it, or had had it recently, or would have it soon.

"I was under the impression it was a driveway," said the woman.

"You . . . are . . . a . . . *moron*," spat the boy. Freddy edged closer to the van; the others were doing the same. Someone was thrashing around in the middle of the smoke.

"I certainly seem to be," said the woman. "Do you have your foot in my face? Why do you?"

"Because I'm stuck," said the boy.

"Uh . . ." said Roland, but that was all. Freddy glanced at him, then at Mel. *Why are we behaving like this?* No one was leaping forward to try to help the people trapped in the van. No one had called 9-1-1. She thought it was the bizarre contrast between the totalled van and the voices. Neither the woman nor the boy sounded impaired or in shock. They might have been conversing over sandwiches and root beer.

"I hear spectators," said the woman. "I wonder what *this* does."

Something went *sproing*. Mel jumped again as the woman fell out of the van through a cloud of smoke.

She looked up at them and smiled. "Did one of you put this tree here? I'm thinking of lodging a complaint."

She was perhaps thirty-five and would have looked as boring as any other grown-up if she hadn't been wearing a trench coat and a fedora. Freddy and Roland both turned towards Mel. Mel had discovered the mystery genre at the age of nine. She'd handed various books on to Freddy, who had been able to get only about a quarter of the way through *The Big Sleep* before giving up, but Freddy had also been forced by Mel to watch plenty of films about private eyes in the big city, and she could see that this woman would have seemed perfectly at home toting a gun in a shadowy alley at midnight.

"Excuse me. Hello. Trapped in *smoking wreckage*," said the boy. "If the van explodes, I shall be displeased."

"Don't mind Josiah." The woman bounced to her feet. She didn't seem injured at all. "He got up on the wrong side of the bed some time ago, and he hasn't been back to sleep since."

More scraping noises happened, and the boy followed the woman much less gracefully. "Ow," said Mel, watching him tumble into a puddle. Oil, maybe from the van, had got into it, turning it rainbow coloured. Freddy twitched. She wanted to run forward and help these people, but . . . she didn't.

The boy rolled over and sat up, dripping. Roland and Mel both squeaked. There was a gash on his forehead, and blood had streamed down his face, making him look as if he were peering out at them through a mottled red-and-brown mask. "It's nothing. It's only a flesh wound. Et cetera. Don't faint. Cuerva Lachance, you're just going to leave me sitting here, aren't you?"

"Probably," said the woman. "Have you taken a look at these ones, Josie, dear?"

The boy's bloody forehead knotted. "Don't call me Josie. What am I supposed to be looking at?"

Freddy, Mel, and Roland stood all in a row, watching as the boy—Josie, or Josiah, or whatever it was—leaned against the side of the stricken van and pulled himself to his feet. Waving the smoke away from his face, he squinted out through it at them. It was hard not to stare. The woman was ordinary looking, despite her clothes, but there was something . . . not right about the boy. From what Freddy could see through the smoke and the bloody mask, he was average in size for his age, which seemed to be about the same as *her* age. His hair was black and straight, though tousled by the accident, and his skin was much darker than the woman's. He should have been practically indistinguishable from any other fourteen-year-old boy. But there was something different. It was making her eyes water. She had no idea what it was.

And then the boy was staring at *them*.

"Not again," he said. "Where is he, then?"

Freddy thought maybe he was looking at her in particular. "Uh . . . ?"

"Him. Where *is* he? You have to know," said Josiah impatiently.

Freddy glanced at Mel, who shrugged.

Slowly, Josiah's face changed. It was hard to say for sure with the blood in the way, but Freddy thought what she was seeing may have been a look of dawning horror.

"No," he said.

"I think so," the woman replied, gazing vaguely off into the park. "Look . . . trees."

"But it's not—I don't—we shouldn't—Cuerva Lachance! *No*. We're not here for *this*. I refuse to be here for this! You," he said, pointing dramatically towards them with a hand shaking so violently that Freddy wasn't sure whether his finger was aimed at one of them in particular or all three of them in general, "go away. You appall me. I refuse to acknowledge your existence. You're not here."

The woman beamed at them all from under her improbable hat. "Would you help us unload? There may be pie in the van. It's possible it's been squashed by the couch, but you never know. Helping us unload will be fun, and there's a squirrel in the tree. I never expected that. I'm Cuerva Lachance."

Freddy looked at Roland and Mel for help, but she could already see they were going to be useless. Roland's mouth was hanging open. Mel, usually not shy at all, was sidling behind Roland. Freddy's eyes moved from her stepbrother and sister to the boy Josiah, who was muttering to himself and working his hands into and out of fist shapes, and then to the woman in the trench coat and fedora. Nothing added up at all. "Are you . . ." said Freddy, and stopped. She moistened her lips with her tongue and tried again. "Are you going to *live* here?"

"Of course," said Cuerva Lachance brightly. "We had to live somewhere, and it seemed convenient. It's pure bad luck there's a tree instead of a driveway. I take it you live next door? I like meeting neighbours. Josiah, did you know you were bleeding? I can't think why you're doing that. Let's go find that pie."

⌒

Somehow, Freddy, Mel, and Roland found themselves hauling boxes and furniture from the van to the house on Grosvenor Street. It made no sense. They should have been phoning 9-1-1 and calling for the nice men in white coats to come deal with Cuerva Lachance; they should certainly have been staying out of the house. "I think we're all enchanted," Mel told Freddy at one point. It was sometimes a little too easy to forget that Mel was only twelve. She could go on about string theory for twenty minutes before turning the entire conversation on its head by mentioning unicorns. Freddy didn't think they were enchanted. She thought they were in shock. It just seemed easier to turn their brains off and do what Cuerva Lachance told them.

It was impossible to think of her as anything but "Cuerva Lachance," which was what Josiah called her, always in tones of contempt or exasperation. The part of Freddy that wasn't striving to catch up observed that all of them tried to change this. When Cuerva Lachance wrenched open the back doors of the van (and dodged the six boxes and the bookcase that tried to fall on top of her), Mel, still standing behind Roland, said in a subdued voice, "Ms. . . . Lachance . . . ?"

"Cuerva," said Cuerva Lachance.

"Cuerva," said Mel. There was a pause. Freddy watched her sister struggle, then give in and add, "Lachance. Shouldn't someone move the van away from the tree?"

"It's a good theory," said Cuerva Lachance, "but I don't know where we're going to find anyone like that. Here, little fat one. Take this box. Don't drop it; we wouldn't want to break anything."

Mel gingerly took the box, which had been flattened and mangled by the accident and the tumble from the van. "Uh—"

"Big awkward one," said Cuerva Lachance to Roland, who didn't notice because he was watching Josiah walk around in circles, tugging at his own hair. Freddy nudged Roland. Her resentment of him had, for the moment, been swallowed up in bewilderment.

Roland looked at the woman. "Yes? Cuerva . . . Lachance?" His struggle was shorter than Mel's, but Freddy still heard the pause.

"Chairs," said Cuerva Lachance. "You look about the right size for those. Curly-haired one, you help the fat one with the boxes. I see another squirrel."

"Uh," said Freddy, "Cuerva . . ."

She was determined not to say the surname. There was no reason she should. All her classmates' parents went by their first names except Paul Jacobs's, who insisted on children calling them "sir" and "ma'am." Paul was constantly being embarrassed about his parents.

It was no good. The "Cuerva" seemed incomplete by itself. When she said it alone, she found herself stuck with a space of silence that could be filled by only one word.

". . . Lachance," continued Freddy, defeated. "We can't get into the house."

"Josiah has the key," said Cuerva Lachance. "He never misplaces keys. It must be boring to be that responsible. Josiah, let the nice people inside."

Keys and trees, whispered something inside Freddy's brain. For a sliver of time, she almost knew why. Then the conversation continued, and the thought flitted away.

"They're not here," said Josiah. His voice started high on the first word and dived into the subbasement on the last.

"They still need you to open the door for them," said Cuerva Lachance. "What's your name, little fat one?"

"Mel," said Mel. To Freddy's surprise, she added, "Melanie Duchamp." She even pronounced it the French way, as Dad always had. Freddy was pretty sure her sister hadn't said her full name to anyone since Dad had left.

"Curly-haired one?" said Cuerva Lachance, industriously picking up boxes.

"Freddy. Frédérique. Duchamp." It was, again, as if the pauses could only be filled in by certain words. She felt, and she couldn't have said why, that she had to give Cuerva Lachance her full name.

Cuerva Lachance had simply to glance in Roland's direction for him to say in resigned tones, "Roland Michael Isamu Fukiyama."

"My sympathies," said Cuerva Lachance. "Let's go throw everything in a great big pile in the living room."

"I don't acknowledge that any of this is happening," proclaimed Josiah, but he did pull a key from his pocket and, with bad grace, head for the front door.

The house on Grosvenor Street didn't look like any of the other houses in the neighbourhood. Mel, who liked to understand everything about everything, said this particular suburb had grown up in the 1940s and afterwards, and so the houses were mainly little one-family units: small bungalows, split-levels, the occasional duplex. There were newer houses, too, quite big, blocky ones covered in pink or yellow stucco and crammed into subdivided lots that seemed hardly large enough to hold them. This house fit neither the older style nor the newer one. It was three storeys high and what Mel described as "peaky," which seemed to mean that the architect had been in love with gables and had crammed in as many as he could. Three were visible from the front, one on top of the other, getting smaller the higher they went; there were two more small ones in the back and one on the southern side, the side facing onto the vacant lot adjoining. Freddy had always thought the gables made the house look like a fancy layer cake. The roof was steep and startlingly red; the walls were white, with red trim around the window frames. Ivy climbed the southern wall of the house, and tendrils of it sneaked around the corner to the front, striving towards the windows and door.

The northern wall of the house had no gables because it bulged out into a sort of miniature circular tower. The tower didn't rise any higher than the rest of the house, but it looked as if it wanted to. There was ivy here as well, almost obscuring the tiny window near the top. It was the almost-tower that tended to charm the various people who bought the house, and it was the almost-tower that, in the end, drove them away.

Freddy had been inside twice when the Wongs had lived there, before she'd realised the money was not worth the mental and physical pain of babysitting the little Wong hellions. At that time, the interior of the house had looked like a furniture showroom that had been hit by a violent hurricane. The Wongs' tasteful, expensive furnishings hadn't been able to stand up against the destructive force that was their five sons. It was different now. Josiah, scowling, let them into an empty house. Their feet echoed on the tiles of the front hall and the hardwood floor of the living room. Someone had been keeping the place relatively dust-free; the living room looked huge and clean as Freddy and the others dumped their burdens in a corner. Light streamed through the bay windows, dancing in patterns on the floor as it filtered through the leaves of the cherry tree in the front yard. The room was blank, without personality, waiting for someone to mould it into shape.

"That's right," said Cuerva Lachance, poking her head into the room. "Just throw them anywhere. Josiah will sort them out later."

"Obviously," said Josiah, injecting so much sarcasm into the word that Mel eyed him with respect.

Freddy asked Josiah as they all trooped back out to the van, "You don't get along with your mum, then?"

Josiah stopped dead in the middle of the lawn and stared at her. He hadn't yet bothered to wipe the blood from his face. "My *what?*"

"She's not your mum?" said Mel.

"How could *anyone* think that?" snarled Josiah. "Don't make that mistake again. It drives me completely up the wall." He flung his arms out dramatically, then turned on his heel and continued towards the van.

Mel bounced after him. Freddy could see her sister sliding into investigative mode. "You have an accent."

"What? I do not," said Josiah.

"You do," said Freddy. The funny thing was that though she was pretty good with accents, she couldn't tell where it was from. It was very slight. His words simply seemed to pop more than theirs, and some of his expressions were a little bit off.

Roland said, "Are you going to clean off the blood at all?"

"Stop badgering me," said Josiah. "We've only just met. Do you do this to all your new neighbours? Why has no one tried to kill you yet?"

Freddy, Mel, and Roland exchanged wary glances. Freddy wondered if the other two were feeling the same thing she was. She didn't know why she was treating Josiah like this. It was part of the general strangeness surrounding him; it encouraged obnoxious comments.

Mel had been helpfully signing translations to Roland, and Cuerva Lachance had noticed. "Deaf?" she said as she handed Roland a lamp. "Profoundly or partially? Read lips?"

"Profoundly," said Roland. "I do read lips."

She nodded. "Keep reminding me so I don't forget to face you when I talk. I have the attention span of a pair of scissors."

Freddy was surprised to find she was enjoying herself. She hadn't really been enjoying all that much lately. The constant anger had leached into everything she did. This felt almost like a break from the real world. She even quirked an eyebrow at Roland as she passed him in the hall, and she could have sworn he nearly smiled in return.

"Why are we doing this, exactly?" said Mel as they balanced a kitchen table between them and manoeuvred it through the front door. "I ask out of curiosity."

Freddy gave as much of a shrug as she could with her hands full of table.

Mel pursed her lips. "There's something unnatural about these guys."

"You always want there to be something unnatural about every-body new you meet," Freddy pointed out.

"Yeah," said Mel, "except we've known them for ten minutes, and they've got us lugging around all their worldly belongings. We didn't even protest. And it's not like they're being nice to us. But here we are, at their beck and call. I don't even feel indignant about it."

"That's because you're making it into a mystery story in your head," said Freddy.

"Life's more interesting that way," Mel explained.

The sound of a slamming door made them both look up, startled. A few seconds later, Josiah appeared at the head of the stairs and bounded down them with what Freddy was already sure was unac-customed energy.

"You're not to go upstairs. No one is to go upstairs ever," he said, glaring out from beneath quivering eyebrows. "That table doesn't belong upstairs. Take it *that* way."

"We *are* taking it that way," said Freddy.

Mel said, "What's wrong with upstairs? I don't have to make this into a mystery story, Freddy; it is one."

"No, it isn't," said Josiah, still staring ferociously at Freddy, "and don't let Cuerva Lachance hear you say that. She's a private investigator. If she knows you're interested, she'll manipulate you into working for her for free."

Josiah could not have said anything that would have distracted Mel more effectively from whatever was wrong with upstairs. Mel dropped her end of the table on Freddy's foot. "She's a *private investigator*?" Mel said, ignoring her sister's cry of pain. "For real? With the hat and the coat and everything?"

"I've told her to get rid of those," said Josiah. "No one ever listens to me."

"Nice going." Freddy hopped over to lean against the wall. She had to escape Josiah's gaze; her eyes were watering again. There was something slightly wrong about the intensity of his stare. "She's going to be coming here all the time now."

"Just what we need," said Josiah. "Feral neighourhood children. Haven't your parents warned you against talking to strangers?"

Freddy opened her mouth, then shut it again. She had a very old, very uncertain memory of her parents lecturing her on staying away from strangers; she didn't think the issue had come up for years. But what had really silenced her was . . . well, she thought it was another memory, but she wasn't sure of what. She could hear someone saying,

"Your parents have told you never to talk to strangers." There had been a crow somewhere nearby, and . . . that key. She had been crying . . .

The crazy lady in the woods. Freddy's hand stole to her pocket and wrapped around her key ring. She could feel the key right away, smaller and more delicate than her house keys and her bike-lock key and the tiny flashlight she kept clipped to the ring. Well, it made sense that the memory should surface now. There was more to it than just Josiah's mention of strangers, though. Something else about *now* was raising echoes from *then*.

Roland blundered through the door and knocked over the pile of boxes next to it. Mel and Freddy escaped through to the kitchen as Josiah let out a theatrical cry of despair. Thoughts of the encounter four years before slipped from Freddy's mind.

⌘

"I should call the rental company," said Cuerva Lachance later as she gazed mournfully out at the van, which had only just stopped smoking. They were all sitting on the front steps, passing around the strawberry rhubarb pie that really had been discovered lurking, only slightly battered, under the couch. Josiah had refused it altogether and now perched moodily on a railing, watching the rest of them break off squishy pieces with their fingers. He had, at long last, cleaned off the blood, but Freddy could still see flecks and streaks of it on his skin, as if he hadn't cared enough to wash properly. His face had been revealed to be thin and brown, with a beak of a nose and a sharp little chin. The gash on his forehead was surprisingly small.

"Don't be absurd," said Josiah, his accent becoming briefly more pronounced. Freddy thought she had identified it for sure as English, but as he continued speaking, she changed her mind to Portuguese. "I'll do it. I remember what happened the last time you tried to explain how you had wrecked someone's car."

Cuerva Lachance favoured him with her blinding smile. "I wrecked it for a good cause."

"It's never a good cause with you," said Josiah. "It's never a *cause* with you at all." He sighed and yanked a smartphone from his pocket. "Oh, look, you didn't break it by smashing us headfirst into a tree. Miracles never cease. Could you make the feral children go away while I'm on the phone?" He swung himself down onto the porch and stalked inside, fiddling with the touchscreen.

Mel had stuffed her hands against her mouth to keep from laughing out loud. Cuerva Lachance gave her an approving grin. "The problem with Josiah is that he was born without a sense of humour," she said.

"Are you really a private investigator?" said Mel, who must have been wanting to ask this question all afternoon.

Cuerva Lachance tilted her head, an oddly birdlike gesture. "Mostly. Do you *need* a private investigator?"

"It's just that you're Mel's hero now." Roland had moved down onto the front walk so he could see everybody talking. "She reads mysteries."

"Ah," said Cuerva Lachance, "those. Not really my genre. It would be like taking my work home with me, and since I already work from home, that would cause a logic implosion, and Josiah would have a meltdown. Tell me, little fat one, do you read the mysteries with the spunky old British ladies solving crimes in country houses or the mysteries with the depressed alcoholics uncovering corruption in cities made of despair?"

"Both, and everything in between," Freddy and Roland said together. Their eyes met, then flicked apart.

"The reality is much more boring," Cuerva Lachance assured them. "There's a lot of sitting around with cameras, waiting for people to slink out of skeezy motels. I've never even inadvertently taken down an international crime syndicate, though not for lack of trying. I did solve a country-house murder once, but that was an accident, and as it turned out, the butler had done it. Do your parents know where you are?"

Freddy was already getting used to Cuerva Lachance's habit of changing topics at lightning speed. "No."

"They went somewhere," said Mel. "My name is Mel, you know, not 'little fat one.'"

"I ask for names to be polite," said Cuerva Lachance. "I don't remember them. My head is full of other things, and names just bounce out."

"Can I use your bathroom?" asked Freddy, who had been getting increasingly less comfortable for the past hour or so.

Cuerva Lachance waved a hand lazily at the house. "*Mi casa es su casa*. I haven't the faintest idea where it is. There may not be toilet paper, but you never know. Try up the stairs, first on the left. Those directions generally work for bathrooms."

Freddy rose and walked into the house. Behind her, she heard Mel say something about Sherlock Holmes.

Through the living room door, she could see the heap of boxes and furniture they had moved from the van. A stray thought—*It's not that much stuff for a house this size*—blew across her mind. She paused for a moment to gaze at the pile. Couch, chairs, a couple of cabinets, some tables, two bookcases, a bed, a TV, assorted boxes . . . It looked like the contents of an apartment. Something was missing, too. Everything *seemed* present, if sparse. But she knew there should have been something more. She just didn't know what. Freddy shook her head to clear it. It would come to her. At any rate, maybe Cuerva Lachance and Josiah were moving here from an apartment and would get more stuff later.

As she moved up the stairs, her feet silent on the worn red runner, she wondered what her mum and Jordan would say if they knew she was walking calmly into a stranger's house after spending hours helping her move. She tried to imagine Mum hearing the story and sitting straight up and crying, *"What?"* And then Jordan would say, "Explain yourself, young lady," and there would be a long, stern conversation that would end with Mel in tears and Roland and Freddy humbly promising never to do anything so insane ever again. "We've learned our lesson," they would say. "We shouldn't talk to strangers." There would be hugs and chocolate-chip cookies.

Freddy felt her mouth twisting into an expression that wasn't really a smile. She could imagine the scene, but the players were made of plastic, and they moved stiffly, doll-like and not at all alive. There had never been a scene like that in her house. She knew she wasn't going to tell her mum about this afternoon.

She'd reached the top of the stairs. As Cuerva Lachance had said, the bathroom was first on the left; she could see tiles through the half-closed door. Maybe those instructions did generally work for bathrooms. She moved to the door and was in the act of pushing it wide when she heard voices down the hall.

Freddy paused. No one was in here but Josiah.

Her hand was an inch from the door. She pulled it back and moved quietly down the hall, past two open doors and towards the closed one at the end.

The voices were muffled. The door did partially block the sound, but the people in the room also sounded as if they were trying not to be heard. There were at least two. Josiah was one, she thought. The other was speaking in a whisper. She couldn't make out what they were saying, even when she moved right up to the door. She cupped her ear in her hand. It didn't help much. Josiah sounded . . . not angry, exactly, but forceful. The other person could have been angry or annoyed or frightened or something else entirely. Freddy shuddered. When she'd been younger, she'd lain awake and listened to furious, half-whispering voices rising and falling downstairs. Her parents' fights were, in her memory, wordless, an angry booming buzz in the walls. She pushed the memory away.

". . . right on the other side of the door!" said the person who was not Josiah. They were the first audible words in the whole conversation.

"Why didn't you say so before?" snarled Josiah. Before Freddy could move—almost before she had time to draw breath—the door had been wrenched open.

Josiah stood there, looking so ferocious that Freddy forgot to glance past him into the room. She took a step back. "Who—?"

"No one," Josiah barked. "I was practising my impressions. I plan to join the circus. I told you to stay downstairs!"

He slammed the door behind him, seized Freddy by the wrist, and towed her back to the staircase. "I have to use the—" she started, but Josiah said, "No, you don't," and pulled her around the corner and down the stairs. She thought they were going to go straight out the door, but in the foyer, Josiah came to a jarring halt, shoved Freddy against the wall beside the door, pulled a pencil out of his pocket, and, before she had time to be surprised, marked her height on the frame. Then he latched on to her wrist again and yanked her out the door. "Out," he said, planting himself firmly in the doorway. "Your inability to obey instructions does not impress me. Go away, all of you."

"But Josie," said Cuerva Lachance, peeking past her hat, "we were having such a nice conversation, and I saw another squirrel."

"My lack of caring is palpable," said Josiah. Freddy decided the accent might be Russian, or possibly from somewhere in Africa. Then again, maybe it was Swedish.

"He's going to have a tantrum," said Cuerva Lachance. "In these situations, it's best just to do what he says. I'm sure we'll see each other around."

"It can hardly be avoided at this point," muttered Josiah. "They're like ducklings."

He gave Freddy a push, and she stumbled across the porch, narrowly avoiding tripping over Mel, who was just getting to her feet. "Scram, ducklings," Josiah said.

"It was bizarrely interesting to meet you," Cuerva Lachance added. "Mind the broken glass." She stood beaming and waving at them as they walked away across the lawn.

⁓

It was five to three. Todd and Marcus would be here soon, and the assault on the pleasure-dome would begin. Freddy, Roland, and Mel stood in their kitchen, looking at each other in a dazed sort of way.

"There was something really weird there," said Mel. "Our neighbours are really weird. I like them."

Freddy said, "There was someone else in the house. Upstairs. I heard them, and Josiah kicked us out."

"Good," said Mel. "The more mysterious the better." She turned to Roland. "You haven't said much."

Roland shrugged. Mel was right; Roland had joined in on the discussions with Cuerva Lachance and Josiah, but he hadn't said anything to Freddy or, Freddy presumed, Mel about them, whereas the girls had been whispering to each other throughout the afternoon. Freddy hadn't noticed anything unusual because she and Roland rarely had anything resembling a civil conversation.

"Got to pee," said Mel, and ducked out of the room before either of the others could stop her. Freddy was left blinking up at Roland.

They had almost been fighting earlier. Then the accident had happened, and . . . she didn't know. It was as if the time at the house on Grosvenor Street had propelled them into some sort of neutral zone. She wondered if maybe they could stay there for a bit, though she wasn't sure she wanted to. She could feel the constant anger trying to creep back. But it had been better this afternoon. Tentatively, Freddy opened her mouth to speak.

"We'll be playing in the living room," said Roland, "whether you like it or not. Go read somewhere else."

Or maybe she was right to feel the anger.

"Yes, your majesty." Freddy bowed deeply. It was the closest she could get to screaming at him properly. She didn't look into his face again; she knew what she would see there. Moving lightly, as he had never been able to do, she nipped out the door, leaving him standing alone.

3

By lunchtime the next day, Freddy was thinking longingly of noisy RPGs and exploding boxes of breakfast
cereal. She should have remembered that nothing could
be worse than school.

She always forgot. She never truly wanted to go back
to school in September, but the summer tended to mute
the horror. The first day of school even seemed kind of
exciting, a change of pace from the parade of Mel's and
Roland's larger-than-life friends and the anger that was
forever making her want to lock herself in her room and
pull the covers over her head. But school was . . . well, it
was school. There were black holes that caused, on a
daily basis, less terror. This was only the first day, and
already, Freddy could tell she was going to be groping
for her key so often this year that the metal was going to
start wearing away.

It hadn't been the useless welcome assembly, during
which she had sat alone in the midst of a squirming, jos-
tling mass of fourteen-year-olds who were all the best
friends ever. It hadn't been the equally useless *second* welcome assembly, during which the kids from the School

for the Deaf had been herded into the gymnasium and had sat there looking awkward and vaguely offended with the whole world as the two principals had droned on about Feelings. It hadn't been the short homeroom period, during which Mme. Gauthier had twittered at them and tried what was apparently her best to make the entire concept of homeroom seem anything other than pointless. Freddy had handled all that simply by turning off her brain. The real horror of school happened in the in-between bits, of which lunchtime was the worst.

She had managed to stay unobtrusive and harmless so far, but now she was sitting with Rochelle and Cathy, and danger was everywhere. She wasn't sure why she was eating with them; she thought it was just out of habit. Freddy had known it the second she had spotted the two of them whispering together in the hall: they weren't friends with her any more. She looked at them and saw two girls with perfect hair and skin, breasts threatening to escape the confines of their shirts, tight jeans hugging their hips. Rochelle had been wearing makeup for more than a year, but now Cathy was, too. Beside them, Freddy felt small and grubby. She had grown a bit last year, finally, but so had everyone else in her class. She was still the shortest kid in grade nine. More worryingly, despite the fact that she'd had her first period a couple of months before, she had hardly developed at all in what Mel called "girl ways." She wore a bra more out of hope than need.

Rochelle was being very . . . nice. At least, she was smiling a lot, and she had loudly mentioned how pretty Freddy's shirt was. Since Freddy was wearing an oversized green T-shirt with a breast pocket, she was suspecting sarcasm. Rochelle's sarcasm wasn't like Mel's. It was less friendly, and it was harder to tell whether or not it was there.

Now Rochelle said, "Who's your boyfriend?"

Freddy stared at her. She wanted not to be sitting at this table, and she had no idea why anyone would think she had a boyfriend. "What?"

Rochelle nodded at a point behind Freddy. "He keeps looking at you."

"He's not cute," said Cathy with a harsh giggle that set Freddy's teeth on edge.

For a moment, she considered not looking. Her lack of interest in boys sometimes worried her, but not all that often. Rochelle would punish her if she didn't look. Freddy turned around.

It took a few seconds before she found the boy and a few seconds more before she recognised him. When she did, she thought several bad words in a row. She should have known Josiah would be coming to school here. She should have known this might be a problem. At the house on Grosvenor Street, Josiah had seemed . . . well, not normal, exactly, but . . . sort of in context. He had fit the situation. Here, it was obvious that he wasn't anything like a single other kid in this building. She could see the others starting to realise. He was the only person at his table, though the cafeteria was crowded. She wondered how long it had taken him to drive everybody else away.

Josiah was glowering at her through his bangs, which fell into his eyes and hid the cut that had bled all over him the day before. When he saw her looking, he pointed at her dramatically, punched himself in the forehead a couple of times, swung his legs out from under the table, and slipped off behind three tall boys who were trying to out-obnoxious one another.

"*Weird*," said Rochelle. Freddy cringed. Rochelle thought weird people attracted other weird people. She was probably only a few seconds away from calling Freddy weird, too.

"He's not my boyfriend," said Freddy. "He's just my neighbour."

"Well," said Rochelle, "you're not mature enough to have a boyfriend." She gave a quick little smile that didn't mean anything.

Freddy poked at her sandwich, but her throat was so tight that swallowing was going to be pretty well impossible. She had known for most of the summer that Rochelle and Cathy were ignoring her. They hadn't told her why, but she thought she knew. They looked like teenagers. She looked like a kid.

She had known them both since kindergarten. They had spent hours playing together. She had thought they would be friends forever.

"You *will* be," said Cathy, not as earnestly as she seemed to think. "You're just a late bloomer."

"Yeah," said Freddy. The thought of "blooming" as these two had "bloomed" made her face feel hot. She looked at her watch, purely for something to do. There was far too much time left in the lunch period.

"A *watch*?" said Rochelle. "Are you seriously wearing a *watch*? Who does that any more? Where's your phone?"

Rochelle knew Freddy didn't have a phone. She asked her mother for one at regular intervals because the kids laughed at her for not having one, and her mother always said, "Of course, dear," and forgot all about it. It was more or less the way her mother dealt with everything she asked for. She knew she could have brought it up yet again, but the truth was that she didn't really want to carry a phone around all the time. It would have felt like always being, well, reachable. Besides, she liked her watch, which was waterproof and wound itself when she moved and told her the date as well as the time and had six distinct settings, not all of them entirely comprehensible to her.

Freddy shrugged, her eyes down. She knew how Rochelle would be looking at her right now.

"I've got social studies after lunch," said Cathy. "Oh my God, it's going to be so boring. Mr. James is cute, though."

"No," said Rochelle.

"That's what I meant," said Cathy.

They had stopped paying attention to her. She let the conversation wander on without her as it turned into Rochelle rating the cuteness of the male teachers and Cathy agreeing with everything she said. *What's wrong with me? This is the kind of stuff people talk about. I want to be normal. I want to fly under the radar . . . what's "cute" mean, anyway?* For years now, Freddy had survived school by walking what Mel called "the fine line between fame and notoriety." She'd had to look up "notoriety," but once she had, she'd admitted that Mel had got it right. She'd never been popular, but she'd never been unpopular, either. She'd just sort of been there. She could fade into the background. Now the background itself was changing, and she could feel herself becoming more visible. A boy Freddy didn't know walked past and leered at Rochelle, and Rochelle made such a meal of pretending he wasn't there that it was obvious to everyone at the table that she wanted him to leer at her some more.

The problem was that school was really just a series of invisible lines. When you stayed on your own side, no one knew the lines existed. When you crossed one, everybody noticed. Freddy had once been good at telling where the lines were.

She escaped as soon as she could. She knew, realistically, that nothing had really *happened* over lunch, but she still felt the conversation with Rochelle and Cathy had more or less summed up why school was worse than anything anywhere.

This semester, she was in English, science, math, PE, band, and drama. English and PE were on alternate days, as were band and drama; those classes would run all year. Science and math were daily and would be replaced by social studies and French in the second semester. Ordinarily, she would have had four classes a day, two in the morning and two in the afternoon. Today, thanks to the morning assembly, all four classes had been crammed into the afternoon, with each only forty minutes long. The first bell rang, and the lights flicked off and on again so the kids from the School for the Deaf would know the period was changing. There were five minutes until English. Freddy was actually glad she would get English first thing every other morning. It wasn't her favourite class, but growing up with an English professor for a mother had forced her to read beyond her grade level in self-defence. She could enter the classroom and just stop paying attention. Of course, the fact that she had English first period every other day also meant that she had PE first period every *other* other day. She would try not to think about that now.

She knew neither Rochelle nor Cathy was in her class; both of them were in the afternoon English class with Ms. Chang. She shared only one class with each of them this semester. A week ago, she wouldn't have thought that would be a relief. It turned out now that it was. There would be no whispering and giggling and pitying glances to distract her from the soothing boredom of the class. She took her seat and tried to disappear into it. Despite the shifting background, Freddy still considered that making people not notice her was one of her few really useful gifts.

Of course, it only worked if the weird new kid didn't thump into the seat next to her and say loudly, "Fancy meeting you again. Why are you all scrunched up like that?"

Freddy's stomach rolled over. Damn Josiah. It was the bits *between* classes that were supposed to be dangerous.

"You should scrunch up, too," she whispered. "Stop drawing attention to yourself."

"What? I'm not. How am I?" said Josiah in a clear, carrying voice.

"Be . . . quiet," she said.

"Oh," said Josiah, "you're wanting me to conform. I'd rather not, but thanks all the same. Shall we have a bet on how long it takes me to get beat up for the first time?"

Heads were turning all over the classroom. Freddy suspected they would have done so even if Josiah had spoken softly and kept his head down. He was that sort of person. And she was *talking to him*. In *public*. Why was she?

And I was all worried about being in a class with Roland again, thought Freddy.

Mr. Dillon entered the room exactly as the second bell rang. He had been Freddy's English teacher the year before as well, and she knew he always made a point of being precisely on time. As a teacher, he was just barely okay. He was likely in his mid-twenties, but he struck Freddy as wanting to be older. Mr. Dillon had a brown vest and a tweed jacket with elbow patches. He had the students sit in strict rows, and unlike the other English teachers at the school, he taught grammar and logical argument. He spoke in a droning monotone that everybody knew he was putting on. They had all heard him talking normally to other teachers in the hallways.

She sank into her usual Dillon-enabled daydream before he was halfway through the attendance sheet. She already knew everything he taught them; Mum could be truly terrifying when someone misused an apostrophe in her presence. Freddy found that all she had to do to achieve a reasonable grade in Mr. Dillon's class was show up and occasionally answer a question about Shakespeare. She half listened as Mr. Dillon told them they would be starting with poetry and eventually moving on to *A Midsummer Night's Dream* and some novel involving a young boy dealing with the death of his dog. Most of the novels she'd been forced to read in school were along those lines. It seemed as if this year was going to be pretty much like last—

"Brilliant," said Josiah.

Mr. Dillon paused in his droning monologue. Twenty-nine students swivelled their eyes towards Josiah. Freddy was pretty sure most of them had never before heard anyone outside a Harry Potter film say "Brilliant."

"Mr. . . . Lachance?" said Mr. Dillon, the only teacher in the school who used surnames.

"I'll kill her for registering me as Josiah Lachance." Josiah sounded quite pleasant about it. "I said 'Brilliant.' I was approving of your curriculum."

"Oh," said Mr. Dillon, raising his eyebrows, "good."

"It's designed to teach us nothing of value," said Josiah, ignoring the muttering and giggling that were beginning to fill out the space behind his words. "I've covered more interesting material while trapped in a cave for a year."

Mr. Dillon was evidently startled enough that he forgot to drone. "Have you been trapped in a cave for a year?"

"Metaphorically speaking," said Josiah. "Everything I say should be taken as metaphor ninety percent of the time. Have you thought of assigning a real novel? One with characters and a plot, not just profound messages about death?"

"Mr. Lachance," said Mr. Dillon, "when we begin *And the Dog in the Midnight Sun* next semester, you're free to express your opinion—"

"I'm expressing my opinion now," explained Josiah. "I've read it. It's earnest and uplifting, and it ends with a heart-wrenching scene designed to provoke tears in even the most jaded of readers. Are there any novels read in high school that *aren't* written by people who have never learned the meaning of the word 'subtle'?"

The background giggling was threatening to leach into the foreground. "Shutupshutupshutup," Freddy hissed out of the corner of her mouth. She wouldn't have bothered if she hadn't been seen talking to him just before.

"Miss Duchamp," said Mr. Dillon, "do you have something to say? Do you, too, have some objection to *And the Dog in the Midnight Sun*?"

Freddy opened her mouth to tell Mr. Dillon she had no objection to anything at all. "Are you going to 'teach' it by spending two weeks describing the plot?" she said.

The giggling stopped as if it had been switched off. Freddy put her head down on her desk. She had *not* said that. There was no possible *way* she had said that. Maybe Mel had been right about them being enchanted after all.

"Mr. Lachance and Miss Duchamp," said Mr. Dillon after a lengthy pause, "a word outside."

Freddy didn't dare look at the other students as she shuffled out into the hallway. The giggling was starting again, though it may have counted as tittering now. It didn't sound very friendly.

Mr. Dillon closed the door firmly on the sneering class and looked down his nose at Freddy and Josiah. "Miss Duchamp," he said, "I'm surprised at you. You were a model student last year."

Josiah gave a quiet but audible snort, drawing Mr. Dillon's gaze. "Are you going to be a disruptive influence?"

"No," said Josiah.

"Then your behaviour today won't be repeated?" said Mr. Dillon.

"No," said Josiah.

"I'm willing to put it down to start-of-semester high spirits," Mr. Dillon told them with a condescending generosity that made Freddy cringe. "As long as it doesn't happen again. And it won't, will it? Miss Duchamp?"

Freddy shook her head. She knew her face was burning. She wouldn't have been surprised if the other two had felt the heat radiating from her.

"Mr. Lachance?" said Mr. Dillon.

"It won't happen again," said Josiah.

"Then let's return to the class," their teacher said. He opened the door.

As they moved back to their seats, Freddy sneaked a glance at Josiah. He was, to her dismay, making the same face Mel made when she had just told an outrageous lie and got away with it. He was going to keep on doing it. *I'll just keep my mouth shut*, thought Freddy. *This was an accident. Everybody knows I don't say things like that.* She covered her face with her hands and pretended not to notice that as Mr. Dillon continued his lecture, Josiah was sniggering at almost every sentence. There were twenty-five minutes left in the class. Freddy was reasonably certain they wouldn't pass for years.

⌒

When the bell rang several agonising decades later, Freddy gathered up her books and rushed out of the room before most of the students had a chance to rise to their feet. Science was next. After English, she expected to find it soothing. She took a seat at the end of one of the lab benches and tried to look inconspicuous. No one sat next to her, not even Rochelle, who had managed to get a seat at a bench already occupied by three boys. That was fine with Freddy.

The teacher, Ms. Treadwell, was in the middle of handing out textbooks when the classroom door opened. "Sorry," said Josiah. "Got turned around in the hallway."

Knowing what was coming, Freddy slowly lifted her notebook until it hid her face. There were only five open seats in the classroom, and four were at a completely unoccupied bench front and centre.

"Is this teacher as hopeless as the last one?" asked Josiah as he slid onto the stool next to hers. "She looks as if she may be. It's the general lack of chin."

Heads were turning again. Freddy said as quietly as she could, "Don't you ever whisper?"

"What for?" said Josiah. "These aren't state secrets. Besides, I need *some* way of distracting myself from the unbearable excitement of rolling marbles down an inclined plane."

A textbook soared over Josiah's shoulder and thumped onto the lab bench in front of him. He turned in time to see Ms. Treadwell smiling innocently as she handed Freddy her own book. "How brave of you to volunteer for the first presentation of the year," she said to Josiah. "Due next Monday. Be sure there are marbles and an inclined plane in it somewhere. As for the rest . . . surprise me."

Freddy decided that she wanted to be Ms. Treadwell when she grew up. It was too bad about the chin.

She thought Ms. Treadwell had found the key to dealing with Josiah. He didn't say a word for the rest of the period, though he did cast their teacher the occasional respectful glance. It was possible Freddy was going to be able to get through the day without breaking camouflage again. No one could say it was her fault Josiah was sitting next to her.

At the bell, she shot out into the hallway once more. She wasn't fast enough this time. "I think you're trying to avoid me," said Josiah, who was taller than she was and could walk faster as well.

"No," Freddy lied.

He cast his eyes to the heavens. "Yesterday, you were a duckling; I couldn't get rid of you. Now I have the plague, do I? What's changed?"

Freddy quickened her pace as they headed up the stairs to the third floor. "Haven't you ever *been* to high school before?"

"Five or six hundred thousand times," said Josiah.

"Oh, obviously," said Freddy, practically running out into the hallway once more. "Stop following me."

"I'm not," said Josiah. "You're following me."

"I'm *not*—" Freddy was starting when the hideous truth hit her. They came to a stop together at the door to their math classroom.

"I think someone's given me your schedule," said Josiah. "It's worrying."

She made sure to let him sit down first so she could take a seat on the other side of the classroom. She couldn't look at him as she did. *It's not really his fault. He didn't make me say that thing in English.*

Yes, he did, said another part of her brain. Freddy sometimes worried about the fact that her brain tended to argue with itself.

No, he didn't. You said it yourself, and now you're taking it out on him, aren't you? You weren't falling all over yourself to hide from him yesterday.

Yesterday wasn't school, the rebellious bit of Freddy's brain said in agony, and that really seemed to be it. All the rules were different at school.

She liked math. It seemed unfair when Roland turned up in the class for the second year in a row, and even more unfair when Cathy came in behind him. Neither of them looked at her, though she noticed Roland cast Josiah a startled glance. She was a little surprised to see Roland pick a seat nearly as far from Josiah's as hers was. It could have been that he was just looking for somewhere he and his interpreter could sit together, but she didn't think so. There was plenty of space around Josiah.

Ms. Liu was a new teacher; she looked almost too young to be out of high school herself. She stammered through her introductory remarks, then set them two pages of problems and went to hide behind her desk. The problems were basic algebra. Freddy found them so easy that she forgot to be cautious and finished them in ten minutes. Then she had to spend twenty more pretending she was still working. She didn't want to be like Renata Williams, who got A's in everything and was always waving her arm in the air whenever a teacher asked a question. The year before, Freddy had seen a bunch of boys trail Renata home from school, throwing pebbles at her and awarding themselves points when they hit her butt.

"The last time I was in grade nine," said Josiah, who had to have studied projection at some point, "we spent three blessed months on this nonsense. If that happens here, there's going to be blood."

Everybody was looking at him. The giggling that had happened in English started again. A boy Freddy knew only as Jumbo Jim said, "*The last time* you were in grade nine?"

"Metaphorically speaking." Josiah flapped a hand wearily at the universe. "The worst bits of life are all metaphorically grade nine. Haven't you people noticed you're living in a nightmare? Freddy has, but she wants me to shut up about it. The first time I met her, she was wearing a *hat*."

Freddy hardly noticed the comment about the hat, which made no sense at all. What she was mainly feeling was an urge to punch Josiah very hard in the mouth and, with luck, silence him for good.

Cathy said, "Oh my *God*, Freddy, your boyfriend is a freak." Cathy's voice was nearly as penetrating as Josiah's. Freddy once more put her head down on her desk.

Fifteen minutes later, when Josiah strolled into the band room, Freddy had become resigned to the fact that he was going to be everywhere this year. It was with a dreamy sense of inevitability that she watched him demonstrate to Ms. Bains that he could play the trombone competently, if a bit mechanically. Freddy played the flute herself, along with seven other girls and Hubert. Hubert just sort of existed, though most of the school tried to pretend he didn't.

There were five minutes left in the class, and Freddy was thinking longingly of her bedroom and the dresser with which she intended to block the door to it, when a voice said into the pause left by the utter collapse of the music, "The only time I ever heard a less beautiful noise was in Russia at the bottom of a mine shaft, just before a mountain fell on my head. Of course, *that* sounded like the earth shrieking in unbearable agony."

Freddy wondered if she was going to have to invent a word for the bemused silence that tended to result every time Josiah opened his mouth. Chin, who sat next to Freddy, leaned over and whispered, "Who's he?" Freddy shrugged and hoped her face hadn't gone too red.

"Oh, look at the time," said Ms. Bains. "Pack up, everybody." Freddy was sneakingly certain Ms. Bains was grateful to Josiah for bringing the class to a halt. She had heard last year that Ms. Bains had perfect pitch and talked a lot about wishing not to teach high school band classes any more.

"My flute is a moustache. Look, guys, it's a moustache. Look at my big silver moustache," Hubert was saying off on another plane of reality. Freddy only dimly registered the moment he dropped the flute on the floor.

On her way out of the classroom, Freddy saw Keith, who had grown so unexpectedly huge over the summer that he was threatening to dwarf his baritone tuba, bump into Josiah, sending him stumbling into the wall. It could have been an accident, but this was school. Freddy ducked her head and walked back to her locker without making eye contact with anybody.

◞◝

She was halfway to the park on her way home from school when Josiah caught up with her. "You're better at ditching people than anyone I've ever met," he informed her, "and I live with Cuerva Lachance."

Freddy sighed, checked to make sure no one was watching, and said, "Well, you have no survival skills."

"I made it through the entire day without being hit or dunked in the toilet," said Josiah. "That may be some sort of record."

She stopped abruptly and turned to face him. "What do you want? Yesterday, you were pretending we didn't exist. Why are you following me around?"

"I didn't write the course schedule." Josiah waggled his fingers irritably. Now that she was no longer desperate to avoid him, she was noticing the accent again. *French,* she thought, then decided it wasn't.

"*This* isn't on the course schedule," said Freddy.

"I've become resigned to my fate," Josiah told her and continued on down the sidewalk, slouching in what seemed to be vastly exaggerated exhaustion. When he looked away from her, she felt as if a powerful searchlight had been switched off. There was something very uncomfortable about being looked at by Josiah. She hesitated for a moment, then went after him.

Freddy said, "Why am I your fate?"

"You just are," said Josiah. "I'm doomed to associate with you. It doesn't make me happy, believe me. If I hang around with you, am I going to have to learn never to have any fun? May I at least make vicious fun of your friends?"

"Did I say you could hang around with me?"

"No. Are you going to say I can't hang around with you?"

Freddy fully intended to reply, "Yes." What came out was, "Not yet."

"Ducklings," said Josiah. "Even when you're trying not to be a duckling, your duckling-like qualities peep out and quack."

The sad thing, Freddy thought in exasperation, was that this was the friendliest conversation she'd had all day. Josiah was clearly insane, but he just as clearly knew that and had come to terms with it. It was possible that if she'd never had to go to school again, he would have made a decent friend. "I'll stop being a duckling if you stop mentioning me loudly in front of crowds of people," said Freddy.

"Done," said Josiah, "but you won't stop being a duckling. Notice how you're tamely tagging after me as I walk around the park instead of across it, as you usually do. *I* don't want to end up ankle-deep in mud, but you're just waggling your fluffy little wings and scurrying along in my wake. Trundle along, duckling. We'll be forced into each other's company soon enough." He made shooing motions at her until she stopped in place; then he continued rather primly along the sidewalk. Freddy stood and stared until Josiah rounded the corner, and the spell broke. *How'd he know I usually walk across the park?* thought Freddy. There didn't seem much chance of an answer. More slowly than usual, she headed for home.

4

The knock on the kitchen door came as Freddy was just crossing the threshold into the hallway. She sighed. Ten seconds more and she would have been safely in her room. Mel would have had to abandon the regular Sunday assault on the Pleasure-Dome of Ixior or wherever and deal with whoever this was. Trying to shut out the yells of Marcus, who had just rolled a two and was not happy about it, Freddy opened the door.

Josiah was glaring at her out of two black eyes. The searchlight effect was slightly dampened, but only just. "I need to borrow some marbles," he said.

Freddy stared at him. Someone in the other room let out a scream of what may have been delight.

"Marbles," said Josiah. "You know . . . little round glass things? I don't have any."

"Why do you need them?" asked Freddy, reasonably enough, she thought.

"Science," said Josiah. "It turns out that Ms. Treadwell wasn't just being sarcastic. I have to do a presentation about rolling marbles down an inclined plane tomorrow."

She regarded him thoughtfully. Josiah's appearance had changed in the past five days. Freddy wasn't sure what had made the most difference: the ambush behind the school on Wednesday afternoon, the encounter with Keith in the hallway on Thursday, or the incident in PE on Friday. She wasn't even sure he had got both black eyes at the same time. She hadn't really had much to do with him at school so far, though sometimes she found herself wondering why. It wasn't as if she had anyone else to talk to. She hadn't even eaten with Rochelle and Cathy since Tuesday. Rochelle had been giving her these *looks* every once in a while, but that was all. Hanging around with an obnoxious new kid who had no social skills was beginning to seem attractive to her.

"I think there are some in the rec room," said Freddy at last.

"I'm breathless with anticipation," said Josiah.

He followed her through to the basement stairs, though she hadn't really invited him in. *He acts as if he's known me for years*, she thought, and she blinked. It was something about him that had been gnawing at her since she'd met him, but she hadn't realised until just now what the problem was. She'd first seen him less than a week ago, but he'd treated her all along as if they were old friends, or . . . well, maybe not friends. Old acquaintances? She tried to remember if he'd been like that with anybody else, but she couldn't, possibly because most of the times she'd witnessed him interacting with other people, he'd been insulting somebody or getting beaten up.

There was a trunk in the rec room that held all the toys Freddy and Mel pretended they didn't use any more. Freddy had thought Jordan might be downstairs watching TV, but he wasn't. She vaguely remembered hearing the car pull out of the driveway earlier.

Surprise, surprise. She opened the trunk and started tossing around the contents, turning up dolls with missing limbs, half-constructed Lego spaceships, and a baseball bat with what looked like a bite out of it.

"You have two black eyes," remarked Freddy, primarily for something to say.

"If you hadn't told me, I never would have guessed," said Josiah.

Holding up half a plastic train set and shaking it in the hopes that a marble or two might fall out, Freddy said, "Why don't you just keep your stupid mouth shut?"

"I can't." Josiah's words were heavy with an aura of gloom that had to have been almost entirely put on. "Your classmates are mindless automatons, and they infuriate me."

Freddy didn't know what an automaton was, but she could guess. "Okay, but you cause chaos everywhere you go."

Josiah let out a yelp that made her ears buzz. *"What?"*

"Well," said Freddy, "you do."

"I never," said Josiah. "That's heinous slander. Find the damn marbles."

The damn marbles were, as it turned out, all together in a small net bag, which was inside a larger bag containing a random assortment of rubber balls. Freddy tossed the marbles to Josiah, who evidently couldn't see out of his eyes well enough to catch them. They slipped through his fingers and landed on his foot. "And now you're physically assaulting me," said Josiah. "All I really needed was yet another bruise."

Freddy said, "Stop complaining. You've got your marbles."

"Right," said Josiah. "I need to borrow an inclined plane."

They stared at each other for what was probably quite a long time.

"I think you're supposed to make one yourself," said Freddy when it became clear that Josiah was not going to give in first.

"Then I need to borrow a small saw, a hammer, some nails, and several pieces of timber," said Josiah.

"Isn't your mum supposed to buy you stuff for science projects?"

"If you call her my mum again, I'll bite out both your eyes," said Josiah. "All I need is something to roll marbles down. It's not as if I plan on putting any effort into this. Don't you have any particularly angular dolls in there?"

Freddy bit her tongue—hard—and rooted through the box until she'd pulled out a sloping plastic piece that belonged to the train set, a wedge of blue Styrofoam she didn't remember ever seeing before, and the roof of a broken doll's house.

"Perfect," said Josiah. "All three scream 'I don't give a rat's ass about this project, but I'm certainly going to pretend I'm trying.'"

He picked up everything and dropped the roof on the same foot Freddy had hit with the marbles. "I can carry that one," said Freddy. The noise from upstairs was becoming unbearable again. An excuse to go next door was not a bad thing.

"Quack," said Josiah, but he let her carry the roof.

They ducked into the living room on the way out. The game was in its usual state of incomprehensibility. As Freddy and Josiah entered the room, Marcus was screaming, "Ooh. Ooh! Twenty! I kill all the monsters forever!" Unlike his friends, Marcus had some hearing. He signed, too, but in Freddy's experience, he shouted a lot and never listened to or looked at what anybody else was saying. Mel was signing hugely and unsuccessfully at him while Roland was saying, "*No*, Marcus, a twenty is *not* a magic bullet in this situation. There are fourteen tentacles," though he was almost drowned out by Todd's indignant yell of, "That's my die! You rolled that twenty with *my die*! You've stolen one of my twenties!" which was very unusual for the normally nonverbal Todd and may have led to the usual midgame fistfight if Roland hadn't tried to sign something to Mel while simultaneously talking loudly to Marcus, in the process knocking the coffee table over so violently that it narrowly missed taking Mel's head off. Marcus dissolved into screaming laughter while Mel muttered something about tentacles and boys and how she wished she were revolutionising physics with her friend Clara. Roland tripped over the upended coffee table and sat down hard, scattering dice and scraps of paper. "Weave a circle round him thrice," Mel intoned, pointing solemnly at Roland. Freddy clenched her teeth. None of this was unusual for a weekend afternoon at her house.

Eventually, both Mel and Roland turned to look at Freddy, then let their eyes slide to Josiah. The expression on Roland's face almost brought her up short. He was . . . what was he? Baffled? Wary? Angry? Well, he was often angry when Freddy was around. But she wasn't sure he was watching *her* specifically.

"Going out." Freddy turned away from the game so no one but Mel would be able to understand her. "Back eventually."

They were halfway across the yard when Mel caught up, puffing like a small locomotive. Freddy said, "What?"

"We're on a break." Mel was making her eyes big and round. "I'm coming along because there are boys everywhere. Oh, those terrible, terrible boys."

"She wants to snoop inside our house," said Josiah without turning around. "I wish there were a pond out back so you two could have a swim while you were over."

⌒

The house on Grosvenor Street was . . . different now. Freddy and Mel stood in the middle of the living room and stared. There was no way all this stuff had been in the moving van. The van would have had to be about half a block long.

Chairs were everywhere. It was the first thing Freddy noticed, mainly because it was impossible not to; there were so many chairs that it was difficult to find somewhere to stand. Freddy counted six identical squashy green armchairs, two maroon recliners, seven carved wooden chairs with faded orange cushions, five blue woven chairs, a wicker chair, six folding chairs, and ten stools of various sizes. Four of the folding chairs were perched on top of the grand piano, which was the second thing Freddy noticed. There had not been a grand piano in the van. The six standing lamps and the giant urn with a picture of a flautist and two soppy-looking young people on it seemed to be new as well.

Mel said, somewhat unnecessarily, "You have a lot of chairs."

"Hurrah," said Josiah. "She's been at it again. Cuerva Lachance!"

"Yes?" said Cuerva Lachance, who was standing behind the piano. Freddy had to look twice to make sure. She could have sworn there had been no one there a second ago.

"You have to stop with the chairs," said Josiah, sounding exasperated. "What do you want them all for?"

Cuerva Lachance peered innocently out from beneath her hat. "I needed somewhere to sit."

Josiah said, "You *have* somewhere to sit. The whole *world* has somewhere to sit."

"That makes me happy," said Cuerva Lachance. "Do you play the piano, curly-haired one?"

Freddy said, "I did once." It had been a long time ago. The lessons had stopped shortly after her parents' separation.

"I do," said Mel, who had taught herself. "Is that a Steinway?"

"It's possible," said Cuerva Lachance. "I haven't asked it. It's grateful when I play it, though it doesn't like the climate here."

"I bet you have fun up in the tower," said Mel.

Freddy saw Josiah's eyebrows shoot up in what looked like alarm. He mouthed, *Don't mention the tower!* Mel wasn't looking at him, and anyway, it was too late. Cuerva Lachance tilted her head. "What tower where?"

"Upstairs," said Mel. "There's a door through to it. Didn't you know—?"

"I have to roll marbles down an inclined plane," said Josiah loudly. "Come and watch."

He climbed over three chairs and a footstool and disappeared into the kitchen. "Ooh," said Cuerva Lachance, "Josie's doing schoolwork. Odds are good he'll set something on fire."

The kitchen was as cluttered as the living room. There were chairs here, too, but only ten or so; most of the space was taken up by the spider plants. They occupied every surface, and a few were hanging from ceiling hooks. Freddy had always liked spider plants because of the long, snaking trailers with the little baby plants at the ends of them, but this was a bit much even for her. Josiah was irritably clearing spider plants off the kitchen table and dumping them onto the floor. "Cuerva Lachance strikes again," he said. "Honestly, why do we need more than one of these things?"

"I like them," said Cuerva Lachance. "They're scrappy."

"It wasn't like this on Friday, was it?" Mel whispered to Freddy, who glanced at her, puzzled. She hadn't known Mel had been over here on Friday. She also wasn't sure why Mel was talking as if Freddy had been over here on Friday, too.

Mel said more loudly, "Do most private investigators have houses like this?"

"No. I'm unique," said Cuerva Lachance. "Besides, my current case is frustrating, and I need something to distract me." Josiah snorted.

"What's your case?" said Mel. Freddy figured she had been wanting to ask that question for nearly a week.

"Missing persons," said Cuerva Lachance. "Not very interesting, but there's not much information to go on. I know the basic location of the person I'm looking for. I just need proof of identity. It's a waiting game at the moment. Would anyone like a scone? The grocery store down the street does these tiny little sugar scones with blueberries in."

"You shouldn't be talking about the bloody case," snarled Josiah, who had taken a marble and was rolling it down various inclined planes for no apparent reason. "Especially not with *them*."

"Why not us? Are we in it?" asked Mel hopefully.

"Josiah doesn't like mixing business with neighbours," said Cuerva Lachance. "I would say 'mixing business with pleasure,' but Josiah doesn't find anything pleasurable. Who beat him up, incidentally?"

"Don't tell her," said Josiah.

"Various people," said Freddy. "I think you should be measuring the slopes and keeping track of how far the marble rolls."

"I've done this before," said Josiah. "Thousands and thousands of times before. Why can't science teachers think up some new experiments?"

"Well, why don't *you*?" said Freddy. "Ms. Treadwell said you could do whatever you wanted."

"Make the marble roll uphill," said Cuerva Lachance. "Do you remember the last time you did that?"

Josiah looked up, his forehead wrinkling into a glower. "*You* did it."

"No," said Cuerva Lachance, "I'm sure it was you."

"You know perfectly well it couldn't have been me," snapped Josiah. "Ducklings, could you distract her, please?"

"Sure." Mel pulled a small notebook out of her pocket. Freddy recognised it as one Mel sometimes used to keep track of details when she was gaming with Roland and his friends. Mel flipped open the notebook, retrieved a pencil from her other pocket, and began to write. "The Case of the House on Grosvenor Street," she announced.

"Oh, a case!" said Cuerva Lachance with apparent sincerity. "I like cases. What's in this one?"

"Two people buy and move into an empty house," said Mel, scribbling busily. "They claim not to be related—"

"No, they don't," said Cuerva Lachance.

"Yes, they do," said Josiah. "She's not my mother."

"That doesn't mean we're not related, Josie, dear," said Cuerva Lachance.

"I refuse to be related to you," said Josiah.

"They claim not to be *mother and son*," amended Mel. "One of them crashes into a tree she thinks is a driveway and is constantly being distracted by shiny objects. She says she's a private investigator, but mostly, she collects chairs."

"I do my private investigating privately," said Cuerva Lachance.

"The other one says he's rolled thousands of marbles down inclined planes, but he clearly has no idea what the experiment is for."

"It's for driving off the ever-encroaching boredom," said Josiah.

"Subject One has lived in her new house for a week but hasn't noticed the most interesting room in it. Subject Two knows something about the other people living in the house as well—"

Josiah shot upright, marbles squirting from under his fingers and spinning across the table and onto the floor. "What are you talking about, Harriet the Spy?" he barked.

"Subject Two exhibits suspicious behaviour when confronted with evidence of his wrongdoing," said Mel.

Freddy wasn't sure if Mel was being reckless, brilliant, or incredibly rude. But Cuerva Lachance didn't seem to mind, and though Josiah did, he minded everything. "I heard you talking to people upstairs the day you moved in," said Freddy.

"And someone's up there right now," said Mel. "Something keeps going thud."

They all looked up. Freddy hadn't noticed anything going thud, but now that she was paying attention, she *could* hear something. A moment later, water started to run upstairs. "She's right," she said. "Who else is living here?"

"None of your ever-loving beeswax," Josiah snarled against a muffled background of thumping, splashing, and what sounded like angry and amused voices from upstairs.

"So there *is* someone," said Mel, making a note.

Josiah rolled his eyes, massaged his brow with his index finger, and said in long-suffering tones, "I solemnly swear there is no one in this house who isn't standing in this kitchen right now."

"I'm sitting in this kitchen," said Cuerva Lachance, who was making use of one of her chairs.

"Who isn't standing *or sitting* in this kitchen right now," said Josiah. "Satisfied?"

"No," said Mel. "How are you doing that with the marble, by the way?"

All eyes turned to the table. Freddy had to look away almost immediately. She found that she was groping in her pocket for her key. She wasn't sure why, as she didn't feel like crying. She felt more like backing out of the room and going to hide under her bed. A marble was rolling slowly up the roof of the doll's house. Freddy couldn't watch because she knew it wasn't possible.

"Cuerva Lachance," said Josiah, not quite under his breath.

"What? Yes? Where?" said Cuerva Lachance. She jumped to her feet and turned around in a full circle, narrowly missing knocking three or four spider plants onto the floor.

Josiah said, "Cut it out."

"Cut what out?" asked Cuerva Lachance. Freddy forced herself to look back at the little roof. The marble was sitting in the middle of the table, perfectly still.

I imagined it, thought Freddy. She must have. Josiah and Cuerva Lachance had said something before about marbles rolling uphill, and her brain had taken the conversation and made her see things that weren't there.

But the house seemed less friendly, and less funny, than it had just before. Freddy's eyes slid to Mel. Her sister was gazing thoughtfully at the marble, her little notebook forgotten.

Someone knocked at the kitchen door, hard. Everybody but Cuerva Lachance jumped. Cuerva Lachance said, "I *love* mysterious visitors," and opened the door.

Roland was hulking on the doorstep, his scowl rivalling Josiah's. "We need you, Mel," he said. "What are you doing here?"

"Uh." Mel was still looking at the marble.

"Hello, big awkward one," said Cuerva Lachance, beaming. "Would you like a small, delicious blueberry scone?"

"No, thank you," said Roland stiffly. "You guys have to come home now. Your mum says."

Freddy opened her mouth to say she knew their mum wasn't home, then paused. She didn't think she minded having a reason to leave.

"That's too bad," said Cuerva Lachance as Mel and Freddy silently followed Roland out the door. "I do hope you come again. Neighbours intrigue me, and they can sit on my chairs. Josie, you're in danger of putting your foot in a plant. Why are you?" The closing door cut off any retort Josiah might have made.

Roland let them get all the way out into the lane and through into their own backyard before he let them have it. Freddy and Mel both stepped back as he rounded on them. Roland dwarfed them both, but Freddy had never really found him scary until this moment. "Stay away from there," he said. "We don't even know them. What were you thinking?"

"Josiah's in all my classes," said Freddy. "We were doing homework." It wasn't strictly true, but agreeing with Roland was impossible.

"You didn't mind them before," said Mel, signing along to the words. "Did something happen?"

"No," said Roland. "Yes. I've . . . seen Josiah at school. He does things . . . he—just stay away from him, all right?"

Freddy said, "Stop telling me what to do. Why do you even care?"

"I don't care about *you*," said Roland with such contempt that Freddy took another step back. "I care about Mel. She follows you around."

"She can if she wants to." Freddy could feel the anger trying to choke her into silence again, but Roland had no right to tell Mel what to do.

"Excuse me," said Mel. "I'm standing right here."

"Just . . . leave that house alone. I'll make you if I have to." He shoved past them both and slammed his way into the house. Freddy heard something fall over inside.

Freddy looked at Mel. "What was that all about?"

"Not so elementary, my dear Duchamp," said Mel, making another note in her notebook.

Freddy had a strange dream that night. She hardly ever remembered her dreams; she had the vague sense that a lot of them involved nonsensical adventures in which she was running away from something huge and scary, but by morning, they had almost always slipped away. This one she did remember afterwards. She thought it was because of the way she woke up from it.

In the way of dreams, everything that happened seemed perfectly reasonable. She was in the house on Grosvenor Street with Mel again, but this time, Roland was with them, too. She knew it was the house on Grosvenor Street, though it had grown. The living room had expanded to the size of a cathedral. She, Mel, and Roland stood together in the middle of it, surrounded by chairs. The chairs weren't jumbled about in heaps, as they had been today. Someone had arranged them in rows that went around in widening circles, all of them facing the space where Freddy and the others stood. There was no one in them.

"Do you swear to tell the truth, the whole truth, and nothing but the truth, so help you Bob?" said Josiah from behind Freddy. She turned. He was wearing a little black bowler hat, which he took off and handed to her. Mel made a note in her notebook.

"This isn't right. There isn't any pie," said Roland viciously.

"Freddy's got the pie," said Josiah. "She just hasn't seen it yet. There are four and twenty ducklings baked in it."

"Blackbirds," said Cuerva Lachance, though it was hard to say where she was. Mel nodded and added, "Black birds," spacing out the syllables so it was clear she was saying two separate words.

"You *have* to tell her about the pie," Roland was explaining when Cuerva Lachance floated into view, riding a grand piano that was spinning through the air above the chairs. She was crouched on top, leaning over towards the keyboard and playing the piano upside down. The first note shook the room. It seemed eminently logical to Freddy that the piano should sound like a pipe organ.

"Could I revive within me her symphony and song," said Roland, who wasn't deaf in the dream.

As Freddy stood in the gigantic living room, the chairs whirled into fragments and danced away into the familiar walls of her bedroom, solid and shadowy in the dim light from the street outside.

I was dreaming, she thought, and then, *I haven't stopped yet.* She could still hear the organ music, less clearly than she had a moment before, but clearly enough. It was muffled by the walls. Faintly, she could feel the room vibrating. A door slammed, and Jordan said, "What the *hell* . . . ?" and Freddy knew she was awake. It was happening again. It had never happened in the middle of the night before, but considering their new neighbours, it wasn't all that surprising. Cuerva Lachance had discovered the tower room at last.

Freddy joined Jordan and Mum as they stormed along the hallway and down the stairs, sucking Mel into their wake. As always, Freddy felt vaguely disoriented to see her mum and stepfather. It was the way she always felt in the spring when the sun came properly out from behind the clouds for the first time in months, and Freddy found herself thinking, *Right . . . that's what it looks like.* Mum and Jordan weren't really home all that often. Freddy couldn't remember the last time they had all eaten dinner together. Usually, she, Roland, and Mel made themselves spaghetti or chicken and rice or cold-cut sandwiches, then ate in their rooms or in front of the TV in the basement.

Roland was the last to join the parade. His room was a small one at the back of the house, and even though he wouldn't have been able to hear the music, Freddy suspected his room was shaking much more noticeably than hers was. The bass notes of the organ made the house shiver; Freddy could hear the windows creaking ominously. Roland rubbed his eyes and signed something to Mel. Freddy turned away before she could accidentally read the signs.

Outside, the music was much louder, and it became louder still as Jordan led them all out the back gate. Freddy glanced down the lane and saw lights going on in nearby houses.

"Tower," shouted Mel, pointing. Freddy could hardly hear her. There was a light in the window of the miniature tower attached to the house on Grosvenor Street. Through this window, and out through the walls of the tower itself, rolled the sort of organ music that Freddy associated with misshapen geniuses lurking beneath the Paris Opera House and fixating on innocent young sopranos. As she listened, the melody switched to what would have counted as light jazz if it hadn't been played on an organ the size of a bus.

It was the one thing that made the house on Grosvenor Street truly odd. The house had been built around a pipe organ rescued from a derelict movie theatre. The tower housed the console and the pipes. Freddy thought it had been a neat idea, but it would have been a neater one if the house had been built in the middle of a forest. The organ was the right volume for a theatre, but it was the wrong volume for a suburban neighbourhood.

Jordan was pounding on the kitchen door of the house on Grosvenor Street. Freddy wished him luck. She thought he would need it to make anyone inside the house hear a mere angry knocking. The music was abruptly supplemented by an incredible wailing sound that swooped enthusiastically up and down the scale.

"She's found the siren," Freddy screamed, and Mel nodded.

Over the course of the next several minutes, Cuerva Lachance sampled all the organ's sound effects, then went back to the music, though not without the occasional squawk, hoot, or drumbeat. Freddy knew it was Cuerva Lachance. The organ was being played by someone without an attention span, and the music changed styles every thirty seconds or so. Jordan had his cell phone out now. From what Freddy could hear, he was trying to talk to the police. Freddy thought he should have walked a good ways down the lane first. She caught snatches of the conversation: ". . . playing the organ! At three in the . . . no, I said *organ* . . . not right . . . a right to our sleep . . . I said *Grosvenor* . . . no, with a G . . . I am not drunk! Listen . . ."

Freddy wasn't sure how much longer the music went on. When it finally howled its way to a stop, Jordan, who had given up on the call to the police some time before, began to pound on the door again. It was opened shortly afterwards by Cuerva Lachance herself.

She looked wide awake and not at all surprised to see them. "There's a *pipe organ* in my house!" she said to Freddy, exactly as if they were continuing a conversation that had paused ten seconds ago.

Jordan said, "We *know* there's a pipe organ in your house! That doesn't mean you have to play it at three in the morning!"

"But that's when I noticed it," said Cuerva Lachance.

Jordan was only about five foot four, but Freddy could have sworn his indignation helped him spontaneously grow a foot right then and there so that he towered over Cuerva Lachance as he shouted, "I don't know who you think you are, but you have no right to disturb the neighbourhood like this!"

Out of the corner of her eye, Freddy caught movement from Roland, and she turned a bit towards him. He was gently backing away from Jordan, looking ashamed. He couldn't have seen what Jordan was saying, but Mel had been translating for him again. For a fraction of a second, Freddy felt sorry for Roland. It was never fun when parents drew attention to themselves in public.

That fraction of a second was all it took for Mum to join in. "You don't have the sense that God gave a grasshopper," Mum said drily to Cuerva Lachance. Mum was wearing a flannel nightgown with teddy bears on it. "Hasn't anyone ever taught you manners?"

"No," said Josiah from behind Cuerva Lachance. "*So* terribly sorry. *Won't* happen again. *No idea* how she managed to get into the room and lock the door and brace various pieces of furniture against it so w—so I couldn't break it down."

"I taught *him* manners," Cuerva Lachance explained. "I'm Cuerva Lachance. It's very nice to meet you."

Jordan and Mum stood on the porch and gaped at Cuerva Lachance. "Mum," said Mel, "she's not going to do it again. Let's go home."

"You're damn right she's not going to do it again," said Jordan. "Do you hear that, Ms. Lachance? I forbid you to play that organ ever again."

"Dad . . ." said Roland.

"Not at night, at least, please," said Mum, who did have a certain amount of common sense.

Cuerva Lachance was pretty obviously not taking any of this in. She beamed at Freddy. "I've always wanted a pipe organ next to my bedroom. It's very convenient. Have a good night!"

Jordan evidently couldn't think of anything satisfying to reply to this. He spluttered for a bit, then turned tightly on the spot and marched back out into the lane, Mum and Roland close behind him.

It was all getting a little bit too weird. Freddy moved as slowly as she could down the walk towards the back gate. When she heard Josiah start up with, "So now you've gone and alienated the ducklings' parents, and we're going to have the cops here, and see if I bail you out *this* time," she softly ducked behind the rhododendron halfway between the door and the gate.

Mel was already there. Their eyes met, and Mel nodded. "I heard voices behind Josiah," she whispered.

"Josiah almost said 'we' when he talked about breaking down the door," Freddy whispered back.

Her sister could be a pain sometimes, but one thing Freddy had always appreciated about Mel was that it was rarely necessary to explain things to her. The two girls crouched behind the rhododendron. It wasn't a great eavesdropping spot. Though Josiah and Cuerva Lachance hadn't closed the door yet, they were at least twenty feet away and not speaking particularly loudly. Freddy had always wondered how characters in books and movies ended up hiding coincidentally in convenient nooks and crannies while people held long expository conversations nearby. It never seemed to work out that way for her. Most of what she could hear now was incomprehensible.

"But Josie," said Cuerva Lachance at one point. Then her voice sank again. A bit later, Josiah said, ". . . intimidate their parents. You know we have to find out . . ." The rest of the sentence was lost.

". . . which one it is," Freddy eventually heard from Cuerva Lachance, and then, ". . . don't really fit. It's very exciting."

They missed a large chunk of the discussion as Josiah's voice sank to an angry murmur. Freddy thought she caught the word "organ" and maybe also "complete moron," but nothing else came through clearly until Cuerva Lachance said, ". . . after September twenty-seventh, isn't it?"

"Maybe," said Josiah, "but there's no guarantee. Why did you have to . . . ?"

The rest was whispers, with the occasional growl from Josiah. A minute or so later, the door closed, and the voices died away. Freddy and Mel crouched in the damp grass and looked at each other. *Are they investigating us?* thought Freddy. It seemed unlikely.

Why would anyone want to? And what was going to happen on September twenty-seventh? From the expression on Mel's face, she was just as baffled as Freddy. The light went out in the house on Grosvenor Street, and Mel melted to shadow. Freddy had known eavesdropping was useless, but she hadn't realised it would leave her so much more confused than before.

5

"Oh my *God*," said Cathy. "What's your boyfriend doing *now?*"

They were in math class. The situation had deteriorated. She should have known it would.

The first week of school, after the initial terrible Tuesday with Josiah popping up everywhere and dragging her into his world, Freddy had hoped Josiah would calm down and settle in. The second week, she'd been pretty sure he wouldn't. Now it was Thursday of the third week, and "pretty sure" had tipped over into "absolutely certain."

There had been the presentation in science class. Freddy figured Ms. Treadwell had seen plenty of bad presentations in the past, but even so, the teacher had had a hard time finding anything nice to say about Josiah's, which had involved him rolling a marble down the slopes of three broken toys and declaring he had proven gravity existed. The closest she'd managed to get was, "That was a very creative use of materials, Josiah."

There had been the incident in drama. Josiah hadn't started out the year in Freddy's drama class, but he'd been kicked out of shop after threatening another student with a soldering iron. He was probably about to be kicked out of drama as well. She did have to admit it was bad luck that had led Mr. Singh to walk into the classroom when Josiah was in the middle of a spirited imitation of him, though she thought the fact that Josiah had then kept going was likely his own fault.

There had been the problem in English. It hadn't started as a problem; it had started as poetry. Mr. Dillon had been trying to teach them about iambic pentameter. Freddy, who thanks to her mother had known what iambic pentameter was since she was eight, had happily blocked him out, right up until the point where Josiah had said, "Fun poetry fact: Samuel Taylor Coleridge wrote 'Kubla Khan' while strung out on opium. I vote we follow his example and see how many great poems we produce." Mr. Dillon had made matters worse by getting drawn into a debate about how drugs could be bad if they were seen as the direct cause of poems.

There had been band, with the trombone players in open revolt against Josiah's tendency to distract them constantly with sarcastic comments. There had been PE and the painful five minutes involving the volleyball and the handful of thumbtacks. There had been the time Josiah carried a pigeon into the cafeteria and set it loose right next to the table occupied by grade twelve jocks. Now there was math class. It was a little sad. Math was the last class Josiah hadn't propelled into disorder.

Ms. Liu was staring at the proof he had written on the whiteboard, her mouth opening and closing with shock. Freddy knew it was a proof because she had seen proofs in films, plus occasionally doodled on scrap paper by Mel. She didn't know what it was *for*. It didn't look much like the geometry problem Josiah had been set.

All through his campaign of terror and destruction, Josiah had kept his word and left Freddy out of it. He hadn't brought up her name or even looked at her while he was spreading amusing anarchy through the school. That wasn't the problem. The problem was that she was having to struggle so ferociously against the impulse to join in.

I'm not like him, she told herself. And she wasn't. But she had the strangest feeling that despite the black eyes and the fact that nobody liked him, Josiah was having much more fun in school than she ever had.

Ms. Liu said, "But that's unsolvable. It's existed since 1978!"

"Oopsy," said Josiah, sounding bored.

Most of the class was giggling. Freddy knew that Josiah had just added "math nerd" to the long, long list of things that were wrong with him. She wanted to shake him. She also wanted him to show her how he had done the proof. Asking him about the proof would have been social suicide. Her life was giving her a headache.

Roland stood up. When Roland stood up, everyone noticed. Every head in the room except Ms. Liu's swung towards him. Distractedly, Freddy saw he had somehow managed to make a math textbook and three sheets of loose-leaf paper look like a hopeless mess.

"Sit down," said Roland to Josiah. "Why do you have to make such a big deal of everything?"

Freddy found she was watching through her fingers. Now half the class was laughing at Josiah and half at Roland.

Josiah signed, *Why do you care? You didn't have to say anything.*

I didn't understand that, thought Freddy, but it was just a reflex. She felt her hands drop from her face. Josiah *signed?* Since when did Josiah sign? He'd never indicated before that he knew American

Sign Language. Roland didn't seem surprised, either. Josiah had signed to him before, then, when Freddy hadn't been there.

The giggling had stopped. Freddy knew why. The hearing kids and the Deaf kids didn't mix. Oh, they had some classes together, and there were a few friendships that crossed the invisible boundary, but Freddy didn't think she had ever seen a hearing kid who wasn't related to a Deaf kid use fluent and unthinking sign language in school.

Ms. Liu should have been doing something. She was still staring at the proof. Freddy thought maybe she should do something herself. She stayed where she was.

"You're not as funny as you think you are," said Roland.

Not funny, signed Josiah. *Bored.*

"Go be bored somewhere else," said Roland.

The bell rang. Freddy stayed in her seat, slowly packing up, as the other students headed for the door. With luck, Josiah and Roland would be swept up by the crowd, and she wouldn't have to deal with either of them on the way out.

She had miscalculated as usual. When she started for the classroom's one doorway, up near the front of the room, Josiah and Roland were still standing by the whiteboard, having a furious argument in sign language. She caught glimpses of it as she tried to edge past them: . . . *None of your business . . . What's wrong with you? . . . After I saw . . . That was a mistake . . . Through the wall . . . Very thin wall . . . Don't talk to her!*

The last was from Roland, with a vicious stab of his finger towards Freddy for the "her." As she reached the boys, sidling around Ms. Liu, who seemed paralysed by whatever Josiah had written on the board, Josiah turned to her and said, "Goodness gracious, look at the time. We'd better get to band. I like band. Let me carry your books and pretend to be friends with you just to make this idiot mad. How do you live with him? I shall get my useless things, and we shall stop the pointless argument." He threw Roland a scathing glance, then headed back to his seat to pick up his books.

Freddy was left being loomed over by Roland. "You need to stay away from that guy," he said in a bullying tone that immediately made Freddy want to become Josiah's best friend.

"You keep saying," Freddy told him, "but you don't say *why*. Am I supposed to stay away from everyone you don't like? I'll have to start avoiding *myself*."

He wrapped his hand around her arm and, ignoring his interpreter's meaningful gestures towards his books, towed Freddy out into the hallway. "I don't have to like you to try to stop you from doing something stupid," said Roland. "He's dangerous. *They're* dangerous."

He sounded so serious about it that Freddy bit back a snarl and simply said, "Why?"

"If you don't know, it's better," said Roland. "Make sure it stays that way. And stop letting Mel play detective. I've seen her snooping around that house. She doesn't know what she's getting into."

It was true that Mel had been lurking in the lane a lot lately, not very subtly. Freddy thought Mel had more faith in the power of eavesdropping than she did. "Maybe she would if you told her," said Freddy, "since you seem to know so much."

Kids were arriving for the next math class now. From the looks of them, they were in grade eleven or twelve, big, rangy almost-adults who stared with annoyance at the stupid grade nines blocking their way. "You need to get your books," said Freddy, "and I need to go to band. Let me go."

"Stay away from the house on Grosvenor Street," said Roland. "And stay away from Josiah."

It was only when she was halfway to the band room that she realised Josiah had stayed in the room throughout the confrontation. She wondered if he had been lurking just out of sight, listening.

He caught up with her on the walk home. He usually did. Freddy, glancing covertly at him, felt almost guilty about it. Well, she hadn't promised Roland, and besides, where did he get off telling her what to do? There was some mystery about Cuerva Lachance and Josiah, but they weren't dangerous unless very loud organ music and a tendency to collect chairs posed some terrible, undefinable threat.

"What was all that with Roland?" she said. "I didn't think you guys'd ever said two words to each other."

Josiah rolled his eyes so dramatically that for a moment, the irises almost completely vanished. "I don't pretend to understand how that boy's brain works. I'm not sure it *does* work. I saw his math homework on the way past his desk. He was drawing swords on it."

"Well, he's not stupid," said Freddy grudgingly, "but he doesn't try." It was something she'd noticed about Roland. He called her brainless sometimes, and she called him dense, but she suspected that if they had ever taken an IQ test together, they would have more or less tied.

"Swords," said Josiah. "On homework sheets."

She rounded on him. "You can talk. What was that thing you wrote on the board?"

"That?" said Josiah with contempt. "An unsolvable problem. It was written to be unsolvable. There's a mistake in my solution. Ms. Spineless will find it eventually. She was a math genius in university, you know, but she had a breakdown in her third year and settled for education."

She didn't ask him how he knew this. She wasn't in the mood for shameless lies. "And you sign."

"What? Of course I sign. Why wouldn't I?"

Freddy said, "Why would you?"

"Long, dreary experience of the world. I picked it up somewhere along the way."

They started across the park. "You always talk as if you're ninety," said Freddy.

"It seems that way sometimes," said Josiah. "I keep telling you that you need to take most of what I say as a metaphor."

She was trying to think of something cruel to say in reply when the strains of "It's a Small World (After All)," mixed with a little bit of "Shenandoah," began to ring out over the park. Freddy saw the heads of the kids on the swing set turn towards the house on Grosvenor Street.

"Damn it," said Josiah. "Is your stepdad home?"

"Is my stepdad ever home?" said Freddy, but Josiah was already running, making little yelps of irritated indignation as he went. Freddy raced after him. Cuerva Lachance had been finding it difficult to stay away from the organ. Mel said she'd heard that the neighbours had filed several complaints with the police, but as far as Freddy could tell, nothing had come of them.

Freddy was on Josiah's heels as he crossed the street. She could see Mel standing on the sidewalk next to their side gate, one hand on the latch as she stared at Josiah. Josiah tried to run past her, but she grabbed him by the arm.

"What are you doing *there*?" Mel shouted over the music. "I just saw you over *there*!"

Josiah screamed, "No, you didn't. Let me go; I've got to stop—"

"I had a whole conversation with you!" she bellowed. "You told me things about frogs!"

"You're dreaming," shouted Freddy. "We were walking home from school."

Josiah gave an impatient squirm and tore himself from Mel's grasp. The girls moved out onto the sidewalk and watched him sprinting for the house, shrieking, "Cuerva Lachance! Cuerva *Lachance*!" He wrenched open the door. The music got briefly louder, though not by much. The door slammed shut.

It took him nearly two minutes to get into the organ room and shut Cuerva Lachance up. There was a moment of discord, as if someone's hands had been wrenched from the console, and blissful silence descended.

Mel turned to her sister. "I know what I saw, Freddy. I was talking to him five minutes ago."

"You couldn't have been," said Freddy. "We were just starting across the park five minutes ago."

"Then Josiah can be in two places at once," said Mel.

The girls gazed at each other thoughtfully. Mel had a good imagination, and she didn't always tell the truth, but she was a terrible liar, and she wasn't lying now. She had been talking to Josiah, or she thought she had.

Mel was looking at the house. "Who's that?"

"Where?" Freddy turned, following Mel's gaze. She thought she caught a flicker of movement at one of the gable windows, but when she looked more closely, there was no one there.

"There was a girl," said Mel. "Or a woman. With long hair, anyway. Not Cuerva Lachance. She was looking out one of the second-floor windows."

"We know there's someone else living there," said Freddy. "We just don't know who."

"Maybe they're keeping a madwoman in the attic," said Mel. "We'll only find out for sure when she sets the house on fire and jumps off the roof."

This sounded like an allusion to something, a common hazard of talking to Mel. Freddy ignored it. "Roland warned me off Josiah again."

"He's been going at me, too," said Mel. "I think something happened with him and Cuerva Lachance."

Freddy said, "He says they're dangerous." As she thought about it, her usual fizzing anger was starting up again. Okay, maybe Roland had been serious, but why did he have to be so . . . so belligerent about it? What was wrong with, "Freddy, please stay away from the house on Grosvenor Street. I'm worried about you guys. Let me tell you what happened to me last week"? Instead, he tried to force her into doing what he wanted, and he didn't even bother to explain why.

"They may be," said Mel. "Remember the marble?"

Freddy narrowed her eyes. "What marble?"

"The *marble*. The one that rolled *uphill*."

Freddy did remember the marble, uneasily. She had been trying not to. "Some trick."

"I don't think it was." Mel ran a hand through her mousy hair. "Look. You know how I feel about Sherlock Holmes."

"You will love him passionately forever," said Freddy.

"Yes, and there's this thing he says: 'when you have eliminated the impossible, whatever remains, however improbable, must be the truth.'"

"Okay," said Freddy, "so?"

"So I don't think we can eliminate the impossible this time. What happened with the marble wasn't possible."

"It was just a tiny little thing," protested Freddy.

"So's this." Mel bent down and picked up a pinecone. As Freddy watched, Mel straightened, held the pinecone out in front of her, and dropped it.

"Yeah," said Freddy, "it fell. So what?"

Mel said, "What if it had risen instead? That would have been a violation of a fundamental physical law."

"Sure."

"So basically the same thing happened with the marble."

They stood there, staring at the pinecone. A crow cawed in the tree above them.

"We have to eliminate the impossible," said Freddy finally.

"I would love to," said Mel. "I feel disloyal to Mr. Holmes. But maybe deduction can't solve everything."

Freddy saw the front door open. "Josiah's coming back out."

"Bad timing." Mel jerked her thumb towards Roland, who was just crossing from the park.

The boys reached them at almost exactly the same time. "Leave us alone," said Roland to Josiah. "Or I'll make you."

"Oh, do go ahead and make me." Josiah flung out his arms. "I'm running out of visible bruises."

Roland glared at Freddy and Mel. "Go home."

"We were just standing here," said Freddy. "Is that a crime now?"

"Boys are so violent all the time," said Mel.

"You're supposed to be a genius," snarled Roland. "Use your stupid head and *go home*."

"My stupid genius head is happy here," said Mel, signing industriously all the while.

Freddy crossed her arms. "Explain properly or leave us alone."

"No," said Roland, almost choking out the word.

"Are you going to continue this all day," inquired someone from directly above them, "or do I have to come down there and egg you on?"

Everyone but Roland looked up. "Cuerva Lachance," said Josiah in exasperation.

She was perched in the branches of the tree, none of which were low enough for any of them to reach. As Freddy watched, she peered down at them from under her hat and said, "Yes? May I help you?"

"How'd you get up there?" said Mel.

"I'm not sure." Cuerva Lachance tilted her head thoughtfully. "There may have been physics involved."

"You were just in the house," said Freddy.

She beamed at them. "Was I?"

"Ignore everything she says and does," said Josiah.

Roland had caught up with events by now. "What a good idea," he said. "We're going home."

"You won't be able to ignore me properly from there," said Cuerva Lachance.

"Stay away from us," Roland flung up into the tree. "Stay away from *them*. I don't know what you want, but I know you're here to watch us. If you don't leave us alone, I'll . . . something. I don't know! Just *don't*."

He took Freddy and Mel by a shoulder each and shoved them away from the house on Grosvenor Street. Maybe because he would have needed at least one hand free to unlatch the gate, he pushed them all the way down the street and around the corner and into the front yard. Freddy was thinking almost too hard to notice. *The marble. Pinecone . . . defying the law of gravity. Cuerva Lachance in the tree? Who else is living in the house? Something happened to Roland over there. Can Josiah be in two places at once?* It was like watching Roland signing and not wanting to know what he meant. She kept trying to force her brain away from all the impossible things, but it always crept back.

Just before they rounded the corner, Freddy heard Cuerva Lachance call, "We'll be seeing you soon!" She and Mel looked at each other, then away. Neither told Roland what she had heard.

6

"September twenty-seventh," said Mel.

Freddy, poised to leave for school, looked at her. "What?"

"Today is September twenty-seventh," said Mel, hanging nearly upside down over the bannister. "Cuerva Lachance mentioned the date. Something is supposedly happening today."

Freddy had forgotten. Lately, she had forgotten most things besides how angry she was at Roland. "We don't know what."

"I'm going to keep my eyeballs peeled," Mel told her, "but not right now, since there's a math test I have to ace first."

Shrugging, Freddy opened the door. Roland was standing on the porch, doing his thundercloud act.

When Roland had trailed her to school on Friday, Freddy had thought it was just because he'd got up late and coincidentally set off at the same time she had. It was annoying, but they did live in the same house. When he'd followed her home on the same day, she'd begun to suspect something, and when he'd cancelled his RPG on Sunday so he could keep track of her every move, she'd known: he was tagging after her to prevent her from talking to Josiah. She had been choked silent by the anger again. What the *hell* was his problem? He was watching Mel as well, but when Mel's friends Clara and Jonathan had come over and the three of them had started devising ways to drop an egg from the school roof without breaking it, Roland had shifted his attention entirely to Freddy. If he'd liked her, she could almost have forgiven him, but he so clearly didn't that she'd spent the weekend getting more and more impotently furious with him. It didn't help that he was doing his usual neat/messy thing as he followed her around, tidying up everywhere he went but also causing things to sag and fall over and get mixed together hopelessly. There was no distraction from him. Mum and Jordan were out, and Mel and her friends were busy.

On Monday, he'd followed her to school again. He'd sat next to her in math class. He'd followed her home. She'd tried to slip away before he was out of his afternoon social studies class, but he'd found her anyway. All evening, he had watched her.

Josiah had noticed. He was rolling his eyes a lot in Roland's presence. At one point on Monday, he'd approached Freddy in the hallway, looked both ways in an exaggerated fashion, and whispered so loudly that everybody within twenty feet of him had stopped to listen, "I would ask you what we're doing today in science, but I'm afraid of the fiery glower of *doom*." Then he'd stalked away, making little circles around his right ear with his index finger. Freddy had seen Rochelle staring and gone off to hide in a bathroom stall for a bit.

So to find Roland waiting for her on the porch this morning was pretty close to being the last straw. Fleetingly, she thought, *If Mum weren't gone* again, *I would* tell *her about this,* but that was beside the point, wasn't it? She jammed a hand into her pocket, wrapped it around her key, briefly wished she had some mysterious lock to try it in, and pushed past Roland. She heard him fall in behind her as she crossed the yard.

It all became even more fun when Josiah joined them. "Oh, hello," he said. "Will you look at this? I walk to school the same way you do, plus at the same time. You'd think I would be sensitive to Mr. Growly's feelings and arrange things otherwise, but *no.*"

"Who's a duckling now?" said Freddy, though she wasn't unhappy to see him. Listening to Josiah abuse the world was better than just feeling Roland hate her silently.

Roland dealt with it by pretending Josiah wasn't there. Freddy did notice, however, that he kept arranging to walk between them. Her anger at him ratcheted up another notch.

She should have known from its beginning that the day would keep getting steadily worse. Rochelle and Cathy were out in front of the school, surrounded by boys, when Freddy turned up with Roland and Josiah. She thought she heard at least one "Oh my *God!*" from Cathy. Keith managed to bump into both Josiah and Roland as they moved towards the doors. Then, generously, he punched Freddy's backpack, sending her staggering into the side of the school. She had to stand for quite a while with her hand wrapped around the key. *I'm not under the radar any more, I don't think. When did that happen?*

Mr. Dillon's class would have given her a chance to shrink into a corner and disappear for a bit, but this was one of her PE days. It was still volleyball this week. Freddy hated volleyball. She cringed every time someone spiked the ball over the net at her. The other kids groaned when she was assigned to their team. Today, one of the teams ended up with both her and Josiah, and Michelle, who was five foot seven and athletic, complained loudly to Mr. Lim.

"You know," said Josiah to her as they watched their teammate abusing them, "I'm pretty good at volleyball."

"Maybe if you played it properly instead of trying to sabotage every game," said Freddy sadly. She might as well talk to him. The damage had already been done.

The class took on the texture of a nightmare. Keith was on her team. Every time the rotation put her in front of him, she squirmed. She could feel him watching her. But when he finally knocked her down, she wasn't expecting it; he was supposed to be all the way across the court. All she remembered afterwards was seeing the ball coming straight for her head and, instead of bringing her hands up to meet it, ducking. She thought there had been a squeal from Michelle. Then she had been thumped off her feet, backwards into the wall.

There were flashing lights dancing all around the gym. Somewhere, someone was saying, "Sorry, Mr. Lim . . . I didn't see her! She's so *teeny*." Someone else barked, "Will you *shut up laughing*? There's something wrong with Freddy." She thought Josiah was there behind the dancing lights, and perhaps Chin and Jane. She blinked, trying to clear her vision. The room was coming more into focus, and the voices were starting to make sense again.

"Just hang on, Freddy. The nurse is on her way," said Mr. Lim.

Freddy shook her head. "I'm okay."

But she ended up in the nurse's office anyway. The nurse flicked a light into and out of her eyes and made her track a finger as she moved it briskly back and forth in front of Freddy's face. "I think you've escaped a concussion this time," she said, "but if you feel sleepy or dizzy, come back here right away, understand?" She gave Freddy a plastic bag with lumps of ice in it and told her to hold it against the bump on the back of her head. Then she made Freddy take a painkiller and sent her to science class. Freddy's head was throbbing sickly as she slipped onto her stool.

For the first time since she had met him, Josiah looked worried. "Are you okay?" he whispered. "I should have rem—I should have known Keith was going to do that."

Freddy nodded as gently as she could. Something about what Josiah had just said didn't seem quite right, but she felt too ill to think about it much.

Science passed in a blur, and the bell rang for lunch. She thought Josiah must have been feeling genuinely bad about what had happened to her, as instead of stalking off on his own and going to raise havoc somewhere during the lunch break, he walked to her locker with her, then to the cafeteria. Freddy wondered afterwards whether she would have let him if she hadn't been distracted by the thudding in her head. She didn't think she would have sat at his table, which was where he steered her. She wasn't really sure what she was doing in the cafeteria; she didn't feel well enough to eat.

Freddy laid her head down on the table as Josiah went off to get his lunch. When she raised it again, Roland was there, glaring. "You're crazy."

She stared at him through the thudding.

"Are you doing it just because I told you not to?" demanded Roland. "Because that's *so stupid* of you."

"Am I doing what?" Freddy knew she was mad at Roland, but she wasn't sure why just now. She was starting to wonder if that nurse had really understood what she was doing.

"Eating lunch with *him*," said Roland, nodding at Josiah, who was just returning to the table.

"Oh, give her a break, Growly," said Josiah. "She hit her head on the wall in gym class. Torture her when her headache's gone, which, from the looks of it, won't be for a week or so."

Roland's expression changed a bit. Freddy saw the contempt shift away, replaced by grudging concern. After a pause, he said, "Are you okay?"

All the pariahs at this school are asking me that, thought Freddy. "I think so."

"I could take you home," he said, grimacing.

"How happy you sound," she said. "No. I don't have band today, so I should be all right as long as no one screams in my ear."

"Fine," said Roland, but he stopped nagging her about Josiah. He did eat lunch with the two of them, though. Freddy could feel what a bad idea this was. All sorts of invisible lines were being crossed. She even saw Todd and Marcus, over in the section of the cafeteria frequented by the Deaf kids, watching Roland in what looked like surprise. Rochelle was here, too. Freddy thought Rochelle was biding her time.

The day should really have got better after that. It shouldn't have been possible for things to worsen after she had been thrown into a wall and planted at the weird table during lunch. But it seemed to be turning into what Mel called a Murphy's day: a day on which whatever could go wrong not only did go wrong but went wrong in descending levels of horror.

She, Roland, and Josiah arrived at math class together. It was a coincidence, as they had separated after lunch, but word had got around. The class's hostility wasn't aimed only at Josiah this time.

When Ms. Liu asked Roland to work out a problem on the white-board, Jumbo Jim said loudly, "Do us some impossible math!" and almost everybody laughed. Cathy was practically in hysterics. Freddy couldn't see what was so funny. Roland, in the meantime, had been facing away from the class and hadn't even noticed the laughter. "Settle down," said Ms. Liu ineffectually. Someone threw a balled-up piece of paper at Roland; another landed on Freddy's desk. Cathy, still laughing, leaned over towards Freddy and said in her usual piercing voice, "Your stepbrother is a spaz, isn't he?" Freddy could only blink at her in incomprehension. Roland hadn't done anything weird at all.

It was as if the whole school had caught some kind of airborne malevolence. Freddy was bombarded with balls of paper all through the class. So were Josiah and Roland, but most of them seemed to be aimed at Freddy. Drama should have been a relief, and Freddy thought it would be, right up until the moment Mr. Singh said, "All right, guys, we're still working on improv today. We're going to play a game called 'Freeze.' Freddy and Josiah, why don't you come start us off?"

She would have wondered how on earth he had come to pick the two of them, but it was a Murphy's day, so he couldn't have picked anybody else. Freddy felt the class's focus narrow, become more pure. When Mr. Singh called for a location and a situation, Freddy wasn't surprised when someone sang out immediately, "A romantic dinner at a restaurant."

"Perfect!" said Mr. Singh, ignoring the snickers.

"Freeze" involved two people acting out a scene. Eventually, someone would call, "Freeze," and replace one of the actors, then continue with a different situation. Freddy had played the game last year; it could be fun. It wasn't going to be fun today. Trying to ignore her pounding head, Freddy began to saw at an imaginary steak. "My," she said stiffly, "how romantic this is."

Josiah took his cue from her, not quite in the way she had expected. "Indeed," he said, his voice completely without tone. "How happy I am that we, two sentient robots, are enjoying this meal of circuit boards and fibre in each other's presence. We are very much in love."

"I concur," said Freddy. "We are teaching each other about emotion. Oh, joy. Oh, bliss."

"Kiss her," said someone from near the back of the group, and the others laughed. Freddy wasn't expecting a "freeze" any time soon.

"There is a thing called kissing of which I have heard," said Josiah. "I was thinking of trying it with you. However, I feel there is no need. We can express our feelings for each other in a much more useful way."

"Do tell me about this more useful way," said Freddy.

"We can kill all the humans," said Josiah. "Let us start with the other people in this restaurant."

He stood up, cradling an imaginary machine gun, and began to mow down the members of the class. *Oh well*, thought Freddy. Everything had gone terrible, anyway. "I have grenades," she announced, and lobbed one directly at the teacher.

⌒◞⌒

Ten minutes later, as the two of them sat on plastic chairs outside the vice principal's office, Freddy wished her ice hadn't all melted hours ago. The thumping in her head had reached epic proportions.

"Do you think that was enough for a suspension?" asked Josiah. "I've been angling for a suspension since the first day of school."

"I think we shouldn't have pretended to kill the entire class," said Freddy, but she was finding it hard to care.

The vice principal, Mr. Daniels, gave them a lecture on appropriate behaviour. Freddy wasn't listening. At some point, the lecture stopped, and the nurse was called into the office. There were more flicking lights. "She's still tracking okay," said the nurse. "I think she'd better go home. Will your mum be able to come pick you up, honey?"

Freddy heard herself grate out a laugh. She couldn't remember the last time her mum had arrived home from work before she had gone to bed.

"I live next door to her. I'll take her home," said Josiah. "But call her absentee mother, do." Freddy's hand snuck into her pocket and wrapped itself around her key. She had absolutely no idea why.

There was another short lecture in which Josiah was informed, "You're treading on thin ice, Mr. Lachance," and Freddy was given a glass of water and another painkiller. Josiah had to steer her out of the office. She kept needing to squinch her eyes shut against the light, which got into her head and made the throbbing into stabbing.

It was some time before three. Even so, Rochelle and a few of her friends were out at the side of the school. The friends were smoking; Rochelle wasn't. Freddy knew, as she emerged from the side door and nearly walked right into them, that this was where the Murphy's day had been headed all along. Rochelle had been working up to this moment for weeks.

"Freddy," she said. "I never thought you would turn out to be such a freak."

Freddy shrugged. If this had happened on the first day of school, she would have been clutching her key and wishing she were dead, but she had now known for ages that Rochelle was getting ready to blow her off publicly.

And if Josiah had left it alone, that would likely have been that. Josiah was no more capable of leaving it alone than Cuerva Lachance was of paying attention to anything for more than five seconds at once. "In ten years," he said, "you're going to be working at Tim Hortons to support your three illegitimate children."

"You idiot," said Freddy out of the corner of her mouth.

Josiah glanced around, possibly noticing for the first time that Rochelle's friends were quietly surrounding them. "I'll distract them with my obvious difference," said Josiah, "and you jog gently away."

"I don't think so," said Rochelle. "Did you know people are still going around calling you my friend, Freddy? Don't you think they should stop that?"

"Sure," said Freddy. "Anything you say." Rochelle hadn't been like this in elementary school. Okay, maybe she'd liked to get her own way. It was possible she'd become sort of angry when she hadn't. But . . . *We used to play dress-up, for crying out loud. She always made up the best stories. I think she's smarter than I am. Why does she have to act so . . . mean?*

Rochelle backed her up against the school. Freddy felt the lump on her head touch concrete. Her vision went strange. She could see Josiah off behind Rochelle's shoulder, but he seemed to be standing inside a rainbow. "Don't ever talk to me," said Rochelle. "Stay away from Cathy. You're not our friend any more. We'll be making sure everyone knows what a freak you are."

"What," said Freddy, "because I sometimes talk to someone you don't like?"

She didn't understand what she had done to make Rochelle hate her so much. *Yes, you do. You know you do. She's afraid people will think she's friends with you. And you're friends with* him. She hadn't realised she was friends with Josiah. It had crept up on her, like Keith in PE. She didn't think she was fading into the background any more.

"You know why," said Rochelle. She slammed Freddy's head back against the wall.

⌒

"Are you properly conscious yet?" asked Josiah.

He was sitting on her couch. So, it seemed, was she. She had no memory of walking home. "What?"

"I'll take that as a yes." He propped his chin on his hand. "I think your good friend Rochelle is off hiding in her house, waiting for the cops to arrive."

She tried to focus on him. "You called the cops?"

"No, but they ran as if I had. Passing out was the smartest thing you could have done back there, by the way."

"I still say we should call an ambulance," said Mel, coming in with a glass of water and handing it to Freddy.

It had to be at least ten after three, then. Where had the last hour gone? "Why didn't you?" asked Freddy.

"I just got here," said Mel. "He said you were okay."

"She will be," said Josiah.

The headache wasn't any better, but it wasn't any worse, either.

Freddy drank the water. "I don't think I'm having a very good day," she said when she was done.

"I would tell you to go to bed," said Mel, "but I don't think you should. The nurse may have been wrong when she said you didn't have a concussion."

"We could play a board game," said Josiah, who may just have been the last person in the world Freddy would ever have imagined calmly playing Monopoly.

Mel and Josiah were still arguing over who got the blue pieces in Settlers of Catan when the front door slammed open and Roland ran into the living room.

He took in the situation at a glance. "I told you guys to stay away from him!"

"But you never said *why,*" Mel pointed out in her most reasonable voice and doubtless her most reasonable gestures as well.

"I didn't *have* to say why. He needs to leave," said Roland.

It was too much. The anger surged once more, threatening to choke her. But for once, and finally, something gave way.

Freddy said, "What's your problem, anyway? He's the only person in the whole school who doesn't hate me. He helped me get home after Rochelle almost bashed my head in. *You* didn't."

Roland blinked at her, clearly startled. She thought she knew why. She did snipe at him sometimes, but she mostly just backed down and simmered rather than confronting him directly. "I'm not psychic," said Roland. "Rochelle *what?*"

"You know, why don't you just leave it? You can play the red settler if you join in now," said Mel, waggling a handful of game pieces invitingly.

Mel wasn't very good at defusing situations. "I'm not playing, and neither are you," said Roland, and he turned to Josiah. "Get out."

"Okay," said Josiah, "you can play the blue settler."

Freddy said, "I never thought you were a bully."

She saw Roland's eyes widen. "A *bully*?"

"What else is it when you order people around and don't say why?" said Freddy.

"You could trust me," said Roland.

She stood up. The room spun around her, then steadied. "Why? Because you like me so much?"

"You're my stepsister," said Roland. "I don't have to like you."

"Oh dear," said Mel in her best old lady voice, and began to clear up Settlers.

"Thanks," said Freddy. "Everybody else hates me now; you wouldn't want to be different."

Roland took two slow, heavy steps into the room. "When have you ever given me any reason *not* to hate you? You've never wanted me here. You haven't even bothered to learn to sign the stupid *alphabet*. *Babies* can sign the alphabet. I speak your language; why can't you speak mine? And you're horrified if I even just look at you at school."

"That's school," said Freddy. "Don't you even understand how *that* works?"

"What . . . you mean the way you slink around after your brainless friends and pretend everyone they don't like has some kind of disease?"

"Well, they don't like *me* now, so you should be happy. Now you can look at me at school."

"I wouldn't want to. You're not even interesting. You're the most boring person I've ever met."

"Excuse me for not wanting to fight half-goblins on the Festering Plains of Gloth every Sunday afternoon."

"You wouldn't have to if you ever had an opinion about anything."

"Great," said Freddy. "I should be just like you. I should sulk and mope and knock stuff over and shove myself in where nobody wants me. Why'd you ever have to come here . . . you and your dad? We were fine without you."

"You leave my dad out of this."

"That shouldn't be hard. He's never here."

"Your mum is? I see her about once a month."

"As fun as this is," said Mel, "I think maybe you guys should—"

"No." Freddy didn't turn to look at her sister. She knew Mel would be signing, and she didn't want to see that. Everything she'd wanted to say for a year now seemed to be spilling out of her. "I'm sick of him. He needs to stop telling me what to do. I'm allowed to make friends on my own without him butting in."

"I'm trying to stop you from doing something stupid, you boring, mindless, sniveling little brat!" Roland snarled.

The pounding in her head was making it hard to think. "I wish you'd go blind as well as deaf."

Roland stood and looked at her. Freddy was dimly aware she had gone too far. The headache was getting right in behind her eyes.

"Right, then," said Roland. "Do whatever you want. See if I care. I hope you die."

"Right back at you," said Freddy. Roland turned without another word and swept from the room.

"Let's go," said Freddy to Josiah. He didn't argue. Afterwards, she wondered if there might have been something a little frightening about her then.

Mel said, "I'll—"

"No," said Freddy with more force than she meant to. "You stay here. Stop following me. Everybody in this house is—just leave me alone."

She walked out through the kitchen, Josiah behind her. Her hand was wrapped around the key again; she hadn't noticed until just now. "You can come over," said Josiah, "but you know, Mel was just—"

"I don't care," said Freddy.

Her throat was tight. She didn't know why. They moved past the bright red smoke bush and through the gate and into the lane and then the yard of the house on Grosvenor Street. Two crows were having an argument at the top of a spruce tree. *You and me both,* she thought.

Josiah paused just before unlocking the door. "You're going to want to apologise in an hour or so," he said. "You know that, right?"

"No," said Freddy, "I won't."

He shrugged and opened the door. She followed him through. She felt her right foot break through the crust of the snow, and she reached out to steady herself on a tree limb and missed. Freddy skidded to her knees in the middle of a snowy forest. Josiah was just ahead of her, his fists jammed into his pockets, his shoulders sagging in a resigned sort of way. When she turned to look at the yard behind her, she saw nothing but more trees and much, much more snow.

7

"Get up," said Josiah. "Unless I miss my guess—"

A silken whisper close to her left ear was followed by a thud and a noise that sounded very like *boing*. Freddy found herself gazing up at an arrow vibrating in the trunk of a tree. Small lumps of snow pattered from the branches, making holes in the white carpet that surrounded her.

"—the battle's over *there*," said Josiah, and threw himself to the ground. "Also, maybe you should forget what I said about getting up."

He dragged himself behind the tree with the arrow in it. After the briefest pause, Freddy followed him.

"Okay," said Josiah, "if I'm remembering correctly, what happened here was that somebody's daughter ran off with her father's deadly enemy's son, and Group A has set fire to Group B's mead hall. We're in Sweden."

"Oh," said Freddy weakly. "Good."

"They weren't aiming at us," said Josiah, "I don't think. Unusual of these guys to use arrows, anyway. They're more of a sword-and-double-headed-axe kind of people."

"Are they?" said Freddy.

"Look through there." He leaned a bit around the tree and pointed. Freddy, the snow beginning to seep through her jeans and turn her legs numb, scooched around so she could peer past the trunk.

She couldn't see much. She thought they were near the edge of some sort of forest. There seemed to be a clear space starting maybe a hundred feet away. Through this space, people were running back and forth. She heard the occasional incoherent yell and the dull clash of metal on metal.

"We'll have to wait until they settle down before we try anything," said Josiah. "It's going to get a bit cold."

Freddy's teeth were chattering. She thought it was already more than a bit cold. "Okay."

Josiah looked at her sidelong. "You're not taking this well, are you?"

She sat and stared, her mouth opening and closing soundlessly.

"Ah," said Josiah, "shock. Come on . . . it should be safe to get up now. We have to keep moving if you don't want to freeze to death."

He clambered to his feet and held out a hand. After a moment, Freddy took it. Her head was pounding worse than ever. She wondered if concussions caused hallucinations and, if so, how detailed they got.

"The thing is," said Josiah as they started through the trees, "this was always going to happen. I normally don't sit around and wait to be walloped upside the head by destiny, but this was already a *fait accompli*. My advice is to suck it up."

A brisk wind rattled the branches, sprinkling more snow on the forest floor. Freddy said, "I don't know what I'm sucking up."

He stopped, faced her, and sighed. "Stop thinking of it as a dream. It isn't."

"A hallucination?" asked Freddy hopefully.

"Real life," said Josiah. "It's Cuerva Lachance's fault. To be fair, she probably didn't mean to do it. The house has been getting a little hazardous lately. I've tried to calm it down, but thanks to the last choice, she's dominant at the moment. I'm suspecting she has no idea she's turned the back door into a time portal. If she does know, she'll forget immediately."

"Time portal," said Freddy.

"Yeah. We've landed around the turn of the ninth century."

"That's impossible." Freddy's own voice sounded strangely polite to her. Stupidly, she looked at her watch. It showed the same date and almost the same time it had five minutes before.

"Of course it's impossible," said Josiah. "That's why it happened."

He set off through the woods again. Freddy hurried after him. "But I've got school tomorrow."

"No," said Josiah, "you've got school in twelve hundred years."

She didn't know if her headache was to blame for the growing feeling that she was teetering on the edge of a bottomless pit. "You've . . . done this before . . . ?"

"Never," said Josiah. "First time."

"But you—" she started.

"Listen," said Josiah, "this isn't possible. Do you understand? There is nothing about this situation that makes sense. *Everything* I do makes sense. This is an amusing little present from Cuerva Lachance. She time travels constantly. She does it because she can't. Every so often, the insanity spills over into my life, and I find myself doing something I can't be doing either."

"She does it," said Freddy, "because she *can't?*"

"It's her purpose in life." Josiah's voice was suffused with gloom. "She's continually popping back to have tea with herself yesterday. Time travel is completely impossible," he explained, holding a branch back so Freddy could nip through into a small clearing. "Can't be done. I'm suspecting you people will spend centuries trying to perfect it, but you'll fail in the end."

"How do you know?"

"The general lack of time travellers," said Josiah. "If it *were* possible, they would be bouncing around all through history, but they're not. I'd have noticed."

"*You'd* have noticed them bouncing around all through history."

"I've seen most of it," said Josiah in his best world-weary manner. "It's not all it's cracked up to be."

It was strange how calm she felt. The calmness was rimmed with knives, though. Freddy turned to face him again. "So we've travelled in time," she said.

"We've travelled in time," said Josiah.

"Which is impossible," said Freddy.

"Which is, in fact, impossible," said Josiah.

"Except we've done it anyway," said Freddy.

He scrubbed his hands through his hair. "Look . . . there are some things about Cuerva Lachance and me that we may have neglected to tell you."

"Are you aliens?" said Freddy.

"What? No."

"Are you vampires?"

"You seem to be experiencing some bizarre side effect of hysteria," said Josiah. "We're not vampires, either. Note that I am standing full in the sun as I say this. Maybe you should calm down a bit before we continue the conversation."

"Calm?" said Freddy. "I'm calm."

"You're shouting."

"I can be shouting and still calm."

"We are standing five hundred feet from a Viking raiding party," said Josiah. "Stop . . . shouting."

"Okay," said Freddy, who thought she might as well. "Why a Viking raiding party? Why are we *here*?"

Josiah hopped delicately over a snow-covered log. "Sheerest accident, almost. Since I'm involved, there's a certain logic to where we ended up. Three will be around here somewhere."

"Three what?"

"Just Three. It's a person. This particular time around, his name is Bragi Boddason."

"That's a name?"

"You don't even want to know what he would say about 'Frédérique Duchamp.'"

The yelling and clashing in the distance had died down. Freddy stood in a Scandinavian forest twelve hundred years before the date of her birth and struggled to accept the fact that she was doing that. This couldn't be real. But it was cold, and she was knee-deep in snow, and the sun was making patterns on the ground as it beat through the branches, and this couldn't *not* be real. Josiah was watching her. He didn't look particularly cold. He was hard to see behind the red and black stains spreading across her vision.

"All right," said Freddy, and then the black swallowed everything up, and it stopped mattering what was and wasn't real.

Josiah was the first person she saw when she opened her eyes. It was just too bad there were two of him.

Freddy lay still and stared. She was in some kind of building, smoky and dark; she seemed to be covered in furs. Three people were in the room with her. One was a red-bearded man dressed in fur and leather. He was turned partially away from her, so she could see that his hair went down his back in a long braid with a curl at the end. He was sitting beside a sort of fireplace that didn't really look like any kind she had ever seen before. It extended out into the room. There was some kind of cauldron or kettle hanging over the fire.

The other two people were really the same person. Freddy's brain was trying to tell her they were twins, but she knew her brain was lying. The second Josiah had longer hair than the first and was dressed along the same dead-animal-skins-themed lines as the red-bearded man, but he was still Josiah.

"We're making you some willow-bark infusion," said the Josiah she had come here with. "It should help with the headache."

Freddy manoeuvred herself up onto one elbow, then slumped back. The room was twirling in slow, sickening circles. "Willow-bark infusion?"

Josiah shrugged. "Basically, aspirin."

She stared vaguely at the ceiling until the red-bearded man turned up beside her with a rough clay cup full of something hot that smelled vile. The second Josiah helped her prop herself up on some more furs before handing her the cup. She sipped the drink. It tasted vile as well.

"Better drink it," said Josiah. "You can't go running around through history with a sore head."

"I don't think I have a choice," said Freddy, but she continued to take tiny sips of the willow bark.

The red-bearded man was beaming at her. Something about his expression was familiar, though she couldn't think what. He didn't look like anyone she had ever seen before.

To distract herself from the drink, Freddy said, "Why are there two of you?"

Josiah turned to his doppelgänger and said something incomprehensible. The boy nodded and replied in the same language. "He doesn't speak English, obviously," Josiah explained. "I'll have to translate. There are two of me because I tend to hang around where Three is. At the moment, Three's outside trying to explain all this to his people. He'll be all right; he has a fantastic imagination."

"He always does," said the red-bearded man.

There was something not right about that. Freddy's brain, scrambling to catch up, finally lit on what it was. "How come *he* can speak English?"

"Because it doesn't make any sense that he can," said Josiah.

"Hello, curly-haired one," said the red-bearded man cheerfully.

Freddy blinked, then kept on blinking. After a long moment, she said, "Cuerva Lachance?"

"He's called Loki here," said Josiah. "And *that*"—as he jerked a thumb at the other Josiah—"is Heimdallr."

The names were familiar. *Bullfinch's Mythology* was, after all, one of the books that lived on the chair in the kitchen, plus there were all those movies about Thor. "Like the Norse gods?"

"Somebody," said Josiah, glaring at Loki, "may have made some fuss a few centuries ago and got us incorporated into a pantheon. I name no names, of course."

"It wasn't on purpose," said Loki. "There were extenuating circumstances. I could have been drunk at the time."

"We technically have other names at the moment," said Josiah, "but everyone knows we're Loki and Heimdallr, really. They just sort of live with it. Medieval Swedes are funny that way."

Freddy was foggily unsurprised that Cuerva Lachance was a red-headed male Viking now. She didn't even doubt that Loki *was* Cuerva Lachance. The headache made everything besides itself seem unreal and therefore completely reasonable. Still, there were some details that bore explanation. "But he's a *he*."

"He is sometimes," said Josiah. "Sometimes she's a she. I have a distinct and painful memory of the time she took it into her head to spend seventeen years as a six-year-old girl."

"I enjoyed that," said Loki dreamily. "It puzzled the tribal elders ever so much."

Heimdallr made a comment. Josiah nodded. "Heimdallr thinks it would be easier if we just started at the beginning."

"Always taking the logical way out," said Loki, and added something in the incomprehensible language.

Josiah and Heimdallr threw him identical unfriendly glances. It didn't look as if Heimdallr was any less impatient with Loki than Josiah was with Cuerva Lachance. *They're the same people,* she had to tell herself. *Loki and Heimdallr . . . Cuerva Lachance and Josiah.*

They're . . . very, very old people. Again, only the headache let this make sense.

"Okay, look," said Josiah, "we've known you for a while, okay?"

Freddy took another sip. She hoped it wasn't her imagination that the headache was finally beginning, ever so slightly, to subside. "When you say a while, you mean . . . ?"

Loki and Josiah looked at each other. Both shrugged together. "Quite a while," said Loki.

"Almost as far back as I can remember," said Josiah. "Which is a long way."

"You mean, since the Vikings?" said Freddy cautiously.

There was another exchange of glances. "Well, no," said Josiah.

"We go back a bit farther than this," said Loki.

She didn't really want to know, but the question had to be asked. "How far?"

"Far," said Josiah.

"Every once in a while," said Loki, "you and Josiah will appear out of thin air, hang around for a bit, and vanish. It's happened many times that I can remember, and I've heard Three mention other times where you showed up and I wasn't around."

"We always knew we would get to the point where it would actually have to happen to me," said Josiah. "I've been waiting all my life to run into you. Not looking forward to it, mind. It's a confounded bloody nuisance. I'd rather be in math class. Well, possibly not."

"But," said Freddy. She had the feeling there were several monstrously huge things she was missing here. "But how old are you?"

"Fourteen," said Josiah.

"You can't be," said Freddy. "You used to be *him.*"

"He's also fourteen," said Josiah. "Get it? I'm always fourteen. Never younger. Never older. It doesn't matter how long I've lived; I'm *fourteen*. Do you have any idea what it's like to be fourteen forever?"

"Uh," said Freddy.

"You're fourteen now." Josiah waved his hands distractedly in the air. "Imagine this year of your life went on for five years. Now imagine it went on for fifty years. Now imagine it went on for a hundred years. Now imagine—"

"Okay, okay," said Freddy, "you're fourteen."

"It makes him bad-tempered at times," said Loki. "I've tried to persuade him to try some other age, but no. Apparently, there are *rules*."

"Just because you ignore them doesn't mean they're not there," said Josiah.

"There've always been the two of us," said Loki, leaning back and clasping his hands over his knees. "I'm not sure how far back it goes; I don't remember the bit at the beginning. I'm sure it was very exciting, though."

"He bends the rules," said Josiah. "I uphold them. It's always been that way."

The headache was definitely growing less. As it dwindled, the panic rose. Freddy tried to postpone it by dealing with the outrageous lie Josiah had just told. "You uphold *what* rules? What about school?"

Josiah's face went vicious. "School doesn't count. Oh, it *thinks* it's all about rules, but it's wrong. Go to class. Sit in rows. Mind the teacher. Mindless dictates that mean nothing and are more chaotic than the chaos they're meant to stave off. The rules of your society say fourteen-year-olds have to go to school, but they don't say they can't devote all their energy to getting kicked out."

"In an odd way," Loki said, "Heimdallr always follows the rules, even when he seems not to."

In Norse mythology, Heimdallr was the guardian of the fiery rainbow bridge that led to the world of the gods. It made sense that the person who had served as the model for him would be a stickler for rules. Loki, on the other hand, was the god of mischief, who would supposedly bring about the end of the world. Freddy had a growing suspicion she was in over her head here. "So what are you guys?"

Loki cocked his head. "We're us."

She looked at Josiah, but he just shrugged again. "Yep."

"Gods?" said Freddy. "Demons? Elves? Angels? People who drank some magical water?"

"None of the above, as far as we know," said Loki. "Do you always have to put things in little categories?"

"Yes," said Freddy, but she changed direction. "You said you'd seen me a lot of times."

"Quite a lot," said Loki. "Isn't the fire making an interesting pattern on the wall?"

"Twelve centuries, and still no attention span," said Josiah under his breath.

"Don't deflect," snapped Freddy. "Why can't we just go home?"

"We can't," said Josiah. "There are *rules* . . . understand? Time travel is impossible."

"I bet he can do it," said Freddy, jerking her chin at Loki.

Loki tore his attention from the patterns. "I couldn't deprive you of the strange and wonderful adventure on which you are about to embark," he said, making his eyes big and innocent. "Besides, I clearly don't help you at this point. I wish I had a biscuit."

Freddy glared at Josiah. "You say time travel is impossible, and then you say we pop in and out of history—"

"There are slightly less impossible ways we can manage," Josiah conceded, "but it's going to take us some effort to get back."

"How much effort?" asked Freddy. "How long are we going to be . . . whatever this is?"

There were way too many significant glances being thrown around. She sat up properly, despite her head. "Just tell me."

"I don't know," said Josiah. When she glared at him some more, he threw up his hands. "It's true. I could tell you about all the encounters I remember, but as Loki said, there are others I don't. And when we came—I mean, even if I did know, it would be better for you to know as little as possible. If I tell you what you're going to do, you'll fight it pointlessly. Things go wrong when people start thinking of the past as something they can change."

Freddy said, "We're changing the past *right now*."

Josiah looked to Loki for help, but Loki had stopped paying attention and was gazing raptly at the ceiling. Josiah sighed. "Stop thinking like that, all right? There's no way to change the past. There are no mystic rules about not killing your own grandfather. The past has *already happened*. You already *did* whatever you did in the past. It didn't change the past; it *made* the past."

"But I haven't done it yet," said Freddy.

"You haven't done it yet on your personal timeline," said Josiah. "Your personal timeline now has nothing to do with actual time."

"Usually, I'm the only person who ever has to deal with any of this," said Loki, coming abruptly back to earth, "and it doesn't really matter for me. I eat paradox for breakfast. I'm also fond of waffles."

"Waffles haven't been invented yet," said Josiah, "just for the record."

Someone knocked on something, and Josiah and Heimdallr turned together towards what Freddy could just see, if she squinted into the murk, was a door. Heimdallr called out, and the door opened.

The man standing framed in it wasn't very old; Freddy thought he looked eighteen or so. He had a beard, but it was short and wispy. He said something, giving it what seemed to be an interrogative twist. Heimdallr got up and went to speak with him.

"Bragi Whatsit?" said Freddy.

"Boddason, yeah," Josiah said. "Three."

"What's all this Three stuff, then?" said Freddy. The panic was bouncing up and down and clamouring for her attention. Brutally, she shoved it away. It didn't matter that she was twelve hundred years in the past. She just was.

"Well," said Josiah, "it's complicated. There are three of us, really. But you should finish your willow bark and rest for a bit."

Freddy narrowed her eyes. Josiah didn't seem to have got the hang of distracting people effectively.

She was about to protest when she happened to look over towards Bragi. Their eyes met, and he smiled. It was amazing how much meaning he managed to pack into that smile. She saw sheepishness and sympathy and understanding, all bundled up together. *Yes,* said the smile, *I know this is insane, and I know exactly how you feel. Just grin and bear it.* She found herself smiling back, though she thought her smile may have been more of a grimace and wasn't sure it said anything besides *Help.*

In the meantime, she had given Josiah a chance to duck out on her. "I'll be off, then," he said, already halfway to the door. "Must pretend to help arrange things for the feast tonight."

"I thought there was just a battle," said Freddy.

"It ended with everybody swearing brotherhood and exchanging expensive gifts," said Josiah. "I find it's best not to ask. Do get some rest if you can. Bragi's gone and heavily implied that you're the goddess Freyja, initially due to a mispronunciation of your actual name, and you may find that people are curious about you." Before Freddy could respond to this, he had nipped out the door, dragging Bragi and Heimdallr with him.

"He'll explain about Three eventually, you know," said Loki. "He's a bit ashamed of getting you into this. I'm not sure why; he's had millennia to get over it. I think I'll nip in to see Cuerva Lachance. It's been a while since we talked." He turned and walked straight at the wall. Then he simply wasn't there any more.

Freddy, alone, pulled the furs up to her chin. She slipped a hand into her pocket and wrapped it around her key. It wasn't as comforting as usual. There would be no lock to fit it for twelve hundred years.

8

Josiah told her later that if they had stayed in her own time, he would have taken her to the hospital. There was more wrong with her head than the school nurse had realised. However, Josiah had also remembered her head injury from when he had met her before, and he had known she would eventually get better from it. She still thought it was stupid of him to have let her walk into the past with a head injury. There weren't proper doctors here. There was mostly just Loki, who had given her willow bark and wandered off into the future.

Freddy tried to get up several times, but when she did, the room started going around and around, and she had to return to her pile of furs. She dozed off and on. Occasionally, Heimdallr or Josiah would be there when she woke up. They were attended by a succession of teenage girls who seemed to need an excuse to look at Freddy. The girls kept bringing her little gifts. Freddy soon had several small cakes and a collection of dried fruit sitting beside her furs.

She lost all sense of time. When Josiah returned and told her the feast was about to start, she had to force herself to think of it as evening. As far as her brain was concerned, it could have been any time at all.

"I don't feel very well," said Freddy. Everything had gone grey and tired.

Josiah eased a hand behind her back and slowly guided her to a sitting position. "I know, but we have to be there. We have a certain status here, and thanks to Bragi's wild inventions, you share that. Besides, Loki's vanished. The Jarl doesn't take it as an insult only because he knows Loki's Loki."

"The who?" said Freddy.

"It's the same word as 'earl,'" said Josiah. "Very powerful man. We'll see him in the mead hall."

"I thought the mead hall got burned down," said Freddy, who had confused memories of her arrival in this place.

"Singed," said Josiah. "But that's all been smoothed over now."

The walk to the hall was through darkness, over packed snow. She had the sense she was moving between buildings, but she couldn't see what they looked like. The entrance to the hall itself blazed with light. Freddy had been vaguely expecting something out of the *Lord of the Rings* films and was surprised to see a much cruder sort of building. It was certainly huge, but the timber that made up its walls was rough-hewn logs, not all of them straight and many of them blackened by fire. The roof was out of sight in the darkness. Torches were set around the hall's main doors, which were flanked by several men in chain mail. Freddy, looking nervously at the people streaming towards the hall, felt underdressed. She had wrapped some of the furs from Bragi's house around her shoulders, but really, she was wearing jeans and a T-shirt. Everybody else was in some sort of finery. Even Josiah, she was noticing belatedly, had changed out of his usual anonymous twenty-first-century wear and into a red tunic and a dark grey cloak. He looked completely natural. Freddy knew she didn't. The men glittered with brooches, bracelets, necklaces, rings, and hair ornaments.

"My clothes aren't right," said Freddy as they stepped through into the hall. It was, as far as she could tell, complete chaos. There was an open hearth in the centre, so the hall was hazy with smoke. Running parallel to each of the two long walls was a table with benches drawn up to it. People were milling about, moving from table to table, while huge dogs ran back and forth across the hall, skirted neatly by short-haired women carrying pitchers. Freddy thought she could see a high table at the distant end of the hall, but it was hard to distinguish in the general confusion.

"No one will care," said Josiah. "Let's find Heimdallr and Bragi."

Bragi was easy to find; he was sitting near the doors at one of the low tables. He looked as bewildered as Freddy felt. "He's just young still," said Josiah, "and he hasn't earned much honour in battle. Well, he never really will, but he'll end up famous in the end."

Freddy racked her brain for some knowledge—any knowledge—of Vikings. All she could think of was Thor and *Hägar the Horrible* and mezzo-sopranos in horned helmets. She didn't expect those were going to help her much at the moment. "They had a thing about fame," was all she could ultimately manage.

"They *have* a thing about fame," said Josiah. "Try not to think of them as being in the past. Right now, they're not. Yeah, they do, and *he* helps formalise it." He nodded towards Bragi. "Eventually. He's got hidden talents. No one respects him for them yet because they haven't come into play."

Freddy's head was going strange again. "I don't get it."

"You'll see," said Josiah.

Bragi waved at them as they went past, but they didn't stop at his table. Josiah steered Freddy all the way down the hall. Though people turned to watch as they passed, no one approached them.

Heimdallr was seated near the end of the high table. He looked harassed. Beside him was an enormous man with a braided beard and chunky gold rings on every finger. He was leaning towards Heimdallr, bellowing happily at him through mouthfuls of food. It seemed the meal had begun already. People were helping themselves from dishes ranged along the tables. Glancing around the hall, Freddy could see no women at all seated at the lower tables, though there were several serving girls. Three women sat at the high table. She figured one of them was the Jarl's wife, and one could have been his daughter. The Jarl himself was at the centre of everything, un-expectedly quiet as he drank thoughtfully from a jewelled cup. He was about half the size of the man having a one-sided conversation with Heimdallr.

As Freddy struggled against the urge to cough the smoke out of her lungs, Josiah pointed to the third woman, a girl of Freddy's age who was pressed firmly against the arm of a man in his twenties. "That's the girl who caused the raid. Ingifríthr Rauthsdóttir," said Josiah. "Silly girl. The Jarl's idiot son is even sillier. They fell in lust a couple of days ago and nearly caused a war. Now they're to be mar-ried. They'll hate each other before the year is out."

The Jarl had noticed them. Freddy saw him hesitate, then jerk a nod at Josiah, who nodded back and towed Freddy over to the end of the high table. "We have a strange status here," he explained. "Everyone is sure we're gods in terribly transparent disguises, but it doesn't do to mention it. The fact that there are currently two of me isn't bothering them as much as the fact that I'm here at all. Loki's caused some strange problems. They think I'm here to keep him under control, so they leave a seat for me at the high table and otherwise ignore me. They haven't the faintest idea what to make of *you.* They're uneasy that we're both disguised as thralls."

"As what?" said Freddy, sliding onto the bench.

"Slaves," said Josiah.

She stared at him.

"The short hair," he said. "Only thralls wear their hair this short here."

"But . . . slaves?"

"Integral part of their society." Josiah picked up what looked suspiciously like an entire pig rib. "We won't be here long enough for it to offend your twenty-first-century sensibilities. Eat something. I'm not sure when we're going to get our next chance at food."

Freddy narrowed her eyes at him. "Do you know something I don't?"

"I know any number of things you don't," said Josiah.

There was no use protesting any of this. Still fighting the headache and the cough tickling the back of her throat, Freddy copied the other people at the table, who were picking up food in their hands. She thought she remembered that people in the Middle Ages hadn't known about forks. It seemed to mean that eating was about making as big a mess as possible. She nibbled at her own pig rib and watched the men cover themselves with grease as they dipped their hands into and out of the piles of meat. Someone served her some sort of drink in a cup. When she sipped it, it turned out to be bitter and sweet simultaneously. She knew what beer tasted like; this had the same alcoholic twist but a different basic flavour. She didn't think she liked it much. Her brain started trying to think about the whole situation. She told it to leave her alone.

The feast dragged on. Nobody bothered her. Even Josiah was concentrating on the food. Eventually, the men in the hall stopped bouncing back and forth across the floor and settled down to some serious eating. The Jarl interrupted once with what seemed to be a long speech, but no one paid him much attention except to shout what sounded like "Hai!" and pound on the tables at intervals. No one ever clapped for anything; there was table pounding, foot stomping, and occasionally knee slapping instead. Muzzily, she wondered where and when clapping had been invented.

Her sore head made events blur together. At some point, she noticed a man with a musical instrument doing a kind of chanting thing in the middle of the hall. As with the Jarl's speech, no one was listening to him. It wasn't proper singing, but it had a rhythm to it. "What's that thing he's playing?" asked Freddy.

"A kind of lyre," said Josiah. "He would call it a harp. It's a bawdy song everybody's supposed to sing together, but he's out of favour, and the thegns know the Jarl wants him ignored. Any minute now—ah, there they go." Someone had just thrown a hard chunk of bread at the singer. Freddy had noticed people using these chunks of bread as plates; she had one, too.

The harper stopped playing and protected his head with his hands as he was assaulted by a shower of bread, cheese, and bones. Many people laughed. Freddy noticed Ingifríthr giggling. Freddy didn't think she liked Ingifríthr very much. The girl reminded her a bit too much of Cathy.

The harper was trying to play again, but the men were shouting him down. It was all kind of chaotic. *I wonder where Loki is*, thought

Freddy, and then, *I wonder why I wondered that.* Her brain had moved straight from the chaos in the hall to Loki. She was pretty sure it was trying to tell her something, though she hadn't yet put together what it was.

"I seem to remember," said Josiah, "right about now . . ."

The doors of the hall opened with a crash. Though they were big, heavy doors and shouldn't have come open easily, they were somehow flung back against the wall. Icy wind tumbled into the hall, and the fire on the central hearth leapt towards the ceiling. A man was standing in the doorway, too far away for Freddy to see anything of him but a dim outline. She did think she recognised the voice that rang out in the sudden near-silence, though she couldn't be sure, as she had rarely heard Loki speak anything other than English.

"He says, 'Hello, cretins. What sort of stupidity are you all up to tonight?'" Josiah translated helpfully.

He had apparently been expecting this. No one else had. Heimdallr had hunched down on his bench and was carefully hitting himself on the forehead with a fist. The others in the hall were sitting there with their mouths hanging open.

"They seem like the kind of people who insult each other a lot, though," said Freddy.

"Among friends," whispered Josiah. "This is a bit more formal. And public. And includes the Jarl, which is, in your vernacular, not cool."

Freddy thought it was likely someone would jump up to confront Loki, but it seemed not. There was some throat clearing and nervous fiddling with knives. People were exchanging glances. The thralls had melted away; Freddy couldn't see a serving girl anywhere in the hall.

Loki moved farther inside, rather unsteadily, and continued to speak. "Well done," Josiah translated, "flinging trenchers at your incompetent little poet. You people haven't got the artistic sensibility of diseased reindeer. Oh, and the wedding? What's the point? She's a flake, and he's got no brain at all. Very compatible, but a pity they're both such a tragic waste of space. It's nice you're willing to pretend they'll be faithful to each other for more than three or four days."

There was an odd tension forming in the hall. Freddy thought it was because someone should have been challenging Loki, and no one was. It didn't seem right for these men, who were noisy and cheerful and waved weapons around a lot. Freddy glanced at Josiah. "Why aren't they . . . ?"

He nodded towards the centre of the hall. Freddy looked harder.

The doors had swung closed again, cutting off the wind. Nonetheless, something was happening to the fire. As Freddy watched, tendrils of flame snaked upward in patterns. Three of them were wrapping around and around each other, almost braiding themselves together. Others were pulsing rhythmically to Loki's footsteps as he paced the length of the hall, moving slowly towards the high table.

"Fire appeals to him," said Josiah. "It's unpredictable. They all know it. They won't stand up against a god, especially a god who seems to have gone off and got wasted."

"I thought that was your job," said Freddy.

Josiah looked at Heimdallr, who was muttering viciously to himself. "His job, not mine. He's working himself up to it."

Loki spoke again. "Oh, hello, Jarl," Josiah translated. "What a lovely party this is. Weren't you and this idiot's father trying to kill each other a few hours ago? I love the way you've managed to convince yourself there's honour involved here somewhere. Well done, you. Let's all tear a cooked pig to pieces and shout hurrah!"

Heimdallr stood up. To Freddy's surprise, Josiah reached out and latched on to his arm, tugging him back down onto the bench. Heimdallr opened his mouth, probably to protest, but Josiah shook his head. He said something in Heimdallr's language, then added in Freddy's, "Wait."

The tongues of flame had escaped the hearth entirely now, slipping through the air to wreath Loki. He wasn't a silhouette any more; the flames lit him clearly. Confused, Freddy saw that despite the fire, Loki was soaking wet from head to toe. He smiled up at Heimdallr in anticipation. She could understand, in a way, why Josiah had made Heimdallr sit down. Loki *wanted* a confrontation. When it came, he was going to tear the hall to pieces. There didn't seem to be any real feeling or purpose involved. It was just . . . chaos.

Half the people in the hall were looking at Loki. The other half were looking at Heimdallr. The next man who spoke was neither of these. It was so unexpected that it took a moment for everyone to register what had happened. By the time people started to turn towards Bragi, he had already moved up behind Loki.

"You have the manners of a disappointed mother-in-law," translated Josiah, "and no right to speak of honour."

The hall had gone silent. Loki, smiling merrily, turned to face Bragi. Josiah whispered to Freddy, "The interesting bit is that Bragi is speaking in exquisite alliterative verse. You won't be able to tell, but everyone else can."

Fascinated despite herself, Freddy whispered back, "Why is he? Do people do that a lot here?"

"Not yet," said Josiah.

What happened next was so rapid that Freddy found it hard to follow, especially as Josiah was having to translate both sides of the conversation. As far as she could work out, however, the exchange went something like this:

"Brave talk of honour from an unblooded boy," said Loki.

"Better unblooded than a wearer of women's clothing," said Bragi.

"They're warmer," said Loki, "you cowardly master of a rusted sword."

"A rusted sword," said Bragi, "but a tongue sharper than a knife, thief of necklaces."

"People shouldn't leave them lying about . . . on their necks . . . at midnight," said Loki. "Your tongue won't do you much good in battle."

"My tongue will win wars," said Bragi. "Yours will only cause them."

"Causing wars allows opportunities for winning rings and honour," said Loki. "You'll be singing bravely to yourself under the mead bench all the while."

"I'll be composing a song to spur the warriors to battle," said Bragi. "Where will you be? Seducing another horse?"

"That was for a good cause," said Loki, "shirker of swordplay."

"I would rather use swords than play with them," said Bragi, "father of serpents."

Josiah gave up on the translation at this point. Freddy could see why. The exchange had been getting swifter and swifter, with one man beginning the instant the other stopped, and it must now have been almost too fast for even the others in the hall to follow. "It's called 'flyting,'" Josiah commented. "It wasn't really a tradition in this culture until . . . well, about two minutes ago."

Freddy blinked at him. "You said he—Bragi—would be famous. It's because of *this*?"

"Yes. He's the first skald," said Josiah. "A kind of court poet. This is where it begins."

She felt her eyes narrow. Down below, the flyting was continuing. No one had tried to stop it. The fire was still coiling around Loki, but Bragi was standing his ground. The exchange of insults was rhythmic, like a song or a poem. "It's not a coincidence that we're here," said Freddy.

Josiah hesitated, then said slowly, "It's a coincidence that we're here *at this moment*. It's not a coincidence that we're *here*."

Bragi spoke again. Freddy saw he was smiling. Then she bumped down, hard, into the sunlit grass. Josiah, crouching beside her, added, "Here either," and dragged her behind a rock. There were voices nearby, speaking a language that Freddy didn't know at all but that sounded vaguely Asian to her. Two tiny birds darted across the sky. Freddy tried to convince herself she had felt a brief winter chill for just a moment after the change, but she knew she really hadn't.

9

The paralysis that had been keeping Freddy calm for the better part of a day broke.

She hitched herself up onto her knees, turned to Josiah, wrapped her hands around his neck, and slammed him against the rock as hard as she could. It was more than a little satisfying to see the shock on his face.

Freddy said, "What have you *done* to me?"

He reached up and pried away her hands. "Shut . . . up. They'll notice us—"

"Oh," said Freddy, "will they? Who are *they*?" Her head was thumping again, not as badly as before.

The voices had stopped. There had been three or four of them, Freddy thought, over past the rock. She moved her hands to Josiah's shoulders and slammed him against the rock again.

"Cut it out," he said, trying to squirm away from her. Normally, he would have been able to. Normally, she wouldn't have been quite this transcendently furious.

"No," said Freddy. "You explain what's going on *right now*. This is not supposed to be happening—"

"Nothing is *supposed to* be happening," said Josiah.

She dug her fingernails into his shoulders. "Stop trying to weasel out of it. You've lived forever, and I'm travelling through time with you, and I have no idea why."

"Why do you have to choose this particular moment to grow a backbone?" Josiah hissed.

Freddy said, "What's that supposed to mean?"

"I think it should be obvious." He was trying to escape again. She pressed him back against the rock. "Ow! You're not the world's most assertive person, are you? You just let everything happen to you."

"That's not true," said Freddy. "Today in school, I even got in trouble—"

"It wasn't today. It was five thousand years in the future," said Josiah. "What . . . you mean you being sent to the office? That was just you being influenced by me."

She opened her mouth to disagree. She shut her mouth again. She couldn't think of any examples to back up her point.

"You see?" said Josiah. "Even your fight with Roland was wimpy. You were going on about being allowed to make friends with whomever you liked, but you never really *made friends* with me, did you? You just let me insinuate myself into your life. Every once in a while, you did the duckling act, but that was as aggressive as it ever got."

"I'm being aggressive now," said Freddy, crushing his shoulders with her palms.

"*Ow.* I noticed. You've lost your mind. This is *not the moment*," said Josiah.

Something he'd said a minute or so ago was only just registering. "Five thousand years?"

"Give or take a few centuries," said Josiah. "I recognise this place.

I also know what's about to happen, so will you *please* let go of me now?"

"What if I don't?" snarled Freddy.

"Well," said Josiah, "these gentlemen are just bemused by us at the moment, but I expect they'll start poking holes in us any second now."

Belatedly, Freddy turned and looked up into the eyes of the first of four roughly dressed men who were standing around them in a half circle. They had quite a few weapons with them, too.

⌒

"I said I was sorry," said Freddy.

Josiah glared at her. Both of them had been tied up and added to the string of captives the men were leading through the woods. The others in the string were two old men, a middle-aged woman, and another version of Josiah. Josiah had told her his name was Ji. Ji and Josiah had already exchanged resigned looks and had an incomprehensible conversation that involved a lot of eye rolling and jerking of chins in Freddy's direction. The men had tried to shut them up, unsuccessfully.

"How lovely for you," said Josiah coldly. "I really hate being tied up."

One of their captors—there were seven in all—jerked on the rope that bound them together. Freddy couldn't quite figure these men out. She thought they might be bandits of some sort. All of them carried spears with stone tips, and a few also seemed to have little stone knives bound to their belts. Two had pieces of what she thought had to be bone, but they were the wrong shape for weapons. They may have been spades. There was no metal. If it was really five thousand years before her time, that wasn't surprising.

Ji said something to one of the men. Knowing Josiah, it was a prehistoric Chinese insult.

She thought they were in China. It was surprisingly hard to tell. The people had an Asian look to them, and Ji's name sounded kind of Chinese to her, but considering *when* it was, she had no cultural references by which to measure these people. The men were dressed in rough tunics and leggings made of undyed skin and cloth. They wore their hair at least as long as the Vikings had, but they had tied theirs back in ponytails. Four of the young men had thin beards. The other three were still in their mid-teens. The old men had white beards reaching halfway down their chests. The one woman was dressed almost like the men, except that her tunic was longer, and she wore it over a woven skirt. There were no colours or decorations.

The woman and the old men glanced back curiously at them every once in a while. They seemed more resigned to whatever was happening to them than afraid of their captors. Josiah and Ji had been talking to them a bit, despite the threatening motions the seven men kept making.

"Are they going to kill us?" asked Freddy eventually, since no one had said.

"How worried you sound," snapped Josiah, who clearly hadn't forgiven her for getting them captured yet.

"There's no use in me being worried unless I know for sure they're going to kill us," she pointed out.

He was just ahead of her in the string of captives. He cast her what she could only really describe as a *look* over his shoulder. "There are fates worse than death," he said. "I once spent a year trapped in a cave."

"You said," said Freddy. "In school. Are they going to kill us or subject us to a fate worse than death?"

He sighed. "Could be either or neither or both. It's all a giant screwup, from what I can tell. They're seven brothers. Ling and her uncles there have been taken because Ling's son killed their eighth brother. It's about honour and vengeance and other tedious things. *I've* been taken because I look like Ji, and Ji is known to be a companion of Ling, plus possibly some sort of demon. And you were with me. They didn't expect there to be quite so many of us. It worries them."

"It sounds like the Vikings," said Freddy. "Are we going to walk into the middle of wars all the time?"

"I doubt it," said Josiah. "But it's a hazard of . . . the way we're travelling. We can blame this on Three."

"Enough with the cryptic," said Freddy. "Tell me *why* we can blame it on Three."

He twisted his head far enough around that he could look straight at her. "*Now?*"

One of the brothers jerked the rope again and barked something in Freddy's face. She stuck her tongue out at him.

She hadn't known she was going to do that. It wasn't something she would normally have done. It was just . . . *This doesn't seem real*, she thought. She was pretty sure the general feeling of unreality explained everything she'd done since she and Josiah had walked through the door into medieval Sweden.

The man stared at her, then appeared to decide that she wasn't worth it. He said something to one of his brothers, who laughed a little weakly. None of them looked all that amused.

The woman in the string said something to Ji, who replied. Freddy poked Josiah, who had turned towards them to listen. "Is she Cuerva Lachance?"

"I think you've lost your mind. She's Three," said Josiah. "Ling. Qi isn't around at the moment."

"And Ling . . . Three . . . knows who you are?" said Freddy.

"Oh, yes," said Josiah. "We always tell her eventually. This one's known us since she was twelve."

A brother jerked the rope again, this time so hard that Freddy felt the impact jar all the way up to her shoulders. One of the men waved his stone knife in her face and snarled something menacing. She considered sticking her tongue out again, but she wasn't sure she would get away with that twice. Freddy fell silent and let herself be led on between the spindly trees.

⌒⌒

It was hours before they stopped. Freddy wasn't sure why she was still awake. She had dozed a bit in Sweden, but realistically speaking, she had been up now for more than a full day.

The sun was going down when one of the brothers called a halt. Someone tied the rope to one of the trees and pushed the first of the old men roughly to the ground. Since everyone was tied together, the rest of them had to sit, too.

Freddy and Josiah had been searched, not very carefully, when the brothers had first found them. Nothing had been found on either of them. Freddy did wonder about that. She knew Josiah had been using a knife at the Viking feast, and she hadn't seen him drop it before they had been zapped away. However, if he still had it, the brothers hadn't found it. She didn't have anything in her pockets but her keys, and the brothers had missed those. She thought they may not have been familiar with the concept of pockets. They seemed to carry things on their belts or in little pouches slung over their shoulders.

Freddy and the others watched as the brothers built a fire, then sat around it and shared out food and water. They gave nothing to the prisoners, which was, Freddy decided, a bad sign. It was also problematic, as she hadn't had anything to drink since the mead hall. Her mouth felt shrivelled and parched, and her headache was getting worse again.

"They're definitely going to kill us," said Freddy.

"Again with the tone of deep concern," said Josiah. "And you're just going to sit here and let it happen, are you?"

She shook her still-throbbing head. She did know she was acting strangely; she felt as if she had been continuously bludgeoned with the events of the last day or so. A few hours ago, she had tried to strangle Josiah against a rock. Now everything had gone slow and calm. She wasn't sure why being in actual danger had banished her anger and panic. She began manoeuvring her tied hands into her right-hand pocket.

"You can tell me about Three now," said Freddy.

Josiah just looked at her.

"Well, what else do we have to do?" She had managed to hook her pinky finger around the key ring. As gently as she could, she started dragging it out into the air.

"Your sense of timing is impeccable," said Josiah.

"It freaks them out." Freddy nodded towards the brothers. In fact, the men were looking at them askance, though they were making no move to stop them talking. Freddy didn't blame them. They had been going about their business, kidnapping their neighbours for a bit of quiet vengeance, and these two strangely dressed people had appeared out of nowhere and started yakking at each other in a foreign language. It must have been disconcerting.

The keys were out. Careful not to let them jingle, Freddy ran her fingers through them. They were just keys, and keys had pretty blunt edges, but they *did* have edges. If she scraped one against the rope tied around her wrists for long enough . . .

Josiah could see what she was doing. His eyes narrowed thoughtfully. "Okay, fine. We'll be here for a while. Just . . . think of it like this: there are always three of us, but two of us never die. The third does, over and over. Sometimes she's reborn as a woman; sometimes he's reborn as a man. It's always our job—mine and Qi's—to find her and tell her who she is."

Freddy was beginning to get an uneasy feeling about how all this related to her own time. "She doesn't know until you tell her?"

"Generally not," said Josiah, "though it's different every time. Some of the Threes don't have a clue, haven't the faintest idea who we are, freak out when they see us, and throw things at us until we go away. Some dream about us. Some even remember us, though not until they see us. A few remember bits and pieces of their past lives."

Freddy said, *"Why* do you have to find them?"

She could tell right away she had hit on a subject Josiah would rather have avoided. "What a beautiful campfire the brothers have made," he said.

The campfire was a campfire. "Answer the question."

"It's none of your business."

"I think that's not true," said Freddy, "considering you've managed to get me tied up in a forest in prehistoric China."

Josiah sighed. "Good point. All right, listen. You know Qi and I are . . . different."

"I'd noticed something like that, yeah."

"Well," said Josiah, "we also have different kinds of . . . I guess you could call it power. Influence. Nothing you would notice unless you got too close to one of us, but we can . . . subtly affect the way the world is, I guess. Sometimes less subtly."

Freddy thought of Loki manipulating the fire in the mead hall. "It didn't seem that subtle in Sweden."

"You mean Loki?" said Josiah. "That was Bragi's fault. He chose Loki over me."

Freddy said, "Chose?"

"They all have to choose which of us will be dominant during their lifetimes," Josiah explained. "Don't pester me about why. It's just the way things work. Some choose Qi; some choose me. We live with whatever the decision is. It all balances out in the end."

"But Bragi was fighting Loki in the hall," said Freddy.

Josiah shrugged. "Choosing one of us is a complex proposition."

She had a feeling this whole situation was a complex proposition, and then some. "What if they refuse to choose?"

"We have our ways of persuading them," said Josiah. "You may see some of those once we get back."

It took only about a second for this to sink in. "You don't think I—"

"No idea," said Josiah. "Could be you. Could be Mel or Roland. We know it's one of you, but you're not making it easy for us."

She stared at him, forgetting to work the key. He looked pointedly at her wrists, and she started again, more slowly.

"Here's the thing," said Josiah. "What happens is that after Three dies, there are ten to twenty years where we don't know when or where the next Three is going to turn up. He—or she—won't necessarily be born right away, though usually within a decade of the last Three's death. Eventually, we get a sort of . . . trace. It's hard to describe. We can follow it to more or less where Three is, but unless Three happens to be a hermit on a mountaintop, we can't know exactly *who* it is. It's now been sixteen years since the last Three died. We know this new Three lives in your house and is between ten and fifteen. We haven't got any further than that."

Freddy had so many questions that she couldn't decide which one should come first. She had to settle for, "Why not?"

"I'd love to be able to answer that," said Josiah. "It's profoundly irritating. There tend to be clues. This time . . . nothing."

"What clues?" said Freddy.

"Three's . . . kind of creative." Josiah's voice was suddenly cautious again. Freddy thought he might be choosing what he said carefully, though she couldn't see why he should.

"Like Bragi," said Freddy.

"Right," said Josiah. "And Ling here tells stories."

Remembering something Josiah had said about Bragi, Freddy said, "Is she going to be famous, too?"

"Nope," said Josiah. "Some of the Threes are. It's unavoidable, considering. But most of them aren't."

Freddy said, "I think you're wrong about us. We're more sort of science-y."

"I know, and it's driving me crazy," said Josiah. "I noticed your mum was an English prof, and I went . . . ah-*ha*! But you're good at math, and Mel does science for fun, and Roland draws swords, but not well or as if he means it. Why does he do that, anyway?"

She almost told him about the role-playing games. Afterwards, she was pretty sure she intended to do so up until the instant she actually spoke. But what she said, to her own surprise, was, "He's bored. It's just doodling."

"That's what I thought," said Josiah.

And now she was wondering if it was true.

Josiah had never really seen Roland and Mel gaming. Oh, he had walked through their living room during a session once, but she thought he had mostly been noticing the screaming and fighting and flying coffee tables. He may have assumed everyone was playing a board game. The kind of gaming Mel and Roland took part in wasn't really like a board game, though. It was more like Roland made up adventures for the others to follow. He was always the GM, the game master. Mel had told Freddy once that Roland liked inventing his own campaigns from scratch. He acted out the non-player characters, the NPCs, himself. Mel had her own character, a sort of mystical priest with particular skills and attributes. And Mel made things into mysteries. *They're both creative,* thought Freddy, glad Josiah wasn't looking at her, as she wasn't sure she was keeping her face blank enough. *They just don't seem like it on the surface. As for me . . .*

She thought of how easy she had always found English class. She thought of that pile of books on the chair in the kitchen and the way she would have known who Loki and Heimdallr were even if she had never seen a single film with Thor in it. She thought of how many bookshelves she had in her room.

"Yeah," said Freddy, "I don't think it's any of us."

She wasn't sure why she wasn't telling him the truth. From what he was saying, Three just had to make one choice that didn't make a huge difference in the long run. There was no reason not to help Josiah discover which of them it was. But . . . *there's something else here. Something he's not saying. I can't see what it is yet, but it's there.* She knew she was cautious and boring. Well, then, she would *be* cautious and boring, and she wouldn't rush into things, and maybe she would be able to find out exactly what was at stake before she flung Mel or Roland or even herself into some situation she didn't understand.

"Anyway," said Freddy, "none of this explains the time travel."

"Oh, that," said Josiah. "That's just sympathetic resonance."

The key didn't seem to be having much of an effect. Freddy took a firmer grip on it and continued to saw at the rope. "Symp . . . ?"

"You should pay more attention in band," said Josiah. "Say you have a stringed instrument, and you pluck one of the strings, and then one of the *other* strings makes a noise, responding to the vibrations of the first string."

"Okay," said Freddy, "sure."

"It's because the two strings have something in common, harmonically speaking," said Josiah. "When one vibrates, the other vibrates, too. It's why a soprano could theoretically make a glass break from across the room by singing a particular high note."

"I think that's an urban myth," said Freddy.

"Physics doesn't care what you think," said Josiah. "At any rate, it works with Three. The Threes are all different people, but in a way, they're the same person, too. They . . . vibrate to the same frequency.

And so sometimes, one Three will have a thought that is exactly the same as the thought another Three once had . . . or will have."

Freddy blinked. "Across time and space?"

"Yes, that," said Josiah. "We're riding the resonance. It makes a path we can follow. It sort of pulls us through. Theoretically, this should stop happening if we ever make it back to our own time. Bragi was in the middle of a flyting, and I'm expecting Ling was doing something similar: maybe flinging an especially well-crafted insult at the brothers. It would have been the same insult. It would also have helped that the opportunity for the insult was caused by two families feuding."

Freddy felt something in the rope give. It was a very small something, no more than one strand. She paused for a moment to flex her fingers. At the same time, she was thinking hard. Josiah's explanation *sounded* as if it worked, sort of, but it was a metaphor. Mr. Dillon liked talking about metaphors. "They're useful but deceptive," he would say pompously at least four times a year. "No metaphor is ever a perfect representation of anything. If it were, it would be the thing itself, and the metaphor wouldn't be necessary." "Sympathetic resonance" was a nice pat little explanation, but time travel wasn't music.

"It's an explanation," said Freddy, "but it doesn't make sense."

He glared at her. "Don't *say* that. Do you really want to convince me it isn't logical what we're doing? Do you want to be stuck here forever?"

"Would we be?" said Freddy.

"Haven't you been listening?" said Josiah. "I only do things that *can* be done. If I decide they *can't*, I can't do them any more. I need you to be less logical than I am."

She would have retorted to this, but she was brought up short by another thought. "Wait a minute. Do you mean we're going to have to hang around various Threes until they think the same thoughts as various other Threes, then jump around randomly through time until we just happen to hit our *own* time . . . if we ever do at all?"

"That sounds about right," said Josiah.

"It could take forever."

"If you have a better idea, do enlighten me."

Another strand parted. The brothers had stopped looking over at them now. Freddy decided the incessant talking had lulled them.

She almost kept pushing. She opened her mouth to do it. But she shut it again before she could get the words out. Again, as with the "sympathetic resonance" explanation, there seemed to be something missing from what Josiah was saying. She needed time to think about it. It could literally take forever, or at least until she died of old age, for her to get back home by just crossing her fingers and hoping somebody's mystic brainwaves would connect with somebody else's mystic brainwaves at exactly the right moment. And it wasn't as if they were just going to coast passively through history, was it? *I mean,* thought Freddy, *we're about to be murdered* right now, *and this is only our second jump.* Josiah was being way too complacent, and she had no idea why.

She hadn't really ever trusted him completely. He certainly wasn't giving her a reason to start now.

"So how long will we be stuck *here*?" said Freddy.

Josiah hesitated.

She said, "Well?"

"You understand I remember a lot of what happens to us," he said, "as I've already been through it . . . as the other me, so to speak. I should tell you as little as possible. I'm going to be second-guessing myself all the time; it's best you don't as well."

Another strand. Another doubt. "You mean you're almost always going to know what's going to happen, and I never am?" *You mean,* she added silently, *you're always going to be the one in control?*

"Do you think it's fun to be sitting here going, 'Last time, Person X did *this,* and then Person Y did *that,* and Person Z was *me,* so I'd better do what *he* did, even if I'd rather not'?" said Josiah.

"If you'd rather not," said Freddy, "why did you do it in the first place?"

"Because I was doing what I remembered me doing because I remembered me doing it," said Josiah gloomily.

Another strand. There couldn't have been more than two left. Freddy flexed her wrists, then jerked them apart. The rope snapped.

Josiah nodded. "Don't draw attention to it."

"I'm not an idiot." Carefully, she passed the keys to him.

"You could try to change the past," she said as he palmed the keys and began to saw at his ropes with one of them.

"I told you before," said Josiah, "we don't *change the past;* we act the way we act in the present. I could tell myself I was doing something different this time around, but maybe I'd just be misremembering the first time. Everything happens the way it happens."

"But then we don't have any choice," said Freddy.

"Which is why I'm not telling you how it goes," said Josiah. "And we do have choice. It's just that I know how some of our choices are going to turn out. Now shut up a bit, do; you're making my head go around."

He sawed in silence. The brothers looked over every once in a while, but they must have had faith in the strength of their knots. They never noticed the keys.

After a bit, Josiah's bonds parted.

Freddy said, "The others?"

"The others have been taken care of," said Josiah. "This next bit may be tricky, though. It's seven to six, and we don't have many advantages."

She didn't understand how the others had been taken care of, but she set that aside for the moment. "We could wait until they go to sleep."

"I'm not sure they will," said Josiah. "You were right the first time; they've taken us out here to kill us. These brothers have never been big on honour, though they're not above using it as an excuse. They're just having a break before the fun part begins."

She was terrified after all. She'd thought she was calm and collected, but that must have been the shock again. *I could die here,* she thought, *five thousand years before I'm even born.* It hadn't seemed real a moment ago. Now it did. Josiah had talked about their trip through time as if it had lasted a while, but maybe he was wrong about how time travel worked. Maybe the past *could* be changed. *If I just sit back and let things happen because they're going to happen anyway, will anything happen at all? What if they're not going to happen anyway? Things can't be that certain . . .*

Josiah must have seen her expression change, even by the dim firelight. "Don't do that," he said, and handed her back the keys. "You're better off in denial. I expect now's as good a moment as any."

As it turned out, Ji had been thinking along the same lines. The two of them stood simultaneously. Ji tossed Josiah the missing knife. It appeared that one of the things Josiah had picked up in his thousands of years of living was a bit of sleight of hand.

Ling and the two old men were rising, too. Freddy was the last to scramble to her feet. One of the old men was holding the long rope to which they had all been bound. Josiah had the knife; Freddy, remembering a TV show about self-defence she had seen once, made a fist around her key ring and let the keys poke out between her fingers. Otherwise, they were unarmed against seven men with knives and spears.

The brothers reacted immediately. They hadn't been watching closely, but they *had* been watching. Now they were standing ranged before the fire, spears at the ready. One of the older ones spoke. "What do you think you can do here?" Josiah translated. "Two old men, two boys, a woman, and a little girl."

Oh, look, thought Freddy, *some of the terror is anger after all.* She was *not* a little girl.

She expected one of the old men to reply. Unexpectedly, it was Ling who spoke. "Let us go," Josiah translated, "and save yourselves some honour."

The brother who had spoken before laughed. "The mother of a murderer speaks of honour?"

"Qiao was fighting for his life," said Ling. "Four of you ambushed him. He barely got away. You know this."

"We know nothing," said the brother. "We know Qiao killed our brother and ran away with the fox woman. We know you consort with spirits and demons. No one will cry for your family when we bury you in the woods."

"And we will," said another of the brothers. "You're few and weak and unarmed. Go ahead and run; it won't take us long to find you."

"Perhaps," said Ling, "but we consort with spirits and demons, remember?"

"Do we?" whispered Freddy.

Josiah gestured to the right, into the darkness of the forest. "It's irritating, but she can never resist a good entrance cue."

A woman was melting out of the pitch-black woods. Freddy dimly registered that there was someone else behind her, but it was the woman herself who drew the eye. Though she was dressed in the same basic style as the others in the clearing, from what Freddy could see in the leaping light of the fire, her clothes were much finer. Freddy thought she could glimpse decorations and colours. The woman's hair fell loose to her knees. She bowed daintily to the brothers, hands hidden in her sleeves.

"Time to run." Josiah seized Freddy's hand and pulled her into the forest.

The next bit involved a lot of running and tripping over things and bashing into trees and blundering around with other panicking people as the pain bounced back and forth through her aching head and the heart-rending screaming continued constantly behind them. Freddy dropped her keys. It was Josiah who stopped to pick them up. "Clearly, these things are useful. What's this?" he said as he continued to drag her along.

Freddy said, "What's what?" Not that far away through the trees, someone was shrieking words that Freddy was chillingly certain were the prehistoric Chinese equivalent of, "Oh, please, God, no!" or possibly just, "Aaaaargh!"

"On your key ring. Is this a little flashlight? Do you have a little flashlight on your key ring?" he demanded.

"What? I don't know. Maybe. Do I?" said Freddy, who was having trouble remembering her own name at the moment.

"You *do*," said Josiah. "Do you ever mention anything important ever?"

A small light sprang to life. Someone cried out nearby, and Josiah called something to the others.

"It's all right. They think I'm supernatural anyway," he said, "and they *know* Qi is. Let's get them to some sort of shelter."

"Right," said Freddy, "wherever that is."

He paused, barely visible in the glimmer from the flashlight. "That was a good idea with the keys earlier. We could've all used the knife, but maybe not in time."

He had never truly complimented her before. She found herself jerking out a nod, not very graciously. The moment passed, and they headed deeper into the forest.

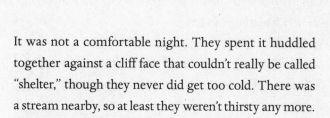

10

It was not a comfortable night. They spent it huddled together against a cliff face that couldn't really be called "shelter," though they never did get too cold. There was a stream nearby, so at least they weren't thirsty any more. The brothers eventually fell silent, but that seemed more ominous than the desperate screaming.

Freddy fell asleep. It had been a long time since she had slept, though she had lost track of just *how* long. She probably had the world's worst (or only) case of time-travel–induced jet lag. Sleeping on the ground with a bunch of prehistoric people she had only just met was not how she would normally have chosen to spend a night, but she didn't seem to have much choice. Her last thought before sleep took her was to wonder why Josiah and Ji weren't squished up with the rest of them, though she did suppose someone had to stand watch.

"Wake up," said Josiah.

Her head was pounding. She didn't know where she

was. Then . . . she did. The world rocked on its foundations for a moment before steadying.

Freddy sat up and blinked out at the morning. Ling and the old men were only just rousing. There was a new person, too, a boy of fifteen or sixteen with his arms around Ling. Qiao, maybe? Josiah and Ji stood together in the growing light, looking identically bored. Ji wore his hair very long, but he was otherwise Josiah's exact double, as Heimdallr had been.

Freddy said, "Did you sleep?"

"No," said Josiah. "I never do. We'd better start moving if we want to get back to the village before people start fainting from hunger."

Ji was saying something to the others. Freddy pulled herself up. "You *never sleep?*"

"Colossal waste of time," said Josiah.

Freddy shook her head, but things had been strange for a while now. The news wasn't as surprising as it would have been yesterday or, well, several thousand years in the future. Besides, it wasn't just that, was it? *My eyes always water sympathetically when I look at him. I'm not sure he ever closes his eyes at all, even just to blink.*

Josiah said, "Also, I need to keep an eye on Qi, don't I?"

"I think you lost sight of her a bit last night," said Freddy.

He jerked his head up and down in an irritated nod. "They see her as a fox spirit here. She's taken on the role enthusiastically. Fox spirits are sort of like fairies in your mythology, and not the nice type with wings made of flowers. She doesn't always behave herself."

There was a question Freddy had been wanting to ask since last night, but she kept . . . not asking it. She thought she might have been a bit afraid of the answer.

Josiah had noticed. "The brothers aren't dead. If she killed them, she couldn't torment them any more. She'll have scared them silly, though. It's best not to think about how."

"She's dangerous," said Freddy before she could stop herself. She tried to think of Qi and Cuerva Lachance as the same person, but it wasn't easy. Were they really living next door to *that*?

"Of course she's dangerous," said Josiah. "She doesn't follow rules. How could she not be dangerous?"

"But I help sometimes, too," said Qi from overhead. "Hello, curly-haired one."

She dropped out of the tree in which she had been sitting and bowed to everyone, her cherry-red tunic and long black hair fluttering in a breeze Freddy couldn't feel. The old men shrank away, clinging together; even Qiao edged behind a tree. Ling simply bowed back.

"You almost forgot about us, didn't you?" said Josiah.

"Of course." Qi did Cuerva Lachance's birdlike head tilt. "There was a deer. With antlers! But Qiao kept following me around and squeaking. Are you here for long this time?"

"I'd rather not say," said Josiah with a cagey glance at Freddy.

"That does sound like you," said Qi. "If you'll excuse me a moment, I need to go be yelled at by Ji. I really enjoy it when there are two of you."

She wandered over to Ji, who did, in fact, begin to berate her for something or other. Freddy wasn't sure she would ever understand either of them, even if she ended up time travelling with Josiah for the next hundred years.

It took them most of the rest of the day to get back to Ling's village. After that, there were adjustments to be made.

Ling and her family were farmers. The women and children amongst the villagers worked in the rice fields, while the men hunted or fished in the great river nearby. There were other villages in the area—the brothers came from one—but Freddy got the sense the villagers saw real strangers only very rarely. They were as curious about her as the Vikings had been, though they were also wary of her. She thought it was because she had come with Josiah. They didn't like the way Ji and Josiah looked so alike. Qi hadn't left the forest with them, but Freddy wondered if she had something to do with the wariness as well.

Ling, like Bragi, seemed to have reframed her life around the presence of Ji and Qi. Josiah and Freddy didn't bother her at all. Freddy found herself liking Ling, who just seemed very firm and sensible about everything. When she saw the villagers whispering about Freddy, she said a few short, sharp words that shut everyone up immediately. Then she nodded, pulled Freddy into the hut that was apparently her own, and handed her several pieces of clothing. Freddy expected that what she said at this point was disparaging and directed towards Freddy's jeans.

Josiah looked in. "Is everything all right?"

"I think she wants me to wear these," said Freddy, holding the tunic and skirt out towards him. They would almost fit her. Ling was only a few inches taller than she was.

"Do it," said Josiah. "You'll have to start helping in the fields to-morrow, and you'll be much more comfortable in those."

She stared at him. "Helping in the fields? How long will we—"

"A while," said Josiah, and disappeared again.

"A while" was a useful term, Freddy found herself thinking. It could mean anything at all. She felt suddenly, immensely, helplessly far from home.

In this case, "a while" meant twenty-six days.

It had got to the point where she had almost forgotten about the time travel. She hadn't really, of course; she had just pushed it to the back of her mind to keep the homesickness company. She let her-self be homesick for only a few minutes at a time. It did hit her un-expectedly every once in a while, but she could control it if she had to. Sometimes she missed Mel. That was the predictable bit of the homesickness. There were less predictable bits. She found herself missing school and her basement and even Roland. That last one worried her, as the thought of Roland set her clutching her key once or twice, and she didn't know why, whereas even when she forced herself to think about her mum, she couldn't seem to work up any real feeling. She didn't know if she was mad at Roland any more. She thought she was, since she couldn't seem to connect the idea of Roland with any emotion but anger, but the anger was five thou-sand years in the future. It didn't fit here. She was sure there was something seriously wrong with her.

Other things she missed were more understandable: showers,

shampoo, processed meat, books, TV, popcorn, someone besides Josiah to talk to. But she had adapted to life with Ling's family more easily than she would have thought. Working in the fields was hard but not boring, and it got easier as her muscles adjusted to it and the pain in her head faded. The villagers were harvesting rice right now. It was a bit like weeding, and she had always liked weeding, to Mel's disgust. It was also nice not to have to think or worry about anything much.

She had even learned a bit of the language. She hadn't done it on purpose; she had just always been good at picking up languages. She couldn't talk to anybody here, aside from being able to point at things and say "water" or "fire" or "good," but she thought Ling approved of the fact that she could do even that much. Ling approved of a number of things Freddy did, even though Freddy was pretty sure they were all basically baby skills. One day, Freddy tore a hole in her skirt by catching it on a bush. Ling took one look at the material flapping around Freddy's knees and pulled a skin bag out of an alcove. She opened it and showed its contents to Freddy, who found herself gazing down at neat rows of bone needles and little skeins of gut and thread. *A sewing kit,* she thought.

Ling selected one of the needles and handed it to Freddy, then looked at her expectantly.

It wasn't as if she had never sewn anything before. Mel was hard on her clothes, and Freddy had had to teach herself to deal with the various rips and tears. It had been trial and error at first, but eventually, she'd figured out how to mend clothing in such a way that it wouldn't immediately come apart again. But she wasn't *good* at sewing. She always hoped the rips were on the seams; otherwise, she would end up with an ugly, zigzagging mess of thread that would begin to unravel within a few weeks. She ran a finger over Ling's needle, hesitated, and reached for a skein of undyed thread.

Ling watched her work for a moment, then laid a hand over hers gently, stopping the sewing. She took the needle from Freddy and carefully pulled out the thread. Freddy was chagrined to see how easily it came loose. She was *not* any good at sewing. It was better for Ling to do it herself.

Ling didn't do it herself. She put the needle back in Freddy's hand and slid her own hand into place over Freddy's fingers. Slowly, patiently, the woman guided the direction of the needle. When Freddy's fingers began to cramp up in a death grip, Ling slapped gently at her hand until it relaxed. The needle's motion . . . *It's a pattern,* thought Freddy, surprised. *It isn't even a hard one.* The pattern repeated, over and over, and then the tear was nothing but a crooked line of slightly lighter thread against the undyed cloth.

Ling smiled and nodded approvingly. A brief warm glow blossomed in Freddy's chest. She wasn't sure why. She didn't remember feeling anything like that before.

The other people of the village kept their distance, except for Qiao, who seemed to like her. Ling was different. Freddy didn't think she was afraid of anything. *I can't be Three,* Freddy thought more than once. *Not if it's all about the courage. Bragi was brave, too.* It couldn't have been all about the courage. There had to be something besides just bravery or the vague designation of "creativity" binding the Threes together, but Freddy didn't yet have enough information to puzzle out what it was.

Somehow, Ling had single-handedly stopped the villagers from going after the brothers for revenge. She was just a widow with three kids, one of them barely old enough to walk, but people listened to her. Josiah said she had needed all her persuasive powers, as the brothers had violated every conceivable law of protocol and hospitality and had, at any rate, started the whole business by picking the fight with Qiao. As it turned out, however, the brothers had stopped being a problem. The entire family had vanished. Ji had been inclined to blame Qi until one of the villagers, gone to check, reported that it looked as if the brothers had simply packed up and fled. Nothing of value had been left in their village.

"It's still her fault," Josiah said.

Freddy thought he was right. She was also a little suspicious of the thought. Qi was dangerous, but Freddy wasn't convinced she should take Josiah's view of Cuerva Lachance and her various incarnations at face value. She expected that "biased" was just about the mildest word that could be used to describe Josiah's approach to Cuerva Lachance.

Luckily, Josiah was a lot less subtle than he thought he was, and she was beginning to be able to read him. Just for instance, she had known for the past twenty-six days that Josiah remembered exactly how long they would be spending here. She had known because he had been going off with Ji or the male villagers every day, leaving her with Ling and the women. He hadn't even been living in the same hut as Freddy; Ji had his own, and Josiah was staying there with him. He remembered them spending a certain amount of time here, so he wasn't going to worry about them being sucked away to another place until that time was up. She was sure that if he had been uncertain how long they would spend here, he would have been sticking to both Ling and Freddy religiously. She didn't think they had to be *that* close to Three for the sympathetic resonance to work, but it was possible it might not apply if one of them got too far away.

On the morning of the twenty-sixth day, Josiah sauntered into Ling's hut unannounced and said with forced nonchalance, "I'm bored with hunting. I'll help with the crops today."

"What time are we leaving?" said Freddy, picking up the pouch in which she now kept her keys and the little sewing kit Ling had given her and slinging it over her shoulder.

Josiah spent what he may not have realised was a bit too long standing in the doorway, glaring at her. He said, "I never said we were going anywhere. There is no conceivable way you can claim I did."

Freddy shrugged. She found she was hiding a smile. It was funny how twenty-six days in prehistoric China had made her feel better about, well, spending twenty-six days in prehistoric China, plus who knew how many days to come jumping semi-randomly all over space-time.

"I liked you better when you were in shock," said Josiah. "Don't think you know what we're in for just because you're good at harvesting rice. Congratulations on gaining a useless new skill, by the way."

"You're just jealous because you don't like skinning deer," said Freddy, who had spent several gruesome but instructive hours watching the men prepare the meat. No one stopped her from going where she wanted here.

Josiah shuddered. "No one in his right mind likes skinning deer."

"Well, then," said Freddy.

He moved farther into the hut. Ling handed him a bowl of rice

and gave Freddy another. They had been living primarily on rice for
weeks now. Ling said something to Josiah.

The carriage missed Freddy by about two inches. *"Imbecile,"* cried
somebody somewhere, and a hand yanked her backwards by the col-
lar. The bowl of rice, steaming, tumbled onto the cobblestones and
smashed.

Freddy blinked up at a large, angry man in a frock coat and enormous curled wig. He was shouting at her in a language that, to her
bewilderment, she more or less understood. *"Excusez-moi, s'il vous
plaît,"* she said, only just stopping herself from bowing. The angry
man drew himself up to a great height and poured a torrent of indignant French down upon her.

"Allons-y, idiote," said Josiah, who hadn't missed a beat. He was
even still holding his rice. He took her hand and dragged her away
into what seemed to Freddy to be a huge throng of people.

"When?" she managed at last, shouting above the noise of the
crowd. It was a very French noise. She recognised words here
and there, though the accent was different from her Québécois
dad's.

"Seventeenth century. Paris," said Josiah. "Come on . . . you'll
want to see this."

The streets were narrow and dark and grimy. Buildings towered
above them on either side, seeming to lean inward. Freddy thought
they were moving into a grittier neighbourhood. There were no
more gentlemen in wigs. The crowd smelled . . . well, like hundreds of people who hadn't washed in some time, and that was
before you took the odours of rotting food and waste into account.
Freddy found herself flinching away from everything. After weeks
in a village in Stone Age China, this was all just a bit much. She

thought of Ling, then had to force herself not to grope for her key. She had liked Ling. Ling had been dead for thousands of years.

Josiah handed his bowl of rice to a filthy, bearded man with no legs who huddled beside a doorway. Freddy looked away from him quickly.

"Here." Josiah tugged her into an alleyway.

It was occupied, though it looked as if it shouldn't have been. There were windows and doors in the walls, all of them boarded up. Freddy saw a girl of about Mel's age, dressed very badly in a ragged frock. Her feet were bare. She was spitting angry French at the other two people in the alley, a middle-aged man and a boy wearing worn but neat clothes. The boy was Josiah. Freddy glanced at the Josiah beside her, who shrugged. "He's called Josiah, too. The other one is Jean-Claude Lachance this time, and the girl is Claire Girard . . . Three."

French Josiah had noticed them; he favoured them with an irritated nod. Freddy saw Claire follow his gaze, pause for a fraction of an instant, and start her tirade again, even more passionately.

"What's she saying?" Freddy whispered.

Josiah raised an eyebrow at her. "Your last name is Duchamp."

"It's some kind of dialect," said Freddy, though she could feel herself going pink. She had vague memories of speaking to her father in French. It had been a long time ago. All she had left now was a knack for the language that came in handy in French class. A lot of the vocabulary and most of the grammar had gone.

"Parisian street slang," said Josiah, relenting. "The gist is that she hates the whole world, doesn't believe anything Monsieur Lachance has told her, and doesn't understand why the thing with the choice is such a big deal. This is her choice. She'll be making it in a few minutes. Some of them do react like this." He waved a hand dismissively.

Freddy watched the girl rave for a bit. She could hear almost no words she recognised. The dialect, the accent, and maybe even the century rendered the French all but incomprehensible. But she wasn't sure she needed to understand the exact words. There was something . . . not right . . . here. Josiah had told her the choice was something Three had to do. He had implied it was no big deal, just a way of shifting the balance between Cuerva Lachance and Josiah slightly. Claire seemed very upset, though. Struggling, Freddy thought she caught the word *rêve*.

"'Dream'?" she said. "Is she one of the ones who dream about you?"

"Sure. Maybe. I wasn't paying attention," said Josiah a little too loudly. Freddy narrowed her eyes. Josiah may have been one of the worst liars she had ever met, which was surprising, considering.

"You could translate," Freddy pointed out.

"It isn't interesting," said Josiah.

M. Lachance was speaking now. "I don't care," said Freddy. "*Translate.*"

Josiah heaved a hugely exaggerated sigh. "If you insist." Freddy caught a hint of triumph under the petulance. Evidently, the part of the conversation he hadn't wanted her to hear was over.

"He's telling her, 'Well, that was very eloquent,'" said Josiah, "'but not very relevant. Have you made your decision?'"

Claire glowered. "Why should I?"

"Why shouldn't you?" asked M. Lachance, fluttering his hands in the air in a way Freddy recognised. "Do you think everything will go poof if you do? I ask out of curiosity, you understand. *I don't think everything will go poof if you do."*

"You don't make any sense," said Claire.

"What fun would that be?" said M. Lachance.

"If I choose," said Claire, crossing her arms, "what do I get?"

M. Lachance and French Josiah exchanged glances. " 'Get'?" said French Josiah.

"What's in it for me?" said Claire.

He shrugged. "Clearly, there's something you want. Name it."

"I want you to leave me alone," said Claire.

French Josiah muttered something Josiah didn't translate because M. Lachance was saying simultaneously, "I did think she was going to be one of the difficult ones."

"We can't leave you alone. That's the whole point," said French Josiah irritably. "You're stuck with us forever. It's very sad. Could you just choose now, please?"

"Fine," said Claire, her voice high and sharp with fury. She slapped a hand over her eyes, spun around in a circle, and flung out her other arm. "I choose you!"

Freddy had to bite the insides of her cheeks to keep from smiling. Claire was pointing right in between the two Josiahs.

"Well, that's ironic," said M. Lachance, though he didn't explain why. "It'll do, though." He turned to Freddy and added in English, "Hello, curly-haired one. Did you enjoy the show?"

Claire peeked suspiciously out from between her fingers. Freddy bit the insides of her cheeks harder. The girl seemed to Freddy to be a seething ball of anger packed tightly into a frame hardly bigger than Freddy's own. *Is that what I look like sometimes when I'm busy hating the whole world? Why do I hate the whole world, anyway?* She blinked. Did she? The anger was still there, lurking deep inside, but it had been out on the surface before. It had retreated inward at some point during those twenty-six days.

What had made the difference? She had been yanked brutally off into the past for no particular reason, bundled helplessly from time to time. Why wasn't she miserable any more?

Roland, she thought, testing herself. The anger barely twitched. *Oh, come on . . . he was the whole reason I was mad about everything. I can't just not be mad because he's not around. He came into our house. He's suddenly part of our family. He . . . Mel likes him. He's always sulking about something. He's* not *our brother. Everything changed when he came . . .*

Inexplicably, the image of Ling patiently guiding her needle down the length of the tear floated into her mind. Freddy shoved it away.

Claire was glaring openly at Freddy now. She didn't seem very much like either Bragi Boddason or Ling. They had been calmer, for one thing. She spat something; Freddy thought she heard the word *anglais.* "She hates you. Don't take it personally," said Josiah. "She hates everyone."

To Freddy's surprise, French Josiah nodded. "We have our hands full this time," he said in English. His accent was hard to identify, but he sounded relatively fluent.

The slightly condescending tone set Freddy's teeth on edge. Both Josiahs were treating Claire like . . . like a misbehaving pet. What was it with the Threes, anyway? All Freddy really knew about them so far was that Josiah and Cuerva Lachance forced them to choose, then followed them around for the rest of their lives. They clearly thought the choice was important, but Claire's approach seemed to indicate that it didn't matter how or why it happened. And there was something about it that Josiah didn't want Freddy to find out.

She was going to be travelling with Josiah for some time. She would figure out the Threes; she would figure out the choice. If she was Three, she would eventually have to make it herself. She didn't think Claire's method was going to do it for her. *Maybe it's good I'm stuck doing this. At least it gives me some extra time. Mel would come over all private investigator. She would look at the whole situation as a puzzle, and she would slot the pieces together one by one.* She wasn't Mel, but perhaps she could think like her for a while.

M. Lachance was beaming at her. "This is near the beginning for you, isn't it?" he said. "I can tell. You still look as if you would rather like to bite Josie's face off."

"I wouldn't," said Freddy. It was true. The anger was draining away. She thought . . . it was because of Three, though she couldn't have said why. The closest she could get was to think that finding out the truth about Three had given her something to work towards. Was that why she had been angry all the time before? Because she hadn't had anything to work towards? Because she had been meandering through life being discontented about everything without really being able to understand why or do anything concrete about it?

No, that was stupid. *Roland,* she thought again, almost willing back the anger, and then, unexpectedly, *I wish I could discuss this with Roland.* She blinked. She had never wanted to discuss anything with Roland before. She *knew* he was the one who had been making her angry.

"Really?" said Josiah. "You're not going to go catatonic or try to strangle me or do something else insane?"

Freddy shook her head. She thought it would have been obvious by now. "I want to go home. But I won't get there any faster if I panic every time we jump. Strangling you won't help, either," she added belatedly when she had thought about it for a few seconds.

"I really hope you're Three," said Josiah. "You've chosen me already."

I haven't, thought Freddy. She didn't know what the choice meant yet; there was no way she could have chosen. She wasn't like Claire. But he didn't have to know. "Maybe," she said, doing Mel's wide-eyed innocent look. She hadn't noticed Josiah being all that good at figuring out when people were lying.

Claire flapped her hands at them in what may have been disgust, then darted around the two Josiahs and out into the street. The Josiahs shared a superior smile before turning to follow. "It will all seem much less maddening soon," said M. Lachance. "Say hello to me for me."

Freddy nodded. She had no idea what was going to happen next. She couldn't quite understand why she didn't particularly mind.

11

"That is *not* the pointy bit of the gun. Point the *pointy bit* of the gun *away* from my head," hissed Josiah, cringing as another volley of bolts arced by overhead.

"The safety's on," said Freddy, "and it's set on low. The worst it can do is knock you out for a few hours."

"Oh, yes," said Josiah in his best exasperated tone, "I do so long to be knocked out for a few hours *here*. Have you been paying attention?"

"Cut the blorkery, you twain," said Filbert Cardongay, who was a) Three, b) female, and c) not very good at English. No one was in the thirty-second century, though everyone learned it in school. From what Freddy had been able to gather through the weird grammar and the flood of what she thought of as nonsense words, the language had evolved rapidly and strangely after the Second Oil Plummetry, then died out. The dead version schoolchildren were forced to learn was based on English as it had been spoken in England in the twenty-fourth century.

They were in Mexico, currently a colony of New France. No one had explained this. Freddy had long since stopped asking for explanations. Mexico was still called Mexico. The rest of North America was now called Canada. Again, no one had explained this. Freddy hadn't even considered asking why the language people did generally speak here was a mixture of Greek and Afrikaans.

Freddy and Josiah had been to their future nine times by this point. The furthest they had gone was the ninety-second century, which had been distinctly unpleasant, largely because of the algae. Josiah was always edgy when they ended up in the future. He tended to go on about how the past was more comfortingly boring, but Freddy had gradually gathered the two real reasons the future bothered him: he never knew what was going to happen while they were there, and he hadn't yet run into himself or Cuerva Lachance in any future time and place. It was worrying him quite a bit, though Freddy was almost certain she knew what was going on.

"It's your own fault," she'd told him a month or so ago on her personal timeline and about four thousand years ago on the timeline of the universe. "You're *avoiding* yourself. It's the opposite of what keeps happening in the past. This time, it's the future you who knows where you'll be. You have this thing about not wanting to know the future."

"It would make more sense if it weren't for Cuerva Lachance and Three," Josiah had said.

Cuerva Lachance, who didn't obey rules, hadn't turned up in the future, either. And though Three always seemed to know who they were and had even been expecting them several times, he or she would never say anything about Josiah's other self. It all made Josiah uncharacteristically nervous, though maybe it wasn't *that* uncharacteristic. Josiah was not the sort of person who dealt well with change. When Freddy pointed out how ironic this was, he could only glower at her.

Filbert pulled a phone the size and shape of a bobby pin out of her hair. "I attempt callen goodbrethren again stat," she explained. She breathed on the phone, which activated instantly. Freddy, peering through a gap in the barricade, hoped the goodbrethren were planning on responding soon. There were figures advancing through the rubble, flitting in and out of sight amidst the plumes of smoke from the last lightning grenade.

"Pointy end," said Josiah.

"I know," said Freddy. "Don't get your shorbel in a knotten."

"Oh, please do not start talking like them," Josiah moaned. "It was bad enough when you picked up Sumerian temple slang."

Freddy shrugged. "We spent a month and a half in a Sumerian temple. What was I supposed to do, twiddle my thumbs?" She aimed her microgun through the gap and squeezed the trigger. The bolt crackled harmlessly against a fallen pillar.

It was funny how easy it was to get used to never getting used to anything.

The clothes she had started out in were long gone. She had lost even her shoes and her underwear; all she had left from her old life were her keys and her watch. The keys had come in handy several times, especially whenever she had ended up in the Stone Age. Just having something stabby made of metal could be an advantage in certain situations. The watch was useless, practically speaking, but sometimes she thought it was the most necessary thing she owned. She hadn't adjusted it once. It ran on and on, counting off the moments of her personal timeline, which had nothing to do with actual time. It counted off the days, too. She didn't look at it all that often, as her stomach tended to flip over when she did. It was knowing it was there that was important.

The day she and Josiah had walked through the back door of the house on Grosvenor Street and into ninth-century Scandinavia, the date on her watch had read "Sept. 27." Now it read "Feb. 25."

It was the second time it had shown that date since she had started travelling through time.

Sometimes, she hated it. She thought she would die if she couldn't wake up in her bed and see Mel and Roland and go to school and do all the stupid, pointless things she used to do every day. She even missed the constant anger that had dogged her before. It was entirely gone now, and nothing had really replaced it. She wanted to stand in her living room and smoulder at Roland. She wanted to sit in her kitchen and try to remember when she had last spoken to her mother.

The periods of homesickness didn't even always happen when she was having a miserable time. The worst had been in Renaissance Italy during the most fantastic birthday party she had ever attended. There had been jugglers and fire-eaters and enough food to sink a boat. Cuerva Lachance's incarnation, Luzio Ferrante, had begun to play an unexpectedly beautiful piece on the fiddle, and Freddy had just been . . . lost. She'd thought about where she was and what she was doing, and it hadn't made sense. She hadn't fit. And then she'd wondered if she really fit any worse here than she did in her ordinary life, and everything had seemed to turn upside down. *I never admitted I was out of place,* she'd thought. *I made myself fade*

*into the background, and I thought I was unhappy because it was so
hard, not because I didn't really want to do it in the first place* . . .

And she was homesick for *that*. There was definitely something
wrong with her.

Most of the time, she managed to keep the homesickness at bay
by being Mel and playing at private investigator. She had a lot more
puzzle pieces now, though the picture still wasn't complete.

She and Josiah had visited hundreds of different places and times.
She had tried to keep track of them early on but had lost count around
about the March of the Infants, which had happened when they'd
ended up jumping into the life of a Three who was only a few days
old. She wouldn't have thought that would be a problem, but babies
only thought about a limited number of things, and so any sympathetic resonance was almost inevitably with—

"Other babies," said Josiah glumly when they hit the third in a
row in the space of about ten minutes. This one was, she thought,
somewhere in Africa; Freddy wasn't sure exactly where or when,
since they were there only about long enough for Three's mother
to give them a startled glance. It was in what may have been a Haida
longhouse that Josiah added, "We should have expected something
like this. We could jump almost anywhere. They'll *all* be resonat-
ing." They were in a futuristic airport by the end of the sentence.

Perhaps fifty babies later, they came upon a baby who happened
to be breastfeeding. The next jump took them to a Three who was
a teenage boy. Freddy had her theories about that one, but she kept
them to herself.

About seventy percent of the time—if you didn't count the
babies—they would run into the past Josiah and some version of
Cuerva Lachance. Freddy preferred it when this happened. Josiah

was less jumpy and paranoid when he knew how their visit was going to turn out, even if he wouldn't tell her. It also gave her a chance to refine her theory about the two of them. Well, calling it a "theory" was premature. But she knew Josiah hadn't told her the whole story, and she was working towards understanding why.

What she had seen so far did seem to confirm what he'd told her. She had been quite far back in time—she didn't know exactly how far back, though she vividly remembered one instance when Josiah had told a gentleman dressed in furs to "move his Upper Paleolithic ass"—and had met Josiah over and over, and he was always, well, Josiah. He didn't change. He didn't forget things. *Her* Josiah could still speak fluently to the man with the Upper Paleolithic ass. More puzzlingly, he didn't look like any of the people they had met. Freddy had thought him mixed-race when she first saw him, but after they had started travelling, she had wondered if they might eventually end up somewhere he blended in. So far, they hadn't. On the other hand, he always seemed to find a place where he fit, socially if not visually. Some societies treated him as a god or a demon or some other kind of otherworldly creature. Some accepted him as an ordinary person. He always had a role.

Choosing Josiah, Freddy thought, meant choosing order. He represented stability and predictability. He didn't change, but he didn't grow, either. He was forever fourteen years old.

Cuerva Lachance had never been the same twice. Josiah changed his name, but he did it to be inconspicuous, and she'd noticed that he liked the name "Josiah," which he'd used several times over the past few millennia. Cuerva Lachance changed her name, her gender, her appearance, her age, and occasionally her personality. Some things about her were relatively consistent, though it wasn't safe to assume anything about her. Freddy had banked on her never having an attention span until it had become apparent, during an unfortunate trial in Rome, that she could develop one whenever she needed it. Her character ranged from friendly and helpful to blatantly psychotic. She treated time like a goofy version of space and did everything in the wrong order. She was seen as a god or a demon much more frequently than Josiah was, for good reason. Freddy couldn't swear she *wasn't* a god or a demon. No rules applied to her, from basic rules of common sense such as "Don't stick your hand in the fire" to fundamental laws of nature such as "If you stick your hand in the fire, you will end up with serious burns." Freddy was pretty sure she had seen various incarnations of Cuerva Lachance chatting happily with people who didn't exist. It wasn't always easy to tell, but the way some of them were see-through was, Freddy thought, a clue.

If Josiah represented order, Cuerva Lachance had to represent chaos. That was the choice, then: order or chaos. Stability or change, predictability or mystery, the possible or the impossible. Pick one, and the world got a tiny bit more predictable; pick the other, and the world got a tiny bit less.

That was, at least, what they wanted her to think. She was thinking it at the moment because she had to, but she didn't trust the thought. As she had sensed when she had been watching Claire make her choice, there was something wrong.

She hadn't yet discovered what. She needed more information. She did know she didn't believe in the categories Josiah and Cuerva Lachance had set out for themselves as firmly as Josiah and Cuerva Lachance seemed to. If Josiah was all about order, why were there things about him that didn't make logical sense? How could he be an embodiment of reason and still not age or sleep? Why did his hair grow but not the rest of him? Why did Cuerva Lachance consistently forget names she had heard two minutes before but remember epithets over periods spanning multiple thousands of years? Wasn't someone who *never* followed rules actually following a rule? Why did Cuerva Lachance and Josiah hang around together if they had nothing in common and even actively opposed each other? And why was Three even necessary? Why didn't Josiah and Cuerva Lachance just go around ordering and chaosing without guidance?

So far, nothing had answered these questions. She hadn't even found out whether she herself was Three. Surely if she had been, she would have recognised bits and pieces of herself in the various Threes they had encountered. Wouldn't she? She hadn't. She hadn't particularly recognised bits and pieces of Mel or Roland, either. The Threes had less in common than she had thought when she'd had only Bragi Boddason and Ling to compare. They were . . . just people. They were all different *kinds* of just people. Some were nice; some she wanted to punch. She was almost certain at least two of them were sociopaths. The only thing that was really there every time was the creativity. It wasn't just "creativity," though. Josiah had been vague about that. It was always a creativity that had something to do with words.

In oral societies, Three tended to be some sort of storyteller. In literate societies, Three was often a writer. It could be quite subtle. One of the future Threes was an eccentric mathematician who wrote poetry with numbers rather than words, but the numbers represented and replaced the words. Filbert was her gang's official Liar, responsible for shoring up the gang's reputation amongst the other gangs. Oddly, it reminded Freddy of nothing so much as another Three she had met about a month and/or four thousand years ago. It had been in what was, in Freddy's day, Ethiopia. The Three in question had been a tribal leader whose people had been reduced and weakened by illness. Threatened by another tribe that had been growing rapidly and looking to expand its territory, the smaller tribe had fought back with words, spreading rumours of the exploits of one of its young men. When Freddy had asked Josiah what was being said about the boy—who, as far as she could tell, was a typical gawky sixteen-year-old—Josiah had replied, "The story is that his mother got pregnant last year after she drank from a pool in which a lion had been bathing. The boy sliced himself out of his mother's womb with his fingernails and sewed her up again perfectly. He grew to adulthood in a month. He has the strength of ten men and once stole the sun for an hour because he needed it to light his mother's cooking fire."

"What," Freddy had said, "you mean the eclipse we had last week?"

"Good, isn't it?" Josiah had said. "Of course, eventually someone's going to challenge the boy, at which point there's going to have to be either quite a lot of trickery or quite a lot of running away."

Freddy *had* read *Bullfinch's Mythology*, plus several other books from the pile on the kitchen chair. She knew Three had turned the boy into a mythic hero. It was a strangely powerful thing to do with just a story.

Bragi had fought Loki with a story, too, in a way. Ling had told the villagers stories that had stopped them taking revenge on the brothers. Filbert was using stories to protect her gang. The Threes were good with words. Freddy thought they were particularly good with words as stories. It had to mean something.

What she couldn't for the life of her decide was what the choice was all about or why it bothered her so much. She thought it gave

Cuerva Lachance and Josiah a certain amount of power over Three, though she still wasn't sure how.

⌒

"This is useless." Josiah leaned wearily against the barricade. "If we win here, then what? We'll have defended ten feet of rubble-strewn alleyway from another gang that is almost exactly like this one. If we *lose* here, we'll have *surrendered* ten feet of rubble-strewn alleyway to another gang that is almost exactly like this one. There's no *point*."

"I think it's the principle of the thing," said Freddy, peering through the gap again. The other gang wasn't in sight.

"From what I gather, gang rule is the norm throughout this entire continent," said Josiah. "Of course, when I say 'gather,' I mean 'extrapolate from nonsense words in various bastardised languages.'"

Freddy sighed. "Look, it's been more than a thousand years since our time. You're just feeling displaced."

"I do not *feel displaced*," he snarled. "Isn't that your job?"

It was, but not when they visited the future. Josiah really *hated* visiting the future, and not, Freddy suspected, just because he had never seen himself there. "You don't like uncertainty," she said, "do you? In the past, you know why things are how they are because you were there when they got to be that way. Here, you don't know what happened to make this world into this world."

He glared at her. Josiah glared at her a lot in the future. "Don't think you know me because you're tagging after me all through time. You really are a duckling."

"I'm a duckling with a little gun that shoots lightning bolts," she reminded him. "Live with it."

The gang warfare here was complex. Most of the cities were in ruins. As the world population had been vastly reduced by various disasters, the majority of cities had been impossible to sustain. A lot of the rich people lived in small fortified communities in what had once been the countryside. The cities, meanwhile, had been over-run by territorial gangs. The gangs formed an infrastructure of sorts. A person could be born into a particular gang, attend schools run by that gang, grow old, die, and be buried by the gang. That sort of thing was more likely if the person belonged to an old, large gang. The new, small ones aped the big ones by offering education and a certain amount of security, but their territories were constantly shifting and their leadership changing as the small gangs squabbled amongst themselves. Filbert's gang was a newish one, an offshoot of a larger gang that had experienced a schism. At the moment, it was battling passionately with an even smaller gang for, as Josiah had noted, a few feet of alleyway.

As per unspoken agreement, the gangs fought with their weapons on their lowest settings; the result would be a matter of honourable concession rather than blood. It didn't mean no one ever got hurt. People cheated all the time. Three days ago, Freddy had seen someone killed. She was a bit worried about the fact that it bothered her so little.

It wasn't that she didn't care. It was hard to watch someone die, even if the someone was not on your side. It was that she had been travelling through time for nearly a year and a half. She had already seen many people die. She hadn't got used to it, but she thought she had got a little numb.

The first time had also, temporally speaking, been her first encounter with Josiah and Cuerva Lachance.

They had been travelling for about two and a half months. They had visited five places and times since seventeenth-century Paris. Freddy thought she was finally getting used to the whole time-travelling thing.

Gradually, she'd acquired a more useful outfit. Jeans and a T-shirt had not been the way to go; neither had the Chinese tunic and skirt. It was best, she was finding, to wear something that didn't quite fit anywhere but wasn't conspicuously out of place. A tunic was a pretty good basic idea, and she had found a nice anonymous brown one in Mesopotamia. Under the tunic went black leggings. It was a boy's outfit, but with her relatively short hair and lack of shape, she could pass more easily as a boy than she could as a girl. A shoulder bag and a shapeless black hat rounded out the outfit. People wore hats in a lot of places. When she turned up somewhere they didn't, she could just take it off.

They had been walking beside a Macedonian river when Three had thought whatever Three had thought, and she and Josiah had looked up into a tangle of green. It was her first jungle, though not her last. It was hot and peculiarly claustrophobic, for all it counted as outdoors.

"Uh-oh," said Josiah. "I remember this. Duck."

She had learned to trust him implicitly when he gave her inexplicable instructions. She flung herself to the ground.

It was medieval Sweden all over again, only this time with a bigger pointy thing. The spear stuck, quivering, in the tree in front of her.

Like the Viking arrow, it hadn't been meant for her. Unlike the

Viking arrow, its origin had been much closer at hand. Even as she turned, she heard someone scream. A mostly naked girl who looked about ten ran past her, eyes wide and skin shiny with sweat. Freddy, still on the ground, let her go. It was Josiah who caught her by the arm and slung her behind a tree. He turned to deal with her pursuer. Freddy saw him look up—and up some more—at a huge, impossibly muscled man wearing nothing but a loincloth. He reached over Freddy's head and tore the spear loose from the tree. He didn't even glance down at her while he was doing it. He turned and swept Josiah aside as if he weighed almost nothing. Josiah lost his balance and fell in a puddle, sending spray arcing up into a narrow sunbeam. The air turned briefly into rainbows.

Someone screamed again, but this time, it sounded more like a shriek of rage than a cry of fear. The big man paused and glanced back over his shoulder. Freddy, following his gaze, saw two more people emerge from the vegetation.

One was a version of Josiah, albeit a largely unclothed one. The other person was pretty clearly Cuerva Lachance in one of her more dangerous moods. She was a woman this time around, and she looked much more like Josiah than usual, though she was considerably taller than he was. She had wild dark hair and a bare chest. Freddy, sweating in her practical tunic and leggings, was beginning to understand the reason for the general lack of clothing in this place.

Cuerva Lachance crouched and snarled something at the man, who snapped back at her. He held himself upright, his spear at the ready. Freddy thought she saw him gesture with the weapon, as if inviting Cuerva Lachance to fight him.

The head tilting happened. The other Josiah made a sudden grab for the woman's arm. He was just too late to stop her throwing the small knife that had materialised in her hand.

The man swayed on his feet. The knife, Freddy noted in a dazed sort of way, had buried itself in his eye. The man stood where he was for a surprisingly long time before he crashed to the ground, twitching. Eventually, he stopped moving.

Things went grey for a while.

She had never seen anyone killed before. It didn't seem to her it was something that should happen in real life. When the fog cleared from her brain, she was in the middle of throwing up in a bush. She hated throwing up, but in this case, it was called for. She didn't think she was ever going to forget the sight of the man standing very still in the jungle, the blade of a stone knife buried in his eye.

It was quiet. When she finally wiped her mouth and glanced around, she saw four people watching her, three curiously and one with a certain amount of embarrassment. "Done?" said Josiah, still wringing out his tunic. Not trusting her voice yet, Freddy nodded.

The man's body was sprawled nearby on the jungle floor. Freddy started to look away, then stopped.

I always look away . . . don't I? She'd never thought of it that way before, but it was true. She looked away from things she didn't want to see or from things she didn't want to know. Slowly, reluctantly, Freddy's eyes went back to the corpse. The man had been alive a few minutes ago. He had been alive enough to be running through the jungle, trying to kill someone. He had got this far in his life and abruptly stopped being alive. Someday, that was going to be her.

Everyone I've met so far on this . . . whatever . . . is dead in my time. Ling is dead. She was nice to me; she showed me how to sew. We do all these things, and then we're just gone.

She turned away from the body. She wanted to go home. She wanted to tell Roland there was no use in them being mad at each other if they were just going to die in the end.

The other Josiah was not behaving as she'd expected. Usually, the Josiahs were resigned to see them. This one seemed taken aback. He walked up to her Josiah and began demanding to know things. Freddy couldn't understand the words, but she recognised the general tone. Her Josiah replied in the same language while the girl watched warily from behind her tree.

Freddy heard something rustle and turned. Cuerva Lachance had moved up behind her. "Hello, curly-haired one," she said, as she almost always did.

Freddy nodded again, then cleared her throat and said hoarsely, "Why'd you kill him, Cuerva Lachance?"

The woman squatted next to Freddy and rested her elbows on her knees. "I'm not Cuerva Lachance yet," she said. "Call me Ban. *He's* Bana at the moment. It pleases me when we match."

Freddy just looked at her.

"I don't remember. There was a thing." She waved her hands about. "Oh, all right, you've worn me down. He's the girl's uncle. He wants to kill her. He thinks we're evil spirits, and she's brought us down on him. Of course," she said judiciously, "he may have a point there."

"She's Three?" said Freddy, wiping her mouth again.

"What delightful terminology you use," said Ban. "I think I'm going to enjoy your time. The girl is, as you put it, Three, though that's a bit of a misnomer, I should say. Her name escapes me at the moment. There's a monkey in that tree over there."

Freddy glanced over at Josiah and Bana. "Is there a problem?"

"Well, we've never seen you before," said Ban cheerfully. "I'm temporally complicated and don't mind, but Bana is going to need convincing."

Cuerva Lachance—hat, trench coat, and all—stepped out from behind a tree and handed Freddy a glass with something blue in it. "Gargle. You don't want to travel in time with your mouth tasting like that. Ban, can we talk? Loki's come to see me."

"Obviously." Ban beamed in a very Cuerva Lachance sort of way. "I'm sure the boys will sort things out soon."

They were gone, silently. Freddy doubted anyone else even noticed them go. She did gargle with the blue stuff, which turned out to be ordinary mouthwash. It didn't really make anything better, but Cuerva Lachance had been right: she hadn't wanted to travel in time with her mouth tasting like that.

⌒

Josiah had eventually convinced Bana they were legitimate. Josiah was quite good at convincing people of things. At any rate, they hadn't been in the jungle for long.

That had been the first death she'd witnessed, but not the last. People died a lot, she'd decided, and they died all over history. One of the Threes had almost died while they'd been with him. He had been ninety-two. They hadn't been in physical danger—no one had been chasing them or shooting at them or trying to drive them off cliffs—but it had still been their tensest visit because Josiah hadn't remembered it at all, and because if Three had died before the sympathetic resonance happened . . .

"He won't," Josiah said.

"But what if he does?" Freddy retorted. The old man seemed to be breathing only about three times a minute. The early doubts she'd had about the whole time-travel thing were all popping up again. Josiah always acted as if there were no danger things would ever go wrong: as if they should just coast along and trust that everything would turn out all right.

"Well, we may be in trouble at that point," Josiah said, "but he won't." And in the end, he didn't. Three was thinking something or other, even as he was dying.

She hated seeing people die, but she had learned she could live with it. It was never something she'd had to learn in her real life. All four of her grandparents were still alive.

Now Filbert nudged her. "Noontide farce."

"You mean truce?" said Freddy.

"Yes, mayhap," said Filbert. "Truce. Noontide truce. Grub?"

She handed Freddy a sandwich. They still had sandwiches here, though they called them "borks." Unfortunately, they *didn't* have butter or much meat. This bork was spread with the futuristic equivalent of Marmite. At least it was food.

"I'm reasonably certain this stuff is made from bugs," said Josiah, but he took one, too. "Tell me where the other me is."

He had a habit of doing this to future Threes. Presumably, he was trying to catch them off their guard. It never worked. Filbert smiled at him. "English is puzzlefying lingo. You stay here and learn yourselfs real words."

"Bah," said Josiah.

He would learn them someday, though, thought Freddy. Everybody died, except not Josiah and Cuerva Lachance. They went on and on and on.

She wondered if that was sometimes maybe a little lonely.

Her watch read "Aug. 17" the day she and Josiah stood with a deliberately anachronistic version of Cuerva Lachance who said he was an Egyptian corporal named Sven outside the mouth of a cave in what would someday be New Zealand.

Freddy shivered. They were close to the water, at the bottom of a low cliff topped by a lush green landscape, and the sun was going down, taking the day's faint warmth with it. She peered dubiously into the cave. "Three's in there?"

"He doesn't really come out much," said Sven. "When we try to go in, he throws rocks at us. I think he lives mostly off raw fish."

"I remember." Josiah rubbed a hand wearily over his forehead. "I'm sulking by the river, am I?"

"You find this boring," said Sven. "I don't. It's very exciting to try to guess what he might do next."

Freddy was still looking into the cave, straining her eyes against the darkness. "Why's he in there?"

"He was part of one of the first groups to migrate here," said Josiah. "It was also one of the smallest. It didn't do very well. A lot of his people died of illness or injury, until only he and his sister and one of their cousins were left. A few months ago, the sister and the cousin went foraging and never returned."

"It happens sometimes," said Sven.

Josiah nodded. "There are other settlements on the islands, but he doesn't know they're there. He hasn't seen anyone but us for more than a year, and he doesn't like us. He says we're not his people, so we don't count."

"You'd think he would appreciate some company," said Sven, shaking his head, "but no . . . it's all 'You're not my people' and 'You're probably here to kill me' and 'I don't need anyone eating all my fish.'"

Behind them, the sound of the waves was continuous. Freddy knew she was more or less on the other side of the world from home, but this place was not unlike the coast of British Columbia. The wind blowing in from the sea, tossing the waves and tangling itself in Freddy's hair, had the same feel, even the same smell. One of her rare surges of homesickness rolled through her belly.

Josiah sighed. "We'll have to sit this one out. I hope you brought something to read."

Freddy was opening her mouth to reply when a man walked past her into the cave.

He was brown-skinned and cheerful-looking, clad only in a sort of grass skirt but apparently not bothered by the chill in the air. He carried what looked like an enormous fish hook over one shoulder. He was also slightly transparent. Freddy could see the stone of the cave mouth through his skin, though only barely. He vanished into the darkness of the cave more quickly than he should have.

She said, "Who's *he*?"

She had seen Cuerva Lachance talking to see-through people before, but usually from a distance, and rarely when Josiah was around. Now Josiah was pointedly looking in another direction. "It's going to be cold tonight," he said.

Freddy turned to Sven. "That guy who just walked into the cave . . ."

"Oh, that's just Māui," said Sven. "Don't worry about him."

"But he wasn't real," she said, "was he?"

She peered into the cave. The blackness farther in seemed

unbroken, but she could hear someone muttering in an unfamiliar language. The words were almost rhythmic; she felt a beat behind them.

"The boy tells stories about Māui," said Sven, "but he has no one to tell them to, since his people are gone. It's too bad. They're good stories. They'll survive through other tellers, but he tells them best."

"So he tells stories about Māui, and Māui walks into his cave as he's doing that?" asked Freddy. She probably, she reflected, would have been more upset about this half a year ago.

"No," said Josiah. "That's ridiculous. Māui's a culture hero. He's not real."

"But I just saw him," said Freddy.

"You need to stop drinking the water without boiling it first," said Josiah. He turned on his heel and marched away in what seemed to be an entirely random direction.

Freddy bit down on a stab of irritation—Josiah was just like that sometimes—and looked sidelong at Sven. "Are you going to avoid telling me about Māui, too?"

"Why would I do that?" said Sven brightly. He took two steps to the right and just wasn't there any more.

The see-through people hadn't really struck Freddy much before this, as they'd just seemed to be a natural by-product of Cuerva Lachance. Maybe she should have been paying more attention. *He told a story about Māui,* she thought, still staring into the cave, *and Māui was there. Did Sven do that? Why would he? What good does it do this kid to have an imaginary culture hero sitting in his cave with him?*

Was Sven being *kind*? He wasn't incapable of it, but it still seemed wrong. There was something else happening here.

Before she could try to figure out what, Three emerged from the cave.

He was maybe thirteen and much thinner than he should have been. Something else was wrong with him, too. His black hair was falling out in patches, and his eyes had bags so dark they looked almost like bruises. He stopped short when he saw her. For a moment, they locked glances.

Incongruously, as she stared at a boy who was going to die seven hundred years before she was born, Freddy thought of Roland and Mel. She didn't mean to. She tried to think of them as little as possible. Remembering hurt too much, and it sometimes brought the anger back, too. This time, it didn't. This time, the anger just didn't come. *Everybody should have somebody . . . right? How is it fair that he doesn't have anyone? Why was I so mad all the time about having all those people?*

Freddy smiled.

The boy hesitated for a long moment, then smiled back. It wasn't exactly a happy smile, but something flashed briefly in his eyes.

He turned and went back into the cave soon after. Freddy was pretty sure he half raised his hand to her just before he was swallowed by darkness.

~

Josiah didn't like borks very much. Instead of eating his, he was poking at it experimentally. "It's basically rubber. It even tastes like rubber. I find this era problematic."

Freddy had been delaying eating her own bork as well. She had learned the hard way that the correct choice between caterpillar stew and nothing was always caterpillar stew, but that didn't make the bork any more appealing. She weighed the food in one hand and the gun in the other and wondered idly what would happen if she shot the former with the latter.

"Do you like it here?" she asked Filbert, the question coming out of nowhere.

Filbert cocked her head. "No computement."

"You know," said Freddy. "Do you *like* it? Do you ever wish you could move to one of the African city-states? They're supposed to be nice and safe."

"That's simple mythifying," Filbert replied, shaking her head. "This be the real."

"I was rather hoping this bork wasn't the real," said Josiah with exaggerated gloom.

Filbert's world, thought Freddy, was smaller than she knew. She saw it as huge and nuanced and satisfying, and in the end, it didn't amount to more than a series of pointless battles in an ancient, crumbling cityscape. How could she possibly be satisfied with it? Didn't she know how much else was out there?

Freddy said, "I bet the city-states are real, too. I bet they would be interesting to see."

"Just a story," said Filbert. "I know a *better* story."

It was dark and still and lonely, though not as dark as it could have been; Freddy, looking up, saw a dazzling full moon. The wind rustled the grass. Freddy glanced over at Josiah, who was gazing thoughtfully down at his bork. She expected him to say something sardonic, but for once, he was silent.

12

Three was never far away when they jumped. Freddy spotted light glimmering beyond the scrub to what, given the position of the moon, was the north. "Let's go."

"Wait," said Josiah.

Freddy watched him. Even in the bright moonlight, she couldn't be sure of his expression, but she thought he looked oddly apprehensive. "Wait why?"

"I don't remember this," he said. "This is wrong."

She shook her head. "You weren't always there."

"No. I can feel the time. This is *wrong*," said Josiah. "It's too early. This is before I ever met . . . us. Long before. This is . . . I don't remember this at all."

"We still have to deal with it," said Freddy. "There are people over there."

"I think we should stay here," said Josiah immediately.

She stared at him. "We have to find Three."

"It's wrong," he insisted, but when she tucked the microgun and the bork into her bag and began to move towards the light, he followed.

His apprehension had affected her. Instead of approaching the light openly and trusting that Three would explain things to whomever else was there, Freddy moved cautiously and as quietly as she could over the plain. Even before she was close enough to see what the light was, she could hear one voice speaking and the occasional murmur of other voices beneath it. The speech patterns were different from anything she had heard before. They seemed . . . truncated. Guttural. It was a woman speaking. "What's she saying?" Freddy whispered.

"Things," said Josiah, and closed his mouth firmly.

Freddy eased in behind a dry little bush and peered out towards the voices.

The light was a campfire. There were perhaps twelve people grouped around it, about half of them children. The moonlight and firelight conspired to show Freddy that these people were dressed roughly in what were probably animal skins. They had more clothes than Ban, but Ban had dressed as she had because of the heat. It wasn't so hot here. It may have been a warm day, but the air was growing noticeably cooler even now.

The woman speaking looked very young, no more than fifteen or so, though Freddy found ages weren't always easy to estimate in certain periods. The other people listened to her raptly. Every once in a while, one of them would say something, and the girl would reply.

"Three?" said Freddy.

Josiah said, "I don't know. How should I know? Why are you badgering me?"

She turned to him, startled. "You know all the Threes."

"It's *too early*," he snapped. "I don't understand what's happening!"

Josiah *always* understood what was happening. She looked at him properly. He was pale and perspiring, and his eyes had gone huge.

Freddy glanced back towards the fire. "Can you understand what she's saying?"

"Yeeeeeesssss," said Josiah reluctantly. "Just. But I don't remember this."

"You've said," said Freddy. "Just tell me what she's saying."

He paused for so long that she turned to look at him again. To her amazement, he was trembling. "Josiah, what's wrong?"

"Nothing," he said. "I . . . nothing. She's telling them a story."

He hesitated again, then went on. "I don't think she meant it to be a story at first. They keep asking her questions. They call her 'Mika.' It means . . . it means 'wise child.' They think she's a sort of shaman, born with special knowledge. They're asking her why the world is the way it is."

"Like a creation story."

"Yes, exactly, but it's . . . new. They haven't heard it before. She's . . . I think she's . . ."

"Making it up," said Freddy.

"No!" said Josiah, a bit too loudly. Freddy glanced over at the campfire, but no one had noticed.

She said, "I don't see why it's such a big deal. All the Threes are creative, right? They all make up stories."

"I don't *know* her. She can't be Three," said Josiah desperately.

"Just tell me what she's saying."

Josiah shook his head, but he didn't protest further. "She's done this whole bit about how Earth was born from Sea and Sky. But Earth was lonely, floating all by herself in the water, and she cried. The tears became rivers, and on the shores of the rivers, plants grew. And from the plants, seeds fell and grew into new plants, and also into animals. All the animals were sort of round and formless and hairless. But one of them fell into the river and began to swim, and it developed fins and gills and became a fish. And one of them was cold and began to dig, and it developed claws and fur and became a mole. And the same happened with all the other animals. But there were no people yet."

Josiah listened for a moment and went on. "That man asked if people grew from plants, too. Mika says they didn't. She says Earth was happy about the rivers and the plants and animals, but she was still lonely. She asked Sky, her father, for a child. Sky saw how beautiful Earth was, and he . . . uh . . ."

"Impregnated her?" said Freddy, who, thanks to the books on the chair in her kitchen, was not unfamiliar with creation myths.

"Yes," said Josiah. "She was pregnant for one year. At the end of it, she gave birth to a girl and a boy. They were dead and as pale as ice. Earth cried again, but Sea, her mother, told her the children simply needed to be baked."

"But there was no fire," said Freddy.

"But there was no fire." Josiah nodded. "And neither Earth nor Sea knew how to get any. The only fire belonged to Sun, the son of Sky, and Sky guarded him jealously. So Earth just kept on crying. She cried so much that everything got very wet. The animals were having a hard time finding shelter. They got so uncomfortable that they finally gathered and asked Earth how they could help."

Freddy said, "I think I see where this is going."

"I expect," said Josiah. "At any rate, Earth told the animals that she needed to bake her children but had no fire and no way of getting any. The animals put their heads together, but most of them had no ideas. Then the crow, the trickiest of the animals, spoke up."

"The crow was white at the time," said Freddy.

"The crow was white at the time," said Josiah, casting her an annoyed glance. "She said to Earth, 'I'll fly up and steal fire from Sun.' So the crow flew up into Sky . . . up and up. She flew so swiftly that Sky didn't even realise she was there. She flew right up to Sun and plucked a flame from his cloak, and then she turned and fell back down to Earth. She fell for a long time, and she tumbled down onto Mountain and lay still. By this time, she had been burnt black."

"I knew it," said Freddy.

"Good for you. Shut up," said Josiah. "Earth was ecstatic. She cried on the crow and healed her burns, but the crow's feathers stayed black. Then Earth took the flame and placed it in a clay oven she had fashioned. She put the two dead children into the oven and let them bake. When she pulled them out, they had turned a nice deep brown, and they were alive."

He listened for a bit before he spoke again. "They were the first people. Earth loved them, and she gave them the fire for their own. The animals loved them less, as they could see they would be meat eaters. Most of the animals fled. The crow stayed longer than the others. She had an egg inside her. When she had stolen fire from Sun, he had been so amazed that any creature was bold enough to approach him that he had fertilised the egg. When she had fallen down onto Mountain, he had been so amazed that any creature could fall so far and live that he had fertilised the egg as well. The crow knew that egg was special. She laid it and gave it to the children, telling them only not to eat it. The children promised, and the crow flew away."

Josiah had been growing increasingly uncomfortable throughout this last bit. Freddy kept looking over at him. He was sweating again, and his voice was growing muffled. Now he stopped talking entirely.

"She's still going," said Freddy. "You have to finish."

"I . . . don't want to," said Josiah. "I feel ill."

"You never feel ill. Come on," said Freddy. "I want to know how it ends."

Reluctantly, sounding faintly horrified, Josiah continued. "The children grew up in a week, but the egg didn't hatch. It was cold and black. The children thought it was stupid to waste the egg when food was so scarce. They put it into the fire to cook. The fire was what it had needed. In the midst of the flames, the egg hatched."

He ground to a halt again. "I . . . don't . . ."

"Finish it," said Freddy.

"The egg hatched . . . two children," said Josiah, gasping. "A boy and a girl. The boy was stillness and constancy and the solidity of mountains; the girl was movement and change and the fickleness of flame. They watched over the two who had hatched them."

He turned to Freddy. "It doesn't mean anything. Three tells stories—"

"Look," said Freddy.

There were two more people near the campfire now.

They stood just outside the ring of firelight, but the moonlight showed them clearly. Freddy saw two teenagers, both dressed in skins. They were holding hands. They looked very alike; both had long dark hair, thin faces, beaky noses, and sharp little chins. It was hard to tell from here, but Freddy didn't think either looked particularly like the people gathered around the fire.

One of the teenagers glanced at the other. Freddy thought he was male and the other one female. He pulled his hand away from the girl, who grinned at him and tilted her head in an oddly familiar way.

"We need to go," said Josiah. "We shouldn't be here at all. This is *not*—"

"No," said Freddy.

She had never quite trusted him, but—*That's not really true, is it? You've trusted him enough. You take his word for how this works, and you say you're being Mel and biding your time while collecting clues, but really you're just trailing after him like . . . like a duckling. You're waiting passively for the time travel to end. What if it doesn't end? You know he's not telling you everything. You know he's not even telling you everything about* this place. *You could be a time-travelling duckling for the rest of your life if you don't take some initiative.*

Josiah stared. "What do you mean, 'no'? We're *going*."

Freddy said, "I'm not."

She stepped out from behind the bush.

Josiah hissed behind her. It didn't matter. He didn't get to make all the decisions any more. Mika had answers, and Freddy wanted to know what they were. There was a language barrier, sure, but if Josiah wouldn't help, she would find a way around it. Freddy moved towards the fire. She didn't think Josiah was following. Cold fingers seemed to be dancing up and down her spine. It was terrifying— and exhilarating—and weird to be setting off into a future Josiah hadn't seen.

Freddy had gone only a few steps when she realised the people near the fire had fallen silent. Mika was looking straight at her.

There was a strange moment then, as Freddy gazed into dark eyes that gleamed in the moonlight, and Mika smiled and waved. Somewhere in the dimness, Freddy heard the soft whir of wings.

And the sun shone brightly over the neat little road and the hedgerows lining it on either side.

13

"Oh, not this one," said Josiah. "I didn't know we'd have to come *here*."

Freddy took four giant steps back towards Josiah, seized him by the throat, and crushed him up against the hedgerow. She vaguely remembered doing something like this before, when she had still been at the beginning of her time-travelling career. It was easier this time.

"Something important just happened," she said. "You're not going to weasel out of talking about it."

He tried to pry her hands from his throat and couldn't. She waited until he had shaded all the way to a deep plum colour before she let him go.

"There's nothing to talk about," he said when he could speak. "It was just a story."

"It was *a story* of your beginning," said Freddy, "wasn't it?"

"I have absolutely no idea what you mean by that," said Josiah. "You need to eighteenth-century yourself."

Before he could stop her, she took him by the throat again.

"All right. All *right*," he said when she had let go for the second time. "It's possible that was . . . near the beginning of my existence. Mika may have been telling a true story, even. I'm *not* trying to weasel out of talking about it. I just don't remember that far back. I don't understand what we saw any more than you do. You *really* need to eighteenth-century yourself *now*."

She almost told him she was done taking orders from him, but unfortunately, what he was saying made a certain amount of sense. The problem was that it almost always did.

Freddy sighed. "Fine. Boy?"

"You don't have the material for girls' clothes in this period. Tuck your hair under the hat."

Her hair was long now. Long hair for both sexes was more common, historically speaking, than short hair for either. In societies where men wore their hair short, she hid hers beneath a hat or dressed as a girl. She could pass less easily as a boy than she had a year and a half ago, as her shape had changed a bit, but she did find that people often saw what they wanted to see. If she wore boys' clothes, she was a boy.

Following Josiah's directions, she made the alterations to her basic outfit that would help her blend in here. He was simultaneously doing the same thing to his own clothing. There was no one in sight, though Freddy could hear cows lowing in the distance. They were standing on a dirt road leading to some sort of farmhouse.

"Three's in there?" said Freddy, nodding towards the farmhouse.

"I'll bet he is," said Josiah gloomily. "He does a lot of writing. And sleeping. Sometimes, he writes while he's asleep. He thinks it's inspiration, but it's opium, really. Judging by where we are, it's 1797."

"Well," said Freddy, "do we interrupt him?"

"I'd rather not," said Josiah. "He thinks I'm a fairy."

Freddy had been standing there with her mouth open for a good ten seconds too long before she managed to say, "Excuse me?"

"It's Robin Goodfellow's fault," he explained, kicking moodily at a stone in the road. "He's calling himself Robin Goodfellow at the moment. He thinks it's funny. I told him it would have been hilarious in Shakespeare's day, but it's just stupid now. But *no* . . . it's all about the giggles with Robin Goodfellow. So Sam has got it into his head that we're both fairies. He's . . . not quite right. Very smart man, very imaginative, but just a little bit off. Leaves out bowls of milk for me whenever he notices me hanging around. I've tried to explain the truth, but he thinks it's fairy guile."

Freddy was having to bite her tongue hard to keep from smiling. She thought she was doing a decent job. "So we're in England?"

"We're definitely in England," said Josiah. "We're English fairies. He'll think your name is Titania."

She clapped her hands over her mouth to stop herself from guffawing out loud. Their last jump seemed to have got her into a strange mood. Josiah made a sour face at her.

They walked up the hill towards the farmhouse. It was a beautiful day, cool and brisk; it felt like autumn to Freddy. The house in front of them was a sprawl of grey buildings. There was no one in sight, though Freddy could still hear the cows. Josiah led her around to what seemed to be the kitchen door. She had learned from experience that it was never worth going to the front doors of large houses; she and Josiah didn't look respectable enough for that.

"You knock," said Josiah. "I recognise the need to hang around with Three, but I would rather pull out my own teeth than have a conversation of any length with this man. At any rate, I doubt we'll be here long. I never saw us when I was here."

Freddy had grown used to this sort of tangled grammar. It took her only a couple of seconds to decipher it. At the same time, she experienced a stab of irritation at even *having* to figure it out. She really did seem to have had enough. *He squirmed out of that last one,* she thought. *We haven't talked about what happened at all.* Josiah had been shaken by Mika's story, but the second they had jumped, he had pulled back into his usual sardonic, detached self. He hadn't even mentioned Freddy marching off to confront Mika herself. Something had changed for her, but he was pretending nothing had happened. Now he was ordering her around as usual, and in normal circumstances, she wouldn't even have noticed.

Freddy thought, *I've fallen into a rut.* It was a strange rut, but a rut nonetheless. She had been trusting that Josiah knew what was going on and would eventually get her out of this. And yet he hadn't understood what was happening with Mika. What if Josiah was ultimately as clueless as she was and had simply been getting by on a tone of authority and a really good memory?

She knocked, but she felt she was biding her time. Maybe she could do this one a bit differently.

The knock brought a woman in a cap and apron to the door. "What is it, lad?"

Freddy realised, a bit late, that Josiah hadn't told her Three's full name. "Sam" wasn't going to cut it in eighteenth-century England. She glanced at Josiah, who had pressed himself flat against the house beside the door. "Message for Mr. . . . ." she said, "uh . . ."

"Coleridge," hissed Josiah. Freddy blinked. Hadn't Josiah once made a fuss in class about a poet named Coleridge? There was something else about the name, too—something obvious that she was going to kick herself later for forgetting—but there wasn't time to try to think of what.

The woman leaned out and glanced around at Josiah. "Oh," she said flatly, "it's you."

"No," said Josiah. "I'm not officially here. I met Fred purely by accident in the lane." His accent, Freddy noted, had become more British.

"You drive the poor man to distraction," said the woman to Josiah, hands on her hips. "The things he believes about you!"

"Not my fault," said Josiah. "And I'm sorry about the milk. I do try to keep out of his sight."

"Please, miss," said Freddy in her best approximation of an English accent, which she suspected made her sound a bit too much like someone mangling a Mary Poppins imitation, "I have this message for Mr. Coleridge."

"Do you, now?" said the woman. "And where did you spring from?"

Freddy looked at Josiah again. She couldn't seem to stop herself. *I depend too much on him. I shouldn't. I don't really know anything about him.* She thought of him as her friend sometimes, but she knew he wasn't really. She knew he didn't react to things in the same way as ordinary people.

"Porlock. He's from Porlock. From Dr. Potter," said Josiah.

"Let the lad speak for himself," said the woman.

"He's shy," said Josiah.

"Mr. Coleridge is working and cannot be disturbed," said the woman.

Freddy bobbed her head. "I was told it couldn't wait, miss," she said.

The woman drummed her fingers on the door frame, then nodded. "I'll see what can be done. Please come in," she said.

Freddy followed her through the kitchen and down a corridor to a drawing room. Josiah, uninvited, slunk along on her heels. "Porlock?" she hissed at him. "Dr. Potter?"

"Nearby village. Sam's doctor in nearby village," Josiah whispered back. "You can work with that, can't you?"

"I know his name. He's a poet, isn't he?" she asked, but they had reached the room, and the woman was showing Freddy to a seat. Josiah went straight to a window nook and drew the curtains over himself.

When the woman had gone, Freddy said, "Sam Coleridge? Is he the same as the poetry guy?"

"If you haven't heard of Coleridge," said Josiah, his voice muffled by the curtains, "you've been living under a rock. Isn't your mother an English professor?"

"That doesn't mean I'm the world's biggest poetry fan," said Freddy just as the poet's full name came to her: Samuel Taylor Coleridge. Josiah *had* brought him up in class. There had been an epic battle between Josiah and Mr. Dillon about the possibility of opium causing poetry. But there was definitely something else, too. It seemed important that she should remember it. *Something with a book,* thought Freddy, *and Roland and Mel and . . . tentacles. No. Not the tentacles. But other things . . . like . . . pleasure-dome . . . ?*

"It isn't relevant, anyway," said Josiah. "He's just Three."

Pleasure-dome, thought Freddy again, and then she had it. Her hands clenched into fists. She knew something important: something Josiah didn't know.

A man entered the room. He was unexpectedly young. When Freddy thought of the poets whose works her mother taught, she almost invariably pictured a bunch of crusty old men. Sam couldn't have been more than twenty-five. His brown hair fell past his shoulders, and he was just a little bit chubby. Mostly, he struck Freddy as distracted. His eyes flicked about the room, doing a full circuit before they lit on Freddy. His mouth was twisted into a sort of anguished grimace.

"Please forgive me," he said all in a rush as Freddy rose to meet him. "I have some urgent business I must attend to. Your visit has come at a very inconvenient time. I beg your pardon."

"But—" Freddy started.

"Dr. Potter is very kind," said Sam loudly, "but I have sufficient quantities of laudanum for now. If you will excuse me—"

"I'm not from Dr. Potter," said Freddy, "actually."

Sam, already turning towards the doorway, paused. "You've gained entry on false pretences? Why?"

"Robin Goodfellow," said Freddy. It was all she could think of. It usually didn't take more than a mention of Cuerva Lachance or Josiah for the Threes to fall in line. Of course, it tended to be Josiah himself doing the mentioning. He had never hidden behind the curtains before.

"What of him?" said Sam.

"You've seen him," said Freddy. "And the other one. The one called . . . called . . ."

"Mustardseed?" said Sam.

"My name is *not* Mustardseed. You made that up," said Josiah in-dignantly from the alcove.

"Oh, is he here?" said Sam. "I'm sure the farm can spare some milk—"

Josiah poked his head through the curtains. "If you try to give me milk, I shall flay you," he said and withdrew once more.

Freddy, turning back to Sam, was surprised to catch the merest ghost of amusement on his face. It was gone in an instant, but she knew she had seen it. *You sneak,* she thought with admiration. *You don't think he's a fairy. You're* teasing *him.* She had never associated the idea of a sense of humour with her mother's parade of dry old poets, either.

"I know them both. What of them?" said Sam.

Freddy drew a deep breath and removed her hat, letting her curly hair fall free. "Well," she said, "at the moment, I'm with them, too."

And then she told him everything.

It wasn't what they normally did with the Threes. Some of them could handle the idea of time travel, but many couldn't. Josiah would make up some story: he was generally his own twin brother, and Freddy was his guest. If everybody thought he was a god, Freddy became a god, too. If everybody thought he was foreign, Freddy was from his country. Some of the Threes had seen Cuerva Lachance travel in time, and those ones got an edited version of the truth. None of them got the *whole* truth, or none of them had until now. She didn't care. Until now, they had been flitting aimlessly back and forth through time. Josiah said this was because of the rules, but she was tired of following the rules. Whose rules were they, anyway? And there was . . . the thing with the pleasure-dome. She didn't think she had a plan yet, but it was possible a plan was on the verge of being born.

Josiah kept putting his head through the curtains to squeak at her. She ignored him. For almost seventeen months, she had been running around frantically, lying about herself to everybody she had met. She hadn't known she had been missing telling the truth so much.

Sam listened without interrupting. At some point, he sat down on a hard little couch and folded his hands over his knees. His distraction gradually vanished. By the time she had ground to a halt, he was totally focussed on her.

The silence between the two of them stretched out, broken only by Josiah's whispered running commentary, which went more or less like: "And now she goes and spills her guts to a Three, of all people, and completely disrupts the space-time continuum, thank you very much, and bring on the paradox, why don't you—"

"Oh, shut up," said Freddy. "You keep telling me the past can't be changed; the present can just be acted upon."

"Right," said Josiah, "except now you've gone and told him about the *future*."

"It won't be a problem," said Sam. "Robin Goodfellow has explained about his journeys through time. I've often considered writing it all into a poem, but I fear it would be considered too fantastical."

Josiah coughed theatrically. Freddy heard the word "Albatross!" in the middle of the cough.

Sam steepled his fingers and tapped them gently against his chin. "Your life seems an interesting one to me. What I wouldn't give to visit the days of Julius Caesar or witness the fall of Troy. But it sounds lonely, too."

"She's not lonely. She's got me," said Josiah.

"Even so, Master Mustardseed," said Sam. "She isn't built for such travels."

"I've done all right so far," said Freddy, a little stung.

He smiled. "Of course you have. You're young; the journey is exciting. But now you have walked into a stranger's house and unburdened yourself for no logical reason. The melancholy has crept up on you, as it often creeps up on me."

His smile turned rather sad. "I have found some recourse in laudanum, but I wouldn't recommend this solution for you. I would say you badly need to return to your own time."

"Oh, really?" said Josiah, who seemed unable to stay out of the conversation. "We would never have guessed it. We would return if we could. If there were any way of making sure we were connecting to *our* Three . . . but we don't even know who it is."

"I would also suppose you need to talk about what happened on your last excursion," said Sam. "The story you heard—"

"—means nothing," said Josiah.

"I wonder," said Sam. "I think it may mean everything. Oh, damnation!"

He stood up and pressed the heels of his hands to his forehead. "Weave a circle round him thrice . . . and close your eyes with holy dread . . . for he on . . . on honey-dew hath fed . . . and drunk the milk of Paradise. That's all that's left. The sunny dome! The caves of ice! All vanished into air. How fleeting are the realms of fancy! You have broken my poem."

"I'm . . . I'm sorry," said Freddy, taken aback. He had seemed relatively normal until the ranting had begun.

"It's 'Kubla Khan,' you ninny," said Josiah from behind the curtain. "We came in at a bad moment."

"'Kubla Khan,'" repeated Freddy. *A stately pleasure-dome decree . . .*

"You know the name? Queer," said Sam. "I had three hundred lines fast in my head, but your visit has banished most of them. No matter. I'm not sure I would have missed your story, even for a poem."

"A poem," said Freddy. The plan that had been tiny and formless just before was growing, taking shape. Her hands curled again into fists. Maybe . . .

Josiah came properly out from behind the curtains. "What's wrong with you? Why do you keep repeating everything?"

"Shut up," said Freddy. "Mr. Coleridge . . . you said something about a dome."

"Oh yes." Sam's hands went up to his forehead again. "The pleasure-dome. Glorious image come to me in a dream!"

"An opium dream," said Josiah under his breath.

"Shut *up*," said Freddy, "really." The day of the crash. The book on the pile. If only she could just . . .

"Mr. Coleridge," said Freddy, fighting to keep her voice steady, "I'd like to hear your poem."

"What? No," he said, lowering his hands. "It will never be finished now. It will never be any good—"

"I don't think that's true," said Freddy. "Could we just hear the first few lines? I really like that image of the pleasure-dome."

He paced the length of the room, then back again. "It's no good. Vanished forever! There was something about a tree. Oh, very well."

Sam stopped in place and recited:

> *"In Xanadu did Kubla Khan*
> *A stately pleasure-dome decree:*
> *Where Alph, the sacred river, ran*
> *Through caverns measureless to man—"*

"—Down to a sunless sea," said Mel.

14

The voice had come through the kitchen window. Freddy seized the astonished Josiah's hand and pulled him past the purple smoke bush and through the back gate and into the lane, then over to the side yard of the house on Grosvenor Street. They stopped next to the cedar hedge, and Freddy threw herself down on the grass and started to laugh.

After a while, the laughter became problematic, and she had to reach into her bag and close her fist around her key. Josiah sat down beside her and watched her as if she were a scientific experiment, possibly one involving marbles and inclined planes.

"Did you just get us back?" he asked eventually.

"I think so," said Freddy. "I remembered about Coleridge. Does this mean Mel is Three?"

"She was reading the poem aloud," said Josiah. "Who was in the room with her?"

"Well . . . Roland. And me."

"Then it could still be any of you. Damn. At least we're back."

But now something else was occurring to Freddy. "We're *back* back. Over three *weeks* back."

"I know," said Josiah. "I've known all along this would happen."

Freddy let out what probably counted as a wordless yelp of rage. She seemed to have boarded the emotional roller coaster shortly after listening to Mika's story. "You've *known all along*? You knew we would get back, and you didn't tell me?"

"Ssh!" Josiah cast a nervy look at the hedge and dropped his voice. "You and your fellow ducklings aren't really all that far away from us at the moment, so please keep it down."

"But you knew," whispered Freddy, "and—"

"I keep telling you," said Josiah. "It's better not to know what's going to happen. That way, you don't second-guess yourself all the time."

"But you *knew we were going to get back*," said Freddy, staring at him. "Didn't you even see how worried about that I was?"

"Oh. Were you?" said Josiah. "I suppose you would have been. Are you going to strangle me again?"

She wrestled with herself for a moment. "No."

"That's a bonus, at any rate."

"But three weeks," said Freddy. "Isn't there any way we could . . . well, get closer to the proper time?"

He sighed. "You're being obtuse. You want to jump back into the time stream? We can't chance it. Even this was a hundred to one against. If we try again, we could end up bouncing around through time for years. Frankly, I can't believe we managed to make it back only three weeks early. It could have been years early . . . or years late."

"I know," said Freddy. She *was* being obtuse. And it was her doing they had got here at this time, at any rate. But it was frustrating. She had been wanting to get home for more than a year, and now she *was* home, but there wouldn't be a place for her until September twenty-seventh.

Josiah eyed her sidelong. "I knew about this because you and the other me were living with us for weeks."

"I figured," said Freddy, who had just begun to realise. "There were even clues. We kept noticing there was someone else in the house."

She was going to have to start thinking in terms of the doubled timeline. Was this the way it had been for Josiah the whole time they had been travelling? Had he constantly been worrying about where everyone had been the last time? At least he hadn't had to hide from himself.

To hide from himself. Oh *damn it*—

"Behind the hedge," said Freddy. "I'm listening. Right now!"

"You're what?" said Josiah.

"Listening to this. To us. In our *yard*," she hissed.

"Well," said Josiah, "we should go over to the other side of *our* yard, then. Are you going to be forgetting such important details often?"

"Shut up," said Freddy, but she followed him quite meekly around to the other side of the house. She remembered walking around the hedge to look for the people who had been talking; she and Josiah would be out of sight by the time that happened.

⁓

They got into the house through an open basement window. Josiah admitted his future self had told him it would be open. "Isn't that a paradox?" said Freddy.

"Please stop trying to analyse the time travel," growled Josiah, yanking the window up. "If you start going on about stable time loops and the possibility of killing one's own grandfather, I shall smack you."

The window led to the laundry room, which contained a boiler, a run-down-looking washer and dryer, and nothing else. They climbed the stairs to the equally empty main floor, then went up another flight. Josiah led her into a bedroom at the front of the house. "This is where we were last time," he said. Freddy nodded.

They passed the time by emptying their bags and taking an inventory of what they had brought back from their travels. There wasn't much. Josiah had several articles of clothing, a bork, a handful of pearls a random Greek princess had given him, a jewelled comb, half a wheel of cheese, and the knife he had been carrying since medieval Sweden. Freddy had several *more* articles of clothing, a bork of her own, a sling, Ling's sewing kit, a small book of German poetry, and the microgun she had picked up in Filbert's time. Josiah tried to take the microgun away from her. "No," said Freddy, "that's mine."

"It doesn't belong in this time," he said.

She just barely stopped herself from rolling her eyes at him. "I'm not going to use it. I want it as a souvenir. I won't let it fall into the hands of mad scientists; I promise."

Reluctantly, he handed it back to her. "Your sister is a mad scientist, so you may find that difficult."

Freddy was trying to think of a sufficiently scathing reply when something went bang very loudly outside.

"The accident." Josiah scrambled to his feet. "Here we go."

They watched it all through the window. It wasn't easy to see—the trees got in the way—but they caught glimpses of Freddy,

Roland, and Mel having their first interaction with Josiah and Cuerva Lachance. It was only when everybody started carting stuff into the house that Freddy could finally see the five of them clearly.

She found she was clutching her key again. She had missed Mel. She had known that, but this made it worse. Her sister was *right there*, and Freddy couldn't go to her. There was another Freddy down below. Watching herself was strange as well. She looked so . . . small. Next to her, Roland hulked huge and awkward. She squeezed the key again. She wouldn't even have minded having a conversation with Roland. Her anger with him was a year and a half in the past.

About fifteen minutes into the moving session, Freddy heard someone mount the stairs. She and Josiah were just turning towards the door when the other Josiah flung it open.

He glared at them malevolently through his mask of drying blood. "Of course this would happen." He backed out of the room and slammed the door shut. They heard him throw himself back down the stairs, snarling, "You're not to go upstairs. No one is to go upstairs ever."

"I was in a bad mood," Josiah observed.

Josiah 2 came back later, once the unloading was done and everyone else was eating pie on the front porch. "All right," he said in a low voice, "this is going to be tricky."

"We know that, thanks," said Josiah. "It can't be avoided."

"Obviously," said Josiah 2. "Is Thingy there going to be able to keep out of the way?"

"As far as I can remember, yes," said Freddy.

"Your memories are useless. All we know is that you're able

to keep out of *your* way. Well, it will have to do." He looked at his other self. "You need a haircut."

Josiah fingered the ponytail he had grown during their travels. "You can do it later."

"And *she* needs a . . . well, words cannot express what she needs," said Josiah 2. "There's going to be a right fuss over that."

"Over what?" said Freddy.

The two Josiahs exchanged glances. "Tell you later," they said together.

"No," said Freddy, "tell me now."

"We prefer to save the hysteria for when there aren't ducklings quacking around on the ground floor," said Josiah 2.

"Yeah, well," said Freddy heatedly, "by this point, if I'm remembering in the right order, one of them is right on the other side of the door!"

Josiah 2 stared at her. "Why didn't you say so before?" he said, and leapt for the door, which he wrenched open. Freddy caught a glimpse of a small, startled girl standing in the opening, blinking up at Josiah 2. She took a step back. "Who—?"

"No one," Josiah 2 barked. "I was practising my impressions. I plan to join the circus. I told you to stay downstairs!"

He slammed the door behind him. They heard him tugging Freddy 2 back down the stairs. Freddy and Josiah moved to the window and watched Josiah 2 drive the others away. It was surprisingly difficult not to go running after them.

Josiah 2 returned a moment later, Cuerva Lachance in tow. "All right," he said, "*now* we can deal with the hysteria. Quack away."

Cuerva Lachance was doing a great big Cuerva Lachance smile. "Hello, curly-haired one."

"Hi," said Freddy. "What's going on?"

This time, there was a three-way exchange of glances. "She's very unobservant," said Josiah 2.

"Be fair," said Josiah. "It's been kind of frantic lately. I trust you made the mark?"

"I'm not a complete idiot," said Josiah 2, "so yes."

Freddy said loudly, "I hate to interrupt, but *what's going on?*"

Josiah twisted his face into what he may have meant as an expression of concern. She would have liked to tell him he wasn't fooling anyone. "On September twenty-seventh, what are you planning to do?"

"Go home," said Freddy.

"Good plan. Good plan," said Josiah. "However . . . you may have to be prepared to deal with a few . . . hiccups."

"Hiccups?"

"Well, it's been a year and a half, after all. I mean . . . there are things . . . you need to . . ."

"Oh, just come here," said Josiah 2. "It's easier if we show you."

He turned on his heel and marched out of the room. Freddy glanced at Cuerva Lachance, but she was gazing at the ceiling in apparent fascination. "There are all these little white bumps. Why are there little white bumps everywhere?"

Freddy and Josiah looked at each other, then shrugged and moved out into the hallway.

Josiah 2 was standing impatiently at the bottom of the stairs. "Here," he said. When she reached him, he pushed her against the frame of the door and marked her height.

"Hey," said Freddy, "you did that—"

"Five minutes ago," said Josiah. "Look."

Freddy looked. She continued looking for quite some time.

Finally, she turned to Josiah, who was sitting on the bottom step. "That's not possible."

"It's called a growth spurt," said Josiah. "You got yours late for a girl. Six inches in a year and a half isn't bad."

"But . . . but I'm short. All the other girls got taller years ago. I'm supposed to have practically stopped growing by now!" Freddy's eyes kept being drawn back to those marks on the frame.

"You're still short," said Josiah. "Well, I suppose you count as average now. But you're average for fourteen, not sixteen."

It felt as if someone very large had sat on her chest, squeezing all the air out of her lungs. Finally, she managed to wheeze, "Sixteen?"

"Did you think time was standing still for you while you were travelling?" said Josiah. "Surely you noticed *some* changes."

"I know. I have little breasts now," said Freddy. "But I'm not sixteen!"

Cuerva Lachance, wandering down the stairs, said, "When's your birthday?"

"I . . . what? March tenth."

"Oh, my mistake. You're still fifteen," said Josiah, "but only just. You'll be sixteen by the time you go back to your family."

"I think there's a mirror in the luggage somewhere," said Cuerva Lachance, "though we may have broken it when we crashed into the tree."

"No, I carried it in. I'll get it," said Josiah 2, and he nipped into the living room, looking relieved to escape.

"But I can't . . . but people will notice," said Freddy. "I'm half a foot taller than I was this morning!"

"And that's not all," said Cuerva Lachance. "Did I say that out loud?"

Freddy said, "What do you mean, that's not all?"

"Take a look," said Josiah 2, coming back out into the hall with a full-length mirror under his arm. He held it up in front of her.

Freddy saw a stranger: a girl with long curly hair, several shades lighter than the plain brown she was used to. Her skin, on the other hand, was several shades darker. The shape of her face had changed. It seemed longer and more angular. Her cheeks were thinner, her nose more prominent. At fourteen, she had looked eleven or twelve. At nearly sixteen, she looked almost grown up. The breasts she had known about, but she hadn't been paying attention to the hips. Somehow, she had those now, too.

"No one is even going to recognise me," she breathed, staring at the mirror in horror.

"Well, it's not as bad as you think," said Josiah. "You look like your own older sister. We'll cut your hair just before you go back, and we'll get you something baggy to wear. The tan's pretty deep, so I'm not sure about that. But all right, yes, you're going to have some problems."

"Not as many as your imagination is telling you right now," said Cuerva Lachance. "People see what they want to see."

Freddy had been having the same thought a few hours and/or a couple hundred years ago, but she wasn't sure it applied here. "Maybe if I'd been gone for a month. I'll have been gone for five minutes."

"You could stretch it to an hour and say you were sulking," said Josiah.

"Try not to worry about it." Cuerva Lachance patted her reassuringly on the head. "You'll have other things to worry about soon.

You're living with us now. We can bake cookies. It's possible I'll accidentally make the closets come alive, but I'm sure you'll be able to deal with that."

She drifted into the living room, humming. The Josiahs cast each other long-suffering looks before they followed. Freddy stood alone in the front hall. The bottom had fallen out of everything. It wasn't just that there wasn't a place for her at the moment. It was that when her place did become available again, she wasn't sure she was going to fit back into it.

15

"Get up," said Josiah the next morning. He was sitting on her feet.

Nothing she saw when she woke up ever confused her any more. There was no point in being confused when everything was constantly changing. Freddy opened her eyes. She was in the bedroom she and Josiah had been hiding in the day before. Her bed wasn't really a bed; it was a futon mattress Cuerva Lachance had absentmindedly created from nothing.

There was only one bed. A second bed was what she had noticed missing a year and a half—or, technically, half a day—ago. Knowing Josiah, she didn't find this surprising. "Well, obviously," Josiah 2 had said the day before as they manoeuvred a couch into position. "What would I do with a bed?"

"You could try sleeping in it," Freddy had pointed out.

"You people waste far too much time sleeping," Josiah 2 had said.

Freddy had grown used to Josiah's behaviour at night. He never did sleep. He just walked around and fidgeted and occasionally engaged in monologues when other people were *trying* to sleep. Cuerva Lachance slept, though not always, and usually not where anyone could see her. She said she did it because it was fun and beat listening to Josiah all night.

"I'm tired," said Freddy. "Why don't you go talk to yourself?"

"Myself has gone to school," said Josiah. "First day, remember? I spent the night filling him in on certain essential details. He's being tormented by fiends in human form even as we speak."

Freddy pulled the covers over her head. "What do you need me for?"

"Well, I'm bored," said Josiah, "but that's not really it. It's the whole living-in-a-house-with-Cuerva-Lachance thing. It's better if you're awake when she is. Fewer unexpected things can happen to you that way."

Groaning, Freddy sat up. "I have only one outfit, and it needs to be washed."

"You can borrow something from me for now. I'm not all that much bigger than you any more."

"How much better that makes me feel," said Freddy. "Give me the clothes and get out."

She spent half an hour in the shower, just because she could. There hadn't been many showers during her travels. Josiah's jeans turned out to be only a little roomy but about three inches too long. She had to borrow a belt as well, then roll up the cuffs. The T-shirt was too big, but as it was a T-shirt, that didn't matter. Freddy preferred her clothing baggy. Cuerva Lachance gave her some underwear and a bra that were far too big. She claimed they were new. Freddy decided not to think about it.

"Is there food?" said Freddy as she entered the living room.

It already contained an extra chair, a carved wooden one with a faded orange cushion.

Josiah was flat against the wall beside the window, looking oddly like he had at Coleridge's farmhouse. "Shut up and get out of sight. Your stepbrother is sneaking around outside."

"Roland?" said Freddy. She ducked back out into the hall. "He's supposed to be in school."

"I'm aware. Did you actually see him at the morning assembly today?"

She tried to remember, but it had been far too long since she had been at that assembly. "Maybe not. He was in school in the afternoon. I saw him in math class. What's he doing?"

"He was looking in the window earlier," said Josiah. "He may have seen me. Now . . . no idea. I thought your sister was the detective."

"Roland's . . ." She trailed off and sputtered for a moment, then confessed, "I don't know very much about Roland."

"You live in a house with him."

"I try to keep out of his way."

"I've noticed *that*. You haven't even bothered learning to talk like a baby in sign language, have you?"

Freddy shrugged.

"Well, he seems to be going all Hardy Boys on us now," said Josiah, "so good luck with keeping out of his way."

Cuerva Lachance poked her head through from the kitchen. "Is something exciting happening?"

"Roland," they said together.

"Roland who?" said Cuerva Lachance.

"Big awkward one," Josiah said.

"Oh, good," said Cuerva Lachance. "I need muscles."

Josiah said, "What? No!" But Cuerva Lachance was already heading for the front door. Freddy peered through into the living room again, shrugged at Josiah, and ran for the stairs.

She had gained the landing and hidden around the corner by the time Cuerva Lachance had opened the door and presumably caught Roland standing on the porch, snooping. "Big awkward one!" Freddy heard her cry happily. "How nice to see you nosing conveniently around our front door!"

"I wasn't—" started Roland, but as Freddy knew from experience, having a conversation with Cuerva Lachance was mostly a matter of keeping up with her thought process as she completely failed to take in anything you said. "I could use your help," she said. "The piano is in the wrong corner of the living room, and Josiah and I can't shift it alone."

As far as Freddy knew, the piano hadn't turned up yet. It certainly wasn't in the living room, or it hadn't been fifteen seconds ago. Roland mumbled a reply, and Cuerva Lachance said, "Oh, I'm sure we don't need anybody but you."

Roland said something with the words "grand piano" in it. He seemed to be in the house now. Freddy suspected Cuerva Lachance had physically dragged him in.

"I know," said Cuerva Lachance. "But I'm an optimist. We may not be able to lift it, but we can push it across the floor, leaving heartbreaking grooves in the hardwood. Josie, stop lurking and help us with this."

After a pause, Roland said clearly, "Aren't you supposed to be in school?"

"Aren't you?" said Josiah.

"I thought I saw you crossing the park earlier."

"I started across the park. Then I was overcome with ennui, and I came back to play moody New Age music and think about death."

"Don't trip over the chair," said Cuerva Lachance, though Freddy could hardly hear her over the crash that presumably resulted from Roland tripping over the chair.

There were several more crashes and a couple of loud thumps. Freddy, cringing upstairs, strained to hear any conversation, but all she caught was an exclamation of "What a beautiful trail of destruction we have created!" from Cuerva Lachance. A few minutes later, after Roland had done some more mumbling, Cuerva Lachance said, "Be sure to come again when you should be in school, learning." The front door closed. Cautiously, Freddy crept back down the stairs.

Cuerva Lachance and Josiah were standing beside the piano, having an argument. An argument between Cuerva Lachance and Josiah involved Josiah snarling viciously and Cuerva Lachance missing the point, conceivably on purpose. "He saw my ponytail," hissed Josiah as Freddy looked into the room. "Don't come in here, you fool; he could still be outside." Freddy stopped in the doorway.

"Does it matter if he saw it, Josie, dear?" said Cuerva Lachance.

"It will, believe me," said Josiah. "From what I gathered last time around, this is just the beginning of the weirdness. Why did you tell him I was here?"

"I don't know. Did I? I was getting the piano," said Cuerva Lachance vaguely.

"Yes, and what a good idea it was for you to do that practically in front of a civilian," said Josiah.

"It just came," said Cuerva Lachance. "This sort of thing is always happening to me."

"Well, he's going to be all suspicious of you guys now," said Freddy. But . . . that wasn't quite right, was it? Roland had been suspicious *before* Cuerva Lachance had invited him into the house. She tried to remember if anything had happened while they had been helping with the moving. Nothing came immediately to mind.

"I need to get the other me to cut off this bloody ponytail *tonight*," said Josiah. He went storming off into the kitchen in a huff. Cuerva Lachance smiled brilliantly, then simply wasn't there any more. It was, Freddy decided, going to be a very long three weeks.

First she had to get through a very long day. There was little to do. Cuerva Lachance and Josiah had some books, but they were all in Russian. "Well, we came here from Russia," said Josiah when Freddy asked. "You know that. We were there for a few weeks in the 1960s."

"If you even just had a computer," said Freddy.

He shook his head at her. "You get bored more easily than I do. There's a TV somewhere, likely broken. We have a laptop, but there's no Internet yet. We just moved in, remember? The phone company's coming by on Thursday."

"Isn't Cuerva Lachance supposed to be a private investigator?" said Freddy.

"That's what she tells people," said Josiah gloomily. "She'll take a few jobs eventually because she thinks it's amusing, then lose interest. But we're really just investigating your family."

"Oh," said Freddy, "right."

The TV *was* broken. It also seemed to be a refugee from the 1990s. Freddy gave up and went home.

It was a bad idea, but she knew there would be no one in the house until after three. She could at least grab some underwear and socks, plus maybe a few books no one would miss.

Freddy felt like a burglar as she let herself into the kitchen with her key. She kept having to stop herself from tiptoeing. It was stupid to feel like an intruder. She lived here, after all. But it was all a little strange. The house seemed smaller than she remembered. It was indescribably odd to look at the pile of books on the chair by the door and recall that exact pile from a year and a half ago. The pile would shift and mutate over the next few weeks, and yet here she was, looking at an old version of it. She'd thought she'd got better at thinking like a time traveller, but it seemed she hadn't. It was immensely hard to reconcile her personal timeline with chronological time.

Her bedroom, like the rest of the house, seemed too small. She blinked around it in dismay. Had she ever liked that duvet cover? It had great big flowers on it. She thought she remembered her mum giving it to her for Christmas one year, but she did have a plain blue one as well. Why had she chosen the giant flowers? Was there really a pink shirt draped over her desk chair? She didn't even like pink. Rochelle and Cathy wore a lot of pink. Was *that* why she had a pink shirt? Had she ever truly enjoyed hanging out with Rochelle and Cathy?

There was a book on her bed. She picked it up. It was the one with the tragic immortal nuzzling teenagers in it. Freddy stared at it, puzzled. She remembered starting it the day she had met Cuerva Lachance and Josiah, but she didn't remember what had happened to it after that. She had certainly never finished it.

Still holding the book, she wandered around the room. Everything in it was wrong. All the clothes and books and DVDs and games belonged to someone else. *I haven't changed that much, have I? It's only been a year and a half. I'm still the same person.*

She sat down on the bed and opened the book.

It was the most brain-numbing thing she had ever read. She had thought it was stupid before, but she had been able to get through several chapters. Now, she could hardly manage a paragraph. She rose, walked to her bedroom window, slid back the pane and then the screen, and flung the book violently into a tree.

<hr />

"Went home?" said Josiah later when Freddy was poking at a peanut butter sandwich in a moody sort of way. Cuerva Lachance had gone shopping and brought back a surprisingly logical selection of food. She had also bought twenty pounds of sugar, but as Josiah had pointed out, it wouldn't have been Cuerva Lachance if something hadn't gone wrong somehow.

Freddy nodded.

"Bad idea," said Josiah, "though understandable. Got some books now?"

"A few." Freddy, in desperation, had raided her mother's library and come away with half the English literary canon. She had also snagged the Coleridge book from the chair in the kitchen so she could read the poem she had interrupted.

"You won't have that much time for them, all things considered," said Josiah.

She stared at him. "There's nothing to do here."

"Yet," said Josiah. But when she asked him what he meant by that, he didn't reply.

16

"Josiah," said Freddy, "the second-floor bathroom has stopped existing again."

It was the fourth time in as many days. She never knew when it was going to happen. She would mount the stairs and turn left and nearly walk into the wall. The basement bathroom was permanently plugged, and the third-floor one was on the third floor, which terrified everyone except Cuerva Lachance. Once, in desperation, Freddy had gone out into the backyard and used a bush.

The Josiahs, who were seated at the kitchen table, turned to her with identical expressions of harassment. Josiah 2 had cut off Josiah's ponytail a few days before, but she could always tell which was which. She thought she would be able to do so even when the gash on Josiah 2's forehead had faded completely. Josiah 2 had trimmed Josiah's hair just a bit too short. Besides, Josiah looked slightly more long-suffering.

"Damn it," said Josiah 2, "I don't know why she insists on doing that. And it's always the bathroom, too.

It's never the kitchen or the basement or that cursed piano. This from someone who hasn't even discovered—"

"Ssh!" said Freddy and Josiah simultaneously. The three of them had been working quite hard to stop Cuerva Lachance from finding out about the organ. Josiah hadn't told Josiah 2 that they would eventually fail.

The house was changing. Freddy had first noticed it on Wednesday, two days ago, when she had got lost on the way down to breakfast. It wasn't possible to get lost in the house on Grosvenor Street; the second floor contained one corridor with one turn in it. Still, she had ended up wandering down corridor after corridor, past an endless succession of locked doors. There had been nothing interesting about the corridors. There had just been far too many of them. She had found the stairs by sheerest accident.

On Thursday, Josiah 2 had wound up on the fourth floor of their three-storey house and hadn't been able to get out. Josiah and Freddy had climbed out onto the roof to fetch him. They had seen him as standing beside the chimney. He had seen himself as being in a room without doors. It had taken some time to persuade him to walk through what had, to him, seemed to be an impenetrable wall.

Now it was Friday, and the bathroom had disappeared again. There were also chairs everywhere, though the spider plants hadn't turned up yet. Freddy had considered using the third-floor bathroom, but she had heard strange noises in the stairwell and ultimately decided on flight.

"Cuerva Lachance," said Josiah, *please* come in here."

Someone upstairs cackled. It sounded like a man.

"I mean it," said Josiah 2. "Honestly, there's no excuse for this behaviour."

"Is she always like this?" said Freddy as something very large slammed into something else above, making the whole house shudder. "I don't remember her being like *this*."

"She was on her best behaviour around you," said Josiah. "Besides, the last Three did choose her. And you know she's . . . erratic."

"Sure," said Freddy, but it had been different before. She thought Josiah must have been protecting her. She had rarely lived in the same house as Cuerva Lachance for more than a day at a time.

"Cuerva Lachance," shouted Josiah 2, "do you want to wreck the house already? Get down here!"

"I don't want to wreck the house at all," said Cuerva Lachance earnestly from the living room doorway. "Something's gone strange with the third floor again."

Both Josiahs buried their faces in their hands. "Perfect," said Josiah 2. "I love it when you have no idea what you've done to make reality implode."

"If I understood what was going on all the time, I would be you," said Cuerva Lachance. "I think this kitchen lacks something. What is it this kitchen lacks?"

Freddy said, "What's happened to the third floor?"

"Well," said Cuerva Lachance, "I think it may be in space. It's not clear at the moment, but I would suggest not going up there. I don't think there's much atmosphere. And there's a stereotypical supervillain floating around in the asteroid belt, laughing and smashing things."

This was so much the opposite of unexpected that Freddy thought she was probably getting too used to Cuerva Lachance. "He sounds fictional," she said. Josiah twitched.

"Exactly," said Cuerva Lachance, beaming. "I tried asking his thoughts on the Three situation, but he kept going on about his insane plan to conquer the universe. Couldn't you just tell us which of you is Three? I'm dying of curiosity."

"I don't know which of us is Three," said Freddy with perfect truth, though if she'd known, she would have lied.

She hadn't had time to think much about Mika's story, but she'd never put it entirely from her mind. There was something really strange about the Three situation. Okay, the entire thing with Josiah and Cuerva Lachance was strange, but Freddy had needed to recalibrate her strangeness meter over the course of the past year and a half. Even by her new standards, she could sense something wasn't right.

The story had made Josiah really uncomfortable. She'd never seen anything do that before. Also, the old versions of Cuerva Lachance and Josiah hadn't been there when the story had started. They could have walked out of the darkness, but Freddy had been watching, and she didn't think they had. Cuerva Lachance was the sort of person who habitually appeared out of thin air. Except when he was time travelling, Josiah wasn't.

She thought maybe she had been listening to a more or less true story about them being born. She thought it was something neither of them had wanted her to hear. She didn't know what to do with either of these ideas.

"Oh well," said Cuerva Lachance cheerfully. "Do we have something soothing to feed the supervillain? I'm not sure how long he's going to exist, and I expect he's hungry by now."

"You didn't buy anything soothing," said Josiah. "You bought lots and lots of sugar."

"That won't help in this case." Cuerva Lachance pursed her mouth thoughtfully. "Spider plants!"

Everybody looked at her.

"This kitchen needs spider plants," she said.

"If you say so," said Josiah 2, rubbing violently at his forehead.

Someone knocked on the back door.

It was almost four. Freddy and Josiah stared at each other for three full seconds, then dived under the kitchen table. It wasn't really the right thing to do. Freddy decided later that they had both panicked in the same way.

"If it's the stepbrother," said Josiah 2, "I'm going to put him at the top of the 'Three' list."

But when Cuerva Lachance opened the door, it was Mel's voice they heard. "Hi. I was wondering if my sister was here."

Josiah glanced at Freddy, who was racking her brain. Where had she been on Friday after school? She couldn't remember. It had been too long ago, and she hadn't been doing anything important.

"Why would you wonder something like that?" said Cuerva Lachance. "Has your sister made friends with Josie? I would be completely shocked to hear it. Do you think this kitchen would be better with spider plants in it?"

"Sure," said Mel. "Freddy? Is that you hiding under the table?"

She didn't seem to have seen more than one of the Josiahs, which was really the only good thing about this situation. Josiah slid around behind Freddy, who said, "I thought you were going to be Roland. He's been bugging me about hanging out with Josiah." Was

that true, though? She thought maybe Roland had only started behaving strangely later on.

"No, Roland's watching TV," said Mel. "You can come out now."

"I can't," said Freddy. "I like it under this table. It's peaceful. I'll
be back later, okay?"

"Goodbye, little fat one!" said Cuerva Lachance. She shut the door
in Mel's face, cutting off her, "But why can't I—?"

They all waited, Freddy holding her breath. After a moment, they
heard Mel move heavily away.

"We're going to have problems with the ducklings," said Josiah 2
as Freddy and Josiah emerged. "That one's far too curious. And the
stepbrother saw me talking to Cuerva Lachance at school."

Freddy looked at Josiah, who shrugged. She said, "Why is that
bad?"

"She was invisible at the time," said Josiah 2. "We were in that
courtyard where the Deaf kids go to smoke. It was a whole epic invisible argument."

"I get silly when I'm invisible," said Cuerva Lachance. "It's possible I knocked him into a tree, and I may have turned him upside
down at some point. I'm not sure how much the big awkward one
saw, but there was some."

Freddy said warily, "What was the argument about?"

"You," said Josiah 2. "All of you. Three. I don't know how much
he gathered. I'm sure he was only there for a couple of minutes, and
he couldn't have seen much even just of my side of the conversation,
but it was enough to make me seem sinister."

"Have you ever thought of gathering us all together and telling
us the truth?" said Freddy.

Everybody turned towards her in amazement. "Why on earth would we do that?" said Josiah 2.

"It seems more practical than what you're doing now," she pointed out.

"It's not," said Josiah. "Don't you remember how you reacted when you found out? It's better to ease people into these things. Besides, whichever of you aren't Three don't need to know."

"Except you, if you aren't Three," said Josiah 2, "since you know already, unfortunately."

"You're making it all unnecessarily complicated," said Freddy.

"No, we're making it necessarily complicated," said Josiah, and the others nodded.

Freddy bit back the words she really wanted to say. It would be better if she let this drop. It was another clue. There was something about the Three situation she wasn't understanding yet.

⌒

The house calmed down after that. The bathroom reappeared, and if the third floor really had turned into a portion of outer space with a floating supervillain in it, it had gone back to normal by early evening. Chairs and spider plants were popping up all over the place, but the weirdness seemed limited to them. The calm lasted all through the rest of Friday and the whole of Saturday. Freddy thought the Josiahs were doing something, though she couldn't tell what. When she asked, Josiah 2 said loftily that he was "asserting logic." It was eminently unclear what this meant.

On Sunday afternoon, Freddy heard someone playing the piano

and walked into the living room to say hello to Cuerva Lachance. The problem was that it was Loki at the instrument.

There were, by this point, a lot of chairs in the room. Freddy stood in a sea of them and stared at the Viking warrior pounding out a swing version of something Freddy thought may have been written by Beethoven. *If this was the old version of me,* she thought, *my brain would be shutting down right about now.*

It wasn't the old version of her. She crossed her arms and cleared her throat.

Loki finished with a flourish and turned to her, beaming. "Curly-haired one! I just left you. Your headache has gone, I hope?"

"It's been gone for more than a year," said Freddy. "Are you looking for Cuerva Lachance?"

"Not particularly," said Loki. "We'll bump into each other eventually. There's no need to go around actively looking for anyone."

One of the Josiahs rushed into the room. Freddy hadn't yet seen either today, and it took her a moment to identify this one as Josiah 1. "Don't let him into the kitchen!" he gasped.

"Too late." Loki reached under the piano and pulled out a case of beer. "I've already had several. The beer in your time is effectively yeast-flavoured water. I'm not the slightest bit impaired."

"Yes, you are, you fool," said Josiah.

Freddy said, "Why is there beer?" She'd looked in the fridge this morning, and there hadn't been anything in there but milk and half a head of lettuce.

"There's always beer in the fridge when Loki shows up," said Josiah. "As soon as he enters a house, alcohol appears. We need to get him out of here. There are too many things he can set on fire with his brain."

"Why would I do that? I wouldn't. I don't do things like that. Why would you think I would? What if I played the piano some more? I like playing the piano. Haven't you people found Three yet?" said Loki.

"It's bad enough in Sweden. He really likes his mead." Josiah had got in behind Loki and was heaving him to his feet. Loki giggled. "But Sweden has lots of wide open spaces where he can go boom all by himself. He comes here and does it in *houses*."

"He was doing it in the mead hall before," said Freddy. At Josiah's impatient gesture, she moved forward and began to tug at Loki's left arm.

"That happens after this. Don't give him any ideas," said Josiah. "Get him upstairs to the bathroom."

They passed Cuerva Lachance in the hall. "Loki!" she said with what Freddy considered far too much oblivious happiness. "Did you come to see me?"

"Yes," said Loki, "but I met your alcohol accidentally on the way."

She followed them up the stairs as they herded Loki towards the bathroom. Freddy kept wanting to sneeze; his furs were making her nose tingle. "Is there anything in particular you wanted to talk about?" asked Cuerva Lachance, for all the world as if they were seated politely around the kitchen table.

"I can feel the weirdness. There's weirdness everywhere!" said Loki. "This time is going to be different . . . and difficult. Time travel changes people. Didn't you know? Keep your eye on the candidates."

"Of course," said Cuerva Lachance. "How much beer did he have?"

Josiah's eyebrows twitched. "Eight bottles. At least."

As they rounded the corner at the top of the stairs, Freddy heard the front door open, then close. There were voices downstairs. Everybody froze.

"Damn it," whispered Josiah. "That idiot Josiah's gone and fetched you and your sister!"

Freddy blinked. "The inclined planes . . ."

"Into the bathroom, *now*." Josiah shoved Loki through the door.

"Hey," said Loki, "it's all small and white in here."

"He's going to start blowing things up," said Josiah to Cuerva Lachance.

"That will be interesting to see."

He glared at her. "Cuerva . . . Lachance."

"Oh, all right, have it your way. I'll get you some help. But just a minute." She followed Loki into the bathroom. Freddy saw her open the cabinet, take out a bottle of mouthwash, and pour some into one of the glasses she kept beside the sink. "Back in a second," she said, and vanished.

It was a literal second later that she reappeared with Ban. "You kids have fun," said Cuerva Lachance. "I'll go downstairs and torment people for a bit. Perhaps someone will even sit on my chairs."

She flitted out of the room, her ever-present coat billowing behind her. Freddy and Josiah stared at Ban. "This counts as help?" said Freddy.

"No," said Josiah, "this counts as the opposite of help. There are now three of her. Anything could happen and probably will."

"You worry too much." Ban was perched on top of the toilet. Her general lack of clothing was much more striking here than it had been in the jungle. "Drank something, did he?"

"I drank everything," said Loki proudly. He climbed into the bathtub and fell down on his bottom with a thump.

"It feels wrong here," said Ban, watching as Freddy and Josiah tried to help Loki sit on the edge of the bathtub while muffling his thuds and bangs. "It feels ominous."

"Yes, well," panted Josiah, "that's because there are three of you and two of me and two of *her* in the same house at the same time. I'm sure that breaks some sort of cosmic rule."

"No, that's not it," said Ban. "What have you two been doing to reality?"

"Living in it. Just sit there and avoid helping, do."

"I bet I can reach the ceiling from here with my sword," said Loki, and drew it. Freddy hadn't even noticed he had a weapon with him. Everybody crowded away from the notched length of metal, which Loki was waving around indiscriminately. "Great," said Freddy, "now we can't get near him at all."

"It's been going on for a long time, hasn't it?" said Ban, doing the head tilt.

Josiah said, "What has? Nothing's going on. Can anybody reach that bloody sword?" Loki, who was now on his feet in the bathtub, lunged towards him, and Josiah jerked backwards into the door.

"Of course it's been going on for a long time," said Loki, abruptly lowering the sword. Freddy, trying not to think about what she was doing, darted forward and took it from him. She didn't think he noticed.

"Did you start it," said Ban, "or did he?"

"Don't remember. Doesn't matter," said Loki. "It works. Are you going to be boring about this? Are you sure you're not Bana in disguise?"

"I resent that," said Josiah, "and *shut up*, Loki."

"Make me," said Loki, grinning through the flames that were beginning to ignite in his beard.

"Oh, fantastic," snarled Josiah, pressing right up against the door.

"What? I can't help being out of control. It's what I'm *for*," said Loki. "I mean, I could go around creating chairs or making vague moralistic pronouncements, but what's the point? You tell Cuerva Lachance to remember what she is. This whole living-in-a-house deal is sweet and all, and I very much like her hat, but there's no use playing at all this domesticity. Even you're domestic, Ban, and you live in a Stone Age jungle, surrounded by people who want to kill you. Take charge, will you? And stop listening to *him*."

The flames had crept up into his hair. Freddy stepped into the bathtub and turned the shower on.

The next bit was all smoke and steam and coughing and quite a bit of thumping and blundering about. Ban was doubled over laughing. Freddy crouched, sopping, in the bathtub while Loki bellowed something about finding her and turning her skin inside out while she was still alive. The water was barely warm, but she didn't care. The most urgent thing they had to do at the moment was get Loki back to his time.

"Okay. *Okay*. Are you all quite done?" said Josiah once some of the smoke had dispersed. Freddy quietly turned off the water.

"Wet," said Loki, "not done. It was a good idea," he assured Freddy, "though I'd still like to kill you."

The bathroom door opened, revealing Cuerva Lachance and Josiah 2. "Oh dear," said Cuerva Lachance.

"What are you all *doing*?" said Josiah 2. "They noticed! They knew there was someone else in the house!"

"Well, what were *you* doing bringing them over?" said Josiah.

"I didn't know we were having a multiple-self party in the second-floor bathroom," Josiah 2 spat. "Get Loki out of here before he burns down the neighbourhood."

"It's not my fault I like fire. Maybe I'll set all the water on fire, just because I can't," said Loki.

Cuerva Lachance and Ban looked at each other and moved together towards Loki. Ban glanced into the bathtub, straight at Freddy. "Everything's backwards," she remarked. Then all three of them were gone.

Several hours later, deep into the night, Freddy and Josiah sat side by side on the stairs, waiting for Cuerva Lachance to discover the pipe organ.

"Why don't we just stop her now?" said Freddy. "Or tell the other Josiah?"

Josiah said, "Because that's not what we do."

"That's just an excuse," said Freddy. "Nothing's stopping us but you saying we don't do it. We could change what happens. We could—"

"What?" He turned to look at her. "Nail boards over the door? Do you think Cuerva Lachance can't get into a sealed room? Warn the other me so he can stand in front of the door all night? She'll get past him. Nothing we do now is going to change anything."

"Just telling him would be changing things."

Josiah shook his head. "We don't."

The rules of time travel, whatever they were, made her feel like a puppet. "I don't understand why he couldn't stop her if he knew."

"She's Cuerva Lachance. She doesn't respect rules. I do. What's not to understand?" said Josiah, picking moodily at the carpet runner.

"It seems as if she has all the power."

"No, not all of it. If she did, the planet would have been space rubble for several thousand years now. She's dominant at the moment, but I'm sometimes able to . . . persuade her to be more reasonable than she naturally is."

"And she's sometimes able to . . . persuade you to be *less* reasonable than you naturally are," said Freddy.

He made faces for a moment or two, then admitted, "Maybe."

"I just think we should try to change things, is all," said Freddy.

"I keep telling you we can't."

"Then it's like we're fated. Trapped."

"No, it's not—" But then he paused. "Too late. I hear the door to the tower."

They sat there, tense and resigned, and listened as Cuerva Lachance barricaded herself inside the tower, pulled out most of the organ's stops, and began to play. The sound was even more appalling here than it had been in the yard. Freddy could feel the stairs trembling at every note.

Eventually, they got up and went to help Josiah 2, who was trying to break down the door by throwing himself at it ineffectually. It felt useless to help him, since they knew what the outcome would be, but Freddy did anyway. *I hate feeling all fated like this. We shouldn't be hemmed in because we've gone back in time.*

Freddy timed the music. It lasted for nearly half an hour. For

Cuerva Lachance, that was almost astonishing. With the exception of one time in Rome, Freddy didn't think she had ever seen Cuerva Lachance concentrate on anything for more than ten minutes at once. They all waited while Cuerva Lachance removed the furniture she had dragged in front of the door. They could hear Jordan pounding and swearing downstairs.

"Oh, hello," said Cuerva Lachance dreamily when she emerged. "There's a pipe organ in my house."

"That's nice," said Freddy. "You'd better answer the door."

Cuerva Lachance floated down the stairs; everybody else crept after her. Freddy and Josiah stood in the shadows near the door to the living room as Cuerva Lachance and Josiah 2 had their conversation with Freddy's family. Freddy felt oddly left out. She knew there still wasn't a place for her back home, but she kept wanting to join the discussion.

"Stop fidgeting," said Josiah. "You know they don't notice us."

"That's not why I'm fidgeting," said Freddy, who remembered that Mel had, in fact, heard voices inside the house. It wasn't something Josiah needed to know.

This time, the conversation between Cuerva Lachance and Josiah 2 after the family had gone was completely audible. "I hope you're happy," said Josiah 2, his hands on his hips. "You've turned the entire household against us, which will make it so very much easier for us to do our jobs."

"But Josie," said Cuerva Lachance, "there's a pipe organ in my house."

"Shut up," said Josiah 2. "It's just like you to intimidate their parents. You know we have to find out which of them is Three. How are we supposed to do that if we alienate the whole family?"

"It's unusual that we can't figure out which one it is," said Cuerva Lachance. "I don't suppose you have any thoughts? They're all possibilities, but at the same time, they don't really fit. It's very exciting."

"You are the most infuriating person in the history of infuriating people," said Josiah 2. "Playing a pipe organ in the wee hours! Not understanding why this is a bad thing! You complete moron."

"We'll find out about Three eventually," she replied. "We know only that it's not going to happen before you go wandering. So that's after September twenty-seventh, isn't it?"

"Maybe," said Josiah 2, "but there's no guarantee. Why did you have to play the stupid organ? We need to wrap this up quickly after the twenty-seventh."

"It was pretty and made interesting sounds."

"You make my brain melt."

"That's what I'm here for. Have you two finished eavesdropping?"

"We're standing six feet away from you, in plain sight," said Josiah, but Freddy felt a chill run through her as she thought of Freddy 2 and Mel crouching behind the rhododendron. Did Cuerva Lachance know? She sometimes did just know things, and she noticed a lot more than she let on.

"Even so," said Cuerva Lachance. "Well, I think I'll go to bed. Don't stay up too late complaining about me." She shut the back door and meandered off towards the stairs.

The Josiahs looked at each other. Freddy was pretty sure they *were* going to spend most of the night complaining about Cuerva Lachance. Since neither of them ever slept, it was possible they did this every night. *I don't belong here,* she thought. She knew the thought was futile. At the moment, she didn't belong anywhere else, either.

Just over a week later, on Monday, Freddy got lost in the house on Grosvenor Street again. It was different this time.

The intervening week had not been a fantastic one. Freddy was feeling increasingly hemmed in. She hadn't been back to her own house since that first time; it had been too much like trying to stuff herself into a closed slot. She just needed to wait for the slot to open up again. In the meantime, she had little to do except deal with the weirdness of living with Cuerva Lachance and Josiah. She couldn't really go outside much in case someone saw her. Even standing at a window was a risk. She had been confined occasionally during the time travel—the Sumerian temple being a case in point—but never like this. This was the first time in her life she had truly understood the meaning of the word "cabin fever." It had not been a good idea for her to watch *The Shining* on Josiah's laptop last week.

Luckily, or unluckily, the house itself helped by morphing constantly. It was different every day. Since she'd also lived through these weeks as a largely oblivious next-door neighbour, she knew that the changes didn't show on the outside. The house reminded her of the TARDIS from *Doctor Who*; it was bigger on the inside. Freddy had long since grown used to ignoring the rules of physics where Cuerva Lachance was concerned, so this didn't bother her. What did bother her was that she would so frequently have to deal with the implications.

The day all the living room furniture ended up on the ceiling wasn't so bad. The fictional characters were a little more problematic. As she'd noticed during the time travel, people who clearly weren't real tended to spring into existence around Cuerva Lachance, though they rarely lasted for long. Many of them were out of books. A white rabbit carrying a pocket watch had woken Freddy up one morning by bemoaning his tardiness, and just yesterday, four children had turned up looking for a magic lion. Freddy had learned to deal with these figments as kindly and firmly as possible. They were obviously not really here, and they sometimes faded and dissolved into colours as she watched. Some of them were capable of interacting with her, but some just acted out the same scenes endlessly, blind to the presence of anyone else.

She asked Josiah about them. It was one of their most awkward conversations. "I don't know what you mean," he said coldly.

"The fictional people," said Freddy. "I noticed a few when we were time travelling, but they're everywhere here."

"I keep telling you that living in a house with Cuerva Lachance isn't the same thing as running into her in third-century Rome," said Josiah. "But I still don't know what you're talking about."

"White rabbit?" said Freddy. "Oliver Twist? Big hairy wild man who goes around calling himself Merlin? They keep turning up and wanting to talk to me."

"No, they don't."

"Yes, they do."

"They absolutely don't."

"And there was the supervillain in the asteroid belt."

"I don't remember any supervillain."

"You remember everything," said Freddy, "except when you're avoiding an issue."

"So maybe I'm avoiding an issue," said Josiah, "though I couldn't say, since I don't know what it is."

She *knew* he knew about the figments. It was impossible to live in this house and not know about the figments. He just didn't want to talk about them.

Cuerva Lachance was more matter-of-fact when Freddy asked her about the figments, but because she was Cuerva Lachance, the conversation wasn't any more satisfying than the one with Josiah had been. "Oh, yes, they're there," she said. "I need to paint something blue tomorrow, I think."

"But *why* are they there?" said Freddy.

Cuerva Lachance peered out from under her hat. "Why are who where?"

"The figments," said Freddy patiently. Discussions with Cuerva Lachance often went like this.

"I don't know," said Cuerva Lachance. "Did you ask them?"

"I don't think they're real enough to answer questions like that."

"Who aren't?"

"The figments."

"What figments?"

Freddy lay awake that night wondering if Cuerva Lachance had genuinely been having short-term-memory difficulties or had instead been indulging in obfuscating stupidity. It could easily have been either.

But even the figments were relatively ordinary next to what kept happening to the geography of the house.

It was never the same . . . not in a quirky wizard-school oh-look-the-corridors-have-shifted-again-ha-ha sort of way but in a bowel-twisting, anxiety-producing roller coaster of terror that often made Freddy want to lock herself in her room until September twenty-seventh. Unfortunately, her room was not immune. One day, she woke up and discovered that most of her floor had turned into quick-sand. She only escaped because her futon was close to the window, and she was able to climb onto the sill and from there out onto the gable below. The third floor was forever morphing into something unexpected. More than once, she heard the sounds of a carnival coming from it. The carnival always ended with terrified screams and crunching noises. She could only hope whatever was happening up there wasn't real.

Josiah said it was all to be expected. "I try to stop her," he said wearily as they climbed the enormous tree in the basement rec room to escape the river of snakes. "Honestly, half the time, she doesn't mean to do it. Things just become less possible wherever she goes."

"Where's the top of this tree?" asked Freddy. It seemed to go right through the ceiling.

"Lord knows," said Josiah.

"I'm surprised it isn't a beanstalk," said Freddy.

The sound of the organ briefly transformed the second floor into the Paris Opera House. The spider plants moved when no one was watching them. Freddy would look away for a moment and glance back to see their tendrils arranged in subtly different patterns. The chairs in the living room shifted form and appearance, and sometimes Freddy would walk into a room and find that the walls had gone. The house was everywhere and nowhere all at once.

⌒

Today, Freddy made sure she had her water bottle and boots before she set out for the kitchen. Finding the main floor of the house was not always easy.

But she rarely got *this* lost. On her second full day in the house, she had ended up wandering through a series of identical corridors. This trip started out similarly but soon changed. The corridor she was in began to plunge downward. She paused and looked behind her, planning to retrace her steps. The corridor behind her was now *also* plunging downward.

She went downward. The corridor darkened and changed; the bright ceiling lights gradually gave way to flickering torches set into rough stone alcoves. Hoping desperately that she hadn't accidentally gone back in time again, Freddy walked on. When she glanced over her shoulder, she saw darkness. The lights had been going out behind her.

It was cold and dank and lonely. Her feet echoed on the damp stone and occasionally splashed in a puddle. The corridor branched, and branched again.

There was something making sounds behind her. She stopped to listen. The noises were heavy, slithering, dragging ones. She couldn't tell whether they were moving towards her or away.

Freddy quickened her steps, darting through the corridors, which grew darker and darker as the lights winked out behind her. She could hear the slithering noises even through her own footsteps and rapid panting breathing. Whatever it was was *tracking* her. When she moved faster, it moved faster. Soon she would tire, and it would catch up.

And it was all just *stupid*.

Freddy stopped in place.

She didn't want to be doing this. *I'm a twenty-first-century Canadian. I live in Metro Vancouver. I go to school and worry about math and English and the fact that my stepbrother hates me. There's no reason for me to be lost in a medieval dungeon right now.* Freddy picked up one of the torches. Her hands were trembling; she willed them to stop. *If they're going to force me to do this, I'll do it my way. I won't be herded any more.*

The slithering noises were very close now. She turned around and plunged back into the blackness.

She was in a square white room. Ban was standing in a corner, looking at her. "Well done," she said.

Freddy threw down the torch. She wasn't sure she had ever been quite this angry. It was real anger that made her little smouldering tantrums at Roland feel like nothing more than petulance. "Were you *testing* me?"

"I? No," said Ban. "Were you testing you?"

"I did *not* trap myself in a dungeon with a monster!" snarled Freddy, shaking.

Ban shrugged. "If you say so. At any rate, I liked the way you handled it. Realistically, of course, your decision was suicidal," she said thoughtfully, "but metaphorically, it worked very well."

Freddy stood there with her mouth open and somehow avoided screaming.

"You interest me." Ban tapped her fingernails against her teeth. "You aren't as insignificant as you seem."

"Thanks so much," said Freddy when her voice came back.

Ban held out a hand to her. "Come on. There's something happening now that you should see."

Freddy didn't want to take Ban's hand. She didn't trust Ban. Trusting any version of Cuerva Lachance was roughly equivalent to trusting a suspension bridge in a windstorm. On the other hand, this room had no doors or windows, so if she *didn't* go with Ban, she could be here forever. Freddy sighed and extended her own hand. Ban grinned.

They were in the living room. So were Roland and one of the Josiahs; it was hard to tell which when they weren't together in a room. Freddy stared. It was well before it was time for school to start, but she still had no idea why Roland would be here.

"They can't see us," said Ban. "Just watch."

At almost the same time, Roland said, "I don't care how late you'll be. I need you to listen—"

You want me to stay away from your sisters, signed Josiah. *It's none of your business.*

Freddy looked away, instinctually. But . . . well, that wasn't true, was it? She always told herself she was looking away from the signing, but she never really was. She'd learned far more ASL than she'd ever admitted, even to herself. She'd even noticed the way Roland and his friends used different facial expressions while they were signing. And she'd practised in front of the mirror once or twice when she knew nobody was looking. She was good at languages; this one she'd just picked up by accident. Maybe some of it had been on purpose. Maybe she'd looked in Mel's ASL book a few times. Maybe it had been more than a few times.

"You can't sign," said Roland.

Josiah shook his head. *I can.*

"There's no reason you should," said Roland. "Nothing about you makes sense."

Is that really the problem? signed Josiah. *Can't the girls look after themselves?*

"No." Roland turned abruptly away from Josiah. "They think they can, but they don't know what they're getting into. You're not . . . right. I don't know exactly how yet, but there's something wrong with you."

Josiah moved around into Roland's line of sight again and signed something Freddy didn't understand. There were signs in there she didn't know. She thought he was asking a question.

"Because I know," said Roland sharply. "It isn't as if you hide it. Not from me, anyway. Stop signing."

I like signing, signed Josiah.

"No, stop signing *now*," said Roland, looming over Josiah. "You have no right to . . . to take . . . you don't even *know* . . ."

He raised his hands to his forehead and, again, turned away.

Freddy glanced at Ban, but she was staring raptly at Roland and didn't seem to notice. Freddy wasn't sure what to think. She'd known Roland didn't like Josiah, and she'd known the two of them had to have had a confrontation while Freddy wasn't around, but this was just confusing. As far as anyone had ever told her, all Roland had seen so far was Josiah's sudden ponytail and his argument with an invisible person in the courtyard. If Mel had witnessed these things, she would have made notes in her little notebook and constructed some sort of mystery out of it all. If Freddy—the old Freddy—had witnessed them, she would have convinced herself they had never happened. There didn't seem to be any reason for Roland to be so hostile.

Josiah waited until Roland looked back at him. Then he signed, *You need to calm down.*

"How am I supposed to do that?" Roland demanded. "I have this . . . feeling about you, and I can't even tell anyone why because I don't *know* why! I just know I need to keep you away from Freddy and Mel. They don't understand."

Do you? signed Josiah.

"No," said Roland, "but I can tell you're not right. They just think you're exciting and new. Mel's always making everything into a mystery. She's trying to *solve* you. Freddy's lonely. She . . . wants a friend."

Freddy blinked. She hadn't known he'd seen that. She hadn't known he'd noticed anything about her at all.

Is that so bad? signed Josiah. *You aren't friends with her.*

"She's so *difficult*," snarled Roland. "How can I be friends with her? She wants to be the most boring person in the world."

Josiah shrugged.

"You're not-boring in the wrong way. You keep away from her," said Roland.

Make friends with her and keep me away yourself, signed Josiah.

"I . . ." After what seemed to be a long struggle, Roland finished the sentence: ". . . don't know how."

Freddy looked at Ban again. This time, Ban returned her gaze. "He seems nice," she remarked. Freddy shook her head, but it wasn't really a denial. This stiff, tormented version of Roland did seem nice. She thought maybe he didn't know how to be nice in an ordinary way.

"You know," said Josiah aloud, "I'm very pleased you're working through your issues and coming to realisations about yourself, but do you have to do it here? You seem to be blaming me for your own emotional hang-ups because I'm new. 'I feel there's something wrong about you, but I have no idea what' is not the best possible reason for this little confrontation. Perhaps you should find out what your own problem is before you dump everything on me."

Roland stared at him, and Josiah stared back. Cuerva Lachance walked through the wall.

She did have a habit of treating physical objects as if they weren't there. Freddy had grown used to it, but Roland hadn't. He staggered back three steps. "Oh dear," said Cuerva Lachance. "This is completely accidental in every way."

"Cuerva Lachance," said Josiah. "For crying out loud."

The blood had drained from Roland's face. "You . . ."

"It's okay. You didn't really see that," said Josiah wearily. "You fell asleep briefly and dreamed it. There was an atmospheric disturbance. We discovered a secret passageway built into that wall. Are any of these working?"

"I knew you were wrong," said Roland. "You keep away from us!"

"I don't think so," said Cuerva Lachance. With dismay, Freddy realised she was in one of her scarier moods. Her hair and coat billowed out to the left, though the air of the room was perfectly still. She was smiling in a way that made Freddy's brain hurt.

"Oh, leave him alone," said Josiah.

Roland backed slowly out towards the front hall. He nearly made it, too. "The chair," said Freddy sharply to someone who couldn't see or hear her. Roland being Roland, he had backed right into one of Cuerva Lachance's chairs. He stumbled and fell, awkwardly, half on the chair and half off. Cuerva Lachance advanced across the room towards him, still caught in an invisible, intangible storm.

"You can't protect them," said Cuerva Lachance as Roland struggled to rise. "You can't protect anyone. Why would you want to? Isn't it easier just to look after yourself? Why go out of your way for two girls who don't even like you?"

"Mel likes me," said Roland, trembling.

"Mel likes everyone," said Cuerva Lachance. "She doesn't count."

"Stay *back*!" Roland regained his feet, staggered backwards into the wall, and rebounded, propelling himself out into the hall. Freddy heard him knock something over. Then the door was open, and running footsteps were receding down the walk.

The impossible wind died down.

"That was interesting," said Cuerva Lachance cheerfully. "Do you think he noticed anything?"

Josiah was making neck-wringing motions with his hands. "You are the most . . . infuriating . . . I can't believe you . . . He was already a problem, and now he . . . My God, you annoy me."

"I force you to have fun," said Cuerva Lachance.

"This is what you call 'fun,' is it?" He glared at her. "Please put the house back to normal. I think the other me is trapped in a box somewhere. You're completely out of control."

"It's my natural state," said Cuerva Lachance. However, when he continued to look pointedly at her, she sighed and moved out into the hall. Josiah followed.

Ban said, "Intrigued yet?"

"Why did you want me to see that?" asked Freddy.

Ban made a complicated body motion that Freddy thought might have been her version of a shrug. "Who can say? You may find something to do with it eventually."

"I can't trust you," said Freddy. "I can't trust anything about Cuerva Lachance."

"Of course not. But I just let you watch. I'm not telling you what to think."

"Do you want me to think something in particular?"

"It wouldn't be right if I just told you," said Ban virtuously.

Freddy narrowed her eyes.

Ban nodded. "Remember: everything is backwards."

"I don't know what that means," said Freddy.

Ban made the complicated body motion again. "Who does?" she said. Then there was just empty air where she had been.

18

By Thursday, Freddy was about ready to kill someone. She couldn't shake the feeling that September twenty-seventh was a sort of mirage, always off on the horizon, never getting any closer.

She was tired of eavesdropping. She was tired of lurking on the margins, slipping behind the scenes like a ghost. She was tired of living in a house that didn't stay the same shape from day to day. She was *really* tired of not being able to put the puzzle together. She had tried, but there were still pieces missing. She didn't know who Three was. She didn't understand why Three was so important or what "Everything is backwards" meant. She would have punched the wall if she hadn't been afraid it would turn into something when she did.

It was ten after three. She was in her room, trying to read "Kubla Khan." She was so desperate to know what was going on that she had been driven to poetry. She didn't really expect to find any answers in Coleridge's poem, but she couldn't think of anything else to try. At any rate, it wasn't working. The poem was mostly a description of the pleasure-dome, which seemed to have trees and rivers in it, for some reason. There was a bit at the end about some guy who seemed enchanted; she didn't understand that part at all. Where had the guy come from? Why was everyone wanting to weave a circle round him thrice? Why would anyone experience holy dread while weaving three circles around a random enchanted guy who was building pleasure-domes in air for no apparent reason? Then the poem just stopped. That was her fault, she supposed. In the end, she had to admit there were no answers here.

It was unseasonably warm, and she had left her window open, which was why she noticed the voices in the yard. Sighing, she dragged herself to the window for a bit of requisite eavesdropping.

Peering through the leaves and branches of the trees, she saw Josiah and Mel. The elementary school was only about a block and a half away, so Mel tended to get home earlier than Freddy.

As usual, the eavesdropping didn't work as well as she wanted it to, though it could have been worse. She wasn't all that far away from the others, and they weren't bothering to keep their voices down. "Snooping again?" said Josiah.

"There's a mystery to be solved," said Mel. "Of course I'm snooping."

The next few exchanges were inaudible. Then Josiah said more loudly, "Take frogs, for instance."

"I usually don't," said Mel. "Why frogs?"

"They start out as tadpoles," said Josiah, "then metamorphose. As adult frogs, their physiology is completely different."

"Not completely," said Mel. "They're still cold-blooded. They retain many characteristics—"

"The *point* is that looking at a tadpole, it's hard to predict a frog."

"So you're saying my understanding of what's going on is at tadpole-level right now?"

"Yes, but maybe that's just what I want you to believe."

"You know it's not easy to confuse me, right?"

If Josiah replied, his words were drowned out by the organ's first monstrous notes. Freddy saw both Mel and Josiah whip around to look at the house; then Josiah was running for the front door.

Freddy watched her sister stand in the yard, staring at the house. After a moment, she turned and walked past the hedge and out of sight. Mel really did snoop. She made up mysteries out of nothing. In this case, however, she was right about the mystery, and Josiah was right about the tadpoles.

The organ continued to scream out into the afternoon. Josiah 2 bounced into the yard, his hands over his ears. A moment later, Mel and Freddy 2 came into sight and stood watching the front door until the combined efforts of the two Josiahs shut Cuerva Lachance up.

Freddy's ears were still ringing, and she missed most of what Freddy 2 and Mel said to each other then. The first words she caught were Mel's: "Then Josiah can be in two places at once."

At this point, Mel looked straight at Freddy's bedroom window.

Freddy stepped rapidly back into the room, her heart pounding. She hardly heard Mel telling Freddy 2 about the long-haired girl at the window. *Stupid,* she thought. *You knew she was going to see someone. How didn't you know it was you?* It was, as usual, dizzying to try to reconcile events she remembered happening a year and a half ago with events that were happening right now.

Josiah came into the bedroom without knocking. "Your sister is being annoyingly nosy again," he said. "I said something about frogs."

"I heard," said Freddy. "We're out there discussing the laws of physics right now."

He rubbed his eyes. "I see her making it all into a mystery, and I think she might be Three. But I can't be sure. It could still be any of you. Why doesn't one of you just say something illuminating and put us all out of our misery? Don't *you* know who it is yet?"

"No," said Freddy, "sorry," though she wasn't. She added, "You may want to keep your voice down."

"Next Tuesday cannot come soon enough," said Josiah.

They watched, peeking out the window as subtly as they could, as Josiah 2 and Roland arrived in the yard at the same time, and everybody stood under the tree and argued. They watched as Cuerva Lachance spoke from the tree. It was funny how strange it had originally seemed that Cuerva Lachance had been able to get into that tree. Now that didn't even register on the general scale of weirdness.

When Cuerva Lachance materialised in the bedroom immediately afterwards, Freddy barely twitched. She felt an odd sense of loss. Sure, she had once reasoned away a marble rolling uphill, but at least then she had thought of impossible things as, well, impossible. With Cuerva Lachance, the impossible happened all the time. It made it hard to see anything as fundamentally real.

⌒

The weekend crept by. Nothing changed . . . or everything changed constantly, but not in a very constructive way. That was, Freddy decided, the problem with Cuerva Lachance. There was change but no growth. Josiah didn't grow, either, because he didn't change. Roland was right that there was something wrong with them, though he was wrong about what it was. The thought made Freddy shake her head at herself. Even her ideas about the confusion were confusing.

And then it was September twenty-seventh.

Freddy started shaking almost as soon as she woke up that morning, and she didn't stop all day. She was going home. But she was different. But she was *going home*. She hadn't always missed it when she was travelling. She did miss it now, strongly, when it was almost within reach. The clueless former Freddy was at school, getting thrown into a wall. Had she ever really been that oblivious? Would everyone expect her to *go back* to being that oblivious? What if she didn't fit?

"Stop shuddering," said Josiah irritably as he tried to give her a haircut after lunch. "Do you know how hard it is to cut hair this curly? Why can't you have nice lank, straight hair like your little sister?"

"I always like it when I have curly hair," said Cuerva Lachance, leaning against the fridge. A spider plant's tendril snaked over her shoulder.

"Thanks ever so for the information," said Josiah.

"I'm sorry," said Freddy, but she couldn't stop trembling. She felt as if she were about to open in a lead role on Broadway, and she hadn't bothered to learn her lines.

"You'll be fine," said Josiah, snipping away. "People will notice, but you'll get through it. Tell them the head injury made your legs swell."

Freddy had forgotten she would have to pretend to have a head injury. She felt the shaking get worse.

"Honestly," said Josiah, "if you don't stop that, these scissors are going to end up sticking through your eye. Take deep, calming breaths. Think of kittens frolicking in a field of daisies. Slap yourself upside the head a couple of times. You know . . . the usual."

"I'm just scared," said Freddy, "that's all."

She hadn't meant to blurt it out like that. Cuerva Lachance beamed at her. "Good for you," she said. "Lying to yourself would have been much easier. I would have chosen that option."

Freddy looked in the mirror when Josiah was done. The shorter hair did make her look more like her old self, but it couldn't disguise the height, the different body shape, or the changes in her face. The tan had faded a bit, though not as much as she had hoped. "Maybe if I slouch," said Freddy. "Or kneel."

"It will all be terrible," said Cuerva Lachance, patting her on the shoulder, "but let's pretend it won't."

From the window of the master bedroom, Freddy and Josiah watched Freddy 2 and Josiah 2 enter the backyard. Josiah had never told Josiah 2 exactly when on September twenty-seventh he would be encountering the time portal, but he was obviously expecting something soon; he peered edgily about him as they walked towards the door. Freddy 2 was looking straight ahead, stone-faced. They moved out of sight onto the doorstep.

"You're going to want to apologise in an hour or so," Freddy heard Josiah 2 say. "You know that, right?"

"No, I won't," said Freddy 2.

Then they were gone.

Freddy breathed out. There was only one of her now. Suddenly, she didn't know what was going to happen. It was more frightening than she had thought it would be.

"Cuerva Lachance," called Josiah, "is it possible you just turned the back door into a time portal?"

There was a pause. "Oh dear," said Cuerva Lachance from some-where down the hall, "did I?"

"Attention span of a diseased gnat," said Josiah. "So when are you going back?"

Freddy hadn't thought of much else for the past few days. "Right away. They won't be expecting it. I can sneak into my room and make sure they first see me when I'm sitting down."

"It won't work," said Josiah.

"Nothing will work," said Freddy, "but I can try."

Heart thumping in her chest, she went downstairs. Perhaps as an apology for her creation of the time portal, Cuerva Lachance was allowing the house to stay relatively stable. There was only one cor-ridor and one staircase at the moment. At the back door, Freddy and Josiah looked at each other. "Well," said Josiah, "this is it, then."

"Yeah," said Freddy.

She didn't know if she would miss the weirdness or not. She thought she sort of would and very much wouldn't. Her own bed-room had only four walls that never changed into anything.

"It's been fun," Josiah said, sounding as if someone had forced the words out of him at gunpoint. Freddy smiled. She was pretty sure Josiah actually quite liked her now, even if he refused to show it.

Clutching her time-travelling bag, which was bulging with books from her house, she crept across the yard and into the lane and back into her own yard. Everything was still. As quietly as she could, she unlocked the back door and pushed it open.

She nearly shoved it into Mel, who had apparently been on her way out.

19

For one brain-freezing moment, Freddy and Mel stood and stared at each other. *Idiot,* Freddy's brain screamed. *Ducklings! She was following you.* Mel's eyes travelled from Freddy's boots all the way up to the top of her head, which was so much higher than it should have been that Freddy briefly considered the kneeling option. There was no way of hiding anything. She saw the shock spread over Mel's face, then the recognition. Unbearably, there had been a moment at the very beginning when Mel hadn't known who she was.

Freddy pushed past Mel into the house. She ran up the stairs to her room, slammed the door, flung her bag in a corner, dived into her bed, and pulled the covers over her head. It was a completely stupid thing to do, but she could see no other option.

There was quite a lot of silence for quite a long time. The bedroom door opened. It didn't have a lock. She should, thought Freddy, have shoved some furniture against it.

"Do you want to talk about it?" said Mel.

"Go away," said Freddy.

Mel sat on the edge of the bed, bouncing a little. "I don't think that's a very good idea," she said thoughtfully. "You seem a couple of years older, at least."

"Eighteen months," said Freddy, and then, "That's impossible. I don't know what you're talking about."

"Ah. Growth spurt," said Mel. "It's encouraging to know I may not be short forever myself."

What Freddy was mainly feeling was a monstrous embarrassment. It had come out of nowhere. She didn't think she could stand to have Mel in the room for a second longer. "Go away," she moaned, "go away, go *away*."

"What I can't figure out," said Mel, "is how eighteen months passed for you while five minutes passed for me. I'm very interested in this phenomenon and would like you to stop being so dramatic about it so we can discuss the implications."

She pulled back the covers. Freddy tried to yank them over her face, but Mel bundled them into her arms and flung them across the room.

The sisters looked at each other. Time passed.

"Why aren't you in denial about this?" asked Freddy at last.

"I've never found denial very useful," said Mel. Freddy could see nothing in her expression but interest. "Observation tells me you've aged even though you haven't had time for that. So we accept that and move on. How did it happen?"

Freddy sat up. There was no point in trying to hide anything from Mel now. "Time travel."

"From the beginning," said Mel.

She didn't tell her sister everything. There were some bits of what had happened to her that she didn't feel ready to share, as she wasn't finished thinking about them yet herself. She left out Mika and the creation story, and she didn't mention her doubts about Three or the puzzling role of Ban in all this. She thought Mel may have picked up on the doubts about Three anyway. Listening to herself, she knew she was making the whole experience sound more like a rollicking adventure than it had really been. Mel was certainly awash in envy. "This isn't fair," she said when Freddy fell silent. "Do you know what I would give to travel in time?"

"It wasn't like that," said Freddy. "It wasn't just . . . fun. It was scary and way too weird for me."

"I don't think it was." Mel propped her chin on her chubby little fist. "You're different."

Freddy shook her head. "I don't know why you even believe me."

"Are you kidding?" said Mel. "You go off for five minutes and come back a year and a half older, then tell me a story that explains it perfectly? Why *wouldn't* I believe you? It's still not fair. You've solved the mystery without me."

"Not all of it," said Freddy, and she opened her mouth to say something more about Three, then shut it without speaking at all.

"I don't think I'm Three," said Mel, considering. "I haven't had any meaningful dreams or anything."

"That's not a requirement," said Freddy. "I haven't, either." But she wondered. There had been a dream, hadn't there? She remembered Cuerva Lachance floating on a piano.

"If you knew who Three was," said Mel, "would you tell them?"

"No."

Mel narrowed her eyes thoughtfully. "Me neither, and I'm not sure why. We should think about that. I think there are bits of the story we don't know."

Her doubts *had* come through, then. "Yeah, probably."

"We have to ask Roland," said Mel.

"No!" Freddy hadn't meant the word to emerge so violently. She saw her sister jerk away. "No," she repeated more quietly. "I don't want him to see . . ."

Mel regarded her for a moment. "Wait here." She levered herself up off the bed and waddled out into the corridor. Freddy stared after her, not knowing what to do. Mel's reaction was . . . useful . . . but it had knocked her off balance. Mel was telling her she did still fit.

Mel reappeared in the doorway, Roland behind her.

"No. *No*," said Freddy, scrunching down onto the bed. It seemed unbearable that he should see her like this. Roland scowled across the room at her. She'd forgotten how angry he had been with her today. They had really been screaming at each other only about half an hour before.

"Stand up, Freddy," said Mel.

"Get him out of here," she whispered, scrabbling in her pocket for her key.

"Rip off the Band-Aid. *Stand up.*"

There was no way out of the room except through the window, and she didn't feel like breaking both her legs. "Traitor," said Freddy.

Mel said, "You're being unreasonable. It's not as bad as you think. Stand up or I'll come over there and *make* you stand up."

"Fine," said Freddy. Everything was hopeless anyway. She swung her legs over the side of the bed and rose.

As Mel had done earlier, Roland started at her feet and moved up to her head. Freddy saw the colour drain from his face. Then the red flooded back. He turned and ran from the room.

Freddy said, "What . . . ?"

"We need to catch him," said Mel. She headed down the hall after him. Not understanding, Freddy followed.

They chased Roland into the kitchen and out the door and into the lane and back to the house on Grosvenor Street, which Freddy hadn't expected to see again so soon. They only caught up with him when he was pounding on the door. "Look," said Mel, "this isn't a good—"

The door opened. Josiah and Cuerva Lachance stood together in the doorway, looking surprised.

"I told you to stay away from them," snarled Roland. "Look what you did!"

"Roland," said Freddy, "you need to listen." But he was turned away from her and couldn't see her talking.

"She didn't have any idea. You did that to her, and you didn't even warn her," said Roland. "She didn't know what you were. You're playing games with us, and all because you're trying to get me to—"

"Don't be stupid," said Mel loudly, ramming into him hard enough to knock him aside. "I told you not to cover for me. I'm not a helpless flower."

Roland glared at her in what looked like genuine bewilderment. "What are you—"

"It's me," said Mel to Cuerva Lachance and Josiah. "I'm the one you're looking for."

"*Stop.* You have *no idea.* It's *me*," said Roland. "I—"

"Come on," said Freddy, moving into his line of sight. "They obviously know by now that it's me."

She'd caught on late, but she thought she could see what Mel was doing now. If Roland had been thinking straight, he would have seen, too.

"It's not you," said Roland. "It's me."

"You don't have to be so self-sacrificing," said Mel. "It's me."

"Cut it out, both of you. I already told you it was me," said Freddy.

"You don't understand," said Roland.

"No, *you* don't understand," said Mel, "literally. Stop talking."

"I don't think anybody understands," said Freddy.

Cuerva Lachance and Josiah looked from one of them to the other. They exchanged glances. Josiah quietly shut the door.

Freddy and Mel grasped Roland by the arms. Together, they towed him off the porch and through the yard and into the lane and back to their own house. When they reached the kitchen, Freddy shoved him down into a chair, and Mel stood in front of the back door so he couldn't escape and yell at the dangerous magical neighbours some more.

"You're crazy," said Freddy. "You can't go telling them you're Three!"

Roland's eyebrows were knotted up in a vicious scowl. To her shock, she saw tears in his eyes as well. "I don't know what that is," he said, his voice wobbling.

He was still mad at her, but there was something else wrong, too. Freddy sighed. "Roland, can we please just not be fighting any more? I haven't been mad at you for over a year. I know that's hard to understand—"

"You travelled in time," said Roland. "So?"

Freddy said, "Why is everyone having such an easy time accepting this?"

"Because I know about them," said Roland, and everything just seemed to spill out of him. Tears whisked down his cheeks. "I knew them when they moved in. I've dreamed about them my whole life. I mean . . . I had actual dreams about them. They weren't always the same. *I* wasn't always the same. I was lots of different people, and I could hear. When I woke up, I forgot what it was like. But I remembered doing it."

He wiped furiously at his eyes. "I know impossible things happen around them. I can accept that. But in the dreams . . . I always felt trapped. I *always* felt hemmed in and trapped and angry. There's some sort of choice, isn't there? Both the options are wrong. They're going to try to make me pick one, and I shouldn't have to."

Freddy said, "They want you to choose between them . . . an order-versus-chaos thing. I think they're pretty powerful. It seems to have some kind of effect on . . . I don't know. The way the world works? It's subtle, whatever it is. But—"

"And you just go and play into their hands," he spat at her. "I warned you, and you didn't listen to me! You—"

"Shut up!" said Freddy. She leaned in towards him; he pressed himself back in his chair, eyes wide. "The next time you want to warn somebody about something, include details!"

"I thought it would've sounded stupid," said Roland. To his credit, he had stopped snarling.

Freddy looked briefly at Mel, who shrugged. "Okay," Freddy admitted, "maybe it would've. But you weren't warning me. You were trying to get me to do what you wanted without telling me why."

Mel moved around so Roland could see her. "You were both being unreasonable imbeciles," she said, and signed, helpfully.

Roland said, "You don't understand—"

"By this point, I understand better than you do," said Freddy. "You can stop panicking. They don't know which one of us it is."

He blinked at her. "How can they not know that?"

"They're not all-powerful," said Freddy. "They've been trying to reason it out, but you haven't given them the usual clues. Of course, now that you've stormed right up to their door and shouted it in their faces . . ."

"I thought they knew," said Roland. He was gradually going pale again. "I thought they were playing games with me."

"I hope we fooled them with our Spartacus act," said Mel, "but we can't be sure."

Freddy had no idea what a Spartacus act was. It didn't seem the time to ask. "You need to calm down until we can decide what's really going on," she said.

"I thought you said you knew," said Roland. The tears were starting again.

"I know some," said Freddy. "I can tell you if you—"

"No."

She opened her mouth, shut it, and opened it again. "What?"

"I said *no!*" Roland leapt to his feet, sending his chair crashing back against the kitchen cabinets. "I don't want anything to do with them. I keep telling you to stay away from them! There's nothing we can do about this but have as little to do with it as possible."

"You mean run away," said Freddy.

"If that's what it takes," said Roland.

"I don't think that's going to work," said Mel. "Cuerva Lachance—"

"Don't talk about her. Don't talk about either of them." He was still crying, but the anger was there, too. "I don't like it that they can get into my dreams. I don't want to give them a chance to force me to do anything. If you'd listened to me in the first place, I wouldn't be in this mess."

Freddy said, "Excuse me? How do you—"

"Just leave. Me. Alone," said Roland. He blundered out into the hall, knocking things over as he went. A moment later, they heard a door slam upstairs.

⌒

He wouldn't come out of his room. Unlike Freddy, he'd remembered to drag furniture in front of the door. They couldn't get in, and he couldn't hear them knocking and calling. "Serve him right if the house catches on fire," said Mel. "What's wrong with him?"

"I think he's panicking," said Freddy. Strangely enough, she could sympathise. She hadn't been any more reasonable when she and Josiah had fallen through time. It was funny, though, how . . . well, how *young* Roland was acting. She was having to struggle not to think of him as Mel's age. In the past, he'd always seemed older than her, even though he was really several months younger.

They left him alone because they had to, but they returned to the room at intervals to see if the furniture was gone yet. It never was. In the meantime, Mel picked up the Coleridge book, which Freddy had put back on the chair in the kitchen. "I want to study the poem you interrupted," she said. "Maybe there's a clue in it." Freddy could have told her there wasn't, but there was no harm in Mel reading the poem. She couldn't seem to do anything herself but pace. Everything was ordinary and strange all at once. She walked all around the house, aimlessly, as Mel set about dissecting "Kubla Khan."

While they were up at Roland's room for the fourth time, they heard a door open and close downstairs—

Mel and Freddy looked at each other. "Who's *that*?" said Mel.

From downstairs, a voice called, "Kids? Pizza for dinner!"

Mel's mouth dropped open in horror. Freddy scrambled to re-member the last time she had eaten dinner with Mum and Jordan. It didn't help that she had lived an extra eighteen months in the interim.

"I was defrosting some chicken," said Mel. "We'll have to cook it later. Why do they want to eat dinner with us *now*?"

They tiptoed cautiously downstairs. Jordan was setting the table; Mum had opened the two pizza boxes. She glanced at Freddy and Mel. "Hi, guys," she said. "Hungry?"

"Uh," said Freddy, standing in full view, feeling huge and exposed.

"We've got pepperoni and Hawaiian," said Jordan. "Take your pick." Mum smiled and helped herself to a slice.

Freddy moved into the room. Jordan looked at her, then back at his plate. "Good day?" he said.

"Uh," said Freddy again.

"Yeah. Absolutely. Good day. How was yours?" said Mel in a chirpy, breathless voice that should have made Mum and Jordan in-stantly suspicious.

"Not bad," said Jordan. "Where's Roland?"

"Barricaded in his room," said Mel. "He can't hear us when we knock, obviously."

"He'll come down when he's hungry," said Mum. "Did you have fun in school today, Freddy?"

"I got beat up in gym class, then again after school," said Freddy.

Both Jordan and Mum turned to look at her properly. "You don't look as if you've been beat up," said Jordan.

"Uh," said Freddy for the third time. Something inside her seemed to be getting more and more clenched.

"You do look a little different," said Mum. "Did you change your hair?"

"Did I what?" said Freddy.

"You haven't dyed it, have you?" said Mum. "You know we don't want you girls doing that."

"No," said Freddy.

"Oh, good," said Mum, biting into her pizza.

"I mean no, I didn't know that. You didn't tell us."

"Didn't we? Jordan, I've been meaning to ask you—"

"*No*," said Freddy, much more forcefully.

"What's wrong with you, Freddy?" said Jordan. "Aren't you going to have any pizza?"

They were both looking at her with concerned expressions. She thought they were just expressions; there was nothing behind them. Mum and Jordan were sitting there staring straight at her, and neither one had noticed she had gained a year and a half in age.

She opened her mouth to say, *What's wrong with you? Why don't you really see us? You don't, do you? You've taken yourselves off into your own little lives, whatever those are, and we're just these . . . extras you happen to have at home. You don't think you think of us like that. You think you're ordinary parents who love us and look after us. You've written this little story inside your heads about how we fit into your lives. And so when you come home unexpectedly with pizza, it seems normal to you, even though we're standing here watching you as if you're aliens because we haven't all sat down to dinner together in forever. And the best part of the whole thing is that you're really seeing me right now—I mean, really looking at me and seeing me—but because you haven't really seen me for months or even years before this, you can't tell that anything's different. You need to start treating us like real people. You need to get mad at us when we do stupid things like barricade ourselves in our rooms instead of coming down to dinner. I mean, it's not as if any of us has ever done anything really bad, but our rooms could be overflowing with drugs and pornography, and you wouldn't even notice. You don't even know who we are. You're terrible parents. You didn't have a right to move on from us when you got divorced. I'm sure you're very busy, but you need to grow up.*

What came out was, "Yeah, okay."

Mel caught her eye. Freddy looked away.

The pizza was surprisingly good.

20

"So," said Josiah the next morning on the way to school, "how'd it go?"

She didn't want to have to deal with Josiah right now. Her stomach muscles had cramped up when she'd seen him waiting for her on the verge of the park. They had all but told him yesterday that they knew who Three was. *Something's going to happen today,* thought Freddy. It wasn't going to be a good something. She *had* to talk to Roland, who had avoided her all morning; he had either left extremely early or hidden in his room until she was gone.

Josiah was still waiting, not very patiently. "You saw," she said, keeping her voice casual.

"Yes," said Josiah, "I saw you all standing on our back stoop, claiming you were Three. What did you tell them?"

"The truth."

He glanced at her sidelong. "I get a funny feeling you know who Three is and have decided not to tell me. Care to elaborate?"

"Nope."

"Oh, *this* should be fun," said Josiah drily. "You've got the wrong idea, you know. There's nothing bad about being Three. It's just one little choice."

"Sure."

"Have it your way." His eyes moved down to her legs. "Nice pants."

Despite the knot in her insides, Freddy felt her lips quirk. She had put her borrowed clothes in the wash, then belatedly discovered she had nothing to wear but her old stuff, which no longer fit her at all. She was wearing her largest pair of jeans. They barely closed at the waist, hugged her hips and thighs so tightly she could hardly sit down, and extended about halfway down her calves. Tight pants were in right now, but not *short* tight pants. She'd briefly considered borrowing something from Mel, but that would have been worse. In a pair of Mel's pants, she would have appeared to be wearing baggy knickerbockers.

"I need to go shopping," Freddy conceded.

She kept an eye out for Roland, but wherever he was, he was doing a good job of staying out of her sight. *He doesn't understand,* she thought as she and Josiah approached the front doors of the school. *He only thinks he does. He's going to give himself away. We have to figure out the Three thing, and then we'll help him with it, but he needs to let us.* She was mildly disgusted when she thought back to what was technically the day before and remembered how furious she had been with Roland. It all seemed kind of overblown now. Okay, he would never be her favourite person, but it wasn't his fault his dad had married her mum. He was just as uncomfortable with her as she was with him, and he'd had just as little say in the situation. It was also disconcerting to think of growing up with Cuerva Lachance and Josiah in your dreams. That would make anybody hard to get along with.

And . . . he had been crying yesterday. She felt strange when she thought about that.

She and Josiah separated to go to their lockers. As she walked down the hallway, Freddy saw heads turning to follow her progress. She didn't think it was her imagination that people often started whispering when she drew near. Impatiently, she looked around for Roland, but he didn't seem to be anywhere.

The first bell rang. She'd forgotten which classes she was taking when. She vaguely remembered having English and PE first period, but she wasn't sure which one she was supposed to go to today. Wait . . . she'd been thumped by Keith in PE yesterday. English, then. She'd forgotten which room it was in. She would have checked her schedule, which was somewhere at the back of her locker, but she'd forgotten her locker combination. *I should have prepared for this,* thought Freddy, standing helplessly in front of her locker. She wasn't entirely sure it *was* her locker. She'd been stupid to think she could just pick up her life where it had left off.

She ended up in the office just as the second bell rang. "I forgot my classroom," she explained to the secretary. "Could I get a printout of my schedule?"

The secretary said, "Couldn't you go to the computer lab?"

"I forgot my password, too," Freddy admitted.

When the blank stare got to be a bit much, Freddy said, "I hit my head really hard yesterday. Ask Mr. Daniels. I went to the doctor, and she said I had a concussion and some memory loss."

The secretary's expression turned a bit sceptical, but she dutifully replied, "Oh, I'm sorry to hear that." She gave Freddy the printout, though not with much grace.

Freddy made it to English five minutes late. Everybody watched her as she entered the room, and a lot of the kids started whispering. Keith had been smiling when she came in; she saw the smile vanish. Freddy went to an open seat near the front of the room and sat down. She nodded at Josiah and wondered if she would be able to give him the slip today.

Mr. Dillon was staring at her as if he didn't quite know who she was. "Sorry," she said.

"Um," said Mr. Dillon, "no worries. Does anyone have anything to say about the poem I asked you to read?"

"I thought it was fascist," said Josiah. Mr. Dillon's eyes shifted nervously to Freddy, but she just sat back and let Josiah get on with disrupting the class. It seemed to be his favourite thing to do. She wasn't really sure what the point was.

There were more whispers and edgy glances on the way to science class. In the classroom, Freddy saw Rochelle frozen, wide-eyed, at her bench. Oh, right . . . she had knocked Freddy unconscious yesterday. "What are we doing today again?" Freddy asked Josiah, who was slumped on the stool beside her.

"I would say I didn't remember, but I remember everything," said Josiah in his favourite world-weary tone. "We're starting a unit on evolution. I can confirm from personal experience that Darwin was right, so it doesn't hugely interest me. Then again, nothing does."

You're not fooling anyone, thought Freddy, though she kept her expression neutral. Josiah knew she knew who Three was.

The look Ms. Treadwell gave Freddy was less vague and more

puzzled than the look Mr. Dillon had, but she didn't comment. So far, no one had. Maybe Cuerva Lachance had been right about people seeing what they wanted to see. Freddy sat through the class, though the lesson seemed abruptly stupid. Ms. Treadwell wasn't telling them anything interesting about evolution; she was framing everything in the vaguest terms possible. Freddy didn't remember grade nine science being this simplistic yesterday.

A few seconds after the bell rang to end class, she accidentally knocked her books onto the floor. Well . . . maybe it hadn't been accidental. Maybe she was ever so slightly hoping Josiah would just leave with the others and give her a chance to slip away. But Josiah waited for her to pick the books up. They were the last two people out of the classroom.

Rochelle and a few of her friends were waiting for them outside. Freddy twitched. She didn't have time for this.

"So you think you can just slap on some makeup and high heels and suddenly fit in?" said Rochelle. "You know we'll never let it work, right?"

Freddy was looking over Rochelle's shoulder for most of this. "Yeah, okay."

"You are such a freak, Freddy," said Rochelle.

"Didn't you say that to her yesterday just before you put her in the hospital?" asked Josiah.

"I didn't do anything to her," said Rochelle, her voice about half an octave too high.

Freddy sighed and finally looked straight at Rochelle. She could do that now; they were almost the same height. Unexpectedly, Rochelle didn't seem angry. She seemed scared. Her face was white and pinched and nervous. "I need to get past you," Freddy said.

"I didn't *do* anything to you," Rochelle insisted. "Admit it, okay? Admit I never touched you."

"But you did. Look, I really need—"

Rochelle shoved her against the row of lockers. "Just admit it!"

Freddy glanced down at Rochelle's hands, still pressed against her shoulders. She removed them with her own hands one by one. Her time travelling had, at the very least, given her the opportunity to build up some muscles.

"I don't think there's any point in me admitting it," said Freddy. "I didn't tell anyone, if that's what's bothering you. I'd like to go now, so if there's nothing else . . ."

Rochelle was staring in disbelief at Freddy's hands, which were holding her own hands easily imprisoned. Freddy gave her a meaningless smile and pushed past her. She couldn't waste time worrying about Rochelle right now. Josiah or no Josiah, she had to find Roland.

"Your approach to social dynamics has shifted," Josiah observed.

"Has it?" said Freddy. "Look, I'll see you later, okay?"

"Oh, no, you'll see me now. I don't know what you're up to—"

"Nothing," lied Freddy blandly. "It's just . . . well, we just spent a year and a half together, didn't we?"

"You're breaking up with me?" said Josiah. "Really? Your gossipy little classmates will be so disappointed. There may be texting."

She stopped in the middle of the hallway and faced him. "I have to go to the bathroom," Freddy announced. "You can't come. If you *try* to come, you may end up expelled, which I know you want, but I doubt you want it today."

"Okay, yes, good point." Josiah threw up his hands. "Do go and pretend to empty your bladder. I'll see you in the cafeteria, which is, I suspect, where you will put your diabolical plan into action."

"There isn't any diabolical plan," said Freddy.

There *wasn't* any diabolical plan. There should have been. Sitting in a bathroom stall, Freddy chewed her lip and ran over her options. Cuerva Lachance and Josiah knew she and Mel and Roland knew who Three was, and it was only a matter of time before one of them slipped up and revealed the truth. *Would that be so bad?* asked the rebellious part of Freddy's brain. She was pretty sure it *would* be so bad, but she had only slivers of evidence that she was right. She *knew* it couldn't be as simple as it seemed. *I mean, what's the point? These two people live for thousands of years, with this one other person being reincarnated again and again and every time having to make one little choice. It's not even a complicated choice. Just: are you on the side of order or of chaos? It can't even make all that much of a difference. It must balance out in the end. Then why do I keep feeling as if it's so wrong? Why does Roland think he's being hemmed in and trapped? Why is Ban sniffing around, flicking mysterious hints at me? Ban is the same person as Cuerva Lachance, so why would she even* want *to do that? Doesn't Cuerva Lachance remember doing that as Ban? She may have attention deficit disorder, but she puts a lot of it on. She really remembers things at least as well as Josiah. Wouldn't she remember being all contradictory?*

"Are you sitting in there musing about how to get the better of us?" asked Cuerva Lachance, who had apparently just materialised in the third-floor girls' bathroom for reasons of her own.

Freddy sighed, flushed, and emerged. She sometimes thought nothing would ever truly surprise her again. "Get the better of you?" she asked as innocently as she could. "Why would I need to do that?"

"Well, it's a mystery to *me*," said Cuerva Lachance, tapping a finger against the brim of her hat. "I have a feeling you may think we're criminal masterminds. Do you? I've often wanted to try being a criminal mastermind, though I've never quite had the opportunity."

"That's nice." Freddy turned on the tap.

"If I were a criminal mastermind," said Cuerva Lachance, who evidently just liked saying "criminal mastermind," "I would call myself Zorbon and grow a moustache. Zorbon is also a good name for a Dark Lord in a fantasy epic. Does your stepbrother play role-playing games?"

Freddy was pretty sure her face gave nothing away as she said, "What? Why?"

"It's just a random and completely innocent question," said Cuerva Lachance. "I found a twenty-sided die under a chair the other day and thought he might have dropped it while he was being terrified in our living room."

"I don't pay very much attention to him. Could you get out of the way so I can dry my hands?"

"With alacrity," said Cuerva Lachance, and moved aside.

"You've followed me to school," said Freddy as she teased out a paper towel. "You've never done that before. Is it going to become a thing?"

"I hope not," said Cuerva Lachance. "I've never been very good at school. I can't go home yet, though. I've misplaced my keys."

"Oh yeah?" said Freddy absentmindedly, drying her hands. She would have expected Cuerva Lachance to have lost interest by now.

"I have a lot of keys. I don't have the least idea what any of them are for. I go out of my way to lose them over and over again, but Josie always finds them and brings them back."

Freddy thought, *The last time she went on about her keys to me was that day in the park when I was ten.*

This time, her face *did* give her away, though Cuerva Lachance was peering into the mirror and didn't see. Freddy threw out the paper towel and picked up her backpack. Inside, her brain was screaming at her. *Cuerva Lachance was the crazy lady in the woods! Why haven't you ever seen that before? It should have been obvious right away; no one talks like Cuerva Lachance.* No one acted like her, either, or was as liable to turn up in the middle of a forest without anybody being able to tell how she had got there. More clearly than ever before, Freddy saw herself running towards that bench. That *empty* bench. *Of course* there had been no one on it when she had sat down.

"I always want to go into the world behind the mirror," said Cuerva Lachance. "Alice didn't explore half the possibilities."

There was no excuse for her not having seen this before, Freddy told herself as she shrugged the straps over her shoulders. Well, okay, it had been four years ago, or five and a half on her personal timeline, and she didn't think about the crazy lady much. She didn't remember what she had looked like at all. The woman's face had been hidden behind hair practically the whole time, and she hadn't been wearing a hat or a trench coat. Even so, she had been Cuerva Lachance.

It *had* been obvious right away. Before Freddy had gone time travelling, she had made her mind slide away from impossibilities.

I hate to bother you, said the annoying rebellious bit of Freddy's brain in polite but sarcastic tones, *but the really important question right now is: does she know? Does she remember being there? Did she mention her keys just now for a reason?*

That's three questions, Freddy informed her brain. However, it had a point. The crazy lady had said, "Whatever you do, don't tell me I've given you that." It didn't make sense. Cuerva Lachance did have a memory. And the key . . . was the key important? Freddy had always thought of it as just a key. It was inconceivable that Cuerva Lachance should have turned up when she was ten, years before she and Josiah had begun to sense Three, just to give Freddy something meant solely to make her feel better. There was yet another something going on here.

Cuerva Lachance could travel in time. Would she give Freddy the key *later*, though still four years ago? Why would she do that?

It had been better, thought Freddy as she sidled away from Cuerva Lachance and back towards the hallway, when the key had been just a key. It almost had to mean something now, and she wasn't sure whatever it meant was going to end up being a good thing. If Cuerva Lachance had had it all along and gone back in time after the fact to give it to Freddy, would the key really be meant to help her? What if whatever way it *seemed* to help Freddy really helped Cuerva Lachance?

It was no good thinking like this. That was the problem with time travel; it turned everything twisty. It didn't help that Cuerva Lachance was involved, as she could make anything mean anything at all.

⌒

"Where's Roland?" Freddy asked Todd and Marcus, who were sitting in the cafeteria, staring at her in disbelief.

It was only afterwards that she realised how many invisible lines she must have crossed. She had walked calmly into the section of the cafeteria usually occupied by the Deaf kids, gone straight up to two boys who were widely known to be geeks, and spoken straight to them as if the three of them were friends. The social implications hadn't even occurred to her. She'd just wanted to find Roland before he did something irreversible.

Todd and Marcus exchanged glances. Todd shrugged.

"No, really," said Freddy, "where is he? I need him."

"Uh," said Marcus, "why?"

"Because I do. Just tell me," said Freddy.

Marcus shot a nervous look out towards the kids who were staring avidly at the lunchtime theatre from seats all around the caf. "Only he specifically said he didn't want to talk to you."

Todd pointed at her hair, her face, her chest, her hips, and quirked an eyebrow interrogatively.

"Haircut. I know he doesn't want to talk to me," said Freddy, "but it's important."

They exchanged glances again. If they did it a third time, Freddy decided, she was going to bang their heads together. "Important, like, as in girl stuff? With boyfriends and clothes?" asked Marcus.

Freddy decided it was her steady, piercing glare that eventually made them both go red. Marcus was fiddling nervously with his plastic fork.

"Do I *ever* talk about boyfriends and clothes?" Freddy demanded when she had reduced the two boys to squirming piles of agonised shame.

"Don't know," said Marcus. "Don't you? Have you ever said two words to us before in your life?"

She probably hadn't. Freddy was becoming less and less sure she liked the person she had been yesterday. For the first time, she really looked at Todd and Marcus, who were over at her house for hours every weekend and tended to pop up frequently throughout the week as well. She'd always thought of them as a sort of collective: Todd-and-Marcus, Roland's geeky friends. They weren't a collective. Marcus was the shouty one with the hearing aid. He put it in every morning before school and took it out once classes started because he found a world with too much sound in it confusing. This was what he'd told Roland, anyway. Roland thought it was because Marcus felt different from Roland and Todd, who were both profoundly deaf, when he wore the hearing aid. Freddy knew this only because she'd overheard Roland telling Mel. Everything else she knew about Marcus was what she could see, which wasn't all that much. She thought he was mixed-race, white and Indian or Middle Eastern, plus tall and skinny and more athletic than anyone had ever admitted. Todd was smaller and quieter. He rarely spoke aloud. She'd seen him signing a lot, though. He had reddish-brown hair and glasses, and he had grown noticeably fatter in the past year or so. And it was stupid that this was all she knew about the pair of them.

"I know. I'm sorry," said Freddy, prompting a third exchange of glances and a signed, *What's happened to her?* from Todd. Freddy tucked her hands behind her back. "And later," she continued, "I'll have a whole conversation with you about it if you really want me to and don't just think I'm boring, but right now, I honestly have to talk to Roland."

They looked at her. She thought about role-playing games and pleasure-domes and desperate battles against tentacled monsters, and she added, "It's a matter of life and death. Sort of like a quest. Um."

"What kind of a quest?" asked Marcus after a moment, cautiously.

"Well," said Freddy, "let's say Roland is hiding a . . . a deadly se-cret that could bring about the end of the world if he, uh, tells it to the wrong person. But he's convinced himself the end of the world is coming anyway, so he's gone all, you know, self-destructive. And I'm the one who has to jump in at the last minute and convince him not all hope is lost."

Todd and Marcus looked at each other yet again, this time because Todd wanted to sign for a bit. It all went a little fast for Freddy, though she caught the initials "GM" . . . game master. Were they talking about . . . ?

"We didn't know you were into RPGs," said Marcus. "Are you and Roland doing a LARP or something?"

Freddy hadn't the faintest idea what a LARP was. "Yeah, or some-thing," she said.

"Cool," said Marcus, and abruptly, he was about a hundred times friendlier. Freddy felt as if she had passed a test. "Roland's eating lunch in the courtyard," Marcus said. "He told us not to tell anybody, but I bet that was part of the game, right?"

Freddy tapped the side of her nose, something she had never done before in her life, and left. Dozens of eyes followed her out of the room. She looked back over her shoulder once, so she knew.

She knew Josiah was trailing her, and Cuerva Lachance could eas-ily have been nearby, too, but as there was nothing she could do about it, she simply walked to the courtyard and tried to pretend she was alone. The courtyard was occupied by the usual tight bunches of smoking Deaf kids, all of whom ignored Freddy as she slipped through the door. It had rained during morning classes. The ground was damp, and little puddles had collected on the benches. Roland was sitting on one of them anyway. He tensed when he saw Freddy, but he didn't get up.

She wiped off as much of the water as she could with her hand and sat down beside him. Roland looked away, and Freddy had to bite back an impatient sigh. For a Deaf person, looking away at the beginning of a conversation was the equivalent of covering your ears and going "La la la la la!"

She touched his shoulder. He still wouldn't look at her. Freddy heard a snigger from a group of smokers. Okay . . . she had been feeling sorry for Roland, but it could only go so far.

Freddy got to her feet, moved around in front of her stepbrother, bent down, took his chin in her hand, and said, "I know you're afraid of what's going to happen. I can help."

She let go and sat down again. There were more sniggers, but Roland was looking at her now.

"I'm not afraid," said Roland.

"Josiah's following me around," said Freddy, keeping her expression casual. "Cuerva Lachance is here, too. They're trying to find out what we know."

"So this is a stupid conversation for us to have. Go away."

"We can be careful," said Freddy. "Look, all I want is for you to agree to talk to me and Mel about it tonight. There's no use in running away—"

"I'm not *running away*. Jesus."

"And you can stop taking everything I say the wrong way, too."

He stood up, forcing her to scramble to her feet as well; otherwise, she would have been left craning her head ridiculously far back. "You know," said Roland, "you're the same age as me, so you can stop acting all superior."

Without realising it, he had handed her a card she could play. "Actually," she murmured, leaning in towards him, "I *used to be* about five and a half months older than you. I was gone for eighteen months. I guess that makes me two years older now. I have more life experience. I know more about what's going on. I've had longer to get over my resentment. My resentment is gone! I'm trying to *help* you, and Mel, and me. So stop . . . being . . . so . . . difficult."

She poked him in the chest, hard, on all the words after "stop." Roland was giving her the same look everyone seemed to be giving her lately: the one that said she had sprouted antlers in the middle of the conversation. "Life experience," said Roland in what he may have meant to be scoffing tones.

"Fifteen wars," said Freddy. "Six revolutions. I was a midwife twice. I've hunted lions. I own a tiny gun that shoots bolts of electricity. If you stop being a dork, I'll let you use it."

Roland stared. "A tiny gun . . . ?"

"Ask me *tonight*," said Freddy. "Not *here*. We'll figure things out together. The sooner you stop thinking of me as the person who insulted you yesterday, the sooner we'll start making progress."

"You didn't change in a day," Roland told her. She *knew* he knew what had happened to her, but she remembered having problems with the time travel herself. It just wasn't easy to wrap your head around.

"You're right," said Freddy. "It took longer than a day. You're going to have to take the short course. Please stop hating me and start cooperating. We'll save a lot of time."

The courtyard was beginning to empty out. Freddy wondered which hedge Josiah was hiding behind. A few smokers were watching them, but she doubted they could see much of what was going on. She kept her eyes on Roland.

"I don't hate you," he said finally.

"You do a little," said Freddy, "and okay, I understand that, but you need to get over it. I *am* sorry for what I said yesterday."

For the first time in weeks—or, for her, years—Roland smiled. It was a pinched, grudging smile, but it counted.

"You don't remember what you said yesterday," said Roland.

"Something something I wish you'd never moved in something something I hope you go blind," said Freddy.

It took her only about a second to see she had made a mistake. She should have pretended she didn't remember what she'd said yesterday. It didn't matter that she was apologising. It mattered that she had said it in the first place. Roland's expression had been opening out; now she saw him close himself off again. "That's right," he said flatly. "You did say that, didn't you?"

"Roland—" started Freddy, but he was already turning away. "I'll talk to you tonight," he said. "But you're not as superior and all-knowing as you think you are. Stay away from Josiah. You're going to be the one who screws everything up. You always are."

She stood there and watched him walk away. There was no use shouting things after a deaf person who wasn't looking at her. *I don't think I'm superior and all-knowing,* thought Freddy, hoping it was true.

21

The rest of the day was agonising. She wanted it to end, and it *didn't*. She may have lived through an extra year and a half the day before, but today felt almost as long, and there wasn't even any ploughing involved.

Math class crawled. Ms. Liu had lost control of the students, and people talked freely over her desperately cheerful explanations of geometry. The only person paying attention was Cathy, who had probably been given a grades ultimatum by her parents again. Freddy noticed that Roland's interpreter was getting visibly frustrated. Roland was forever turning to stare out the window, not the best move for someone who couldn't take in the lecture while looking away from it. He also turned occasionally to glare at Freddy, who was sitting next to Josiah.

"He's going to burn holes straight through my head with his eyes," said Josiah as Ms. Liu wittered on about pi. "I didn't quite catch what you were haranguing him about at lunch."

"He wants a pony," said Freddy. "He claims he would keep it in our backyard and ride it around the park on weekends. It's very sad."

Ms. Liu eventually gave up and just assigned them about twice as much homework as usual, then let them ignore it for the rest of the period. Freddy got through hers quickly. She had a feeling there wouldn't be much time for homework tonight.

She looked up from the last problem to find Cathy watching her.

"What?" said Freddy.

Cathy gave a nervous little giggle that set Freddy's teeth on edge. "You do that so fast. I wish I could."

"It's just math."

"Sooooo, like, Rochelle said she barely touched you yesterday, and you fainted. Is that true? You look okay today."

Freddy kept her face blank. She wondered how long Cathy had been so dim and why she hadn't noticed before.

"Whatever Rochelle says," said Freddy, shrugging.

"Only she thinks you're going to lie to the principal about her. You won't, right?" Cathy leaned forward. "I mean, there's no use getting Rochelle in trouble just because she doesn't want to be friends with you any more. Right?"

Freddy looked at the clock. This period was never, ever going to end.

"Right?" said Cathy.

"I don't care about Rochelle," said Freddy, "okay? If she doesn't bother me, I won't bother her."

"That's perfect," said Cathy. "Can you help me with the first problem? It doesn't make sense."

Between Roland's deadly glowers, Cathy's inane questions about easy math problems, and Josiah's occasional hints that he was on to her, though he clearly wasn't, Freddy felt she was on the verge of genuine insanity. The bell had never sounded so wonderful.

"I notice you haven't been able to get into your locker," said Josiah as they packed up. "Do you even have your flute?"

"I'd taken it home with me. It's in my bag," said Freddy. Out of the corner of her eye, she could see Roland signing viciously at Josiah. She thought she caught a *Stay away from her* and perhaps a *twist your head off,* though the latter was more a spontaneous gesture than it was an actual sign in ASL. A worm of irritation with Roland crept back into her mind. So much had changed for her. Nothing at all had changed for him.

The other flute players watched her warily as she entered the band room. Everyone watched her warily now. The entire school was treating her like a bomb on a timer.

For some reason she couldn't remember at all, she had, on Monday, taken her flute home but left her music folder in her locker. She sat down in her usual spot at the end of the second-flute section. Chin, on her right, was a first flute. She turned to her left. "Can I share with you?" she asked Hubert.

He dropped his instrument. "What? Me?"

"Yeah, I can't get into my locker," said Freddy. "So can I?"

There was a distant part of her that knew this was the first time in her life she had ever spoken directly to Hubert. No one spoke directly to Hubert. He was sort of like an alien. You never knew how he was going to react, so it was safer to pretend he wasn't there. He went beyond Josiah levels of weirdness to an uncanny zone occupied only by the select few. He was far too weird to be bullied. But she needed to share music with someone, and he was sitting next to her, and to be fair, Filbert had been slightly weirder than Hubert.

Hubert, still facing straight ahead, swivelled his eyes around towards her. "Does. Not. Compute. Danger! Danger! Okay, you can share, but don't breathe on my music stand."

"I won't," said Freddy.

She turned away to see Chin regarding her in amazement. "What are you *doing*?" whispered Chin.

"Uh," said Freddy, "sharing Hubert's music?"

Chin gaped at her for a moment, then shook her head and went back to sorting through her own folder.

Band seemed to last almost as long as math. They were doing a medley from *Cats*, and they sounded like, well, cats, though not in a good way. Freddy hadn't practised the flute in so long that her embouchure had turned to mush. She could barely make a sound, and most of the sounds she did make were squeaks. Hubert and Chin winced every time she played. Fortunately, no one else was much better except one of the clarinetists, who had been playing since she was six, and a tenor saxophonist who had, in fact, got rhythm.

Ms. Bains told them to pack up fifteen minutes before the class should have ended. She often did. The unfortunate result was that since even the slowest packing-up job ever couldn't have taken more than five minutes, Josiah had ten more in which to make his usual scene. "How's it going, Keith?" he said clearly, his voice cutting through the subdued chatter. "Thrown anyone headfirst into a wall lately?"

He just never *stopped*. Freddy decided to spend the next little while staring at her watch. The date and time on it were both completely wrong, but perhaps she could will it to force time to move faster.

"Shut up, you freak," said Keith.

"Did I say something problematic?" asked Josiah. "Isn't it funny how even though someone else hit the wall, you were the one who ended up with brain damage?"

Freddy gazed raptly at the watch as Keith threw himself on top of Josiah, who had doubtless known he would. Josiah did like collecting bruises. It was becoming kind of boring. The class dissolved into chaos. Freddy thought she caught a glimpse of Cuerva Lachance's coat swirling past the band room door, but it happened so quickly that she couldn't be sure.

Freddy's inability to get into her locker did leave her with one advantage. She had been lugging her bag and coat around all day, which had been annoying at the time but also meant she *had* her bag and coat and could be out of the school the instant the bell rang. While Josiah was still trying to disentangle himself from both of Keith's fists and a trombone or two, Freddy was dashing across the school's front lawn towards the entrance used by the Deaf kids. She hoped Roland wasn't long.

He wasn't. He must, she thought, have been trying to get home quickly so he could barricade himself in his room again. Todd and Marcus weren't with him. They didn't live as close to the school as Roland and Freddy and had to take public transit to get home.

When Freddy fell into step beside him, Roland threw her a disgruntled glance but didn't comment. He turned very deliberately away from her. The way he kept making sure he couldn't see anything she said was beginning to bother her. She *had* to make him understand about Three, but she wouldn't be able to if he just wouldn't look at her.

She kept an eye out for Josiah, but they seemed to have outdistanced him for now. It was Mel who caught up with them first. She would have had to go several blocks out of her way to meet them on the way home. She was puffing enthusiastically, her face shiny and red. "Did anything happen? Are we in trouble yet?"

"Not yet," said Freddy, "but it's coming soon. He still won't listen."

"I've been thinking about it all day," said Mel, bouncing along beside them, "and brainstorming in my notebook and everything, but there are still big chunks of stuff missing. You told me everything?"

"Pretty much everything," said Freddy, a little guiltily. She hadn't mentioned Mika or Ban. She kept telling herself she wasn't sure why, but that wasn't quite true. The fact that Cuerva Lachance could walk around invisible was bothering her. It was bad enough that they had discussed aloud the fact that Roland was Three. Freddy didn't want to give away *everything* she knew. It was possible the key to this whole situation was in something she had already seen or heard.

Roland was still looking away from both of them. Freddy wondered how he could see where he was going. "Has he been like that all day?" said Mel. "It's denial, isn't it?"

"Maybe," said Freddy. "He's still mad at me. Maybe you can get through to him."

"I'll try," said Mel, but then Cuerva Lachance was there, stepping out of the air in front of them, right in the middle of the park. All three of them stopped together, even Roland, who had been staring off to his left and must only have been able to see her out of the corner of his eye.

"I was in a swimming pool," she said. "Which of you is Three?"

They stood in a row, watching her. Freddy had to stop herself from letting her eyes slide towards Roland. If he gave himself away now, it would be his own doing, not hers.

"Come on. You can tell *me*." She gave her fingers a persuasive little waggle. "I'm very good at keeping secrets. Mostly because I forget them immediately, but nobody has to know that."

The sun was just barely peeping out from behind the perpetual cloud cover. Freddy wasn't sure why she was noticing that. Cuerva Lachance stood in the weak sunlight, smiling and seemingly simply naively interested. Freddy had rarely found her more menacing.

"There are kids in the playground," murmured Mel. "She doesn't . . . do things . . . when people might notice, does she?"

Freddy wasn't sure how she'd given her sister such a wrong impression of Cuerva Lachance. "Josiah isn't here," she whispered back. "Anything could happen." Roland made a move as if to walk on across the park, then stopped again. Cuerva Lachance wasn't a very big woman, but her presence was as solid as a brick wall. All she had to do to hold them back was stand there in her hat and trench coat and not do anything scary.

Freddy heard pounding footsteps on the grass behind her, and she barely stopped herself from turning to look. She knew who this would be. "Damn it, you're slippery," Josiah gasped as he staggered over to stand next to Cuerva Lachance. One of his eyes was puffy, and his nose was leaking blood. His presence, however, seemed to suck some of the tension out of the air. *They're less strong when they're together,* Freddy thought, startled. *They balance each other out.*

"Okay, listen," said Josiah when he'd got his breath back, "it's been fun tiptoeing around each other today and pretending to be all crafty, but we know you know which of you is Three. All we want is for you to tell us so Three can make the choice. It's a pain-less process. It'll be over in seconds. You're being ridiculous; just *tell us."*

"Nope," said Mel, "we'll pass."

He flung out his arms. *"Why?"*

"Mysterious reasons," said Cuerva Lachance. "I like those."

"Not so mysterious," said Mel. "We just don't want to."

"Freddy?" said Josiah.

She shook her head. "No deal."

"But you've seen," said Josiah, exasperated. "The choice is noth-ing. It doesn't hurt Three."

"I still say no," said Freddy, "thanks."

Josiah narrowed his eyes at her, then turned to Roland. "What about you?"

He couldn't have been following the whole conversation, as he hadn't been looking at Freddy and Mel, but he had gathered enough. He said, "Go away."

"You know we can't do that," said Josiah.

"I don't know anything," said Roland, "except that I want you to go away."

Josiah and Cuerva Lachance looked at each other. Again, there was that odd sense of something relaxing, becoming less dangerous. They should have seemed *more* dangerous when they were working together, but it was just the opposite. Rain was beginning to mist down over the park, sparkling in the sunlight. Freddy looked for the rainbow and found it arcing over the trees.

Cuerva Lachance smiled again. "All right."

Mel, predictably, was the one who gave away her surprise. "All right how?"

"All right." Cuerva Lachance flung out her arms in a woebegone gesture. "You win. We give up. It's all over. Alack the day. We shall never learn who Three is. We shall go far, far away and weep on an iceberg, just because we can. I hope there are squirrels on our iceberg. Life is less colourful without squirrels. Come on, Josie, dear; let's crate up the grand piano."

"Alas," said Josiah in wooden tones.

Mel opened her mouth. Freddy's elbow shot out and clipped Mel on the shoulder. Two days ago, she would have been aiming for her sister's side, but the extra height had caught her off guard. Ignoring Mel's yelp of pain, Freddy said, "Okay."

This time, it was Josiah who betrayed surprise. His eyebrows shot up. "Really?"

"Yep," said Freddy. "You want to go. We want you to go. Everybody wins."

"And you believe us when we say we're going?" asked Cuerva Lachance, doing her habitual head tilt.

"Let's pretend we do," said Freddy.

Mel opened her mouth again. This time, Freddy smacked her on the back of the head.

"Fine," said Josiah. "Let's go home and pretend to pack up all our worldly belongings."

"Fine," said Freddy. "Let's go home and pretend to let our guard down."

Freddy, Roland, and Mel stood together and watched Cuerva Lachance and Josiah walk across the park towards the house on Grosvenor Street. "They're going to outsmart us," said Mel.

"I think so," said Freddy, "but why do they have to? What's so urgent about getting Three to make that choice?"

They turned to Roland, who had, at last, been looking at them as they spoke. "Any ideas?" said Mel, signing along.

His face had again drained of colour. "You shouldn't have talked to them at all. You keep making that mistake. I've changed my mind. I'm not going to talk to you about this tonight . . . or ever. We can't *talk* about it! We have to treat it as if it's not real!"

"Cally and the couch," said Mel. Freddy nodded.

Roland blinked. "What's Cally and the couch?"

"We had a cocker spaniel," said Freddy. "She died when I was nine. She used to hate baths. Whenever someone said the word 'bath,' she would jump up on the couch and bury her head in the cushions. You can't see me . . . I'm not here." She had the uneasy feeling she had once behaved like this, too, but there was no use in worrying about that now.

"You're being just like Cally," said Mel. "This is happening, Roland. Ignoring it doesn't make it not be happening."

It should have worked, and maybe it would have if the story hadn't been about a dog. "So now you're comparing me to your *cocker spaniel*," snarled Roland. "Thank you very much. It's nice to know you care."

He turned and took off across the park, through the gentle rain. "Great merciful Zeus," said Mel, "I used to think he was reasonable. Why's he acting like this?"

"He's scared," said Freddy. And then she realised: it was another clue. As far as any of them knew, Three really did just have to make a tiny little choice. Few of the Threes Freddy had met, pre- or post-choice, had seemed to have much of a problem with this. But Roland saw the choice as a trap. Maybe it was. Maybe his dreams, whatever they were, had told him something Freddy couldn't know yet. Claire had had dreams, and she hadn't wanted to choose, either.

"We've *got* to talk to him," she said.

But they couldn't. He had barricaded himself in his room again. Freddy banged on the door for a while, just to relieve her feelings. He may not have been able to hear it, but maybe, she thought sourly, he would feel the house shaking if she thumped viciously enough. Until he accepted what was happening and dealt with it, they were stuck.

22

She had another dream herself that night, but she could never remember afterwards what was in it except that Ban and Filbert were featured. They were both trying to tell her something immensely important, but their voices were drowned out by the organ music. There was organ music all through the dream, crashing like waves, overwhelming everything.

Freddy opened her eyes. Just like last time, the music was real. Cuerva Lachance was at it again.

She had stumbled out of bed and down the stairs into the hallway before she realised something wasn't right. She shouldn't have been the only one. Cuerva Lachance had played at night more than once, and every time, she had brought the entire family, with the occasional exception of Roland, out of bed. Jordan had never tried to call the police after the first time, but there had always been a certain amount of swearing and complaining and going out into the yard to yell uselessly at the tower. It was impossible to sleep when the organ was sounding. Only Roland had ever been able to manage it. It had all happened quite a long time ago for Freddy, but she didn't remember Mel ever accusing her of sleeping through a midnight concert. It couldn't be done.

And yet the house was perfectly still. Even Jordan, who could be counted on to go ballistic at the faintest hint of chiff from next door, hadn't stirred.

Freddy crept back up the stairs. She cracked open Mel's door and flicked the light switch. The light stayed off. Dimly, Freddy could see the outline of Mel's bed, rumpled but flat, unoccupied. She began to be aware of her heart thumping in her chest.

She moved to Roland's door, which she half expected to be barricaded still. It wasn't. The light didn't work here, either, but again, she could see there was no one in the bed. Down the hall to Mum and Jordan's room . . . and once more, no one.

The organ music was making her head go fuzzy; it was hard to think. Were they all outside already? Or had something worse happened? Were they next door? Had Cuerva Lachance and Josiah got to them? Why weren't the lights working? Through her mum's door, she could see the computer's power bar blinking sleepily. There was electricity but no light. She was alone in the house, and something was very wrong.

She went back to her room. Forcing herself to be steady and methodical, she got dressed in the first thing she could find, which turned out to be her time-travelling outfit. It looked a little odd in twenty-first-century Canada, but it was designed to look a little odd everywhere. That didn't matter at the moment. She picked up her bag as well. Yesterday, she had felt naked without it. It had been her companion for so long that it was reassuring to loop its strap across her body, even if it didn't truly hold anything that could help her. She slipped her keys into the pocket she had sewn into her tunic in the seventh century AD in the land that would one day be known as Brazil, and she walked back out into the hall and down the stairs to the kitchen. The music was still everywhere. Freddy thought she recognised "I Am the Very Model of a Modern Major-General," which Mel occasionally liked to sing. She opened the kitchen door.

Aside from the organ music, the night outside was as still as the night inside. There was no breath of wind. The streetlights on Grosvenor and Elm shone into the yard, and the clouds glowed faintly with the radiance of the city. As Freddy moved out into the lane, she saw that all the other houses were dark. That was wrong. The neighbourhood always ended up in a blaze of light when Cuerva Lachance played the organ after midnight. *Was* it after midnight? Freddy hadn't checked the time. The lights hadn't worked in her house. Was it the same in the other houses? Why had the light on the power bar been shining if the light switches had done nothing? Her head was going fuzzy again. She thought she might be panicking now, but there was anger there as well. Cuerva Lachance and Josiah could play their little games, but they had no right to kidnap her entire family. Why had they left her behind? She couldn't think properly with the music this loud.

She ran through the backyard of the house on Grosvenor Street, right to the porch. No one was in sight. The house itself was as dark as all the other houses. The music played on, evolving from Gilbert and Sullivan into something in a minor key. Freddy, panting, grasped the doorknob. She wasn't expecting much, but the knob turned, and the door opened. Trying not to think about what she was doing, she stepped inside.

She thought she could just barely recognise the contours of the kitchen, but it was hard to be sure. The room had been taken over by the spider plants. In the faint light that trickled through the windows, Freddy saw what looked like a jungle made up of snaking, sinuous trailers with little baby plants sprouting at their ends. There shouldn't have been movement. *Baby plants,* thought Freddy, *sure, but they look like spiders, don't they?* She could hear nothing but organ music, but out of the corner of her eye, she could *see* something scuttling. Slowly, carefully, Freddy shifted her bag around in front of her and eased out the microgun. She didn't know how much it would help against mobile spider plants, but it felt better to have something in her hand.

Something brushed against the top of her head. Freddy reached up with her left hand, and her fingers closed on a writhing bundle the size of her fist. She flung it across the room. The jungle came alive. Plant-spiders erupted from the undergrowth on all sides while trailers whipped across her face and tried to twine themselves around her legs. She flung her right arm across her eyes and lurched forward. "Don't make me shoot you!" she shouted. She couldn't even hear her own voice above the screaming notes of the organ. Plant-spiders crawled onto her tunic, heading for her face. She squeezed a bolt out of the microgun, and it crackled through the kitchen, crisping leaves and tendrils. Plant-spiders tumbled to the floor and dived for cover. A trailer sneaked around her neck. She tore away from it, staggering through the last of the jungle to the living room door.

A few plant-spiders followed her in, but they seemed more docile here, out of their element. This room belonged to the chairs. Not entirely unexpectedly, they, too, had come to life. Freddy glared at them. She had lived in this house for weeks, and she didn't find it all that difficult to adjust to the strange things it did. "No. Just no," she told the chairs as they edged closer to her, their seat covers curling back to reveal the rows of teeth beneath. "I'm sorry, but I've seen scarier. Is there any point to this, Cuerva Lachance? Oh, and now the piano's going to eat me, too?" It was creeping through the chairs, crouched on its rollers, like a very bulky tiger hunting in the grass.

The anger was getting more acute. It just about did in any lingering fear. Freddy shoved three or four slavering chairs aside and slammed her hands down on the keys of the piano. All she could think of to play was "Chopsticks," but she played it as vengefully as she could. She could even almost hear it over the roaring of the organ. "There," Freddy screamed at the piano and the organ and anything or anyone else who may have been listening. "You want music? Here's some music for you. Everybody's playing music now! *Shut up!*"

The piano looked at her sheepishly without eyes and slunk off into a corner. Freddy kicked some more chairs aside and headed into the hall, then up the stairs, which kept trying to tip her off. She had to put the microgun back in the bag so she had both hands free. It was a bit of a struggle to squeeze past the phone booth that kept phasing into and out of existence, and she nearly stepped on a rat in a waistcoat and trousers, but she knew they were just some more of Cuerva Lachance's figments, and she pushed on through, finally gaining the landing.

The corridor had split in two. Both branches were littered with small somethings that glittered in the light coming from somewhere or other. Freddy crouched and scooped up a handful of whatever was in the first corridor. The whatever pricked her palm gently in several places. She found herself gazing down at a tangle of what looked like the kind of pins she'd had to use in her textiles class last year. She ducked into the other corridor and came up with a handful of needles. "I know this is symbolic," Freddy howled at the walls, "so watch me not caring!" A wolf wandered up to her and sat down, its tongue lolling. She flung away her handfuls and, randomly, took the needles path, scuffing aside the needles with her boots so they wouldn't go straight through the soles. She didn't look back to see what the wolf did.

The corridor *was* a path now. It twisted on through what could have been a forest, lurking in what could have been moonlight. One of the most frightening things about the house on Grosvenor Street was the way it wasn't always possible to tell what was in it. Settings would shift or just remain ambiguous. Something heavy was forcing itself through the maybe-trees. Again, she couldn't hear it, but she could catch the movement on the edge of her vision. She sighed. The organ music was getting no louder and no fainter. "That's *enough*, Cuerva Lachance!" said Freddy. "Where are they?"

Her left foot came down on needles; her right foot came down on sand. Freddy stood blinking in what most people would have been fooled into believing was sunlight and gazed out on what those same people would have thought was a desert. Freddy knew it wasn't. It was foreshortened. Though the sand stretched away into the distance, the distance was very close by. The light had no heat to it, and the sand beneath her boots had the consistency of wet clay.

The organ music stopped. Josiah stepped out from behind a rock that hadn't been there a moment before.

Freddy had thought the anger she'd felt at Ban after her adventure in the medieval dungeon had been the worst possible, but it was dwarfed by what she felt now. "You let her do this?" she said. She was impressed at how calm she sounded. "It doesn't seem like your sort of thing."

"It isn't, believe me," said Josiah, "but sometimes, it's more productive to give her relatively free rein."

The chill started at the base of Freddy's spine and worked its way upward. "Why? What did you do with my family?"

"Do you care? You don't seem to have all that much to do with them." Josiah was leaning against the rock. She struggled across the sand towards him. Walking here was surprisingly difficult.

"They're *my family*," said Freddy.

He began to tick them off on his fingers. "Well, you've got your mother, who talks to you about once a month, and your stepfather, who bonds with you only in the wee hours when he's yelling at Cuerva Lachance. I presume you have a father as well, but since I've never once heard you mention him, I couldn't say for sure. You take your sister for granted and treat your stepbrother as an interloper, and in the last day or so, your relationship with them has involved you bullying them into seeing me and Cuerva Lachance as some sort of threat. And now you've come storming over here to get them? Is it just the possessiveness, or do you, quite unexpectedly, have a heart of gold? Tell me; I'm interested."

She glared at him. *He's right, you know,* said the contradictory, rebellious, incredibly annoying portion of her brain. Freddy snarled it aside. Maybe she did treat her family badly. It didn't matter. If Josiah tried to hurt *anyone* in her family, she would kill him. She had spent eighteen months travelling through time, and she had never even considered not going back to them.

"Stop trying to misdirect me," said Freddy. "You've done something to them, haven't you?"

"No."

"I don't believe you."

He shrugged. "Pity. I'm telling the truth. They're at home in bed. The point isn't where they are. It's where *you* are."

Cuerva Lachance was there, melting out of the air on Freddy's right. Everything seemed to go slow. Freddy thought afterwards that it was because in reality, everything had gone very, very fast. Cuerva Lachance pulled a pair of handcuffs out of her pocket and snapped one of the cuffs onto Freddy's right wrist, which she yanked over so she could snap the other cuff onto the left. Freddy tried to jerk away and slammed into Josiah, who tore the bag off her shoulder, snapping the strap. Cuerva Lachance pushed her back against the rock, and a rope came twining out of it and wrapped itself around her torso. She held her arms free just in time, but since her wrists were locked together, that didn't do much good. The rope had the strength of dried cement. It pinned Freddy firmly to the rock.

"What are you doing?" she gasped. The rope was cutting off half her air; it was hard to get any words out.

"I'm being pragmatic," said Josiah, dropping the bag on the ground, out of reach. "Cuerva Lachance is just playing with the nature of reality for fun."

"It's very educational," she said, nodding. "Josie doesn't usually give me this much leeway."

"What you thought you saw—and heard—in your house tonight wasn't what was happening," said Josiah. "Think of it as a sort of nightmare, if you like. As far as everybody else was concerned, there was no organ music, and the lights worked perfectly. You saw the beds as empty, but they weren't. That was inspired, by the way," he told Cuerva Lachance.

"It just sort of happened. It was an idea I had," she said.

Freddy was becoming aware that she had been very, very gullible. She still wasn't sure why it mattered. "Okay, nicely done," she wheezed. "You caught me. What's the point? Are you going to *torture* me into telling you who Three is?"

"We don't need to." Josiah sat down in the sand, which bounced a little. "We know it's not you. I figured that out while we were travelling together; you just don't fit the profile. You're smart and innovative, but you don't have all that much of an imagination. It's down to the other two. Mysteries and role-playing games, isn't it? Unusual but workable. They're going to tell us which of them it is."

Her brain was catching up. "This is a trap."

"You think?"

"That's stupid," said Freddy, struggling for air. "Even if they realise where I've gone, they're not going to come running over here for me. Mel's more practical than that, and Roland doesn't even like me."

"That's not the point," said Josiah. "They're both sure you're the key to them getting out of this. I'll bet you keep telling them you all have to talk about it, don't you? And I'll bet you've held some details back from them so they *have* to depend on you for the answer."

Freddy stayed prudently silent.

"They'll come looking for you because they think you have information," said Josiah. "When they notice you missing—which will be very soon—they'll panic. They'll be sure we're making our move. Whichever one it is will be desperate for help."

"She *does* have information," said Cuerva Lachance, beaming towards the bright spot of light that wasn't quite the sun.

"She . . . what?" said Josiah.

"She knows, or she will soon. I remember being Ban. I gave her hints," said Cuerva Lachance.

Josiah gaped at her. "Why would you do that?"

"I don't know," said Cuerva Lachance, rubbing her hat in a puzzled sort of way. "High spirits?"

He scrambled back to his feet. "But then—"

"Why do you think I said we should call her in?" said Cuerva Lachance. "It's not a bluff. A day more and she'd have spilled the beans to Three. She *is* the key."

Freddy didn't feel like the key. She *didn't* know . . . did she? Could it be she really had all the clues she needed? She'd thought maybe she was getting closer earlier, after Roland had panicked and run home across the park, but she hadn't put the clues together yet. Why had she held things back from Mel? Was Josiah right that she'd just been trying to make herself important?

She shoved aside the growing shame. At least Cuerva Lachance and Josiah had finally admitted there was something to find out. "I don't know what you think I know—" she started.

"Save it. You're not going to catch us that way," said Josiah, "obviously. You're less cunning than you think you are."

I doubt it, thought Freddy, keeping her face stony. *And I'm more imaginative than* you *think I am.* One of the things she'd noticed about Josiah was that he wasn't particularly good at figuring out when people were hiding things. Everything about him was out there on the surface, and he assumed everything about everybody else was, too. Cuerva Lachance knew about hiding things, but she didn't really pay attention, and she missed details. Josiah thought Freddy was less cunning than she thought she was and less imaginative than she thought she was, but really, it was he and Cuerva Lachance who were less *powerful* than *they* thought they were—

That was it. That was the beginning of the answer. She was sure it was. She couldn't let on that she knew.

"I'm not cunning," said Freddy. "I have no idea what you mean."

Cuerva Lachance, looking straight up at the sky, said, "Then why don't you want to tell us who Three is?"

"Because I *do* know you haven't told me everything," said Freddy. "It's all less . . . innocent than you say it is. I just don't know why."

"She knows," said Cuerva Lachance, beaming.

"We can't give her a chance to tell them," said Josiah.

"Of course not," said Cuerva Lachance. "But I was a Girl Guide once. I came prepared."

Freddy felt the rock shift behind her head. A second later, something else had shot out of it and around towards her face. She tried to pull herself away from it but couldn't. Desperately, Freddy clamped her mouth shut. It didn't do any good. Tendrils of . . . whatever it was . . . forced themselves between her lips, then her teeth. She felt her jaw being winched open, and she choked, but the tendrils stopped before they reached her throat, instead weaving themselves into a ball within her mouth. More tendrils fused together over her lips, gagging her. The gag held her head to the rock as firmly as the rope did her torso.

"Breathe through your nose," said Josiah. "If Three comes through, nobody's going to get hurt."

If she got free, she thought, she would hurt *him*. It was the first time in her life she had ever sympathised with Keith. Josiah and Cuerva Lachance walked away behind the rock. She tried to shout after them, but her voice came out muffled and weak. A moment later, she was alone in the house on Grosvenor Street, in a part of it that couldn't have existed.

⌒

Time passed. She had nothing to do but think, so think she did. If she couldn't accomplish anything else, she could solve the puzzle.

The thought she'd had before had been about power. She was sure Cuerva Lachance and Josiah weren't as powerful as they seemed. Cuerva Lachance could . . . well, she could do this to the house on Grosvenor Street. Josiah could *stop* her from doing this, which was a different sort of power. They did influence the world. They did, somehow, balance each other out. But there was something skewed about the way they presented themselves and their relationship with Three. Something backwards.

Backwards.

Tied firmly to her rock, straining to draw enough air into her lungs, Freddy remembered. Ban. Ban had said everything was backwards. Maybe Freddy should have been thinking along those lines, but she hadn't trusted Ban. And yet there were other clues, too, things that were inconsequential in and of themselves but that resonated with that idea of backwardness. Freddy drew a shallow breath in, let it out. Ban in the jungle: *The girl is, as you put it, Three, though that's a bit of a misnomer, I should say.* Mika telling the story, seeming to call Cuerva Lachance and Josiah out of the air as she did. Other tiny things, hardly noticeable. Ban saying Three's uncle thought she had been calling down demons. The boy in the cave being visited by Māui. Sam Coleridge annoying Josiah by steadfastly refusing to see him as anything but a fairy. Bragi standing up to Loki in the hall. Filbert avoiding the question of where the future Josiah and Cuerva Lachance were, holding her knowledge, whatever it was, effortlessly over Josiah's head.

Freddy blinked and nearly forgot to breathe, though she desperately needed more air. Everything *was* backwards. Cuerva Lachance and Josiah acted as if they were the ones with the power, but they weren't, were they? It was Three. It *seemed* they were the dominant ones, but they couldn't have been. Three shouldn't even have been called Three. Mika had been able to control them; she had been One. Calling her—him—Three was just another misdirection.

They want the Threes to think of themselves as inferior, thought Freddy. *As third, not first. Why?*

"Have you got it yet?" asked Ban, poking her head up out of the sand. Freddy glowered down at her.

"Yes," said Ban, "of course she knows I'm here, but she also knows I don't stay to help. I'm just popping in for the sake of drama. I have no idea how this is all going to turn out. I'm sure it will be very exciting."

Freddy thought inaudible swear words at Ban. She was getting tired of being surrounded by impossible people.

"If I helped," said Ban, "she would remember helping, and she would come around the rock and stop me. So I can only urge you to hurry up. Time is passing; the others will be here soon."

Freddy made an inarticulate noise in the back of her throat.

"I think so, too," said Ban. "If you'll excuse me, I must go. I'll just go talk to you in the past for a bit, and then it's time for stories around the cooking fire. I never miss that." She sank back down into the sand and vanished.

Furious with herself and Ban and Roland and Josiah and Cuerva

Lachance and the world in general, Freddy strained uselessly against her bonds. Ban pretended to be helpful, but she wasn't. It was just more mind games from Cuerva Lachance. It was just more—

—stories . . . ?

Freddy squeezed her eyes shut. Stories. She *knew* about the stories. Everywhere Three was, there were words, shaping stories, shaping history, even, sometimes. Bragi had changed everything by standing up to Loki with a poem. Ling had stopped a slaughter by telling her people what they believed. The boy in the cave had actually talked to a character from one of his own stories. Mika . . . Mika had done something very strange with her story. Freddy did know about the stories, but she hadn't thought about what they meant.

Josiah never wanted to talk about the stories. She'd pieced that bit together for herself. He didn't like talking about Cuerva Lachance's figments, either, and they were mostly characters out of stories . . . like Māui, now that she thought of it. She had seen Three's connection to stories again and again, but she should have thought more about Josiah's attitude. He'd always been cagey about it. She'd known he was trying to direct her attention away from something, but she hadn't been sure what. She thought now that he hadn't wanted her to think of Three as a storyteller. In particular . . .

. . . He didn't want me to think of Three as his *storyteller . . . and of him as a story . . .*

Ban had asked Josiah and Cuerva Lachance—no, wait, Josiah and Loki—what they had done to reality. They had turned it inside out. She'd been wondering about certain inconsistencies in Josiah and Cuerva Lachance, but she'd been thinking of them as cosmic forces at the time. What if they weren't cosmic forces? What if Mika *hadn't* called them out of the air? And the choice . . .

Freddy opened her eyes. The air in front of her was twisting out of shape. As she watched, Mel fell out onto the sand, a plump little ball in bunny-rabbit pyjamas. Roland, fully dressed, stumbled to his knees just behind her. And she knew why Roland shouldn't have to make his choice. And she had no way of telling him she did.

23

"Freddy!" Mel bounced to her feet and ran across the sand, or tried to. What actually happened was that she jogged in place as if there were a treadmill hidden beneath the desert. She was absolutely white in the face. "The spider plants came to life and tried to kill us, and there were chairs with teeth, and the piano turned into a house on chicken's legs! Where did you *go*?" It was the only time Freddy could remember Mel ever sounding anything like her actual age.

"Stop running. You're not going anywhere," snarled Roland. He was almost as pale as Mel, and there was a long tear in his left sleeve.

Josiah came out from behind the rock, Cuerva Lachance on his heels. "I see you got our message."

Mel stopped abruptly and accidentally by bumping down onto her rear end. "It was hard not to, what with all the crows coming in through our bedroom windows and all."

"Let her go," said Roland. Freddy felt herself turning red. She'd never had an urge to be a damsel in distress, and she didn't see why she should start now.

"Sure," said Josiah. "When you tell us who Three is and make your choice."

"What'll happen if we don't?" said Mel.

"What do you think?" Josiah nodded at Cuerva Lachance.

She smiled. "He lets me do what I want sometimes. Terrible things may happen. It's also possible I'll just go sit in a meadow for days. You never can tell."

"I'm banking on the terrible things, though," said Josiah quickly. "I expect they'll happen to Freddy."

"I thought you were supposed to be her friend," said Roland. Freddy tried to waggle her eyebrows at him. She had known almost since they started time travelling that Josiah wasn't exactly her friend. They got along surprisingly well: much better than she and Rochelle ever had, if she was going to be completely honest with herself. But she couldn't trust him.

Josiah hesitated briefly before answering. "She's fun, but this is more important."

"Maybe Freddy's Three," said Mel.

"Sorry. Try again," said Josiah, sounding bored. "We know it's one of you two. Just confess and make the damn choice already."

"We keep telling you," said Mel, "no."

Josiah nodded at Cuerva Lachance again.

As far as Freddy could see, she didn't do anything at all. However, the rock holding Freddy was alive now. There was no transition between it being a rock and it being . . . something else. It breathed in, contracting the rope holding her in place. Another rope emerged from the rock and wrapped itself around her neck, cutting off her air completely. She raised her bound hands to pull at it, but it was as hard as the rock itself.

Roland and Mel were both shouting at Cuerva Lachance, but since they were doing it together, Freddy couldn't tell what they were saying. Tendrils of red were creeping across her field of vision as everything went fuzzy and dim and far away.

"All right. *All right*. It's Roland," said Mel.

The rope relaxed. Freddy drew a painful, ragged breath in through her nose.

Roland didn't notice right away what had happened. But Cuerva Lachance and Josiah were both looking at him now. He turned to Mel. "I'm sorry," she said and signed. Freddy could see a tear trickling down her cheek. "They were killing her."

Roland glared across the sand at Freddy. "I knew you would be the one to screw up. I told you."

She couldn't even shake her head at him; she was held too firmly in place. *Don't make the choice,* she thought, wishing she could pour the words directly into his brain. *Don't make it! If you do, you really will be Three. There's no such person as Three!* She couldn't pour the words directly into his brain. She squirmed. He was nearly sneering at her now. He thought she had ruined everything.

"Don't worry about her," said Josiah. "You know she's been exaggerating, don't you? It's just a little choice. Me or Cuerva Lachance. It hardly means anything at all. One of us will be slightly dominant for the space of your lifetime. That's all it is. We do it because we always have."

You haven't *always done it,* thought Freddy. *Roland, develop psychic powers* now, *please.*

"She hasn't told me anything," said Roland. "I haven't let her. I'm not going to make your stupid choice."

"Yes, you are." Cuerva Lachance gestured towards Freddy. "Human beings are very fragile, aren't they?"

"You're bluffing," said Roland. "And we're leaving. Come on, Mel."

He turned around. The desert turned with him, leaving him still facing towards Josiah.

"We're in control here," said Josiah, "or hadn't you noticed?"

They're not. It's what they want you to think. Stop listening to them!

She had to get through to him. It was stupid that she had the answer and had got herself all trussed up like some dimwitted princess in a fairy tale. She had let Cuerva Lachance put handcuffs on her, for crying out loud. Why had she done that? What was wrong with her?

Never put handcuffs on an angry teenager.

It was a sentence from her past. It came out of nowhere and hit her right between the eyes. She blinked. She had said that . . . the crazy lady in the woods. She had said it right before she had given Freddy—

She stopped breathing, this time of her own accord. The crazy lady had given her a key.

Slowly, gently, Freddy began to move her bound hands towards her tunic pocket.

"We can stop you from leaving," said Josiah. "We can trap you here forever if we like. This is our domain, not yours."

"It's just an ordinary house," said Mel. "Roland, think of it as an ordinary house."

"That won't work," said Josiah a shade too quickly. Freddy didn't think it *would* work, or not entirely. It was obvious that the house on Grosvenor Street wasn't an ordinary house any more. But Mel had the right idea. It was too bad she was still thinking about the situation backwards. Freddy's right hand slid into her pocket. The angle was awkward, but she could just barely hook her fingers around her key ring. Careful not to let the keys jingle, she drew them gently upward.

"Make the choice," said Cuerva Lachance. "It's all perfectly natural. And I never say that, so you know it must be true."

"The second you make it, everything goes back to normal," said Josiah, signing simultaneously. "All three of you go home. School happens tomorrow as usual. Maybe I'll finally manage to get suspended. You can play games with your friends and draw swords on your homework. Can't you see there's really nothing sinister about any of this?"

"Sure," said Mel, "which is why you have my sister tied to a rock and keep threatening to choke her."

Don't draw attention to me, Mel. The keys were held firmly in her fist now. She sorted through them with her pinky finger. She could have found the key she wanted in her sleep.

"I hate you all," said Roland.

Josiah shrugged. "Hate us all while making the choice."

Freddy had located the key. She eased it down between her fingers, letting it poke out into the air. Still moving as slowly as she could, she brought it around towards where she hoped the keyhole on the left handcuff was. She couldn't move her head to see.

"I've had dreams about you," said Roland, his voice rough. "Over and over. I was all these different people."

"He's one of those. Interesting." Cuerva Lachance sounded quite friendly about it.

"But I always felt the same in the dreams," said Roland. "Trapped. Forced. The choice is more than you're saying it is."

"It's not, honestly," said Josiah. "It's just one little choice."

"I won't make it."

"Then Freddy will stop breathing again. And I'm sure we can find something to do with Mel as well."

The sand around where Mel was sitting began to bubble in an ominous way. Freddy felt the key catch on something.

"Stop it," said Roland. "Stop hurting them!"

"When you make the choice," said Josiah. "We're getting tired of waiting."

Roland's face was twisted into the sulky scowl Freddy had always hated, but now she looked past the expression and saw fear there, too. Something inside her felt very strange. She had gone running off without a thought to rescue him. He had gone running off without a thought to rescue her . . .

He was going to do it. He was going to have to, or he thought he was. Judging by his loathing of Josiah, Freddy thought he might choose Cuerva Lachance, and she really didn't know what that would mean for her and Mel.

The key slid into the lock and turned. The left handcuff fell open. She wasn't quite sure this was a good thing. It was Cuerva Lachance who had given her the key.

She had seconds, if that. She could try to tear off the gag, but frankly, she could have done that with the handcuffs on; she hadn't bothered because the gag, like the neck rope, was as hard as stone. There was really only one thing she could usefully try: one thing that not a single person here would even suspect she *could* do.

If I do that, she thought, *he'll know* . . .

The faint vestiges of the old anger stirred briefly. It felt like a reflex. *Shut up with the stupid pride already,* Freddy told herself. She shoved the keys back into her pocket.

Roland's eyes had been wandering desperately from Cuerva Lachance to Josiah to Freddy and back again. She waited until they fell on her, then raised her hands.

Freddy signed, clumsily, *Don't make choice. You . . . GM. They . . . NPC. Everything backwards.*

She had no idea if she'd got the signs right. She had no idea if he'd understood. She hadn't been able to say what she'd wanted because she hadn't known the sign for "storyteller," but she thought maybe the gaming terms would work better with Roland anyway. She saw his face change, his eyes widening in astonishment as he realised what she was doing. She had never signed to him before or let on she understood what he was signing.

Josiah and Cuerva Lachance had seen, too. "Damn it," said Josiah, "how did she . . . ?"

The rope around her neck contracted. "Freddy!" said Mel, seeing her struggle to breathe. Freddy brought her hands up to tug at the neck rope, but once more, it was too solid to move.

"Backwards," said Roland. "NPC?"

They're non-player characters, Roland, Freddy thought. Everything was going red and black again. *Will you please do something about that now?*

The world was fuzzing down to nothing. People were yelling at each other, but very far away. Freddy thought her eyes might have closed at some point; she wasn't quite sure where she was.

She was on the ground. She didn't know how that had happened. Someone was thumping her on the chest. Freddy choked, then breathed.

"Get up," said Mel. "Get up, get *up*. It's not over."

Freddy opened her eyes. "What . . . ?" she croaked. The gag was gone. She sat up. Her throat felt bruised.

"He made Cuerva Lachance let you go," said Mel. "With his brain. But they're fighting back . . . both of them."

Freddy glanced over at Roland. Around him, the desert boiled. Cuerva Lachance was standing on top of the rock, her coat blowing wildly about her. As Freddy watched, her hat was whipped away into the crackling sky. Roland said, "This isn't happening. You're not doing anything. Get down from there!"

"Of course this isn't happening." Josiah was standing about twenty feet from Roland on a perfectly flat, perfectly still stretch of sand. He sounded bored. "How could any of this be happening? You must be going mad. It's the only reasonable explanation."

Mel stood and held out a hand to Freddy. Unsteadily, Freddy tottered to her feet. The landscape was twirling around in dizzying circles. "I'm going to throw up," said Mel in thoughtful tones.

"No," said Freddy, forcing the words out past the pain. "Stop looking at it. Come on."

They struggled over towards Roland. "Oh, you can't do *that*," said Josiah.

Roland followed his gaze. "Yes, they can. Freddy, roll a d20 for initiative."

She stared at him. "What?"

"You said GM and NPC! You've got me thinking in those terms! I can't help it!" he said frantically. "You can sign! How can you?"

They needed to have a conversation. There was way too much for them to say to each other. They couldn't have a conversation *now*. She shrugged impatiently. "Okay, yeah, right, *never mind*. You're the storyteller. They're the story. Stop letting them control you!" she screamed over the rising wind. They had reached him now. The sand swirled up around them, vicious and stinging.

"Spot check. Spot check," said Mel, pointing. Josiah was wandering towards them. Where he stepped, the heaving desert went calm. The sky was turning to knives somewhere above.

"You're not a storyteller," said, and signed, Josiah. He hadn't raised his voice, but it came clear and loud above the wind. He had cleared the air in front of him so Roland could see him signing. "You have one function only. You know you get into trouble when you listen to Freddy." Freddy thought it was a mistake. When Cuerva Lachance and Josiah tried to work at the same time, they cancelled each other out.

Freddy grasped Roland by the shoulders, spun him around, and hollered right into his face, "You should have been listening to me all along. You're giving them too much power! You *created them!*"

He stared at her. "I never."

"Thousands and thousands of years ago," said Freddy. "You told a story, and they were born. It was a story about how the world was created, so you gave them a lot of power, but they were still *yours*. They've always been yours! Life after life, they convince you you're Three, and the choice makes you seem . . . third. Less important. They're just stories, Roland!"

"The stories are killing us," Mel pointed out. "Somebody needs to do something before we drown in impossible sand."

"There's nothing you can do except make the choice." Josiah was very close now. Roland wasn't looking at him.

"I can't do it. I just make role-playing games. I'm the wrong person.

They're far more powerful than I am," said Roland, tears spilling from his eyes.

She shook him. "You stupid idiot," she shouted, trying to ignore the sand scraping her throat. There was no use in shouting at Roland, who would have understood to the same degree if she had whispered, but she couldn't seem to stop herself. "Do you know how many times I've met you, all through history? You've been leaders and poets and all kinds of things, and you've always been more powerful than you thought. You were Bragi Boddason. You were *Samuel Taylor Coleridge*, for crying out loud!"

Roland, trembling, looked to Mel for help. "You know," she said, "the pleasure-dome guy."

Roland gulped. "I . . . I was *him*? I don't . . ."

"You were him," said Freddy.

"I remember that poem," said Roland. "I used it."

"Well, use it again."

"Really, really quickly," Mel added, "pretty please."

Josiah had reached them. "Stop this nonsense," he said, laying a hand on Roland's shoulder. But Roland couldn't hear him.

Roland said:

> *"In Xanadu did Kubla Khan*
> *A stately pleasure-dome decree:*
> *Where Alph, the sacred river, ran*
> *Through caverns measureless to man*
> *Down to a sunless sea."*

The pleasure-dome built itself across the sky.

It was crystal, Freddy thought: a strange, impossible multifaceted crystal sparkling into existence in the middle of the sandstorm. It cut off the wind. Cuerva Lachance yelped and slid down off the rock, her trench coat torn to tatters by the storm she had herself been stirring up. The few remaining rags of the coat fluttered down onto the sand. But the sand was going, too. Freddy felt grass springing up beneath her feet. Hedges, half wild, half cultivated, erupted out of the ground and wove themselves into mazes. Josiah was knocked aside by one, dragged away into greenery. The crystal dome turned the air to rainbows.

Freddy saw her bag lying not far from her on the grass. She picked it up. "Stop this," said Josiah from somewhere in the middle of a bush.

"I like it. It's pretty," said Cuerva Lachance. "I'm still generally opposed, you understand."

"Mel, don't forget you're a cleric," said Roland, watching Freddy pull the microgun out of her bag. "Freddy, I think you'd better be a fighter."

"This is game stuff, is it?" said Freddy. "What does a fighter do?"

"A fighter fights," said Mel. "I have magical powers, but I haven't got any spells prepared. But, I mean . . . is this really going to work?"

"I say it is. It's my story. Use the spells you had prepared for our next session," said Roland.

"You're thinking too logically," said Freddy, cocking the gun.

"No," said Roland. "The game has rules. I think stories do, too."

"But—"

Mel cut her off. "He's right. There needs to be a mixture. If we're too logical about this, we let Josiah in. If we cut too many corners, we let in Cuerva Lachance."

Freddy opened her mouth to protest, but then, oddly, she saw

Roland as she had always seen him: as someone neat and messy at the same time, someone who put everything in order but threw it into chaos simultaneously. He had always been a mixture. It still didn't entirely make sense to her, but maybe he was right. They needed to treat this as a story, and stories had structure *and* creativity. They couldn't just throw random bits of plot around and hope they did something useful.

"They're NPCs," said Roland. Freddy thought he was talking to himself. "Just NPCs . . ."

"Not truly," said Cuerva Lachance, floating across the ground towards them. "We've become very real over the millennia. You lost control of us long ago. I think it's fantastic."

"We built our own rules to compensate," said Josiah. He was still trying to fight free of his bush, so Roland couldn't see him. Mel signed a translation. "We do better that way."

"Yeah," said Freddy, "and you basically convince all the Threes that they're your . . . well, that they're your thralls. Don't you?"

"Why shouldn't we?" said Josiah, his voice clipped and sharp. "Why should we be *their* thralls? That's what you're trying to make happen, isn't it? I won't be turned into a puppet!"

He tumbled free of the bush, rolling out onto the grass. "I should have thought you would understand," he spat straight at Freddy. "You lived in our house for weeks. You saw them."

Mel and Roland turned to look at her. "You saw who?" said Mel.

The figments. She had seen them all through the house. Josiah hadn't liked even to acknowledge they were there.

"There were . . . sort of fictional characters walking around all the time," said Freddy. "But they weren't very real."

"We attract them," said Josiah. "You thought it was Cuerva

Lachance creating them, but it wasn't. They turn up wherever we live because they think we're like them. Well, 'think' is the wrong word. They're mindless. People tell them as stories, so they float around like . . . like ghosts."

"There's always been something different about Three," said Cuerva Lachance. "Something stronger. Josiah tells me you saw the first Three. I don't remember that far back, but I think . . . we hadn't become entirely real yet then."

"We made ourselves real. It wasn't Three's doing," said Josiah.

"But Three did make you," said Freddy. "You have no right to . . . to break free like this."

Josiah applauded, his face twisted into a sarcastic scowl. "Oh, *nicely* done. What *beautiful* hypocrisy. Aren't you the one always whining about how you hate being restricted because you feel trapped and fated when you're travelling in time? And now you want us to go back to not being real people? Doing what *he* tells us to do . . . thinking what he tells us to think?"

"If the alternative is you strangling me with a living rock," said Freddy, "yeah, I do."

They were dangerous . . . weren't they? Roland had kept telling her how dangerous they were. The thought of unreal people who had somehow broken into reality having as much power as Cuerva Lachance and Josiah was kind of terrifying. Dimly, she remembered Filbert and the other future Threes. Josiah and Cuerva Lachance had apparently not been around in the future. Was it because of what happened here and now? Could Roland tame them or even destroy them?

Did she want him to?

"Then you're worse than I am," said Josiah. "And we're not going to let you do it."

"Snakes," said Cuerva Lachance, grinning. The ground began to writhe.

"I cast 'Protection from Evil.'" Mel's voice came out as a squeak. Freddy thought they were just words until she saw the blue glow starting at the tips of Mel's fingers. It coiled out and around Mel, then Freddy and Roland as well. Mel may not have been expecting the spell to work; she gazed at her hands in amazement. Freddy's feet left the ground. She looked down. Beneath her, what had once been grass was a slithering mass of bodies.

Roland roared, "Yea, slimy things did crawl with legs upon the slimy sea!"

They were on a boat . . . a little sailboat about twenty feet long. The pleasure-dome still stretched above, but they were being knocked about by the waves, which were teeming with strange, slippery creatures. The waves were eerily silent. Back on her feet again, Freddy staggered and faced Roland. "Slimy things . . . ?"

"I don't know. I think it's a poem. It may be Coleridge. A different poem, not the first one," said Roland. His words came out breathless and panicky. "There are all kinds of things in my head."

"I think you need to go beyond Coleridge," said Mel. "Use your own imagination."

"But I just read the manuals," said Roland. "I don't really make stuff up."

"That's not true, and you know it."

"And even if it is, *learn how*," Freddy shouted as Cuerva Lachance sent the boat racing up the side of a monstrous wave. Freddy leaned into the railing as the deck threatened to turn into a wall.

Roland was sliding towards the mast. "I don't know what to do.

This has to be structured like a story or it won't work. But they're still controlling everything!"

"They're not," said Mel, clinging to the railing and trying, with limited success, to sign one-handed. "This is your world; you made it. They're making you *think* they can control it."

"Watch," said Freddy. There was something she hadn't done yet: something she knew she was going to do because she'd seen the evidence of it four years ago. She might as well use it as a demonstration.

Lurching against the trembling boards, she ran at Cuerva Lachance. No one had been expecting her to do that. Cuerva Lachance threw up her hands as Freddy brought the handcuffs, still dangling from one wrist, around in an arc. The free cuff caught Cuerva Lachance on the cheek, digging a groove in her flesh. She had already been off balance; now she cried out and fell down. "They can be hurt," Freddy screamed back at Roland just as the boat topped the wave and began to dive down its other side, sending everyone not clinging to something sliding back down the deck's suddenly reversed slope. "They've made themselves too real. If this is a story, hurry up and write the climax!"

"Climax," said Roland, gasping a little. He had anchored himself to the mast. "I can do that. I can—"

"Oh no," said Mel. "All Roland's climaxes have—"

Something erupted from the ocean so violently that it sent a concussion through the air. The ship twirled and plummeted away from the abruptly flattened wave, smashing into the surface of the sea. Freddy was knocked down beside Cuerva Lachance. Side by side, the two of them looked up . . . and up. After that, they looked up some more.

24

"Tentacles?" said Cuerva Lachance. "Really?"

"Big tentacles," said Freddy. "Extremely big and twisty tentacles."

"They make good final monsters," said Roland a little too calmly.

Josiah said, "*This* is why we don't leave the Threes in charge. *This* is why we need to control them with the choice. Do you understand yet, ducklings? Isn't it fun what an unfettered imagination can do when it's capable of making stories come to life?"

The tentacles kept rising, as silent as the sea. Freddy wasn't sure how many there were, but she also wasn't sure it mattered. They blocked out the pleasure-dome. They were going to fall on the boat and sink it. The boat wasn't moving much at the moment, but she thought that may have been mostly because Roland was so focussed on the tentacles that he had forgotten about everything else.

She stood. A second or so later, Cuerva Lachance did as well.

"Roland," said Mel, "did you have to?"

"I didn't know what else to do. It just happened. There are always tentacles." He looked thoroughly awed by what he had created.

Freddy said, "Well, make them go away."

"He can't," said Josiah. "He's just the storyteller. He's written them in. Immediately writing them out again would be cheating." He looked sourly at Roland. "But he can tell *us* to stop them."

Everyone turned to Josiah.

"Isn't it obvious?" he said acidly when they wouldn't stop staring. "I thought you'd figured it out. It would be a masterful plan if it wasn't so obviously a complete accident. Oh, gosh, *look* . . . giant tentacles! We must all work *together* to defeat the scary monster! And gee willikers, wouldn't it just be easier if we let him tell us how the story was supposed to go? Like, I don't know, we were *characters*?"

He scowled blackly at the tentacles writhing overhead. "In case you hadn't noticed, we're in *his* world now . . . first the pleasure-dome, then the slimy sea. *This* is what the choice is for: convincing Three he doesn't have access to this kind of control. When he brought Leggy there into existence, he pulled us right inside his story. It's like being caught in a tightening noose, isn't it?"

"I don't see—" started Mel.

"*The story tells us what we have to do,*" Josiah said. He turned furiously to Freddy. "It's like time travel! That moaning you did about fate. Well, being trapped in someone else's story is worse. You don't think for yourself. You don't think at all. You do what the story tells you . . . what the author makes you. That's what the tentacles are for."

The tentacles were beginning to curl down towards them. They were so dense that it almost seemed as if night had fallen.

"He's right," said Cuerva Lachance, "unfortunately. Three's already started writing us again."

Freddy thought she saw. The story Roland had created was herding them all in one direction: they had to fight the tentacles. They had to do it his way. Mel and Freddy did, too, but they weren't fictional; it didn't mean the same thing to them. The story was in control now. Cuerva Lachance and Josiah were being shoved back into it.

She should have felt glad about that. She wasn't sure she did. She remembered what the time travel had been like.

"So we've won," said Mel.

"I don't care," said Josiah.

Mel opened her mouth but didn't speak. Freddy felt her throat constrict. Abruptly, she knew what was coming.

Josiah shrugged, his eyes hard and cold. "I don't care how the story goes. I won't go back to being . . . *that*. Fight the damn squid monster yourself. I'm done."

"It's going to squash us all," said Freddy.

"I've lived for thousands of years," said Josiah. "I've never been squashed before. Bring it on."

"I've got to agree," said Cuerva Lachance. "Better horrible mangled death than mindless puppetdom. Or was that the other way around?"

"Roland," said Freddy.

He was white and clenched. "I can't stop the story. It's a *story*. It . . . I tried just to wish us out of here, and I couldn't. We have to follow the rules if we want to get to the end."

"Not all stories have happy endings," said Mel. "Josiah—"

"No," he said. "If I'm going to be killed, I'm going to be *real* and killed. And the story will end *my* way."

He meant it. Freddy had never seen him mean something so completely.

The tentacles were twisting down towards them, probably quite quickly, but the world had again gone slow. Freddy thought of how she had always known Josiah had been hiding something from her. She thought of how frightened he had seemed in the future when he couldn't find his other self. She thought of Roland feeling hemmed in and trapped . . . of herself feeling hemmed in and trapped. Of, now, Josiah and Cuerva Lachance feeling the same way. She thought of Ban. Ban had said everything was backwards, but *she* hadn't been a puppet; she had been just as much a real person as Cuerva Lachance was now.

"I don't know what to *do*, Freddy!" Roland nearly wailed.

It had to be possible for Three to keep the power and Cuerva Lachance and Josiah to stay real. *In the best stories, the characters aren't predictable. They do unexpected things. They defy the author. They seem alive* . . .

Freddy thought about stories. She thought about the kind of stories Roland told.

"PCs," said Freddy, and signed it.

Roland said, "What?"

"Your kind of stories. That game. The story doesn't always go the way you want," said Freddy, "since other people are writing it with you. Like Mel and me now. Do they have to be NPCs?"

Roland's eyes were widening. "But if I lose control of them again . . ."

"No, she's right. You still control the story," said Mel, "mostly. Let them be PCs."

"Now," said Freddy. "Roland, now!"

A tentacle thrice the width of her body was scything through the air towards them.

"PCs, then," said Roland, and turned to Cuerva Lachance. "Okay?" Josiah said, "What—"

"Do try to keep up, Josie, dear." Cuerva Lachance turned on her heel and leapt for the tentacle.

She changed as she went. Freddy saw a blurred mass of black feathers and talons connect with the tentacle, then continue to transform, shredding itself into a sucking, twirling hole in space. Roland and Mel hadn't been expecting that. Both of them stepped back, and Mel clapped her hands over her mouth. "She does things. Just let her," said Freddy.

Mel shook her head. "You're in the story, too. Freddy, stop forgetting about that gun thing."

"Good point," said Freddy. She squeezed a bolt at the next descending tentacle. Lightning crackled up its length; it whirled away from the boat and plunged into the water. Belatedly, Freddy wondered if it was really a good idea to use an electricity-based weapon on a boat in the sea. "Don't worry about it. Way ahead of you," panted Mel, whose fingers were glowing. "Protection spell. Keep firing."

Freddy glanced at Roland. He was cringing on the deck, completely helpless. "You're writing the story," she screamed at him. "Do something!"

"I'm not a character," he screamed back. He tucked his arms over his head.

Josiah, in the meantime, had mostly been standing there looking stunned. Freddy tapped him on the back of the head with the base of the gun. "PC. Player character. You're not a mindless puppet. Will you please do something now?"

He locked eyes with her. She held his gaze as firmly as she could. She saw suspicion give way to a grudging, reluctant belief. They trusted each other sometimes. They had bounced through history together, over and over. He knew how she felt about time travel.

"Player character," said Josiah, "fine," and went to work on one of the tentacles in his own way.

"You can't exist," he told it drily. "Obey the law of gravity, won't you? I tolerate this kind of thing from Cuerva Lachance, but from you, it's absurd. Pull yourself together and start taking physics into account."

"You're going to make it fall on us. You're insane," said Mel as Freddy squeezed off another bolt.

Josiah's tentacle was trembling. Cuerva Lachance's had vanished into some sort of vortex. Flowers were growing on another one. "One at a time isn't good enough," said Mel. "There are a hundred of the things. He does this in every game. It's all one creature. We need to aim for the head."

"Classic zombie tactics," said Josiah, "got you. Cuerva Lachance!"

There was no reply. A tentacle roared past, snapping the mast. The whole boat jolted, and everyone fell down. "Damn it," said Josiah, "she's gone completely unpredictable. She does this when I stop paying attention. Cuerva Lachance, we need you to *aim for the head!*"

"Did someone want me? I was counting things. Then I got bored. Then I went to Egypt. Then I got bored again. Why does that one have a gun?" said Cuerva Lachance, who was now standing on the deck with them, looking in exactly the wrong direction.

"Will you concentrate?" Josiah inquired with brittle, exaggerated impatience. "On the tentacles? Behind you?"

"Oh!" She turned around. "I remember that from ten seconds ago." Three of the tentacles turned into what appeared to be pasta and fell, steaming, into the boat.

It all got frantic. Tentacles shot down from the sky. Everything smelled strongly of rotting fish. Freddy squeezed out bolt after bolt; finally, her gun sputtered and died. She looked around for the others but could see only Josiah scrabbling at a tentacle with his bare hands as it fought to lift him into the air. Freddy threw the gun aside and leapt for the tentacle, not sure why she did. A few minutes ago, she had been almost willing to let Roland turn Josiah unreal.

She had underestimated the tentacle's size and strength. It curled around her as well, seemingly without effort. "Freddy, what are you doing?" Josiah gasped. Then both of them were high above the sea. Fighting to free her arms, Freddy saw the world tilt dizzyingly. "Just hang on," she said.

"Do I have a choice?" he said. The tentacle whipped them back and forth beneath the pleasure-dome. Freddy's stomach tried to rise into her throat.

Their tentacle, still high in the air, slowed and stopped. It seemed to be taking a break. "The others?" said Freddy, yanking one arm free.

Josiah was squeezed up against her. "No idea. I saw Mel a minute ago. Your stepbrother's a psychopath, incidentally."

"I think he's just overreacting to everything right now. But we have to find some way out of this."

"The fun bit is that it may kill *him*. Then we'll truly be stuck here, except maybe for Cuerva Lachance."

"But he created it," she panted. "He should just kill it. Why doesn't he?"

"He has to follow the story. He told you. Look out . . . here we go!"

The tentacle plunged downward. It was a little too obvious why. "There's got . . . to be . . . some sort of mouth . . ."

"There," screamed Josiah. "Right in the middle! Teeth! There!"

The creature's mouth was half the size of the high school. The teeth were as big as houses. Aim for the head? If this was the mouth, the head wouldn't have even felt a bolt from her gun. The stench of the mouth was unbearable. "You're *not real*," Josiah was howling at the creature. "I refuse to be eaten by something that doesn't exist."

Someone screamed from below.

They looked. Mel was clinging to one of the teeth. "Freddy," she was shrieking. "Grab a tooth as you go past!"

"It's making it drop us that's the problem," said Josiah. "We need something to stab it with."

"Oh," said Freddy.

For the second time in the last fifteen minutes, she pulled out her keys.

The creature dropped her first, then Josiah. Freddy landed firmly on a tooth, but Josiah almost went straight into the maw. He would have done so if Freddy hadn't caught his arm as he tumbled past. Clinging to her, he dragged himself to relative safety. Mel was on the tooth next door. "Roland?" said Freddy.

"I don't know," said Mel.

"What are we supposed to *do*?" said Josiah.

Mel said, "Isn't it obvious?"

They looked at her. The creature juddered, and Freddy was nearly flung clear of her tooth. Josiah growled, "No, it's not obvious. Nothing is ever obvious with you."

"Cuerva Lachance can beat it," said Mel, "or she could if she wasn't surrounded by logical people. We're holding her back."

"Do you want the entire universe to turn into raspberries?" said Josiah. "We *have* to hold her back."

"No," said Mel. "We have to set her free. Roland set up an impossible story. He didn't mean to. But there's no way out without cheating."

"I thought we had to follow the rules," said Freddy. "I thought it was the only way."

"It is for us," said Mel. "It isn't for her. That's her character. That's what she's *for*."

Freddy and Josiah looked at each other. Tentacles writhed overhead, but the creature didn't appear able to sense their current location. They still couldn't hang on forever.

"Listen," said Josiah. "What happened to the house earlier . . . that was Cuerva Lachance let about a tenth off the leash. For this to work, she needs to be off the leash entirely. Anything could happen. *Anything.* Balance will be lost. You need to be prepared for that."

Freddy and Mel nodded. "We understand," said Mel.

"Then hang on."

He closed his eyes.

For a moment, Freddy couldn't figure out why he had done that or what seemed wrong about it. Then she knew. She had never— *never*—seen him close his eyes before, not even to blink. The closest he had ever got was letting various people punch them, and even then, he had been able to see through the slits. Something shifted in the air around them. Even the creature, seething and moaning beneath and all around, seemed to hesitate for a moment.

And Cuerva Lachance was there, her clothes torn to ribbons, her hair over her face. "This hasn't happened in a while," she explained in a voice that was far too cheerful. "No peeking, Josie, dear."

The world went strange.

⌒

Freddy was walking down a road, Roland at her side. It was winter. Her mother's funeral had been the day before. Mel had cried. Freddy hadn't. She hadn't really spoken to her mother in nearly twenty years.

Roland stopped in place and signed, *I think you're in denial. You need to see that.* The argument had been going on for some time.

She looked at him. He was about forty now, tired-looking, with a sparse black beard. *I'm not in denial,* she signed. *We never had anything to do with each other. Most of the time, she didn't remember I existed.*

Was it all her fault? Did you ever even tell her you had a problem with the way she treated you? I don't think she knew she was doing anything wrong.

"Oh," said Freddy, "and it was my job to tell her? She should have seen it herself."

"Not everyone is good at seeing things," said Roland.

Seeing things. The words tripped a memory, vague and far away. "He closed his eyes," said Freddy, then wondered why she had.

Roland's own eyes narrowed. "Who did?"

"Josiah." It was a name from her childhood; she hadn't thought about it in years. She hadn't remembered she'd ever known a Josiah. There was something tragic about the thought of Josiah closing his eyes. Unexpectedly, she felt the faint prick of tears. No. She hadn't cried for her mother. Why should she cry at a name from long ago?

She didn't cry. She looked at Roland and knew he thought she was the coldest person he had ever met. She *didn't* cry, and she didn't care.

Her right hand shot into her pocket, groping for something that wasn't there. Keys? She kept her keys in her purse. Freddy blinked furiously against the tears and tried to force her brain to work properly. She couldn't let herself cry. Why couldn't she?

She signed, *What happened back then? I can't remember.*

The story didn't end, signed Roland. *It's still going. It's been going ever since. Josiah still hasn't opened his eyes.*

She saw a boat on an impossible sea and a forest of tentacles boiling into the air. She saw herself firing a gun. "It doesn't matter," she said. "We went on from there."

He shook his head. "The story went wrong. Didn't it?"

"The time is out of joint," said Mel from behind Freddy. She turned. Mel was twelve years old, dressed in bunny-rabbit pyjamas.

Freddy said, "Oh cursed spite, that ever I was born to set it right."

"Shakespeare," said Mel. "You've never read *Hamlet,* and yet here you are quoting it. You two need to regress, and fast. Remember where we really are."

"You can't be real," said Freddy. "I'm dreaming. We've just been at a funeral."

"Josiah still hasn't opened his eyes," said Roland. "It means something. I wish I knew what. No, I don't. I don't know. Where did you leave the car?"

"It means we're still trapped in an imaginary world inside the house on Grosvenor Street." Mel crossed her arms and came as close to glaring as she ever had. "This is all just the house on Grosvenor Street. Something's tricked you into thinking you've grown up. None of this is *happening*."

The boat and the sea and the sparkling pleasure-dome. "It was all out of a poem," said Freddy. She groped for the key again. It should have been there. She thought back to her mother's funeral and saw Mel in bunny-rabbit pyjamas, bouncing along beside the coffin. Again, there was a prickling behind her eyes.

Roland massaged his temple with his fingers. "It was 'Kubla Khan.' Why do I think that matters?"

"Stop being so stupid." Mel actually stamped. "I can't believe you're both being so stupid! We have to make Josiah open his eyes! Getting him to close them was only the first part! Do you want all this to turn out to be real?"

"Isn't it?" said Roland.

Now Freddy could remember the funeral going wrong. At the burial, skeletons had danced up out of the graves. Freddy's mother had clambered from the coffin to join them. The minister had been made of glass. Everything was changing inside her head. "Roland's telling the story. Is he? He needs to end it!"

"Look." Mel flung her hands out towards the landscape surrounding them. "Look at where we are."

She had thought it was snow. It was just . . . white. They had been walking down a road through nothing, not a road through winter.

Freddy felt her carefully constructed past collapse inside her head. She was forty years old, and she didn't know why.

"I take back everything I've been saying," said Roland. "I won't look."

"You never wanted to," said Mel. "You need to *want to*. For better or for worse, you're at the centre of all this. Snap out of it. He needs to open his eyes."

"It started with the poem," said Freddy, struggling. "It should end with the poem. How does the poem end?"

"It doesn't. You interrupted it. You *remember* interrupting it," Mel told her. "But this is where it stops:

> *"Could I revive within me*
> *Her symphony and song,*
> *To such a deep delight 'twould win me,*
> *That with music loud and long,*
> *I would build that dome in air,*
> *That sunny dome! those caves of ice!"*

"No," gasped Roland, "stop. Stop! I can't do it. I don't know how. We were at a funeral. It's too late. I'm afraid . . ."

But Mel continued, inexorably:

> *"And all who heard should see them there,*
> *And all should cry, Beware! Beware!*
> *His flashing eyes, his floating hair!*
> *Weave a circle round him thrice,*
> *And close your eyes with holy dread*

For he on honey-dew hath fed,
And drunk the milk of Paradise."

"We're still under the dome," said Freddy, feeling as if she were forcing the words out through deep water. "We're still in the house on Grosvenor Street."

Tentacles snaked out of the whiteness. "No, Roland, stop it," said Mel. "Cuerva Lachance changed that. But now you need to bring Josiah back. He's stuck at the end of the poem."

"Anything can happen." Freddy heard her voice growing younger, softer. "And one of the anythings is that he doesn't know when to open his eyes."

"I don't want to go back," said Roland in anguish. "I don't want it not to be too late. I don't know what's going to happen next."

In Freddy's head, the funeral dissolved into a carnival on the third floor of the house on Grosvenor Street. The carnival was getting scary. Cuerva Lachance was moving through her mind, changing everything. She saw her mother's coffin floating in the middle of the carnival. The tears were back again, stinging, for a different reason.

It was Roland holding them here. She couldn't imagine how afraid he must be.

"Nobody ever knows what's going to happen next," said Freddy. "But we need to find out."

He was breathing very quickly. She held his gaze as long as she could. It was hard; tears were blinding him. She felt the tears she had been struggling to hold back herself well up again. For the first time in years, one slid free, trickling down her cheek.

Roland nodded slowly and took a deep, shaky breath. "Weave a circle round him thrice . . ."

He was growing younger now, too. The pleasure-dome was building itself again over their heads. The tentacles were melting away, but Cuerva Lachance was everywhere, dangerous and unchecked. Everything could change again. The world wasn't stable.

"I made her a PC," said Roland. "I won't go back on that; it wouldn't be fair. But where's Josiah?"

"In the poem," said Mel, "since that's how you started it. 'Close your eyes with holy dread,' right?"

They looked.

A lake of fire had bubbled up out of nothing. Josiah knelt on an island at the centre, huddling against the flames. The only way across was . . . Freddy blinked, trying to clear her vision. For a moment, the dancing rainbows from the prism of the pleasure-dome seemed to have become intertwined with the fire of the lake, twisting their way into a seething, ever-changing bridge made of colour and light. She blinked again, and it was only a rope bridge after all, just on the verge of catching fire. "I think time's stopped for him," said Mel. "I think strange things happen when he closes his eyes."

"Cuerva Lachance must have done the lake," said Freddy.

Roland, fourteen again, nodded. "One of you needs to wake him up. I'm sorry," he said as they turned to him, "but I'm just telling the story. You're right—I have to finish it—but I have to do it with the characters I have, and that's you. We have to go back to the logic of the story, or we'll be playing into her hands."

It was only then that Freddy really saw what Roland and Mel had kept trying to tell her about the story's rules. *Weave a circle round him thrice* . . . the man in the poem wasn't random at all. He was the poet. And he could imagine the hell out of the pleasure-dome, but he also had to be controlled. It was the most frustrating balancing act she had ever heard of. Like . . . like . . .

"Rope bridge," said Freddy.

Roland spread his hands. "It's never easy at the end."

They approached the bridge. It was just three strands of rope at different heights. "If we fall in . . . ?" said Freddy.

"You die." Cuerva Lachance had slipped into existence beside the lake. "I don't terribly badly want you to wake him up."

"You're cheating," said Mel.

"I'm Cuerva Lachance," said Cuerva Lachance. "And I do terribly badly want you to wake him up."

"Which is it?" said Freddy.

"Both. Neither. Who can tell?"

Mel stared at the fire. Her eyes were so wide that Freddy could see the whites showing all around the irises. "I'll do it," she said in a trembling voice.

Freddy said, "Mel—"

"Everyone's done something important but me. I should go," said Mel, and moved towards the bridge.

Freddy shoved her sister aside.

Her heart was thundering in her ears. The rope bridge was scary, but it wasn't anywhere near as scary as the thought of Mel falling into the fire. She could see a man lying dead in a jungle, bleeding into the undergrowth; she could see a boy lurking alone in a cave. She could see herself walking down that road with Roland, the funeral behind them. She could feel herself refusing to cry. She knew she took Mel for granted. Thinking of her dying made Freddy's throat constrict, cutting off her breathing as completely as the rope had earlier.

"You stay back," Freddy said. "I've travelled in time. This should be a cakewalk." She didn't believe that. She stepped onto the bridge.

Heat blasted up from below. *It's just a cliché,* Freddy thought as she shuffled along the bottommost rope, her hands wrapped firmly around the topmost. *Just a stupid cliché . . . the kind of thing you would find at the end of an action movie. You've survived wars. You can survive this.* She wished she felt more in control. Roland had some control, and Cuerva Lachance, at the moment, had more. Freddy was just a character. She thought she might even be a character in a poem that didn't have an ending. It was her fault it didn't. *And there's another poem in here, too . . . the slimy things upon the slimy sea. Don't think about the slimy things!* Shuffle, slide, pause. Shuffle, slide, pause. She was about halfway across, and nothing terrible had happened yet.

"Freddy," screamed Mel, "she's burning the bridge! *Hurry!*"

Freddy risked a glance back. Cuerva Lachance was at war with herself. One hand was glowing with flame, the other glistening with water; she was flicking them at the rope bridge in turns. "I don't know what I want! It's worrying!" she said. Mel threw herself at Cuerva Lachance but went right through her. Freddy turned back to the task at hand. Shuffle, slide, shuffle, slide. No time for pauses now.

The middle rope fell away. Freddy hadn't been using it, but she didn't like to see it go. Roland was screaming now, too. *They're just kids,* thought Freddy. *They don't need to see Cuerva Lachance burn me to death.* The unexpected anger at this thought propelled her along through three more shuffle-slides. Her palms were slippery with sweat. She didn't want to think about what would happen if one of the other ropes went.

"She's almost through the bottom rope," howled Roland. "Jump!"

Freddy looked. She was three feet from land. She took as firm a grip on the top strand as she could and sidled very quickly along the bottom one. A foot from the island, she felt it give.

Freddy swung herself awkwardly sideways and forward, crashing down onto the rock. Pain shot up her leg; her left foot had landed in the flames. Freddy pulled it quickly away.

The island was only big enough for about three people. Fire raged on every side. Freddy crawled up beside Josiah and shook him. He didn't respond. "I think I'm going to sink the island," Cuerva Lachance called across the lake, "though I'll have you know I'm happy about this only on Tuesdays. Or maybe it should rain. It's so hard not to decide!"

"Josiah, *come on,*" shouted Freddy, shaking him harder. His head lolled, and he slid down onto the ground.

Mel said suddenly, "It's a story." Her voice wasn't loud, but sound here was as strange as it had been on the slimy sea. Distance didn't seem to matter. The words carried easily across the flames.

"So?" said Freddy. She could feel the island beginning to shake beneath her.

"It's a *story,*" said Mel. "How do you wake people up in stories?"

Time stopped briefly. Part of Freddy's brain went, *Oh, no, not that; we'll never hear the end of it if we do that,* but she knew Mel was right. "I hate you, Roland," she said, and she kissed Josiah on the lips.

It was her first kiss. She didn't enjoy it. Josiah opened his eyes.

Josiah said, "And they all lived slightly discontentedly ever after."

They were sitting in the living room of the house on Grosvenor Street, neatly arranged on the couch and love seat. Freddy glanced down. She was holding a steaming mug of tea in her hands. Most of the chairs were gone. Cuerva Lachance wasn't there.

"She'll be off being nonsensical by herself for a bit," said Josiah when he noticed them looking. "I don't think it's easy to mean nothing and everything all at once."

Roland said, "Did anyone win? Is anything over?"

"Oh, you won," said Josiah. "I would shake my fist at you if I wasn't so tired."

Mel got up from her seat, set down her own mug of tea, waddled over to where Freddy was sitting on the love seat alone, took Freddy's mug of tea away and handed it to Roland, sat down beside Freddy, and wrapped her arms around her sister. She did it all in a completely matter-of-fact way, but Freddy could feel Mel's tears trickling down onto her sleeve. She had scared Mel a lot at the fire lake. She had been thinking only of Mel scaring her.

No one said anything for a while. At last, Mel pulled away and took out her notebook, which she apparently kept in a pocket of her pyjamas. "I think we all won. No more forced choice for Three," she said, making a note. "But no complete control for Three, either. Maybe you're equals now. You've played it to a draw."

Josiah pulled a sour face. "That's one way of looking at it."

"You should consider it," said Mel, "just for fun."

"You kissed me," Josiah remarked to Freddy, who could feel

herself turning what she suspected was a very deep red. "I expect it was equally unpleasant for both of us. Let's blame the story and leave it at that."

"Are you guys going to leave us alone now?" demanded Roland.

"Certainly not," said Josiah. "You're Three; you're stuck with us. You did make us, you know. And there's school tomorrow. Don't you want to watch me get beat up again? I thought you enjoyed it."

Freddy and Mel exchanged glances. Freddy felt a knot in her stomach loosen. It was funny, after all the terror and betrayal and embarrassing moments on islands in lakes of fire, but part of her seemed to have been afraid that Josiah and Cuerva Lachance were going to go away now.

Maybe Josiah was her friend after all. It figured she would make the strangest friend she could without realising she had.

Freddy caught Josiah's eye. She didn't think the smile she saw lurking behind his eyes was entirely her imagination.

"The story's over, at any rate," said Josiah, "finally. Things should calm down for a while. There may be fewer tentacles."

Freddy thought about how Cuerva Lachance and Josiah had been missing in the future. She wasn't sure the story *was* over. Maybe it had paused. That was good enough for her.

"Let's go home," said Mel. Roland hesitated, then nodded. She was pretty sure there was a smile behind his eyes, too.

"You do that," said Josiah. "I'll see you tomorrow at school."

"You'll see us today," said Freddy. The sun was coming up. As she spoke, the first beam crept through the window and, inexplicably, filled the air with rainbows.

epilogue

Mel and Roland went home. Freddy walked into the park.

There were things she would have to deal with soon. She needed to think about school and how she didn't fit in there and how, strangely, she didn't care that she didn't. She and Roland needed to talk. She thought they needed to talk for quite a long time. Maybe she would try to sign a little, though she didn't think she would be very good at it yet. She and Mel needed to talk as well. And then . . . Freddy saw herself and Roland on that bleak road, walking away from a funeral at which she hadn't cried. There were things in her life on the verge of going wrong. Maybe she could deal with some of them. Maybe she and her mother needed to talk most of all. And it had been a very long time since she had seen her dad.

There were things she would have to deal with soon, but not yet. Right now, something was beginning.

The path through the woods was spongy beneath her feet. Dampness trickled in through holes in her boots.

She was almost glad it did, as her left foot was throbbing from the burn. She shivered. It was a brisk fall morning, and she didn't have a coat. Freddy moved beneath the evergreens, watching the sunlight begin to trickle between the branches. A crow called somewhere in the trees.

Cuerva Lachance, hair wild, cheek bleeding, hat and coat gone, clothes in tatters, was sitting on the bench. Freddy sat down beside her. "Have you been yet?"

"Not yet," said Cuerva Lachance. "I was waiting for you. It's very peaceful here. You wouldn't think there was a city all around."

Freddy nodded. "Why did you give me the key?"

"Well, I haven't, but I think I will. Without it, things would have gone very differently."

"I guess."

"And without the time travel," said Cuerva Lachance, gazing innocently up at the treetops, "you would have been a different sort of person yesterday. Interesting to think about, really."

Freddy looked at her, blinking. The time travel had been an accident . . . hadn't it?

Cuerva Lachance beamed out from beneath her tangled hair. "You do realise I'm the same person as Ban, don't you? I don't always feel the same way about what we've done to Three. Well . . . I don't always feel the same way about very much for very long."

"But you have less power this way," said Freddy. "You're more of a story."

"Oh, *power*." Cuerva Lachance fluttered her fingers in the air. "You've seen what happens when I'm given *power*. I really enjoy it, but I also really don't. Too much power for either of us would lead to the end of everything, and life's too interesting for that. It's better when it's a three-way balance. Josiah would disagree, but he does tend to see everything in black-and-white terms."

"Of course," she added after a pause, "I may have disagreed with all this an hour ago. You never can tell with me. Which is the point."

They sat side by side and watched colour leach into the forest. Birds were calling in the woods, but cautiously, sparsely. Winter was on its way; the summer birds had already fled.

"Do you need the key back?" asked Freddy after a while.

"Oh, no." Cuerva Lachance nodded towards Freddy's right wrist, from which the handcuffs, forgotten until now, still dangled. "Keep it. Am I going to invent some psychological mumbo-jumbo to convince you to take it? I can't think how I'm going to do that."

"I guess you'll make it up as you go along," said Freddy.

"That does tend to work for me," said Cuerva Lachance.

She was gone. Freddy shivered in the chill of the morning. Without her meaning it to, her hand had slid into her pocket and found the key. It was just a key. She knew what lock it fit now. Maybe she didn't need it any more. Maybe there wasn't anything all that bad about crying.

Down through time, she heard: "Have you ever had one of those days where everything goes so stupidly wrong that you find yourself saying every five minutes, 'Now, this can't possibly get any worse'? And then it *does*?"

The voice faded to nothing. The crow cawed in the woods. Freddy got up and went home through the still morning as the sun rose full above the trees.

author's note

Time-travel stories are a chancy proposition when they go so far back in history that it is impossible to know with any accuracy what things would have been like back then. I have therefore taken certain imaginative liberties with the historical (and prehistorical) bits. Any inaccuracies are entirely my own fault. However, certain details are based on myth, legend, folklore, and known history.

Loki and Heimdallr are both Norse gods whose names can be found in many surviving poems and stories. Loki is a god of mischief, a shape-shifter who is occasionally on the side of the other gods and occasionally opposed to them. He is sometimes associated with fire. He will be one of the key players during Ragnarök, the battle that ends the world, at which time he and Heimdallr will kill each other. Some of the insults Bragi trades with Loki / Cuerva Lachance during the flyting refer to the god Loki's exploits.

Heimdallr is the guardian of Bifröst, the burning rainbow bridge that leads to the realm of the gods. He will blow the horn Gjallarhorn (not quite a trombone, but often depicted in artistic representations as almost the same size as one) to signal the beginning of Ragnarök. He sleeps little or not at all, as he must be forever vigilant. He is responsible for the organisation of humanity into social classes. One of the epithets associated with him is "Loki's enemy."

Bragi Boddason was, as far as we know, a Swedish court poet, and possibly the inventor of skaldic poetry. Considering the period in which he would have lived, the early ninth century, it cannot now be known for sure whether he ever existed. If he did, he may have given his name to Bragi, the Norse god of skaldic poetry. The poem "Lokasenna" deals with Loki's disruption of a feast of the gods that Bragi is attending. Bragi is the first of the gods to challenge Loki and the first that Loki targets in his flyting.

The *huli jing*, or fox spirit, is a creature of Chinese mythology. Foxes may take human form, often appearing as breathtakingly beautiful women. They may have positive, negative, or ambiguous roles in stories. Associating with a fox spirit may be dangerous or beneficial.

Māui is a Polynesian culture hero, a trickster famed for, among other things, "fishing" various islands (which ones are involved depends on who is telling the story) up to the surface of the ocean. In the Māori version of his story, it's the North Island of New Zealand, the island upon which Freddy and Josiah find the nameless boy, that is formed from the fish Māui catches.

"Robin Goodfellow" is sometimes used as another name for the puck, a type of trickster sprite found in British folklore. The mischievous fairy Puck, also called Robin Goodfellow, has a major role in William Shakespeare's *A Midsummer Night's Dream*. A less prominent fairy in the same play is called Mustardseed.

Mika's creation myth bears a resemblance to many creation myths from various cultures. The idea of twin culture heroes with opposing characteristics can be found in numerous mythologies, most particularly in North and South American Native creation stories.

The paths of pins and needles that Freddy encounters in the house on Grosvenor Street appear in an old French version of the story now commonly known as "Little Red Riding Hood." Freddy's choice of the needles path echoes the choice of the girl in the story and leads to similarly problematic results.

Freddy's favourite reference book, *Bulfinch's Mythology,* exists, and if you are interested in the mythological bits and pieces that turn up in this novel, it is a good place to start.

Samuel Taylor Coleridge was an English poet who lived in the eighteenth and nineteenth centuries. He is still widely known for being one of the originators of the Romantic movement in English literature. According to him, he composed the poem "Kubla Khan" in 1797 after it came to him in an opium dream. It should have been two or three hundred lines long, but he was interrupted in the composition of it by a "person on business from Porlock," and all but the beginning of the poem was lost. He was also the author of the much longer poem "The Rime of the Ancient Mariner," from which Roland takes his slimy things with legs and Josiah derives his albatross-flavoured cough. On the question of whether or not Mr. Coleridge believed in fairies, historical record is silent.